# A Switch Made in Heaven

## EVA PHILLIPS

This book is a work of fiction. Any references to historical events, real people, or real places are used fictitiously. Other names, characters, places and events are products of the author's imagination, and any resemblance to actual events or places or persons, living or dead, is entirely coincidental

Copyright © 2023 by Eva Phillips

All rights reserved.

No part of this book may be reproduced in any form or by any electronic or mechanical means, including information storage and retrieval systems, without written permission from the author, except for the use of brief quotations in a book review.

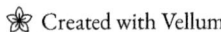 Created with Vellum

*For Chris and Julia*

## CHAPTER 1
## *Selina*

I'm squeezing tightly the steering wheel of a rented Honda CRV, from time to time slightly releasing my hands so I can energetically tap my fingers on the leather, which still smells brand new. I'm trying hard – so hard – not to just put my head on the wheel and fall asleep. It was five in the morning when I picked up the car from Heathrow, which was almost two hours ago. Actually it was five in New York but ten in London, it always takes me a while to combat my jet lag. I don't ever change my watch for the first two days in a new place – it's more out of habit than anything else, a habit that I believe sometimes brings me luck. Although I spent last night at a hotel near the airport, I'm still exhausted. I keep wondering maybe it has something to do with the free champagne I had on the plane. I have such a wonderful husband. When he heard I wanted to fly to England and take my mum to Paris for our birthdays, he immediately used his miles to upgrade me to first class. I bought the flight from the last of my savings, and when he heard I got economy he looked at me terrified.

"Do you know what kind of people fly coach?" he practically shouted.

"Yyyy... people, who can't afford to blow their money on business?"

He didn't seem to listen, "Do you want to get a fungal infection from their showers?"

"I'm afraid that there are no—"

"Let's get you a normal seat."

Leo is a bit of a snob, which is the less wonderful side of him, but compared to his friends he is only a moderate snob. He is just particular about flying economy or getting non-VIP seats for big events, hardly snobbery.

I switch on the air conditioning and cool the car to sixteen degrees to wake up. Mum doesn't know I'm coming home. It's supposed to be a surprise. Normally, she would be the one renting a car as she doesn't own a vehicle of any kind, excluding the second-hand red scooter that she bought on a Facebook children's sale. She lives in the centre of Oxford, less than a mile from her gallery, and when she really needs to go anywhere else it's usually by plane. The lack of a car stems also from her conviction to lead an environmentally friendly life. Each time she buys a plane ticket she pays to offset all the $CO_2$ emissions. Leo never does it when he books our flights, I don't think he even believes in global warming, which recently has become a sensitive topic between us.

I stop at a drive-through to get a double expresso and a chocolate muffin. Last time I was driving at five in the morning was nearly ten years ago in a mad dash to get the best possible seats at Wimbledon. I don't get up before nine, except occasionally in the middle of summer, when I feel like an early run along the beach.

Minutes later I'm back on the road. I drink the entire coffee in just three sips and munch my muffin in a similar number of bites. I feel a bit sick but it should give me the kick that I need.

"So soon?" I say to myself, as my phone suddenly rings. I can see my mother-in-law's name flashing on the dashboard display. "To answer or not to answer, hmm..." I can't decide whether she'll help me to wake up or just distract me from driving. I have Bluetooth so I can talk hands free. "To answer or not to answer..."

"Hi Leona, is everything all right?" I'm trying to sound cheerful, otherwise she's going to interrogate me on why I'm anything less than super happy, as if it was some sort of a crime.

"Yes, yes, everything is fine. I'm just calling because I wanted to ask what you're up to today, and whether you could run a few errands for me..." she doesn't wait for me to answer, but continues in one breath, "I've been so busy lately I haven't had time to wipe the sweat from my forehead. Anyway, could you design an invitation for the charity gala Emil is organising in August? I'll send you all the details later. They also need to be sent to everybody by post and email. I'll provide you with the guest list. Obviously then you'll need to collate the returns. Then—"

"Yeah, right," I say more to myself than her.

"Really?" There's surprise in her voice, she didn't expect me to agree so quickly without making an excuse. "That's fantastic. I've also had to fire my gardener. Do you think you could find somebody to replace him? I don't even know where to start looking for a decent gardener. Ideally a woman because the last one tried to flirt with me, can you believe it?" she says proudly, and I can tell she is more flattered than outraged.

"No, I'm sorry Leona," I say, while taking a junction and passing a sign to Oxford. "I've already got three summer parties to organise for Leo, and I also promised to manage his calendar and plan his press meetings."

"But you just said—" now she is outraged.

"Besides, I'm in England and going to France in a couple of days."

"What? You didn't tell me."

"Should I?" I asked flippantly, smirking to myself and thinking she must be getting more and more pissed off. "Can't you ask Emily or Faith to help out?"

"Emily is a working mother, and Faith has school," she snaps. *And I have nothing to do, of course,* I think while gritting my teeth.

"Why are you going to France?"

"Mine and mum's birthdays."

"What's wrong with celebrating your birthday in America? Especially now, when—"

"I also need to do some research for my book," I only say it because I know she'll hate to hear it.

"Darling, the last thing that I want to do is hurt your feelings," she says in an annoyingly pretentious tone. "It's really the last thing..." *Yeah, I'm sure it is!* I think tightly squeezing the wheel. "You're thirty-one.

Don't you think you're at an age when you must stop dreaming and start making real plans?"

"Sorry, what are you saying? That I should give up on my dream of becoming a published writer?"

"No, I meant—"

"Sorry Leona but I can barely hear you. I need to go. Byeee." I can still hear her perfectly well – too well – saying she will send me an email because she won't need it all tomorrow and I will definitely have some time to do it on my European holidays. I press a button on my wheel and hang up.

*Over my – or rather your dead body Leona!* I'm thinking and take a few deep breaths. *Breathe in and out...*

I could have been a pediatrician. I used to be a straight-A-student with a great ability to memorize. I'm empathetic, I like children and I don't lose my head under pressure. I would be doing something meaningful, which nobody would ever question. No matter how much money I made, people would respect me and instinctively like me. Wherever I went in the world people would recognise my career and appreciate my hard work.

I could have been a cake maker. My mum has never been a good cook and she's an even worse baker, so I've learned it all by myself – first from cookbooks I borrowed from a local library and our neighbour, then from some Internet's blogs. I made the best apple pie and baked cheesecake, which I first brought to the school fairs and then to all the offices where I used to work. I could have had my own cute cake shop, where I would also sell fancy sandwiches and coffee. People would complement my baking, and I would be glad to see their smiley happy faces coming back to me over and over again. I would feel that I do something useful, and people love my work and crave for more.

I could have been a lawyer, yoga instructor or gardener spending my days outside. I could have been anything but... "BUT NO!" I scream to myself and punch the wheel with my right hand. "Of all the things in the world I decided to be a fucking writer. I decided to pursue a career as a novelist to be constantly dismissed."

When people hear what I want to do for a living, my answer instils a whole range of different feelings and reactions, and none of them qualifies as desirable. Some pity me, repeating at every possible occasion how lucky I am to have my husband, so I'm not going to be one of those artists who starve themselves to death for their dreams and idealistic visions. Nobody says my husband is lucky because he gets home-cooked dinners. When was the last time somebody made me dinner? Mum, when I was still at high-school, and my dear husband once, but it was only when he wanted to propose. When did somebody make me an edible dinner? I honestly don't remember.

I wanted to take a year to try and write a book between having a full-time job and having a child. It was an idea that we knew we could afford. My husband has a very busy job and appreciates that I'm almost always there when he's got some time off. Initially, we planned to give it a year and see what happens. My idea proved to be an offence to many – in particular to other women. Those women, the ones who work, snarl at me and say that they couldn't voluntarily stay at home and do nothing. In their eyes I do nothing. I'm a housewife who does nothing – which they don't even seem to realise is a contradiction in itself. I betrayed the cause. I sinned as an emancipated woman who chooses to temporarily not make money – I'm a kept woman. Shame on me. They never resist asking whether I'm not afraid I'll get cut out of the job market. Forever! "Do you really want to have a gap in you CV? How will you describe the lost time on your LinkedIn?" I was asked only a week ago when an old friend caught me writing in a café. What's emancipation about if I'm still not allowed to make my own decisions? Then there are those women who stay at home to look after their children – they also play an important role in telling me who I am. They couldn't just pass me indifferently. No! They feel obliged to let me know how frivolous and lazy I am, and how meaningless my whole existence is. I don't remember how many times I was asked whether I wasn't afraid I might find it hard to get pregnant, and how many times I was warned that when I leave it late it might turn out to be too late.

Last week I was standing at the queue to a juice bar, where two women were gossiping about *Alice's husband*. Apparently, he was in jail for tax fraud. Nevertheless, they seemed to be in awe of how clever, educated and hard-working he was. I decided to be a writer and I get less respect than a criminal, at least he was making money.

I drive around Oxford and keep getting lost because I'm absorbed in my thoughts about Leona. She successfully stole another twenty minutes of my life. I couldn't be any happier we're separated by the wide and deep waters of the Atlantic Ocean. I stop at a crossroads for a red light, impatiently tapping my fingers on the wheel. I look right at a woman with long blonde hair, who's sitting behind the wheel of a vivid green Aston Martin; and a man in a black SUV in a lane just next to her. He's wearing a black leather jacket and large sunglasses that he's adjusting on his head, while bluntly staring at her. They suddenly get a green light but neither of them seems to be thinking about moving forward. They're too busy flirting. He lowers his window to wave and say something to her. I can't tell what her face expression is because she is throwing her hair back and forth, her hands moving everywhere except on the wheel. Suddenly she's got two cars behind her. They start beeping for her to go, but her light is already amber. "Sorry darling, it's too late," I say and put my foot on the gas.

## CHAPTER 2

## *Lily*

Sometimes I wonder whether I could've been adopted, which would make perfect sense considering both my appearance and general attitude towards life. There is almost no resemblance between me and my two-years younger sister, who looks like a perfect mix of our parents. Emma laughs that she's exactly fifty percent dad and fifty percent mum, while I'm a hundred percent myself. Just like our mother, Emma is a slim, petite, girlish-looking brunette with deep green eyes. She inherited dad's dimples, curly hair and small straight teeth. And then there is me – the only real blue eyed blonde in the whole family. I'm also the tallest – at five foot seven inches I'm one inch taller than my father, and two inches taller than my grandfather – before he got old and started shrinking. I've also got the longest eyelashes and the biggest boobs, but the latter is a result of the brilliant work of my surgeon. Just to make it clear – I don't have massive boobs, I wanted them a couple of sizes larger so I would look better in all the glamorous dresses I wear to work, and for all the big galas and cocktail parties I get invited to by my clients.

My parents and my sister believe in science, early procreation, employment that makes an impact in the world, saving a lot of money for a rainy day and Sundays spent with the family on long walks and board games. I love them and respect their beliefs, but to their despair, I've never exactly shared their life ideas. I believe in luck, beautiful objects, having children in your late thirties, or not having them at all, and a job that makes you happy. I don't save, I'd rather invest and use the rest of the cash to live my life Here and Now. If I feel I need to work on a Sunday I do, but I love my job as an interior designer, it's like a hobby that brings me money – a lot of it. When I don't work on weekends, I buy a lastminute flight on a Friday evening to get away somewhere in Europe, returning straight into the office on Monday morning. I often spend my Sunday morning running in the Swiss Alps, on a Tuscany beach or between some narrow streets of a historic town. If I go with anybody, they normally stay in bed till ten, and we typically meet for breakfast in a café that I find on my way back to our hotel. The only exception is Nathaniel – he always goes for a run with me and has a strong opinion on where we're going to eat – no matter whether it's breakfast, dinner or just cake and coffee. Despite being twelve years older than me he's the fitter one – he regularly runs marathons and is a very active member of a rowing club. Those are also reasons why he isn't a frequent companion on my weekend escapes. Those and his two kids, who I haven't met yet. He hasn't met my family either; they don't even know about him. Why? Because my parents strongly believe in condemning their children's choices if they don't fit into their self-made scale of ultimate perfection.

---

"If you're not drinking wine, maybe you would like a beer?" mum asked me innocently as we sat down to dinner the previous night. I would've happily skipped the whole Saturday event, making some excuses to save myself from being constantly compared to my sister and constantly reminded of how much personal growth I need to undertake. But, it was my niece and nephew's fifth birthday party. Charlie and his sister Chloe are my favourite members of the family, and I couldn't refuse an invite to their party. They are also my only hope if I never have a husband and children of my own. They will visit me in a care home – I sort of joke, sort of not, which is probably the result of spending one evening too many with my parents and sister, who always makes me feel like I'm a thirty-one-year-old spinster. *Thirty is the new twenty*, I want to scream, but I know it wouldn't change anything.

"No, thanks mum," I said with a forced smile, because I knew exactly where her kindness was coming from.

"Are you sure?" she asked, and Bob, my sister's husband rolled his eyes. "Not even a gin and tonic?"

"Since when did you promote drinking alcohol so much?" I snapped.

"I don't. I just think you look tense, and it could help you relax. Besides, you don't plan on driving tonight?"

"No, I don't," I gasped. "So, it's what you prescribe your patients when they're tense?" I asked flippantly knowing it would irritate her. "Just have some booze and everything will be all right," I said with a deep voice, making everybody except mum laugh, meaning Emma, Bob and dad because all the other guests had gone after lunch.

"Fine, I won't say anything more about *booze*," she said with an annoying smirk on her face. "Oh, I bought a delicious goat cheese today," she said less than a minute later. "Would you like to try?" mum pointed it out on a cheese platter that was lying on the heavy wooden sideboard waiting for its time after dessert.

"What? Now? I'm still having my starter."

"This cheese would go amazingly with the tomato soup. You could melt a slice on the top," she said and asked dad to pass her the platter. He looked a bit confused, but did what she asked without a word of protest. Bob and Emma exchanged looks and took long sips of their wine.

"Mum, are you kidding me?" I exploded.

"Oh, I'm sorry. I didn't mean anything rude or wrong. I just—"

"You just wanted to find out whether I'm pregnant. The wine wasn't enough proof so you had to see whether I would have a slice of moldy goat cheese. Well, I'm sorry but I'm not pregnant. Can I enjoy my soup?"

"I'm sorry. I'm really sorry," mum said with a panicky voice. "It wasn't only the wine, but also your loose top, tired eyes and... I would never try to test you if you weren't so secretive about your personal life," she sounded like she was about to fall apart.

"Fiona, would you like me to pour you some more red?" Bob asked with his mouth full of bread. He could see that his mother-in-law was on the edge of bursting into tears any minute.

Mum only nodded, and Bob made her glass so full she had to take a sip before raising it.

I wanted to add that I wasn't drinking because I got absolutely smashed on Friday night with my friends in Chelsea, and even the thought of a drop of alcohol could dangerously twist my stomach. I was dying to say I'd drunk so much because I was so nervous about coming home, but I stayed quiet not to make a scene. Over the main course everybody talked about the usual, hospitals. Emma and Bob are also both doctors so nobody could resist a good rant about the NHS, its tight budget and annoying patients. All eyes returned to me and mum during dessert, when I politely refused a home-made lemon tart.

"Oh, okay. I've only spent hours making it with all organic ingredients because I know how important that is for you," mum said looking at me with puppy eyes.

"Thank you, I really appreciate it, but you know I don't like lemon tart." *You've known for thirty-one years the thought of lemon tart makes me sick, so why don't you finally give up on trying to convince me to like the family's favourite dessert? Why would anybody want to make something naturally sour into something so sickly sweet?*

"I only hope it's not because you're worried about your waist. Have you lost weight recently? You look so slim."

"No mum, my weight hasn't changed in six years," I said calmly. Another argument that favours me being adopted. Everybody in the family is naturally slim, my body is the result of hard work and much sacrifice. "Can you pass me the cheese platter now?"

"Can't you wait till we eat dessert?" mum asked innocently, but I knew she wanted to punish me for not trying the damn lemon tart.

"I just wanted to save you from wondering in agony whether I'm pregnant or not by trying that delicious cannot-wait goat cheese," I snapped.

"Girls, please stop," dad said calmly, passing me the cheese platter.

Mum chastised him with her eyes, but he wasn't even looking at her. *Poor dad*, I thought, *I know what you're going to talk about tonight before falling asleep.*

"Tell me mum..." I started while stuffing my face with very average goat cheese, "would you actually be happy for me to be pregnant now?"

"Of course, I would be happy," she said without a hint of doubt in her voice.

"Even when I'm not married?"

"Obviously I would prefer you to be married but... well, it's better than... I mean, I'm sure you've got a boyfriend and the child would certainly provide some motivation for him to propose."

"Mum, Lily has lovers, not boyfriends," my sister suddenly jumped into the conversation. She was giggly and tipsy, but it was no justification for her acting like a bitch.

"Emma!" mum looked at her outraged. "Apologise to your sister."

"I'm sorry," she whispered without even pretending to mean it.

"She didn't mean to offend you," Bob tried to rescue the situation.

"I'm sure honey you've got a lovely boyfriend, and if you don't, you're going to find one soon. You're *still* young and beautiful," mum said putting an emphasis on *still*.

"That's a relief, so I've got something like one year of youth and beauty, although my organic food should get me one more year and..." mum wanted to say something, but it only made me speak louder. "And Emma is right. I don't *do* boyfriends, I only do lovers. That's why Nathaniel wouldn't propose to me if I got pregnant. Well, at least not immediately because he's still married. Funny story actually, he got married young when his girlfriend was pregnant with their first child. He loves his kids, but he also knows now that they shouldn't be the reason to tie the knot," I said and took a large gulp of Emma's wine.

Poor mum gave such a snort that she managed to spit red wine on her ivory silk blouse, dad's light blue shirt, and their new white table runner.

"When you ask me next time, why I wear black or navy to children's birthday parties and other non-funeral family events, I'm going to remind you of this moment," said Bob with a smirk.

"Liliane Rice, you're not being serious," my mother finally got her voice back. She knew I didn't like the name Liliane. She only used it when she was angry with me. I didn't like it so much I officially changed it to Lily.

"I'm afraid she is, darling," said dad, sounding disappointed but still reasonably calm. Damage was done, he must have been thinking, they failed as parents, or maybe my adopted genes were stronger than the values they had tried to instil in me for all those years.

I'd never seen my family sitting in silence, except the time when we saw our gay cousin Colin appear on the X-factor stage in London. Yes, my parents called him *the gay cousin*, which they didn't think was offensive. Colin was pretty and eventually became a model thanks to another TV show, but he was a terrible singer.

Taking advantage of nobody saying a word I slowly pushed myself back from the chunky dark wooden table, which I'd found for my parents in Italy and arranged to be shipped to them for one of their big wedding anniversaries. I stood up feeling dizzy – despite not drinking anything but the one sip of wine, and despite not being pregnant – and I headed towards the main door, carrying just my handbag. As I left the house I thanked my resolve that I didn't drink so I could drive. I was equally grateful I'd been late to the party so my lime green Aston Martin didn't get blocked by anybody. I quickly looked for a good hotel in Oxford and typed its post code with shaking hands. Nobody was even trying to stop me from going, they must have been too busy processing the bombshell I dropped in their perfect home and impeccable family.

After only ten minutes of driving, I made it to the five-star spa hotel, where they provided me with all necessary toiletries, pyjamas, slippers and robe. I felt like I was flying first class on one of the world-renowned airlines – the only thing disturbing the whole experience was the turbulence in my head. I lay in bed till two in the morning, imagining how everybody was getting drunk in my absence and discussing for the rest of the night my pitiful and shameful love life.

---

Now I'm driving back to my apartment in Chelsea, sipping a skimmed latte with a double shot of expresso and swearing loudly to myself about the eventful meal I *enjoyed* last night with my family. *Was it my last supper?* I think, and smirk to the mirror revealing my professional but subtle make-up done in the hotel's spa. *Definitely my last supper, or at least until I officially declare that I'm breaking up with my married boyfriend.* I'm relieved I finally don't have to pretend about Nate. It's so liberating! I feel like I can finally let myself be Me, and I don't need to lie anymore about the relationship. God, lying is so exhausting when you have a mother and sister like mine – unlike most people they actually listen, which forces you to remember every tiny detail of what you say to them.

"Are you going to Venice alone?" my sister asked me a couple of weeks ago.

"With a friend of mine," I said, and I quickly added, "a female one. Why?"

"Nothing, it's just… it's such a romantic destination."

"As romantic as any other Italian historic town. I go there because I love its art and architecture. I'm looking for some inspiration for a villa I'm going to design in Cornwall. Their new owners lived in Italy for a couple of years, and they loved the local style."

"How much do they pay you for the project that justifies travelling all the way to Venice?"

"They paid for the three-day trip," I lied. If she heard I was about to take at least three hundred grand for a three-month job, she would be unable to resist her usual tirade about how unfair the world was, and that I was the living embodiment of the unfairness.

"Oh my god, I don't know why…" she would say over and over again, "I don't know why I went to medical school and spent years, and all those sleepless nights learning, revising, doing my masters, then the specialisation…" she would be counting out and gasping heavily. "I could've had fun and at the same time make plenty of money from a hobby."

"You don't have any other hobby except your job," I would reply, trying not to rise to the fact she thought my job was a farce. I wouldn't explain anymore that I also did a masters at a prestigious university in London and never stopped learning or attending courses. I wouldn't say a word about working nights, on weekends and during holidays. My clients pay staggering sums of money but many of them expect my complete devotion, no less than if I was their doctor on shift in a private hospital.

"I love it but it's still a job, it's hard work."

"Of course."

"By the way, as you make so much money..." Emma said to me a couple of weeks ago, "you know, I thought that you could afford to freeze your eggs. I think it's a brilliant idea for somebody like you." I was a bit shocked but on the other hand what could I expect from my always-blunt sister who specialized in fertility treatment and is a fan of early twenties procreation.

"Somebody like me? Is not having a child in your thirties a disease?"

"You know that's not what I meant," she said defensively when we were sitting on a bench outside her hospital, having packed sandwiches and coffee from a vending machine for our lunch. "You're still not committed to anybody and it might take you some time to meet the right person, so I thought you could save your eggs for later. It's what I would do."

"I'll think about it, thanks," I said to stop her from coming out with more arguments that I really didn't need to hear.

Telling the truth to my family was liberating, but it was also like throwing a snowball down a mountain, knowing that it will most likely cause an avalanche. *Oh, dear god, what was I thinking? I'll never hear the end of it.* I know that even if I broke up with Nate, mum, dad and Emma would never stop preaching to me about the potential consequences of having an affair with a married man and destroying somebody's family. They would never be able to understand that their family was already damaged, and what Nate and I have is real. For my family everything is just black and white, there is nothing in between. They have no appreciation of how lucky they were that they found their love when they were very young and had no doubts about each other. My life has always been complicated – partly because I don't tend to chase easy and straight-forward solutions, but also because it's just the way it is.

I'm waiting at a red light, resting my chin on the wheel and humming a song that is playing on the radio. I'm tempted to *shazam* it, but then I would have to bend down to reach my bag and search for my phone. I manage to fight the temptation before the song is over because the last thing I need are people beeping at me. I feel like I'm being watched. I look to my right and it turns out to be true. An average looking guy in his thirties is bluntly checking me out through the ajar window of his massive black SUV. I lightly turn my head to see who is sitting on the back seat of his car. There is nobody there but he's got two children's cars seats and a colourful sunblind in the window. I look at him still smirking at me but clearly unhappy I noticed the seats. My eyes fill up with tears from the midday sun shining to my right. I regret not having one of my thirty pairs of sunglasses with me. The guy opens his window a bit more and is saying something to me. *Have I been staring at him too much? Does he think I'm interested?* Somebody beeps at us. The guy is still not moving but waving to me and asking me to open my window. I look up, the light is amber. I wonder how long I didn't notice it was green. I press my foot on the gas and all I can hear is a terrible bang. My head violently hits the seat, my hands are flying in the air. I feel pressure on my chest. I can't breathe.

# CHAPTER 3
## *Selina*

I scrutinized my reflection in a mirror, long hazelnut hair messed-up by wind and put up with a pair of designer sunglasses, lightly tanned radiant complexion without even a gram of make-up and a tight pastel yellow dress that stopped just above my slim knees. I was so struck by my look – the new-old-me looking like I was in my early twenties – that it took me a few long minutes to acknowledge that the mirror I was staring at wasn't the only one in the room, or rather in the chamber. A line of mirror-clad arches, opulently embellished with gold and marble, were reflecting large arcaded windows overlooking a golden sunset above truly royal gardens. Candles were flickering in crystal chandeliers – some hanging from a ceiling heavily decorated with paintings and some held by golden sculptures of half-naked women. The sunlight was amplifying various shades of gold from the women's bodies and their skimpy robes. *Beautiful but totally sexist*, I thought.

I felt a delicate warm breeze on my naked shoulders, but I had no idea where it was coming from – just like the music gently playing in the background, which I realised was Jason Mraz singing 93 Million Miles.

"Why would Jason... Oh my dear almighty freaking god, am I dead?" I screamed and scared myself when my hysterical tone returned as an echo. "The Hall of Mirrors in the Palace of Versailles, isn't it my mother's vision of heaven?" The sudden discovery made my stomach queasy, and then the recent events started coming back to me like an avalanche – I couldn't stop them, and it was too late anyway. "The car accident! What's the day today? How long have I been here? Is anybody listening to me at all? How did I get here?"

"Oh, just stop panicking!" said a tall blonde woman, who appeared out of nowhere, and definitely wasn't there to comfort me. She had tiny hips squeezed in dark blue jeggings and perfect perky boobs covered with a tight pink T-shirt. "If you're already dead, you're dead and there's nothing you can do about it," she said flippantly.

"So, God is a Barbie? When I was a child I spent hours trying to convince everybody who was eager to listen that God was a woman and looked like one of my dolls but... this is not happening. I'm just going crazy, am I?"

"No, it is happening, you've just passed out several times, every time they tried to tell you, you were—"

"Hold on a minute! You drove into me and killed me! Now I remember! If you'd been less focused on flirting with the guy at the green light, I'd be alive now!"

"I had a green light so if you hadn't been such a shit driver and driven so badly..." she screamed out of her lungs, then stopped abruptly to take a breath and run her slim fingers through her long straight hair. "Anyway, I'm not sure whether you've noticed, but I also didn't come out of the accident unscathed..." she paused to add whispering, "from the accident that you caused, anyway—"

"Anyway? You killed me! It's your fault we're here!"

"Oh, stop being so emotional. I really can't stand overemotional women" she snapped.

"And who are you? One of those people who are so proud of keeping their emotions in check, when in reality you just let those carefully hidden feelings poison you on the inside, permanently wiping any smile off your face and replacing it with a smirk? Yeah, I know that being sensitive, compassionate and emotive is nowadays passé and reserved for uneducated plebs... but I'm allowed to be emotional! I've just died, and I'm an artist – I'm a writer!"

"Wow," she said flatly. "What books have you written? I bet some crime stories for housewives," she giggled having amused herself.

"I haven't published anything yet but—"

She smirked, "So you're not a writer."

"Another one! You're just like my mother-in-law. I'm currently working on my third book! The fact I haven't sold anything yet doesn't mean the books don't exist and I haven't spent months writing them!"

She cleared her throat, "Sorry to disappoint you, but the only way you'll get published now is if somebody finds your *work of art* and uses your death as a selling point. On reflection, the fact you're dead could add real value – less people would bother to write negative reviews on the Internet knowing you can't read them, and what's the point? Even if you annoy them, you're not going to create anything else, right?" she said, again amused with herself.

"I thought the Hall of Mirrors was supposed to be a heaven, but now I'm afraid it must be hell and you're my torturer. Tortured by a Barbie doll – what does it mean? Is it some kind of allegory?"

"Are you always so overdramatic?"

"Are you always so stoic when you find out you're dead? You must've truly hated your life."

"You're rather judgy for a writer. Maybe that's exactly your problem – people don't like when somebody is preaching to them."

"Enough, stop torturing her," a man-in-white said decisively. Like Blondie he appeared out of nowhere, or was I too focused on myself to notice when he flew into the middle of the chamber on a broom or materialised out of thin air.

"Thank you," I said relieved. "I think we can both agree I don't need purgatory and should go straight to heaven. If I ever did anything less than good, people deserved it, and if I'm not good enough for heaven, who is?"

Barbie laughed out loud but she wasn't looking at me, she was completely absorbed with sizing up the man. He was dressed in a white T-shirt, white linen trousers and skin-coloured sandals. I wasn't sure whether the fact that he was coming from somewhere hot comforted or tormented my un-beating heart.

"God, and I thought I used to be arrogant at times," she said.

"I'm not God, sorry he's—"

"Too busy to see me after I've just died?" I screamed. "Does he even know how much I learnt about him just so some priests would let me have my first communion?"

"Wherever you're taking me, can you please promise to separate me from this woman?"

"That's one thing I can promise you right now," he said with a smirk. "I'm Frederick – not Fred, not Eric – but Frederick," he said overaccentuating his name. "I'm going to accompany you on your journeys. Let's go to my office and talk about what happened and what we can do for you."

Before either of us managed to say a word, Frederick snapped his fingers and all three of us were suddenly standing on a fluffy cloud in which our feet were submerged. It looked like we were standing in cotton candy.

"This is more like my vision of heaven," said Blondie.

"It is your vision of heaven," said Frederick while putting his arm-long blond hair in a ponytail. "We try to meet your human expectations, well... at least some of them. The board agreed a while ago that it's helpful to present soothing and familiar images when you face such a challenging moment like... like—"

"Like death," snapped Barbie.

"Why do you have to keep saying that ugly word?"

"Firstly, there are no ugly words and you as a writer should know that. There are only ugly meanings that people add to them. Secondly, I'm trying to adapt myself to the current situation by repeating *death* and *dead*. I still can't convince myself it's all over... but on the bright side I'm glad it wasn't painful, I have no memory of my final moments, no flashbacks and I'm on a cloud – I mean my whole life is on the cloud but this one doesn't have any *i* at the front, which is rather something. Just a shame I can't make it into an Insta Story."

Frederick sighed, "Sit down. Contrary to what you're thinking right now, we don't have an eternity to work through this."

"Just one question," I said raising my forefinger as if I was at primary school. *Am I getting younger, am I Benjamin-Buttoning after I died*? I thought, but said, "How do you want us to take a seat on the cloud?"

Frederick rolled his eyes, "You can sit down exactly like you do on a chair. Just because you can't see any chairs doesn't mean they don't exist."

"Copied," Blondie murmured and put her arse down in *the air*, crossed her legs and bent back comfortably in *the air*.

I watched her for a while with curiosity, she was acting like she'd done it many times before – was she one of those people who are very adaptable, or did she die well before me and have plenty of time to adjust?

I lowered my bum by an inch but quickly stood up distracted by a mesmerizing view of the Italian boot below the cloud. I gasped just like my mother did when she saw the Hall of Mirrors for the first time. It was during our birthday trip to Paris – on the thirteenth of May when mum celebrated her fortieth, and three days later I turned twenty-one.

"It's what I expect to see in heaven," my mother – artist, painter and hopeless romantic – said when we were standing in Versailles' *Galerie des Glace,* her with a radiant and contagious smile and me with a headphone in one ear listening to Jason Mraz. We loved the Palace and Paris so much that we made a resolution that we would always try to pop back there for our birthdays. But we never did.

I felt a tear rolling down my cheek. "Couldn't you just wait with the whole damn death one month, and let me have a last birthday with my mum?" I yelled throwing my hands in the air. I inherited from my mother a tendency to be overdramatic, expressive and emotional, along with other character traits that probably made my life fuller, more vivid and colourful, but also so much more difficult that it needed to be. "Why? Oh, why couldn't you just wait?"

"Why couldn't you just wait and let Lily have the damn road?" snapped Frederick. "Take your seat and listen before I lose the last traces of my angelic patience and make you go straight to hell, so I can move on with my busy schedule."

"So, are you an angel?" asked Barbie whose real name to my surprise turned out to be just Lily.

"You can call me that," he snapped and tapped something on his newly-arrived transparent glass tablet. He flicked his fingers a couple of times and three glass chairs suddenly appeared, as well as a one-piece glass desk. "This is only so you stop whining that you can't see any furniture."

"Love your tablet," said Lily.

"This model will be available on Earth in twenty-six years. The next Steve Jobs will be conceived..." he paused and stroked his wrist, which made the time to display on his hand, before disappearing as soon as his eyes were again set on me and Lily, "in three minutes... unless his mother-to-be gets suddenly enlightened to use any form of contraception, but she's too smitten by her professor, who is twenty-three years older..."

"Wow," I said.

"Yeah, wow!" Frederick slightly raised himself from the glass chair, rested his elbows on the desk and pointed his fingers at me. "Down on Earth you always assume that Heaven is stuck in time, and all progress only happens in your human yard."

"Fascinating," I said, nodding my head with my mouth wide open. "I wish I could see this and then return to Earth to write all about it or..." I looked down at Earth again, "I wish I spent less time looking at my computer... I wish I'd become an astronaut."

"Too late to be an astronaut, but the good news is that you're not quite dead yet," he said and paused while we both screamed simultaneously:

"What?"

"So then you're not the angel of death? What are we if we're not dead? What's going on with us? Are you trying to say we're about to die soon? Is there something we can do to get back? I'm only thirty-one and never really been in love! I mean, I think I love Nate but is he really the one?" I listened to Lily as she vividly gesticulated, her face suddenly full of genuine emotion.

"I haven't had a proper career!" I screamed.

"Exactly, she's only like nineteen and hasn't lived her life yet either. She hasn't even had a chance to get a real job."

"Selina is actually thirty-one too, married and decided to stay at home to fulfil her dream as a writer and mother," Frederick was explaining while Lily's eyes were getting rounder and rounder.

"Oh well, she made her choice then," she snapped.

"What do you mean I made my choice? You made your choice not knowing what love is at the age of thirty-one. I bet you put your career first and forgot to live."

"You bet I did, and what? I was an executive in a top company, travelled the world, met thousands of interesting people—"

"Your friends are on Facebook, and you have no one to love or even talk to. What a sad existence," I yelled as loud as I could, feeling a few drops of water landing on my head. I couldn't tell whether it was my shouting that shook the cloud into releasing rain or I just spat on my own face.

"What a sad existence YOU had! If you hadn't died in the car accident, you'd have probably ended up as a miserable, unfulfilled and misunderstood writer."

"What have you been through that made you so bitter?" I asked calmly and in the corner of my eye saw Frederick's smug face.

"Finally, you're getting to the point. You both encountered many obstacles in your lives – I mean at least according to your own judgment."

"Yeah, I bet it must've been tough being happily married and enjoying your hobby while other people had to go to work."

"I'm sure it was tough being a successful woman, who..." I paused because I felt I needed to come up with a more vicious comment, "who collected pins on the map and faces on social media!"

Frederick raised both his hands up in the air creating a glow of light between them "God help me, women don't stop talking even when they're dead!"

"You said we weren't quite dead!" Lily screamed.

"You're totally sexist," I snapped.

"Yeah? So, what? Do you want to file a complaint?" he laughed so much his whole body was shaking.

"No way! Are you saying God is a man after all?" I said disappointed. "Oh well, maybe he'll have more mercy for me, women have never particularly liked me. Men, on the other hand—"

He interrupted me with a grin on his face, "You're currently in a place we call *Up There* or *Up Here* – depending on your current position. You're suspended between Heaven and Earth and..." he was explaining, but I was in such shock that I missed at least half of the sentence.

"Sorry, did you *just* say *Hell*?" Lily asked matter-of-factly.

"Yes, your souls are suspended between Heaven, Earth and Hell," he said loudly. "And your bodies are currently being operated on in a hospital in Oxford, which gives me a little time to decide what to do with you."

"Just you? You're not God but you're the only one making the life and death decision? How is this fair?" Now Lily was the more emotional of the two of us.

He gasped, "I phrased myself wrong. I've already had a meeting with the board and together we've come up with some suggestions. Now I see that the majority was right... I mean, the normal procedure would be..." he hesitated and then pressed his open palms to his mouth.

"What board are you taking about? Can we speak to them? Do we have any right to defend ourselves? And what about God?" Lily was trying to keep calm, but she was talking through a squeezed throat.

"I was going to start by explaining all this to you earlier, but you were too busy arguing, which really sums up your entire existence on Earth – you were always too busy to NOTICE certain things. I work for a company called Soul Management Ltd. We deal with life and death matters including human resource management in Heaven, Hell and Purgatory. Our contract is limited to Earth."

"I knew there is life on different planets! I was about to write a book about another Earth!"

"Shut up and listen," Lily snapped nervously. "Let him talk."

Frederick gave her a beaming smile and convinced me that whoever he was, he would flirt with her in a heartbeat if I wasn't there. "There's life on other planets but there is no other Earth and none of the living species exist in your galaxy anymore."

"Anymore? How did they die?" Lily asked arching her eyebrows.

"The usual reason – their own stupidity. Apparently, stupidity is more difficult to stop from spreading than any other disease, and more difficult to shoot than an asteroid."

"Okay, but let's get back to us," I suddenly realised that we were stuck somewhere in the back of beyond of the universe, with a sexist man who had our fate in his hands.

"During the last board meeting I was appointed as the executive manager of the most innovative and heaven-shattering project," he said proudly and full of enthusiasm.

*Great, he's got our fate in his hands and he's new to his job!*

"Congratulations," Lily murmured. "My boss was right – the whole universe is ruled by one corporation or another, and there is no way out."

"I'm sorry but I still don't follow. What does it have to do with us?" I asked, feeling more and more confused, and I wondered for a moment whether I would have understood the whole situation any better if I had worked in a large company on Earth. *Maybe, work-experience wasn't as overrated as I thought!*

"Long story short. Hell is overcrowded, Purgatory is not quick enough at processing Lost Souls, and we can't go against our fundamental rules and send to Heaven those who don't deserve it."

"What are you trying to say?" Lily was fiddling with her beautiful sapphire ring, and I wondered whether she had bought it herself rather than wait for a prince on a white horse to choose one for her. "Can we just get a yellow card, so we get back on the pitch?"

Frederick put his palms into a pyramid and pressed it against his lips while scrutinizing Lily and me for a moment. I held my breath, imagining how it would be if I stopped breathing and what he was about to do with our literally lost souls. "I'm not going to lie, we're going through a crisis on Earth and *Up Here*. Humans are one of the most challenging species. We don't want to invest in expanding Hell. We were brought in to reduce the number of people going there. That's why we're carrying out innovative research and trying something that hasn't been done before in the entire universe..." I looked at Lily who swallowed hard. She had lost her bravado and annoying ambivalence. "I think you two are perfect to become our first guinea pigs."

"Guinea pigs? Is it punishment for me designing offices for that cosmetic company, who did tests on animals? I swear I didn't know about that when I started the job and then I had to carry on to get paid."

Frederick stood up, flicked his fingers to get rid of his desk and chair, and started strolling on the cloud with his hands behind his back, "It's your chance. I'm giving you a chance that nobody else has had before you and..." he raised his forefinger, "if you mess it up nobody else might get such a chance in the future."

"In other words, no pressure," I said.

"Does it mean a warning and a miraculous return? Just please tell me, that we'll be back in one piece, all healthy?" Lily was whispering.

"You will," he gave her a friendly smile, "and no less beautiful." Lily gasped with relief, looking like she was going to burst into tears.

"But I wouldn't mind if my car is a write-off," I said, and Frederick chortled knowing what I was talking about.

"What?" Lily looked staggered.

"I rented the car from Ewis. When I picked the car up at the airport, the guy serving me added the cost of CDW insurance, despite the fact I refused it, loud and clear, a couple of times."

"So, you drove into me deliberately?"

"Of course not, who do you think I am?"

"No idea, and I'm not interested anymore. When can we go back to our lives?" she looked at Frederick in anticipation.

"Have I said that you can go back to YOUR old lives?" Frederick smirked.

I felt like the whole world was closing in, and the other clouds flying around us were about to suddenly surround and suffocate me, "Reincarnation? I whispered. "Are we going to come back and experience some worse existence to appreciate our old lives? Will we return as humans?"

"You both have a tendency to assume and get ahead of the facts."

"I wouldn't call it reincarnation," he hesitated, and I thought he was taking every little opportunity to torture us. "The board refers to it as Soul Recycling and as of today it is the official name of our new program. I'm the executive project manager of Soul Recycling," he said proudly exposing his large white teeth.

Lily hid her face in her right palm and bent in half on her chair.

"The good news is that if you complete your tasks well, you can return to your old lives!" he said cheerfully, and Lily and I jumped up from our chairs – she shedding tears of joy and relief, and me clapping my hands and repeating, "thank you, oh thank you."

"My advice to both of you is – be *vigilant* because the seemingly easy every-day issues are going to turn out to be more complicated than you could have ever imagined. Don't underestimate your role in shaping the fate of the person whose life you're going to have. And finally, last but not least, you're not there to judge anybody, but simply guide their lives on better paths."

"Copied," said Lily. "But what's going to happen with my life? Will you keep us in a coma for the time being?"

"Nope," he said flippantly. "We'll erase the whole car accident, at least temporarily."

"So, who will live my life while I'm fixing somebody else's problems?" Lily looked petrified again.

"Selina."

"Me?"

"You've got to be kidding me! Her?" she asked so outraged that normally I would take offence, but actually I was more than happy to become a successful beautiful woman who travels the world and meets interesting people.

Frederick shook his head, "She's perfectly capable of putting your life on the right path, and you can do the same for her."

"Perfect," she rubbed her hands. "I'm good with people and I can sell myself. I can get her a decent job."

"How do you know that's what I want or need?" I asked outraged before quickly realising I was about to be in charge of her life, so I said calmly, "Don't worry my dear, I'll find you a decent husband, so you won't end up an old spinster, who brings home every stray cat she meets and eventually leaves her fortune to a local pet shelter or museum."

"That would actually be a good thing to leave your fortune to..." Frederick didn't finish, suddenly noticing Lily's sulky face. "So, what was I talking about? Ah, I'm glad you like the idea of switching lives—"

"And what if we don't?" asked Lily.

"I can't tell you what's going to happen with you *Up Here*. As long as you're not officially dead, you're not allowed to learn anything more about the Other Side."

"How convenient for your new innovative project," Lily snapped.

Frederick gave us a wicked smile, "Are you ready to make a deal?"

We nodded hesitantly not knowing what to expect – a hand shake, a seal of our mixed blood or maybe immediate catapulting into each other's bodies.

I didn't notice if Frederick flicked his fingers, but when I blinked we were all standing again in the Hall of Mirrors. The only difference now was a gold and marble desk standing in the middle of the room. Frederick's glass tablet was resting on top of it.

"I won't bother with chairs. It shouldn't take us much time. Sign the terms and conditions at the very bottom with your finger," he pointed on the tablet.

"Are we allowed to read it first?" Lily asked irritated.

"Of course," Frederick forced himself to smile. "But I've already told you everything."

Lily and I bent above the desk trying to read all fifty points of the terms and conditions."

"What the hell? It says here that if we don't manage to fix each other's lives we might get stuck in them till we die," Lily said while standing with her hands on her hips and looking straight into Frederick's eyes.

I thought that I wouldn't really mind if the worst-case scenario was life on Earth as Lily, and the simple thought really surprised me. I didn't know much about the woman, but still in my mind there was enough there to suspect that her life was way more enjoyable than mine.

"It is a possibility but only if you both fail. The next point down says that if you successfully fulfil your task, then you can be back to your old life."

"And what will happen if one of us fails?" I asked.

"She will have to give back the life and..."

"And?" Lily and I asked simultaneously.

"And the project is still a work in progress, so we haven't decided yet. I'm optimistic and I do believe that you'll both do well."

"But what if one of us doesn't?" I wasn't going to give up. "You must've talked about it?"

"The very last point says that if we fail, we will have to accept the consequences but it doesn't say what they are," Lily said.

"Firstly..." Frederick started irritated, "if you lived your life as decent human beings, we could've sent you straight to Heaven, and there would be no problem right now. You seem to forget that we're giving you a second chance here, so I think it's rather inappropriate to expect we give you a third one, or that you deserve some mitigating circumstances."

"If you managed your firm better, I could go to Purgatory and there would be no problem now," Lily snapped, and I elbowed her gently, thinking it wasn't wise to make him angry. To my surprise, she didn't explode with more anger but gave me a sympathetic look – for the very first time I felt like we understood that we were not running against each other, but we were on the same boat and had to fight to rescue both of us.

"Trust me, your idea of Purgatory is much better than it currently looks," he said, and I saw fear painted all over Lily's beautiful face. "Look, if you fail, you're definitely going to come back to me, and we can talk through your options, which of course I would have to discuss first with the board. Also, it would depend on why you fail, so whatever you do – you must know that ends don't always justify the means."

"Oh god, so if I fail, I'll be stuck in Selina's life, or I go straight to Hell! How bad is her life that you compare it to Hell?"

"I haven't said anything like that," he gasped. "You might spend the rest of your life as Selina trying to save yourself from going to Hell, and if not – another option might be taking somebody else's life and continuing to try..."

"Something like Purgatory on Earth," she said.

"Exactly."

"How much time do we have to put each other's lives on the right paths?" I asked.

"We'll review your progress in a year."

"Haven't you read all the conditions?" Lily looked at me disapprovingly and turned to Frederick, "Fine, I'll sign it and what's next? Are we switching our lives straight away or will we have a preparatory course before we start in our new roles?"

"No, it wouldn't be fair – nobody gets a preparatory course before being born, but I'll give you each an assistant who will provide you with some guidance. They will appear when you need them, but they won't always be able to help beyond listening."

"Will they materialise each time we think about them?"

"You'll get company phones that are visible only to you. You can either text or call your assistants," he said, while opening a drawer in the desk and handing each of us an identical glass smartphone. "Check your phones regularly because your assistants will send you helpful tips regarding your new lives. We don't want you not to recognise important people, miss birthdays, dental appointments or suddenly enjoy some food you normally hate or are allergic to."

"Brilliant," I said pressing my contact lists and seeing only one name, "Gabriel... Won't we get your number?"

He shook his head.

"Basil?" Lily said through clenched teeth.

"It's not the Basil with whom you slept in high-school," Frederick explained calmly.

"I hadn't even thought about that, it's just..." she hesitated, while staring at Frederick, "I think Gabriel sounds more professional than Basil."

Frederick sighed. I could tell he had enough of the two of us, so we were soon going back to Earth. I wasn't sure, however, whether I was more excited or scared. "I can assure you they went through the same training and both passed their exams with flying colours. They're equally professional and experienced."

"And they're men again. Is the whole place *Up Here* run by men?" I asked.

"I've told you, I'll have to kill you if I tell you," he said amused.

"Fair enough," Lily snapped.

"Now..." Frederick pressed his palms together and positioned them between his toned biceps, "before we all go separate ways, you've got a chance to give each other a brief few words of advice."

"Right..." Lily started, "take a week of leave and go to a spa hotel somewhere on the coast of Spain or Italy to relax. Then when you come back..." she was speaking faster and faster as if she had it all prepared, "find in my diary a number for Meredith, my psychotherapist, call her and say you would like to start seeing her again once a week, ideally on Friday evening somewhere between work and seeing friends for a drink in town. You'll be able to track my whole weekly schedule from the same red diary I keep on my bedside table. Try not to meet up with my sister and my parents for another couple of months, which shouldn't be too difficult as we don't have any events like birthdays or weddings coming up. When you finally meet up, ignore most of what they're saying – anyway they'll be saying the same things over and over again," she rolled her eyes.

Lily wanted to say something more, but Frederick stopped her with his open palm. "That's enough, thank you," he said matter-of-factly and looked at me encouragingly.

"A whole year..." I sighed.

"At least," said Frederick.

"Okay, in that case accept all corrections that Virginia Russel will make to my book. She should email me this month. I don't always agree with her, but I trust her more than I trust you, and the book can't wait a year. Then pay her as much as she wants and send the book to all the agents from the list that I keep on my desktop."

"That's all?" Lily looked surprised. "Any clues on how to deal with your husband and kids?"

"I don't have any children. One more thing – try not to kill my mother-in-law."

## CHAPTER 4
## New Selina

I didn't start my new and hopefully temporary life by waking up in someone else's bed. Not that it would be the first time I woke up next to a man I didn't recognise – but I was very grateful to Soul Management Ltd that they saved me the pleasure of meeting my husband while exchanging our morning breath. Frederick *dropped me off* in East Hampton on Long Island. Actually, what he called dropping me off was more like violently pushing me off the cloud, while I was still talking to him.

"I'm sorry, but I'm running late, and you need to move on with your life girl," he shouted while I was already falling.

I landed like a cat on four paws, completely unscathed – the only issue was that I jumped straight into Selina Woodhouse's body. When I first met the New Me, I was squatting on a wooden terrace and staring at my long fingers and toes, covered with matching pastel pink varnish. Initially I felt dizzy, so it took me a moment to stand up and take in the rest of my appearance. I was wearing a light floral dress that probably contained every conceivable colour in all different shades and variations. It stopped at the middle of my calf and made me feel like I had transformed into my great-great-grandmother from a family album, one so old that it had started falling apart and losing pages. I stretched my arms in front of me and bent down to look at my legs. I pinched my stomach and touched my boobs. I was still in the slim bracket, but I wasn't as toned as I had managed to get used to during all those years of running, spinning and skiing. I thought with nostalgia that I wouldn't feel comfortable anymore in any of my old super-tight designer outfits. The only smaller part of my body was my breasts.

The terrace was huge, more square footage than most UK houses. One part was covered with a steep roof, which protected a floor-to-ceiling stone fireplace, a long dining table for twelve as well as a low square table surrounded by four wide armchairs. The roof was held up by several long white pillars. The uncovered part of the terrace was even bigger, and I noticed six sun loungers with umbrellas and small tables. All furniture was modern and made of grey rattan covered with ivory cushions. The only people who I knew had white or ivory cushions outside were those who had a full-time housekeeper or ran a laundry business.

The exposed part of the terrace also had plenty of space for guests to walk around with their drinks and admire the view, and there was a lot to admire even for a well-travelled interior designer. On that side of the house the only thing separating the terrace from a deserted sandy beach was a line of low but very dense dark green bushes. The sun was high on the cloudless sky with a gentle breeze. The sea was shimmering like a crystal glass, completely undisturbed by people swimming. I suspected that even if the beach wasn't private, the nearest access to this particular piece of sand was likely several miles away from the house, protecting the mansions of the wealthy and uber-wealthy.

"I think the house is in a pretty good state after last night. Juana did a great job cleaning it all in three hours by herself," I heard a male voice and turned back to see Leo, my husband. He looked exactly like the photo that Frederick showed me just before he pushed me off the cloud. Leo was a tall, well-groomed, thirty-five-year-old with gelled dark dense hair, a Hollywood smile and a toned body. He was wearing a light grey polo T-shirt, a pair of blue jeans and dark blue trainers.

"I agree, she did well. Maybe we should give her a pay-rise," I suggested flippantly, and he looked at me like I was mad. *Rich Scrooge*, I thought, *the worst type. When a man appears to act like a penny pincher but doesn't have much money you can at least hope he's economical and thrifty, and that once he gets wealthier his attitude will change. There is no hope for a rich Scrooge.*

Leo stood right next to me, his left arm gently dabbed mine, and I felt like I was on our first date – slightly smitten, insecure and not knowing what to expect next. I took a breath, thinking I liked his perfume, maybe a bit overwhelming but pleasant and fresh. A friend of mine who used to analyse men's aftershave would have probably said he smelt confident, masculine and powerful. "I've just been on the phone with Rick," he gasped, "a sudden change of plans I need to be in D.C. tonight."

I nodded with understanding, not having a clue what his initial plans had been. "When are you coming back?" I asked hoping that it was in the very distant future, so I wouldn't have to deal with him straight away.

"I won't be back home this weekend. I'll be working late on Friday, and my father is right, if I'm serious about the job I should really be attending more social events. I mean, I know what you're going to say…" I said nothing giving him an opportunity to give me as much detail as possible. "I know you're thinking that we had a big event last night, but a Hampton's cocktail party is still more of a casual social do than actual work. It's not the same when you spend most of your evening chatting about your vacation in Aspen, boarding schools in Switzerland and… but having said so, the dinner on Saturday…" he hesitated again, while rubbing his chin, and looked at me like he wanted to make sure I was still listening to him. I felt like he got used to his wife finishing his sentences for him. More! He expected it.

"What about the dinner on Saturday?"

"Yeah, the dinner," he paused to clear his throat, "you can go with me if you want. There is an early flight on Saturday morning. The dinner doesn't start till eight o'clock."

"I'll stay at home unless you really want me to be there. I've got so many things I would like to do, so many things…" I said imagining searching through the whole big house to find out as much as I could about my husband and myself.

"It's what I thought," he said enthusiastically. "You could do some writing, go to the beach. Take advantage that the season still hasn't started."

"Yeah, sure. Exactly what I would like to do," I smiled, relieved that he had provided me with an excuse.

"But could you also finally fill out the papers?"

"Do you mean the papers that..."

"Yes, the papers," he snapped slightly irritated. "If you haven't changed your mind, they're on my desk. We've got no reason to wait. I don't think that the campaign is standing in our way – it's more of an excuse that we've both been using to postpone what's inevitable. Besides, if everything goes according to plan, we could be done with the whole thing before the campaign starts."

"Done?"

"Whatever you want to call it. We've been trying for the last two years, and you're soon thirty-two."

I swallowed hard, feeling an invisible string wrapping around my neck. It had crossed my mind that Leo would want to have sex with me, and knowing the circumstances of being a wife to the same man for nearly eight years, I suspected he might like to have a child sometime soon. My initial plan was to have occasional sex with my beloved hubby, while taking contraception without telling him – but just like that during the first few minutes of our first conversation he managed to ruin my whole plan. He wanted me to get pregnant without having sex with him! I had absolutely zero chances of fighting his sperm when lying under general anaesthetic.

"They're actually saying now it's best to have your first child by thirty-five, not thirty."

"Who is saying that?"

"American scientists," I said with enough doubt in my voice that he immediately caught on and used it to his advantage.

"It doesn't matter anyway. It's best when we both want it, and I thought it was what we both—"

"Of course, I want a baby..." I interrupted, "a baby with you," I added, again I couldn't remove that hint of doubt from my voice.

"So, don't you think we've been trying long enough?"

"I think there are some alternative methods that can help to increase fertility. Acupuncture or—"

"Bullshit," he snapped. I didn't believe in what I was saying so I found it hard to build up an argument without preparation. "Is it about the injections? I get it that you're not good with needles, but don't you think it's worth the sacrifice? Mum kindly offered that she could come and do the injections every day when I'm away."

"Wonderful, how sweet of her. Is she a nurse?"

"Oh, stop. You don't have to be a nurse to do it, you just have to be brave enough."

"Right. I just have to stop being a coward."

"Look, you always say how much it annoys you that people don't consider your writing as a job of any kind... How they keep asking you what you're really doing during your days, especially when I'm away; or they're quizzing you with smirks on their faces on the number of hours per day you spend on your book. You could cut all the nonsense by getting pregnant," he said with a smug face. "Everybody understands that a woman wants to stay at home to look after a baby."

"But everybody is always questioning how you can stay at home to write a book."

"Exactly," he exclaimed happily as if I had already agreed to have in-vitro with him. "Do you know that Melanie said to Roger that your book was just a little hobby and something to distract you while we're trying for a child? Now, you'll be able to prove them all wrong by writing and having—"

"You don't say," I snapped. "Have we got any other friends who need me to make lifechanging decisions just to prove they're talking nonsense?"

"I think we should implant two embryos at the same time," he said totally ignoring me. "I know they say that it doesn't increase the likelihood of getting pregnant, but it significantly raises the chances of having twins, but—"

"But who cares, right? Especially when you're away with work and I have to deal with them on my own."

"Don't be silly, you're not going to be alone," he said and for a moment I felt better. "My mum will help you." Leo's arguments for having a child with him would probably kill me if I wasn't already dead, or half-dead.

"I'll have a look at the paperwork," I said, meaning exactly what I said, that I would *have a look* at them. "How's the preparation for your campaign?" I asked only to change the topic because I wasn't that interested in whether he was campaigning against raising taxes for the rich, or he was fighting for his right to purchase the beach in front of our house. I wouldn't necessarily support these ideas, but at least in my current state I would have personally benefited from both.

"As usual, we need more money but we're getting there... Oh, have I already told you that Marcus Van de Berg is most likely to support us with a very generous donation? Apparently, he's moving towards RepDem now. He never liked Republicans, and now he apparently had enough of the Democrats. I'm going to see him personally next month at his apartment on Fifth Avenue and try to convince him to go all Violet now..." Leo said in one breath, his eyes shining, and hands vividly gesticulating.

"Are you joking? RepDem?" I was not much into politics, but I had listened to enough of my parents' conversations to know that... that my mother would never give her vote to Democrats, or my father to Republicans. When I was ten, and my sister was eight we moved for three years to Chicago, where our parents got their surgical residency. I witnessed countless conversations with their work colleagues and neighbours about the importance of better access to healthcare and limited access to guns. Inevitably such issues always led to discussions about politics, but luckily, they never got particularly vicious. I was convinced it was partly due to the fact that people were exchanging their views with full stomachs and pleasantly intoxicated heads, while getting toasty over sizzling sausages on our barbeque. Who would have the energy? The discussions weren't purely theoretical because my parents were entitled to vote in the USA. Mum had American nationality that she gained when born on a holiday to the US, a deliberate effort by my cunning grandparents. Dad had previously studied at Harvard and subsequently spent a few years working in New York. After getting US nationality he would have never returned to England, if it hadn't been for one Christmas holiday spent in Cornwall, where he met my mother. At the time the centrist RepDem didn't exist, so it was better for them to move to England. Their marriage didn't need any more reasons for friction. But that was Lily's life, which I needed to forget for a moment.

"Yeah, right? I would never guess... although he's got a house in the Hamptons and would like to buy a long strip of what is currently a public beach, and of course he's against raising taxes for the richest. He knows that I'm not going to be the one who opposes that, right? Even if I've somehow mentioned it somewhere."

"Why would he care so much about your opinion?" I asked flippantly, annoyed with his arrogance.

Leo laughed out loud, "I love your sense of humour. "As the future President of the United States people tend to be interested in my opinion."

I laughed, which he quickly took as me being amused by his joke. *President? Of the United States? And if that's not enough he wants me to have kids with him – ideally twins, ideally pronto, and ideally in a long-distance relationship with him and very close commune with his mother. How is this fair? If Selina wanted to have children, she should be the one carrying them. Frederick gave me a year here! It's totally unfair that I would be the one feeling nauseous and then pushing the kids through my perfect vagina, just in time for Selina to get back on the act!*

"I've got one more question…"

*Oh, my dear god, no more! No more questions and revelations from YOU! I'm emotionally drained.*

"Yes?" I asked sheepishly, feeling afraid of the next bombshell.

"You did a very good job with my last speech. Keep your fingers crossed because if we get some money from Marcus Van de Berg, I'll employ a professional speech writer, but because we're still not there yet, could you run through my next one? You know… use your magic."

"How long is it?" I asked matter-of-factly.

"Twenty pages, maybe twenty-five."

"You said I should spend the weekend on my book and relax on the beach, but now you're asking me to fill out the in-vitro papers and work on your speech," I snapped more irritated than I intended to be.

"Well, it's just improving it, I've already written it. Do you know how much time, energy and consideration it takes to write such works? A few corrections is the easy job."

I burst out laughing, which only intensified the redness of his angry cheeks. "I have no idea, I'm not the one running for President."

"Since when have you become so... I don't know, so..."

"Since today, and imagine what I'll become when you put me on hormones and keep asking for more favours? Oh, no wait! You won't even be here."

"I see," he nodded with understanding, *his* understanding of the issue because he quickly added, "you're on your period. It's not a good day to talk about anything important. I'll call you when I get to the city. I'm not going to ask you for anything more now, but mum would be grateful if you could put her pillow covers in the laundry today," he pointed to a couple of sun loungers stained with red wine.

"Why can't Juana do it? And what? Are they her pillow covers?" I asked angrily forgetting that I should have been more careful in what I was saying.

"You won't stop, will you?" he looked at me disappointed, and I thought that there was probably no rescue for me anymore – it was signed and sealed, I was going to Hell. "I've told you so many times that we're not lying to anybody, we just don't get into the details. It's my mother's house, which in practice makes it mine, and what's mine is yours so it's not really a lie. We couldn't do such grand parties in our Southampton house. Where would you squeeze the people? And yes, I bought my parents all the garden furniture but we use them the most. Mum could never afford it, and you know that my father is very careful with money. It's enough they let us throw the parties here. If it wasn't for us I don't even know whether they would keep such a massive house. They can barely afford the property tax.

"Oh, so—"

"So, Juana can't do it, we can't afford her more than once a week in this house."

## CHAPTER 5
# New Lily

I was sitting in a sports car at a traffic light in Oxford and staring with curiosity at a guy in his black SUV, who was stopped at the same red light just next to me. He was vividly gesticulating with a grin on his face. Despite him putting his window down, I couldn't hear what he was saying. There was something arrogant about him, but I couldn't put my finger on what exactly it was – his smile, large designer sunglasses, leather jacket? Eventually my curiosity won over, and I lowered my window an inch. What was he about to say – *hey babe, fancy a cuppa?* Or more like, *good morning, beautiful day, isn't it? Would you let me invite you for dinner?* Nobody had flirted with me so openly in years – I wondered whether it was because of my large wedding band and even bigger diamond engagement ring, the fact my husband could become the next President of the United States, or just because nobody fancied me anymore.

"Lady, you've got a dead animal all around your front wheel. I'm only telling you that so you won't freak out later. There is a car wash less than a mile away from here, they will be able to sort it out for you. Do you want me to drive in front to show you the route?"

I nodded. I was shocked, and he didn't even know how much. Somebody beeped behind me. I still had a green light in front of me. I looked around, the road was clear, so I put my foot on the gas and drove behind the black SUV. After a few minutes of slow driving in traffic, we turned into a petrol station, which had a small supermarket, car wash, and coffee shop. The man driving the black Land Rover got out of his car first and headed towards a young guy in blue overalls working at the car wash. The guy first made a disgusted face, then put on a pair of rubber gloves and laughed.

"Thank you," I said to the owner of the Land Rover. "Can I at least buy you a coffee?"

"It's very nice of you but I need to pick up my kids from pre-school. My wife will kill me if I'm late again," he smiled.

I glanced at my wheel from a safer distance. It looked horrendous. I didn't need to see more details, so I went to the coffee shop, got a double take-away expresso and a halloumi wrap to eat in a small garden outside. I thought it was ironic that I was so close to home but couldn't see my mum or any of my friends. *I wasn't at the traffic lights*, it suddenly struck me. I must have stayed in the Hamptons. *It's not your home anymore. You're Lily now*, I heard a voice in my head saying.

I walked back to the car to pay the guy for cleaning up the mess. "Can you tell what I killed?"

"A couple of squirrels."

"So, there were two of them, oh god," I squealed.

"Don't worry. If it makes you feel any better, I'm sure they were running away from a fox, and you offered them a quicker death."

"Thank for trying to make me feel better," I said forcing myself to smile.

I got inside the car and sat there for a few minutes breathing heavily, before I switched on the engine and saw the route on my satnav. It was taking me to a place in Chelsea as my final destination, so I concluded that must be home – my new home. Frederick had said I lived in a posh area of London, and he had mysteriously instructed me to follow the signs that appear. I suspected he was having loads of fun with the project and us as his puppets.

I stopped in front of a row of white brick townhouses in the middle of Chelsea, pressed a button on my wheel and said, "Call Gabriel."

"Hello, how can I help you my dear?" I heard a warm voice.

"It's Se... I mean it's Lily Rice."

"I know, who you are," he laughed. "Don't freak out, but I can also see you."

"Amazing! Silly me. What's my flat number? Where do I park my car?"

"Drive towards the underground car park on your right. Stop just in front of the gate so the computer can read your number plate. When it does, you'll see a green light and that's when you need to put your right palm on the screen so it can read your fingerprints."

"Are you kidding me?"

Gabriel laughed. "Your apartment is the top two floors of the building, and there are only four floors, so you won't get lost. It's number 3."

"I've got a two-floor apartment in Chelsea? I can't wait to see it!" I started getting excited. And it's all for myself! I'm single now! Whoa!"

"Not quite single."

"But I live alone."

"You do. But a couple of quick reminders. You told your family last night that you're going out with Nathaniel, right? Nate, as you normally call him, who is still married and has two kids that you've never met. Your parents and sister expressed their dismay and you left their house late at night in a rush—"

"Gotcha, married Nathaniel—" I tried to rush him to finally get into my apartment, only mine. I was going to order some take-away, get a bottle of wine, put my legs up and for a while do nothing. I had been through a lot recently, I deserved a moment of relaxation. It was also what the principle owner of this body had ordered me to do – to relax! That reminded me, I was also supposed to book a week in a spa hotel somewhere on the coast of Spain or Italy...

"Are you listening?" Gabriel asked, but I didn't have a chance to reply because a smart-looking man knocked on the driver's window. "Oh no, don't tell me I've taken his damned parking space."

"Don't—" Before Gabriel managed to say anything else I lowered my window.

"Hey, do you always have to make me wait for you?" he said cheerfully. "Who are you talking to?" he arched his eyebrows.

"Not that I feel I need to tell you, but a friend of mine," I said and heard Gabriel hang up.

"A male one?"

I nodded, "But you have nothing to worry about. He's totally out of this world."

"Who isn't nowadays?" he murmured and got into my car without invitation.

He was a tall brunette, probably in his early forties, wearing a plain blue shirt, beige chinos and navy boat shoes with no socks. He smelled of a mixture of red wine and chocolate cookies.

"Have you already been drinking?" I asked surprised. "It's only two in the afternoon."

"Just a glass of wine. I couldn't go through a Sunday pub lunch with my family totally sober," he laughed and kissed me on my cheek. Suddenly I wished I hadn't cleaned dead squirrels from my wheels but had gone straight home to have more time to discuss details with Gabriel. *How far does Nathaniel live from me?* I was thinking nervously. *God, I hope we're not neighbours and I don't see his wife every day. No, it can't be. How did he get here from Sunday lunch?*

Nate was crazy handsome with wide strong arms and long fingers with manicured nails. He was definitely looking after himself within reason. He looked younger than most people in their forties.

I drove into the spacious and well-lit underground car park, quickly found number three and parked my super-duper car in a space twice as big as was necessary. I got out of the car first, while Nathaniel was writing an email on his phone. It gave me a moment to realise I had been driving an Aston Martin. *Leo would love that, although not in lime green. But he would also say that it was an utter waste of money and completely inappropriate for a respected politician.*

"Sorry, I needed to reply to a client who's been pestering me recently," Nate said, slowly getting his legs out of my Aston. "Seriously if not for the money she's paying me, I would tell her to buzz off. She's happy about the first two floors of the house, but she keeps changing her mind about the third. First, she wants to put a large freestanding bath in one of the five en-suite bathrooms, then she wants the bathroom to be smaller and to have the bath in the middle of the bedroom, then she doesn't want a bath on the floor at all. And she has to inform me about every little idea like ten times a day."

"So, what have you told her this time?" I asked heading towards the car park lifts. I was surprised at how comfortable high-heels could be, until I looked at my feet and saw I was wearing flat pink pumps. *Wow, so this is what tall people feel like*, I was thinking, *it's like constantly wearing super-comfy high heels*. I quickly examined the rest of my body to avoid further surprises. I was wearing light grey jeggings and a loose white blouse that had a couple of small stains from the wrap I had for lunch. *Loose clothes look the best on super slim people... Like me!* "Sorry, what have you just said?"

"You seem to be quite distant today, is it about the phone call? Is it about the guy?" he asked suspiciously but I ignored the question. "I've told her that I'm an architect and maybe she should discuss certain things with her interior designer first, before I re-draw all the walls again. She's insisting on solid walls and concrete floors, so it will be really hard to make changes later."

"Makes sense to me," I nodded entering the lift. "Why are you laughing?"

"I'm pretty sure you're going to be her designer. I heard the boss' secretary saying Naomi only chose our company because of you. She watches your TV show every Tuesday and she's got the set of cushions from your latest collection."

"What?" I mumbled, making big eyes like an owl. *My own TV show? My own collection of cushions? W-h-a-t?*

"That's right," he laughed. "You've got such a great reputation for dealing with very difficult clients that you would probably get her anyway, even if she didn't mention you specifically to the boss."

"Wonderful," I said, not having more time to reflect on it. I had to find my key to the apartment, and it wasn't in my handbag.

"What's wrong?"

"I think I left my keys at my parents."

"Don't you always have them with your car keys?" I put my hand into my snazzy pink crocodile Birkin to touch the car keys, but there were no keys there... although... *It's a smart lock!* I suddenly got enlightened, took out the door fob and put it against the lock.

"You need to fix it so you can use the code," Nate said as we stood in my hallway, me flabbergasted at seeing the apartment, him confused at why I looked so stunned.

"I need a glass of water with ice, it's so stuffy I'm getting dizzy," I rushed through the enormous hallway, past the grand piano and wide stairs straight into an open plan kitchen and dining room. All the appliances were inbuilt and hidden behind pastel grey cabinets so I was glad to see Nate going to the toilet. It gave me enough time to search through the floor-to-ceiling cupboards to find the door to the American-style freezer.

"Feeling better?" he asked, taking a glass from one of the cupboards and pouring himself water from a tap different to the one I had used just a minute before. *Great, I'm probably drinking water that has gone through a water softener. Well, I've just come back from the dead, so they won't send me back on my first day. At least, you would hope so!* "You need to take some rest after what happened last week."

"Yeah, I've actually been thinking about taking a week off and going somewhere sunny. Would you like to go with me?" I said, immediately regretting inviting him on a trip that would give me some time to adjust to this new life, new body, new everything.

"Lily, you know I can't go with you for so long. If I take a week off, I need to go with my wife—"

"You know what? Forget it. I need some time on my own anyway."

"It's exactly what I thought," he said cheerfully. "You mentioned you spent so much time around other people that you need some time on your own, and I think it's a great idea. Take a couple of days off and fly somewhere nice."

"A week or two."

"I'm not sure you'll be able to convince anybody that you should take a whole week when we're so busy at the moment, but if you take Thursday and Friday off then you've got four days and—"

"You're right," I said certain that I would ignore his advice. "Have a drink and grab some food, I'm going to change my top and have a quick shower." I made a few steps towards the staircase. I had a quick glance around. The whole downstairs was a massive open plan space with a kitchen, dining room and a lounge with two L-shaped sofas. The kitchen island was like half of my Hampton's kitchen, and the whole floor was bigger than my three-storey house. It wasn't as cosy as my place, but grand, light, fresh and breath-taking. *You're Lily now*, I heard a voice in my head.

"Do you mind if I assist you?" he said, and I felt a shiver down my spine. "I could use a shower."

"Okay, so I'll have a bath, and you can have the shower," I said, convinced a house like this would have a shower separate to the bath.

"I see you're not in the mood today," he said almost offended like he had flown all the way from Papua New Guinea just to have sex with me. "Do you want to grab a glass of wine and talk about it? We don't need to talk about last week if you don't want to, but I just—"

"Fine," I snapped and walked towards the grey L-shaped sofas. *I need to know what happened last week.* I sat down with my legs crossed looking straight at a marble chimney with a large modern painting above it. I had no idea what it depicted but I liked it – it was full of bright oranges, red and yellows and made me feel good. Nate took a couple of glasses and a bottle of red wine from my wine fridge or rather wine cellar that a minute before I hadn't even known existed. He had opened a round glass and metal door in my wooden kitchen floor and then gone several steps down till I could only see the top of his head. He looked like he had been going into the deck of a boat. I wondered whether Lily had bought somebody's closet in the flat below just to have space for this cellar.

"I feel like white." I always preferred white wine or rosé. I rarely had red, very rarely without a three-course dinner.

He gasped, "I wish you told me that when I was in the cellar trying to choose the best wine for the occasion. But it's definitely more like you."

"More like me?"

"Yeah. Picky, demanding and totally inconsiderate of my time," he smiled.

"I don't actually need any wine. A glass of water would be better."

Nate obviously decided I needed some wine, so he brought me

both, a bottle of French Sauvignon Blanc, and a glass of water. "Thank you," I said putting one cushion on my lap, and one between me and Nathaniel.

"So how are you feeling?" he asked not even looking at me but pouring himself a whole glass of red.

"Not bad."

"Okay, that's a good start... So how was your weekend? I mean the weekend is still not over I'm sure I can make you feel better," he said with a wicked smile to which I didn't respond. "I mean more like... yyy... how was last night with your family?"

"Terrible."

"That bad?" he asked in disbelief like I was obviously exaggerating.

I nodded. "I told them about us. I really didn't mean to, but they pushed me."

He put his glass on the coffee table in front of us and wiped his mouth with his hand. "You did what?" he yelled.

"That bad?" I asked with a smirk.

"I don't know how you can find it so amusing? Oh, wait..." he raised his finger, "I know. You find it amusing because you don't have your own family!" he stood up and started walking nervously around the lounge, his feet practically invisible, hidden in the deep pile of the soft pastel pink rug. "And now what? Do you want me to attend another dinner party at your parents? Drink beer with your father at his barbeque?"

"I hadn't thought about it but it would be nice," I said only to provoke him and see what he really thought about us.

"That wasn't the deal. I thought we were having fun, not playing boyfriend and girlfriend. I've got a wife and children."

"Shouldn't you have thought about them before you got involved with me?" I asked flippantly, touching my smoothly manicured nails.

"Involved? So, are we involved in anything here? God..." he put his head in his hands, while walking in front of floor-to-ceiling glass doors, leading to a long narrow balcony with a garden view. "Derek was right, you can't just have a good time with a woman. It's always got to be something more."

"You can relax, my parents won't post a photo of us in bed on their Instagram."

"You don't understand. We weren't supposed to tell anybody. We've talked about it, and I thought we both agreed that as soon as somebody knows about it, about us... it—"

"It makes it feel more like an affair?"

He let his hands fall along his body and nodded. "Look, I think we need to have a break. What do you say?"

I hadn't expected it would be so easy to get rid of the married guy from my life in order to direct it on a better path. The only thing I was regretting was not knowing what sex with him would be like. My sex life with Leo had left a lot to wish for in the last couple of years. I sized him up, he was handsome but, on reflection, not half as attractive as he appeared to be at first sight. I took a deep breath, "I think your chinos are a bit too short for a guy with such hairy legs."

## CHAPTER 6
## New Selina

I woke up to the sound of the ocean and wind playing with the white plantation shutters in my windows. I looked at an old black plastic alarm clock that was taking the entire space on a dark wood bedside table. It was ten am – a time at which I was always working at full speed in the office or at a client's house. Alternatively, I could be browsing through a furniture store or sitting on a plane and flying to see another pad I was going to totally transform. I never slept till ten even on weekends or during holidays as it was my time to go for a run or have my hair and spa appointments. I felt thirsty, so I stretched my arm to reach for the glass of water I'd put the night before on the floor under the bed. The bedside table, which was reminding me more of an antique kitchen stool, was not only too small to hold anything else than the chunky alarm clock, but it was also constantly moving on uneven wooden boards. While I was reaching for the glass, I caught a glimpse of large plastic boxes under the bed. *Why do people buy smart-looking beds with space underneath if they are just going to use them for storage? Wouldn't it just be better to get a bed with storage? Eh...*

I slowly raised myself up from the large squeaky bed, my back aching from a mattress as hard as a prison's floor. I walked through a double glass door and stepped out on the balcony. The beach was empty with the exception of two women dressed in colourful raincoats, strolling slowly with a dog the size of a squirrel. Light rain was disrupting the smooth surface of the sea, towering waves were violently hitting the shore creating mounds of white foam. The sky was getting dark with seagulls noisily flying to shore. There was something ominous and glowering in the view, but I enjoyed it. I liked standing there alone and being able to gather my thoughts. My husband wasn't supposed to be back for two weeks from D.C. Perfect! I had no work. Perfect! Peace and quiet – exactly what the doctor ordered – well, at least what he ordered for Lily.

---

The house wasn't so grand, spacious and private like my new mother-in-law's, but it was in a quiet and affluent location. It had a high wooden fence separating it from neighbouring houses on both sides, and a large gravelled driveway with a double gate at the front. Yesterday, when we came back from Leona's, I parked my Tesla on the drive behind Leo's sports car and watched as my husband rushed to one of the immediate neighbours to pick up a parcel. While he was frantically pressing the doorbell, I was reflecting on how much I liked my car. I had been thinking about getting one in London, but then, well... life... or rather death happened, and now I had one HERE! It was just a shame it was Leona's car, not mine. Apparently, she had broken her arm in mysterious circumstances, so I became her driver.

"That guy is nice but completely antisocial," said Leo, while opening the door to our house with his right hand, a big flat parcel squeezed under his left arm. "I'm going to stop sending him invites to our parties, he always only sends regrets. What's the point? All I'm doing is making him uncomfortable."

"Have you ever tried to just invite him here for a beer?"

Leo dropped the parcel on the floor in a small narrow hallway, and quickly walked into an open-space lounge with a modest kitchen. "Why would I do it? I told him we were only using this house as an office and for storage."

"Come on, the house is not that bad," I exclaimed. "It needs some love and care and some paint and—"

"And a serious extension that would involve buying out the neighbours on both sides," he snapped angrily. "It's a perfect little house for a perfectly average American family, but it's not a house to show people around when you want to be President of the country."

"Right," I nodded. It was a three-bedroom house in the Hamptons, and as far as I knew an average American family would never be able to afford it. "Maybe it would do some good to show this house instead of your mother's villa, to get the message out there that you're a normal guy who's able to understand normal people."

"No matter what people say, they don't want a normal guy from next door ruling their country."

*Ruling the country, hmm...* I was thinking, while going across the corridor on the first floor to have a look at Leo's desk and the speech he had printed out for me. *So, I'm the one who spends time here, the one who actually lives here. I'm supposed to be writing my books and correcting presidential speeches, but my husband is the one who's got his man cave, his office in one of the three bedrooms.*

"I think I'm going to use the guest bedroom as my study," I said last night to Leo.

"I've told you before it's not a good idea. That's going to be the baby room... unless of course all the procedures take so much time that we move to the White House first. Anyway, there's no point getting used to the space and then—"

*The procedures. The White House. Was he even listening to himself?*

"Okay, so can I share your study?"

"You know how much I NEED the space to be mine. I like to have everything in order exactly as I need it. You've got plenty of space to write. What about the terrace downstairs, the lounge or the balcony in our bedroom? All you need is the laptop, right? I don't know why you're so argumentative today. Is it because I'm not going to be back for two weeks?"

*Right, men have their studies, and women have their dressing tables! Actually I'm going to change mine into a desk – it's big enough. I'll throw the mirror away, chop the pink mini drawers under the table, which only block my knees, and ta-da. Decided!*

I was about to enter the study when I heard the doorbell ring. I looked at my pyjamas, which with stretched trousers and a long-sleeve baggy top, reminded me of a well-worn tracksuit. "I'm not opening any door wearing this", I whispered as my hands stretched the bottom of the top, examining its material. "Nice, soft cotton, at least". I sat behind Leo's desk as large as our kitchen table, and reached for the twenty-something pages speech, when I heard my phone ringing next door. Reluctantly I moved back to the bedroom to pick the phone from the floor and saw that it was Leona calling me.

"Hello," I said grudgingly. I wasn't in the mood for my first encounter with my mother-in-law, but I was curious of what she was about to say. *Is it about taking the cushions to the laundry? Or does she want me to drive her somewhere?*

"Hi Selina," she said with a cheerful singing voice. "I'm just opening your front door so I'm calling not to scare you. Are you still in bed, love?"

"Yyyy..."

"That's what I thought," she said, and I heard somebody turning a key in the main door and treading around downstairs. I ran to the bedroom closet, but before I had a chance to find a suitable outfit, Leona was standing in my door. She was staring at me disapprovingly, her head shaking, hands resting on rounded hips.

"I was just about to get dressed. I've been working on Leo's speech since first thing this morning and I got soooo into it that I've forgotten to change and have breakfast." I didn't know why I was even explaining myself. Was this the effect she had on people? She should have been the one explaining herself to me – she was trespassing! People got killed for doing this in America.

"Yeah, I bet," she murmured and took a deep breath, while still staring at me, now with her arms crossed. She was wearing a light pink costume, with a pencil skirt covering her knees and an unbuttoned jacket with white blouse underneath. The left sleeve of the jacket was slightly folded because of the cast, which began just above her nails and ran all the way to her wrist. Her mostly grey hair was shaped into a perfectly round bun, with a pair of glasses on a string imitating a hairband. Leona was only fifty-six, but she seemed to be determined to age herself at least another decade, if not two. Her white sandals were granny-style – flat and chunky with high straight soles they looked like orthopedic shoes. Her face had barely any make-up on with the exception of a very shiny lip-gloss and a bit of pink blush.

"How's your hand?" I asked just to make conversation and distract her from staring at my pyjamas.

"As you can see," she snapped. "Immobile, useless and impatient to recover. But that's not what you're really asking right now. Don't worry, I haven't told anybody and I've already forgiven you."

"Forgiven me?" I whispered. *What does that mean?*

"I didn't do it to myself, did I?"

"Oh. I'm sorry, I wish I could turn back time." *And you have no idea how much! I want my old life back!* "How did you get here?"

"How do you think? It's called Uber," she snapped. I thought that if she was a dog, I would be trying to walk away slowly without making eye contact.

"Okay," I clasped my hands. "How about you let me change and then I make us some coffee?" I forced myself to sound cheerful.

"I don't know why you think I'm stopping you from getting dressed," she snorted, then yawned and rubbed her eyes but didn't move an inch, continuing to stand at my bedroom door.

"Leona, can I have some privacy?"

"I'll make myself some coffee. I hope you've remembered to get some normal full-fat milk," she said and finally walked away swaying her hips.

I glanced around the small closet that I shared with Leo. His shirts, trousers and jackets were perfectly ironed, while most of my dresses looked like they were pooped out by a rhino.

"Where do you keep your sugar? You know how much I hate any substitutes!" Leona shouted from downstairs. I could hear her frantically opening and closing the kitchen cupboards. She handled them so aggressively that I wondered whether the furniture could lose some paint in the process.

"I don't know."

"What?" she yelled irritated.

I clenched my fists, "Try the cupboard above the fridge," I shouted knowing exactly what would happen. I didn't have to wait long to hear Leona's screaming and coughing. It bought me some more time and eventually I decided to go for the same awful flowery dress, which I was wearing when I landed on Leona's terrace.

"Oh, I'm so sorry," I said covering my mouth with both hands trying not to laugh. "I told Leo last night not to squeeze all the bread flour in the cupboard where we keep the spare sugar. I told him this would happen. I can't even reach it there."

Leona was still coughing. She must have rushed to the sink to rinse her face because the water made it even worse – she looked like she had noodles all over her face.

"Well, a good housewife would let him have his way so he can feel happy and masculine, and then when he's not looking, she would go and correct everything," she said pulling a compact mirror out from her bag. She made a pout like for a selfie #AnotherFightWithMyDaughter-InLaw #TheBitchWhoStoleMySonDidThisToMe #MoreHateLess-Love. Then she quickly shut the mirror with a bang, but kept the pout. "You'll need to drive me home so I can take a shower before meeting Barbara for lunch. I might also need a hairdresser and pedicure later. You've totally destroyed my hair."

"Has it ever occurred to you that I'm not aspiring to be a perfect housewife?"

"You don't have to be perfect my darling... but it would be useful if you were at least not terrible. For example, you could save a lot of money if you did Leo's ironing or..." she spread her hands and looked around the kitchen, "or cleaned his apartment in Washington when you're there so we don't have to pay Mimi. Once you move to the White House, you can afford to be lazy, but—"

"I do my own ironing, which is enough. He's a big boy... Hold on, who is *we*?"

"What do you mean?" she asked baffled.

"I'm sure you used the word *we* in reference to paying Mimi."

"Oh, I pay Mimi to clean Leo's apartment. He's got a job, so obviously he can't do any cleaning himself."

"And he pays Juana to clean your house, how nice!"

"Yeah, we're a good team," she said with a smug face, and I quickly realised there were three of us in this marriage. "You know, sometimes, you could surprise him and pop to D.C. with a fresh pie or—"

"And ideally I would fly there on a broom to avoid the economy fare," I laughed and started looking for a coffee machine, but couldn't find one. There was only a percolator, and I had no idea how to use it. I'd forgotten many Americans still preferred brewed coffee. "I'm busy with my book," I said taking two mugs from a cupboard and preparing us tea. "Sorry we ran out of coffee."

She frowned her bushy eyebrows, "You should always have both coffee and champagne in case of unexpected guests."

*I'm starting to realise you're hardly unexpected.*

"Sorry," I said flatly.

"And as we're talking about your book. I don't mean to hurt your feelings, but darling..." she paused to take a deep breath, "you're nearly thirty-two. Don't you think it's time to stop dreaming and start making plans?" I deliberately punctured her teabag with the teaspoon and not taking it out passed her the cup. She took a sip and coughed. "Let me make myself some coffee. I think I saw a whole bag up here," she said opening a cupboard above the kettle.

"Have you come all the way here by Uber to tell me that?" I smirked. "Next time, you should call to save us all the trouble."

She made herself the coffee and started drinking it with no milk or sugar. "I wanted to ask you for a favour. I would do it myself, but of course I've got a broken hand and..." she paused, probably expecting me to apologise, but I wasn't so convinced it was my fault. "Could you design some invites for the charity gala that Emil is organizing in August? I'll send you all the details later. Then, could you send them to everybody by post and email? I'll provide you with the guest list next week. Then, I need you to make a new list of only the guests who can make it, including their plus ones and any information you can find about them. Oh, and recently I've also lost my gardener. He tried to flirt with me, which I find very unprofessional. Could you find me a new one? It can still be a man but maybe younger than fifty. And..."

"I'm sorry but even if I wasn't busy with my writing, I've still got Leo's speech to rewrite and—"

"And the IVF paperwork, I know. I can help you fill out your medical history and the like, so you've got more time to do the invites and find me a gardener," she said eagerly as if she was offering me a free holiday to the Caribbean.

"Thank you ever so much, it's so kind of you," I said in a singing voice and she gave me a beaming smile. "But no, thank you. Can't Emily or Hope, I mean..." I paused because I almost forgot the name of her younger daughter, "Can't Emily or Faith help you?"

"Emily is a very busy working mum, and Faith has to study to get to college this year," she snapped. "You could actually take example from Emily. She's writing a beautiful blog about being a mum of three small children and running a house. She always cooks a three-course dinner, so she does something for her family and at the same time she creates fantastic content for her website. Isn't it wonderful?"

"Admirable," I mumbled.

"If you really want to be a writer, you need to sell yourself first, then the book. It's how it works now. If you have to show a little bit of your butt and bosom to the public, why not? Doesn't the end justify the means in this case?" she was speaking enthusiastically. "To make it all the more interesting, it should have a bit of real life like when your groceries were delivered to the wrong house... And if you don't sell your book, who cares? You can always get some good marketing deals out of it? Some freebies like cosmetics or nappies."

"And sanitary pads?" I said with a grimace.

"Yes, sani... Fine, you can laugh, be as arrogant as you wish and think you're better than all of us! But Emily is likely to get a cookbook deal and it's all because her blog is blossoming."

"Good for her. Maybe she could create handmade invites and show them later on her blog?"

"Fine," she snapped. "You don't need to help this family."

"Fine, give me the guest list and I'll see what I can do."

Leona smirked and pulled out of her bag a pile of papers rolled into a thick tube and fastened with an elastic band. At the same time, she accidently dropped on the floor an invitation to a party. My eyes lingered on a gold font saying Leona and Emil Woodhouse. I picked it up before she noticed that she had dropped it. I read it out loud, "Divorce party, June 22th."

"Are you getting divorced?" I screamed and she looked at me terrified. Her cheeks and neck went red, her shoulders hunched up and head bent down. I was surprised, she suddenly appeared so small and vulnerable.

"Technically, the divorce hasn't been finalised yet, but it should be in less than a month. It has taken us a while to agree on how we share our money and assets..." she was speaking quickly and nervously. "Emil finally agreed to give me the Hampton house, but only under the condition that no matter what, our children inherit it. I can give it only to them and I can't sell it myself. I think it's fair enough. So, don't you worry. You will still be able to party at my villa," she smiled bitterly.

"For god's sake, I hadn't even thought about that. Are you okay?"

"Absolutely fine. It's what we both wanted," she said matter-of-factly, but I wasn't convinced it was what *she* wanted.

"Does he have someone else?" I asked automatically before I realised my question was nosy, intrusive and completely unnecessary.

"Who doesn't at our age? Or rather, what man doesn't have someone else after such a long marriage? We got married young. We quickly had children. There wasn't much time to contemplate on how much or how little we loved each other," she said, pushing her tears back, but she quickly cleared her throat and got her confidence back. "Emil is still good looking in his sixties. I wasn't really that surprised to find out he had a lover. I just couldn't believe he would leave me for her. She's only thirty, which makes her younger than Emily. What do they have in common? What do they talk about? Or maybe they don't really talk – I guess that's the point. Anyway—"

"I'm so sorry."

"Don't be. Women can be real bitches, they have no morals. Can you believe that a beautiful and educated thirty year old woman wants to marry a sixty-year-old man? I just wonder what her true motives are.

She was the one insisting on Emil taking our Hampton house. She wrapped him around her little finger. Poor Emil."

"I don't know whether I would call him *poor*. Besides, it's as much his fault, as hers."

"Don't be silly. Men are like children. They can't resist temptation, and cunning foxes like Ariana use it to their advantage. I heard about a rich old man who was poisoned by his much younger wife. I told Emil about that, but he only laughed – it's how blind he is! That man was much richer but—"

"Let's hope Ariana is not a killer."

"Anyway, please, please..." she held her hands like at prayer. "Don't tell Leo and my daughters. Don't tell anybody."

"I don't understand—"

"We didn't want them to worry. They've got such busy lives. It's best they find out when it's all over and in more pleasant circumstances, like a good cocktail party," she smiled pointing at the invite. "Who doesn't like a good party, eh?"

"Right."

"Oh, by the way you look gorgeous in that dress I gave you. I told you that more conventional clothes would suit you and I was right. Now, you look like the wife of the President of the United States."

"Yeah, in nineteen-thirty-two," I murmured

"Sorry?"

"I said I love the dress."

## CHAPTER 7
## *New Lily*

Gabriel provided me with a name list of my work colleagues along with pictures and character traits, but after the argument with Nate I wasn't in the mood to memorize them. As apparently relaxation helps our memory, I first lay in a hot tub, which had a view of a wall-sized tropical aquarium, and then in my huge soft canopy bed. I couldn't stop thinking about why a beautiful successful woman would ever get involved with such an arse – a married arse. *Do I love him?* I was wondering. *What's there to love? Was it the first time he acted like that? Was it because his amazing but secret sex life was at risk of being exposed and would have to be over?* At two in the morning, I felt exhausted with my own thoughts and went to search for some sleeping pills. I quickly found them in a bathroom and after taking two I slept like a baby. On the downside, I didn't hear my alarm clock and had very little time to get ready for work. I definitely didn't have enough time to try all the clothes in my boutique-size closet. I chose a simple navy pencil dress with short sleeves, natural tan tights and skin-coloured small heel shoes. Monday was supposed to be one of the hottest days of the year and later when I was standing in front of my office building I prayed for working air-con and deeply regretted not choosing sandals or a lighter dress.

I glanced at the tall red brick building with some glass extension at the top and took a deep breath, *Go girl! You've got it! Oh, no you don't! – you left Gabriel's phone at home! And it has the name list!* The phone didn't just miraculously travel with me, I had to carry it around all the time. It was too late to go back home. Way too late! I rubbed my fingers through my loose hair and adjusted the bottom of the dress that was restricting my movements. *Never mind, you've been on the Other Side – you can handle a day at the office!* I managed to convince myself to go through the main door, slide a magnetic card at a gate and get into one of four lifts. Before I took the courage to leave my lift I went up and down three more times with my heart going so fast I thought I would have to call an ambulance.

The door opened with a ding straight into an open-plan office, but unlike anything I had experienced in my old life, everybody had plenty of space around their desks. You couldn't talk to your neighbour without taking a walk.

"The dress is a bit overkill," said a woman with a ginger bob who suddenly appeared out of nowhere in front of me. She was wearing a green sundress, which looked expensive but casual, and gold strappy high heels.

"Yeah, I've got the feeling I'm going to be a little hot wearing this today."

She rolled her eyes, "That, and why are you covering absolutely everything? Where are your boobs, girl? Where are your knees and your toes? Don't tell me you even vaguely care what Molly says about you?"

"I don't but do you think I should?"

"Amanda, I need to talk to you pronto," said a tall man passing by. It was only for a moment but when he gave me a brief look my heart skipped a beat. He was one of those people who didn't have to do much to make their presence felt. Confident walk, perfect cheekbones, gentle but decisive eyes and the voice – he could easily work on radio talking about anything and people would want to listen.

"You see, even he thinks the dress doesn't suit you. Where did you get it anyway, on *join.a.convent.com*?

The man turned back and laughed, first glancing at Amanda, and then at me. I just wanted him to go away as I could feel I was starting to blush. "Oh, buzz off, it's just a dress."

"Your wish is my command," he said still laughing and disappearing behind a milky-glass door at the back of the open plan space.

"Shut up!" said Amanda with her mouth wide open. You might be wearing different clothes, but your attitude hasn't changed! I know we don't do the whole hierarchy stuff here, but to say *buzz off* to our boss?!" I must have looked like I saw a ghost because she quickly added, "Don't worry. He's got a good sense of humour. Anyway, I need to go. The boss is calling. And don't be bothered by what Molly said. It's better to dress a la *Affair Provocateur* than *become.a.nun.com*".

---

"Lily, here you are! I've been looking for you all morning." I heard a female voice behind my back before I had a chance to say anything back to Amanda, who was already toddling towards the boss' office. *Affair Provocateur? What a bitch! Or maybe I'm the bitch now – the one who's seducing a lovely and innocent married man? I'm sure my old mother-in-law would put the entire blame on me! She always did, just like she always made women into cunning and calculating monsters, while men were silly, nature-driven and blameless. More importantly, how much does bloody Molly know about me and Nate?*

"Oh, hi..." I said with a smile, turning to look down at a petite slim woman, who even in her high heels was barely reaching my shoulders. She had dark hair put into a high ponytail, chunky glasses, and a dress made of the same material as mine, but with no sleeves and with the hem above her knees. "I couldn't get a parking space so I'm a bit late," I explained in case I reported to her.

She looked at her smartwatch flashing as messages kept popping up, and raised her eyebrows, "I thought your walk to work was only ten minutes... But anyway—"

"It is but I can't walk quick enough in this dress. It would take me at least an hour," I said seriously, and she burst out laughing.

"I wouldn't worry about Molly. She's just jealous of you," she said waving her hands. "So..." she typed something on her watch. "I've got a few phone calls from Naomi Fonda and Roxana Jones. Both very disturbed..." she rolled her eyes, "because they couldn't get in touch with you on Friday evening or for the rest of the weekend."

"Oh, I had some family meeting and—"

"You should have said. I'd have put it in your calendar so you wouldn't have been pestered. I can't be your assistant if you don't tell me your plans. To be honest, I was surprised to know you were coming to work today. I thought that you would take some leave after last week, but of course that's none of my business... So, Naomi Fonda and Roxana Jones wanted to schedule meetings. I've checked, you've got some space tomorrow at the end of the day..." I felt I was involuntarily squeezing my fists, and she must have noticed that, or I just looked generally nervous because she quickly tried to rescue herself, "I can call them right back and make up some excuses. I wouldn't have scheduled anything, but Susana said you were fine and coming back today an—"

"That's fine," I said calmly trying to relax. "Do you know what the urgency is about? Have they said anything?"

She nodded, "They said a lot, like really a lot," she gasped. "Long story short, Naomi needs some advice on her bathroom and she wants you to design her house in a slow style." I gave her a quizzical look. "Really, slow style? I've asked around and none of the designers here know what she means. Amanda suggested maybe a countryside style, and Susana said something about pastel green and blue walls."

"And Roxana?"

"Roxana wants you to completely change the style of her villa. Apparently now she hates anything Italian. Her exact words were *effective immediately*," she laughed. "You see, she just found out her husband was cheating on her with an Italian student when they were living in Tuscany."

"She told you all of that?"

"I had to listen to her all Sunday evening but it's fine, it's part of my job and that's why we're the best design company in the country and we're getting that award next month. Our clients just love us," she said proudly. "So, where was I? Ah, Roxana is now in love with a Spanish hacienda style. I've made some more notes for you that I can send... or scan and send because I wrote it all down in my notebook..."

"Don't bother, can you copy them now and leave them on my desk?" I asked, hoping she could guide me to my desk.

"Sure, would you also like some coffee?" she asked cheerfully.

"That would be great, thank you," I said, not moving even an inch, instead I took out my mobile from my handbag and started pretending I was reading some messages. Then I realised the phone was still on airplane mode so nobody could have got in touch with me. Lily must have done it deliberately after the family meeting. Or she did after the thing that happened last week that everybody knew about except me. When I changed the phone mode, my mobile immediately started beeping with messages like mad and I had to put it on silent. I raised my head up and was glad to see my assistant heading towards a glass door with coffee and some papers. *I've got my own office where I can hide from the whole world! Hurrah!*

"We ran out of the caramel capsules, so I made you a standard latte. If you don't like it I can pop downstairs, I'm dating a guy from that estate agency on the ground floor," she giggled. "He also likes caramel latte."

"No that's fine. Thank you," I said hearing a knock on my door.

I sat behind my desk on a pearl white leather chair and looked up to see the boss again. "Jane, I was just about to email you but as you're here – could you re-schedule the morning meeting tomorrow for eleven, arrange a room and let everybody know?"

*Was she also his assistant?*

"Of course," she said and left us alone. *Please don't go!* a little girl was screaming inside me. *Jane, don't leave me with him alone!*

"Look, I'm sorry for the *buzz off* earlier. I've had a long weekend, and last week was even longer," I said, while tapping my fingers on my huge white gloss desk and moving the swivel chair from one side to another with my bum, uncomfortably hot in the warm tight dress. I also felt a zip digging into my back and I decided I had to bin the stupid dress – surely it was against all health standards, it was preventing my blood circulating.

"Not an issue," he said and crossed his hands. He was wearing a white shirt with sleeves rolled up almost to his elbows and a pair of grey cotton trousers with silky patterned pockets. The trousers weren't tight but still perfectly adjusted to his long legs. "I'm here to warn you that Susana wants to talk to you in less than an hour. I've asked her to give you one more day to fully digest what happened last week, but she's insisting that it has to be done today. I—" he didn't finish because we were interrupted by the sound of the phone ringing on my desk, and a loud knocking on my door.

"Please come in," I shouted. *What's next? Can I have one minute for myself? Is this my office or a train station?*

"Good morning, Lily," said a woman with a very serious face expression. She was probably in her mid-forties. Women like her were often described as handsome, but never beautiful or pretty. She was tall, slim and had a short boyish haircut. Her breasts were hidden under a white blouse, which was tucked into a high beige skirt. "I knew you couldn't stop yourself from letting her know that I wanted to have a word with her," she looked at my boss with disapproval. I wondered whether she was the boss of my boss or they were peers. "Can I?" she pointed at a round table with four blue velvet armchairs in the corner of my office.

"Please," I said, as something squeezed my throat and I stood up after seeing my male boss heading towards the table.

"Should I ask Jane to bring us all something to drink?" the man asked. He was looking at me with mercy, which was making me even more unsettled. The last feeling I wanted to instil in this deadly good-looking man was pity.

"I'm fine," she said and looked at me.

"I still have my coffee," I said, and Mr Full of Mercy immediately rushed towards my desk to pass me the drink.

Susana straightened back on her chair and laid her arms on the shiny wooden table "Look Lily, I have no intention of getting into the details of why it all happened," she suddenly raised her hands and drew circles in the air. "I don't need to know. Our relationship is strictly professional and I'm not going to interfere in your private life as long as it doesn't affect your work. You've got a lot to think about and consider, but I want to present you with a couple of options and see where you stand with them."

"There is nothing to worry about," said the man.

"Not yet," she snapped, and he chastised her with his eyes.

"I said, there's nothing to worry about," he raised his voice at her. "We're here to help, not threaten." I felt relief, concluding they were more likely to be partners, and the stern looking woman wasn't his boss after all.

"The way I see it at the moment is that your best option is to relocate to New York. I've already spoken to Mike Henderson and they're very keen to work with you."

"Of course, they are! Who wouldn't be? She's our best interior designer bringing this office huge profits. With all due respect Susana, it's not her best option. Lily has the TV show here, and a long waiting list of rich clients, who live in Europe and aren't going to relocate with her. They'll just change company because some of them have already been waiting several months to work with her," the man stood up behind his chair with his hands holding tightly to the backrest.

"Lily might lose all of that if Molly decides to press charges against her and the case goes viral. It's not going to be pretty, and it'll bring bad publicity to all of us. I've spoken to Molly," Susana paused to clear her throat, "she's already spoken to her lawyer, but she agreed not to sue Lily if she leaves for New York."

"Of course, she—"

"What's the other option?" I asked calmly. I actually liked the idea of being a single woman with loads of cash in New York.

"Make an official apology to Molly, and by official, I mean it will have to go on our intranet. And you'll have to say it in front of everybody in the office. She'll also demand financial compensation."

"Which is ridiculous considering the circumstances. There has been no damage," he snapped irritated, his pale cheeks suddenly getting red.

"No material damage but there so easily could've been."

"But there wasn't," he suddenly released the chair from his tight grip and walked across the room to take a plastic cup and pour himself some water from a dispenser standing next to my desk.

"How much money are we talking about?"

"Paying her money only makes you look guilty," he said, and drank the whole cup in one big sip.

"Two hundred thousand," she said. The man tried to interrupt her, but she stopped him with her open palm and raised her voice, "I appreciate it's a lot, but you're a wealthy woman Lily. Your reputation won't suffer much."

"Is there any other option?" I asked.

"Not that I'm aware of. If the case ends up in court, you might need to pay even more and it will go public. If any of you have a better solution, I'm here to listen," Susana crossed her arms.

"I need more time to gather my thoughts," the man said looking into the distance.

"If I relocate to New York, she won't ask for any money or apology?"

"That's right," Susana said looking content, thinking I was leaning towards her desired solution.

"It's odd that she's ready to forget about it if I go away."

"She claims she's afraid of you and all she wants is to feel safe."

"But why would she be less afraid if I pay the money and apologise?"

Susana sighed, "She claims that when everybody knows how..." she put her hands like for prayer and pressed them against her mouth, "how dangerous you are, then you'll stop. I think she's very emotional and I'd be afraid if you take that option, she might do something to embarrass you further ... If I were you, I would just relocate."

"You mean you'd run away," the man snapped.

---

I lay down on my front – my big boobs making me feel like I had two melons squeezed under my neck. I was wearing only a pair of black panties, while a tanned, well-built man was rubbing lavender oil onto my back. Large chunky candles were spread around the room, mostly on its dark wooden floor and above the stone fireplace. They were constantly flickering, playing shadows on the walls, and bringing a delicate citrus aroma, which perfectly complemented the lavender smell.

"Don't worry, the candles aren't real, your floor is safe," Donald said with a beaming smile after I opened my eyes and gasped. "There is no fire hazard. You can close your eyes and relax," he whispered and pushed his warm fingers into my tense shoulders.

When I got back home from my first day at work, all I wanted was to shut the door, switch off the phone and be left alone. But being alone wasn't a given with Lily's busy schedule. I had to fight to have a minute for myself. As soon as I put my handbag on a chair in the hallway, the sound of my intercom made me jump. I pressed an orange button and immediately saw on the screen an incredibly good-looking man. He was wearing a pair of jeans, a grey hoodie, and had a sports bag with its strap across his trunk. *Am I going to be constantly surrounded by beautiful men now? What a tough existence!*

"Hi," I said.

"Hi Lily," he said singing. "Have you forgotten about your massage tonight?"

"Yyy... I'm not sure whether it's a good time..."

"I can come back in fifteen minutes if that's more convenient. You pre-paid me for the whole month and I've already spent the money," he laughed in a friendly manner. "But I won't be able to make any other days this week."

"Okay," I said and buzzed him in.

All in all I was tense, and the massage could be something I needed the most. Well, maybe except a lawyer! If I was this dangerous individual, who had to choose between exile or public humiliation and a two hundred thousand pound fine.

Donald gave me a kiss on my cheek and moved quickly to my spa room, which I hadn't even known existed. It was the only room in the attic, as he called it, but for me it was big enough to be called a third floor. The room had a non-working fireplace and a high bed with a hole at one end for my head, when I was lying on my front. There was also a modern metal and leather rocking chair, a small coffee table, a sideboard with towels and various cosmetics, and a sliding door opening onto a roof terrace. *I don't want to leave this life! I still haven't had a chance to enjoy it,* I was thinking while lying on the bed with my eyes closed, while Donald was preparing the room. He said he had a surprise for me, which turned out to be the electric candles. Apparently, I was afraid of real ones, and he considered candlelight crucial for ultimate relaxation.

I didn't know how much I was paying for the massage, but it was worth a lot of money. Initially it was painful on my neck and shoulders but by the end I felt like I was floating a few feet above the bed.

"I've finished for today," Donald whispered in my ear and covered my back with a warm towel. "I hope you enjoyed it. Would you like me to bring you a drink, switch off the music or pass you a robe? Or would you just like me to sneak out?"

"That was amazing," I murmured. "I think I'll just lie here for a little longer."

"Okay," he whispered and a few seconds later I heard him gently opening and closing the door.

I must have fallen asleep because the next thing I felt was a light breeze on my leg. I heard the sounds of a street with some voices in the distance, melting into one hum. I opened my eyes and saw that the door to the roof terrace was ajar. I didn't remember Donald even touching it. I raised myself slowly from the bed, but before I managed to reach my robe hanging on a wall, I heard somebody moving the terrace door. I jumped on my bare feet and almost slipped because they were still covered with lavender oil. When I turned back, I saw a man's figure standing in the door. Outside was already dark so I couldn't see his face. I covered my breasts with my hands and screamed.

"I'm sorry, I didn't want to scare you. I've tried to call you and left a couple of messages, but I think you switched off your phone," he was saying while entering my room. "We need to talk," said my...

"Boss?" I involuntarily covered my mouth with my left hand and showed him one of my boobs. I must have looked terrified because he rushed to pass me a robe.

"I love it when you call me that, but not in these circumstances," he said seriously, while standing behind me and helping me to put my hands into the silk cream robe, in which I still felt rather exposed. "Let's stick to Nate tonight."

"Okay," I whispered with my left hand holding tight the top of the robe. I felt even more naked than before.

"I need a drink," he said rushing downstairs.

I found a pair of funky white feather flipflops under the massage bed, slid them on and followed him slowly downstairs. *If he is Nathaniel, who did I see last night?* I was thinking, while standing in front of a large mirror in a hallway on the second floor, my feet immersed in a deep soft rug, hands spread on a console table around a crystal vase of fresh flowers. I touched them to confirm they were real. Then I realised the place was definitely tidier than on Sunday night. *Of course, I've got a cleaner!* I looked at my reflection, my make-up was still in a pretty good state, but I wouldn't expect anything less from the expensive cosmetics I used in the morning. My hair was a bit messy, so I tucked them behind my ears. *I still look presentable. I could get a bra because the robe is a bit see-through, but he has probably already seen me naked so it would be weird!*

"I thought you don't drink red," he said, sitting on one of the high-chairs behind the marble island in my kitchen. He already had one new bottle of red and one bottle of white open in front of him, as well as two empty glasses and some kale crisps.

"No, I don't," I said and leaned back against the kitchen cupboards. So, *the new and old Lily have something in common!*

"Yeah, it's what I thought," he said looking at me with anticipation.

"Sorry, I've just woken up. What are you trying to say?"

"That somebody drank my twenty-year old vintage bottle of red that I got from my godfather."

*Sorry, but even if I wanted to, I can't tell you with whom I've been sleeping. The good news is that we're over and it was just sex!*

I cleared my throat, "I doubt it, have you had a good look around the wine cellar? I might've moved it."

"I saw the empty bottle in the recycling bin," he snapped. "Look, I know that I've still got a wife and that's why we agreed we can't be exclusive – fair enough. But now when I'm officially separated with Melania, I thought you'd want..." he hesitated, "you know, a proper relationship... Of course, not officially yet but—"

"I get it, but it took you how long to separate from your wife?" I said with my arms crossed.

"Fine," he snapped. "I haven't come here to talk about us tonight. And I really don't want to know more about the guy who drank my wine. He's clearly got amazing taste in wine and women, but that's all I need to know about him right now."

"So, what do you want to talk about?"

"Lily, are you kidding me? What the hell have you been thinking by not picking up the phone to me all weekend? We need to talk. We need to come up with a solution. No matter what's between you and me, we need to talk about Molly. She's ready to press charges, and she's got twelve witnesses. Besides, Susana is livid, and she's never particularly liked you – partly because she's jealous and partly because you've always been too proud to try and butter her up even a little," he was speaking louder and louder, nervously picking up an empty glass and putting it back down, doing it again and again. "You should be grateful you haven't been suspended. I know the conflict with Molly has been going on for ages and trust me, if not for Susana, I would have fired her already a thousand times, but—"

"I don't know. Maybe I should just go to New York."

"What's going on with you? I've been going crazy not being able to talk to you since Thursday! You're obviously not well yourself."

I shrugged, "I'm fine."

"Really? You're fine? Is this some sort of self-denial? You were out of your fucking mind on Thursday! You threw a chair at a pregnant woman!"

## CHAPTER 8
## New Selina

I pressed the intercom to Leo's apartment, anticipating that at eight in the evening he would finally be back home. It was the second time that day I was standing in front of his house, stubbornly pressing the same button as if it had the ability to catapult him back to the house just so he could open the door for me.

I got to D.C. early in the morning by train hoping to catch him before he left for work as he'd said he would have a late start. At nine he was already gone. He had no idea I was coming. I was afraid he would've asked me to wait till the weekend, and it was too urgent to wait. I couldn't tell him about his parents' divorce over the phone and I had to do it as soon as possible. He would never forgive me if he ever found out I knew about it and kept it from him. I was sure Leona would find a way to use it against me. Also I needed a good excuse to run away from her errands! She gave me the perfect pretext, so how could I not go?

I pressed the intercom again. Nobody was answering. I had the key, but I didn't want to take him by complete surprise. What if he entered the flat late at night, saw me sitting on a couch and had a heart attack? What if he shot me thinking I was somebody else? On the other hand, I was exhausted lugging around my massive handbag, along with several bags full of new clothes and cosmetics, which I bought while waiting for him. I hadn't packed much to take on the train. There was nothing suitable in my closet, and I gave myself a rash just thinking about using any of the cheap cosmetics that I had in the bathroom.

Leo said he had been renting a cheap flat for the last three months, but the address that I found on his desk, and confirmed with Leona, led me to a beautiful terrace townhouse in Dupont Circle. It was three-storey with a large bay window on each floor. I carefully sat down and distributed my bags on the stairs, which were covered with dust and dry leaves. I was wearing a pair of washed bootcut jeans that I was going to bin as soon as I jumped into one of the new dresses I bought. I was just pulling out the phone from my pocket to text him, when in the corner of my eyes I saw a sign saying 'Sold'. *Does Leo really live here or is it just one of Leona's tricks?* I was thinking, with anger filling up my body. She was so happy when I told her I would like to surprise her son with a home-made-pie. "A woman should never stop working on her marriage," she said preachingly, which gave me shivers thinking of how she always liked to blame women. *Does she feel guilty Emil is divorcing her? Does she think it's her fault he cheated on her? Poor woman,* I thought and started writing message to Leo.

> Are you home? xoxo

The reply came instantly:

> Yeah, but very busy. Call u tomorrow!

> I just wanted to ask, what's your address in D.C. xoxo

He typed the address, confirming what I'd already known. I hesitated for a couple of minutes, mulling over my options and then wrote I was next to his door and just about to go in. If he wasn't there, it was already too late for him to get back from wherever he was, and I would catch him lying red-handed. I turned the key in the lock – it worked, which assured me it was the right house. I was tired, dreaming about throwing myself on a couch and having some coffee. I wondered whether the house had a bath so I could use my new Himalayan bath salt mixed with lavender body oils. Oh, I miss Donald so much!

I stood in a tiny hallway separated from the rest of the house by an oak door. After looking around I decided to take my bags further inside, because all hangers in the hallway were taken by men's coats of different lengths and colours, matching scarves, and hats. Underneath the hangers there were two benches, both covered with magazines and junk mail. I pushed the door. The downstairs wasn't big, but it was cosy and more stylish than our Hampton house. The centre of the lounge had a traditional chimney with a large TV above and two ecru double sofas. A small and open-plan kitchen looked newly done and completely unused. I left the bags on one of the sofas and headed upstairs. I was about to shout 'Leo', when I heard somebody moaning behind one of the three white-painted doors. "You've got to be kidding me," I whispered, standing on the top of the stairs afraid to make a move. I reached into my pocket to get my mobile and I pressed video. *At least I'm going to have proof of him being unfaithful when it comes to our divorce!*

I listened to Leo's moans of pleasure for another few seconds, trying to identify where the sound was coming from. *The first door on the left!* It was slightly ajar. I pushed it lightly with my left hand, my mobile in my right hand aimed straight at a large bed with silky white bedding, my legs and hands shaking like jelly. Leo was lying on his back with his eyes closed, arms stretched down both sides of the bed and squeezing the sheet. From the height of his belly button he was covered with a duvet, with somebody underneath. He gave a loud groan. *Damn it!* I wished I reacted quicker and ruined *his bliss*. Unfortunately, he was already mission-accomplished when I shouted, "I'm going to chop it off! Or I'll find somebody who will do it for me!"

Leo sat up like he had been electrocuted. The duvet slowly slid down on a slim tanned back and revealed a perfect muscly arse. The owner of the fit body turned to look at me and sat petrified not able to say a thing.

"What the fuck are you doing here?" Leo shouted, which gave me a kick of adrenaline and I got my voice back.

"That's all you've got to say after I caught you in bed Fifty-shading another man..." I screamed my lungs out. "Or to be more precise after I caught him Fifty-shading you?" I said more calmly.

"I told you, sooner or later it had to come out," said the man who was sleeping with my husband. He had dark brown hair pulled into a short ponytail, long legs and shaved-everything. He was at least thirty but he had that boyish, fresh look that was going to keep him looking young for much longer than his peers. "My name is Keanu. I'm sorry to meet you in such circumstances," he was saying while looking straight into my eyes, pulling up a pair of shiny yellow boxer shorts and putting on a red T-shirt with a Harvard logo.

---

"I'll call you tomorrow babe," Leo screamed as I was walking out of his upstairs bathroom. He was standing at the top of the stairs and waving to Keanu, who was shutting the main door.

"Babe?" I chortled. "You're not even going to try to hide it by saying it was a one-time thing, that you were just experimenting after taking some cocaine or..."

"What's the point, eh?" he said, still wearing only a pair of red boxer shorts, his hands on his hips, red fluffy handcuffs dangling on his right wrist. "You're an intelligent woman. You've already seen two toothbrushes in the bathroom, two different types of shampoo and conditioner, two different male shower gels—"

"I haven't actually," I snapped, thinking how good it was that his real wife wasn't here to witness it. "While I was peeing, I was too busy thinking about my husband being gay or bisexual and probably never really loving me. So excuse me, if it hasn't crossed my mind to check your bathroom cabinet!"

"I'm not bisexual, sorry. I'm a hundred percent gay."

"Oh... I appreciate your honesty – better late than never! So why the fuck did you marry me, and you've been making so much effort to have kids with ME? Can't you just adopt with your golden-tanned Keanu?"

"He's not tanned, you're being racist."

"Sorry, I haven't had as much time as you to examine the origin of his beautiful body."

"Let's have a glass of wine downstairs," he said calmly. "Or something stronger if you prefer."

"Fine, but can you please get a robe or something and take the handcuffs off? I find it rather distracting."

"I would need to call Keanu to tell me where he put the key..."

"Fine, don't bother," I snapped.

"Let me grab my dressing gown," he said going back to the bedroom.

We went downstairs in total silence. The only sound was the wooden stairs and floor cracking under our bare feet. Leo was now wearing a silky purple gown with long sleeves covering the handcuffs and was taking a lot of deep breaths, like he wanted to say something, but he didn't quite have the courage yet to do so."

"Shall I start? Because you look like you're overwhelmed by the sheer amount of information you're soon going to offload on me," I asked taking a seat on the couch, which was submerged by my bags.

He gasped, "I wanted to tell you the truth, just not like this."

"Yeah, I bet," I said watching Leo, who was holding a bottle of something between his legs, struggling to open it. "I bet you did. That's why you asked me to fill in all the in-vitro paperwork – it was your way of preparing me for this revelation," I burst out laughing thinking it was so easy to laugh when I felt absolutely nothing for the cheater and the liar, who happened to be my husband. Otherwise, I would be devastated. *That's why I'm never going to get married. I'd rather be dumped by a man than find out he's cheating on me!*

A cork suddenly shot out and flew across the lounge hitting and smashing a delicate glass vase that had been standing above the fireplace. "I've never liked the vase, but mum insisted on me keeping it here. It's a family heirloom," he said, passing me a wine glass of something bubbly. *Prosecco?*

I took a quick sip, "Are we seriously drinking champagne? Is it to toast our divorce?"

"Look..." he started to sit but when his bum nearly touched a bag, in which I had a couple of new dresses, I screamed, and he stood up straight. "Is that all yours?" I nodded. "Have you bought them today?"

"I thought that I should use your credit card while I still can," I said with a smug face.

"So, you already knew? How?"

"No," I sighed. "I needed some new outfits. My wardrobe is terrible, that's all."

"I think it's fine. You're not working, you don't need so many new clothes," he said outraged. "We need to save for the IVF. Our insurance policy might not cover it and my campaign—"

"Are you serious, Leo? Is me buying a few new outfits the biggest concern of our marriage? Have you already forgotten you've been cheating on me with a man, who I've just met? We're getting divorced."

"We don't need to get divorced," he said sheepishly leaning against the fireplace.

I couldn't believe my ears, "What?"

"Look… 'All the world's a stage'," he said while drawing an arc in the air with his left hand, right palm holding the already-empty glass.

"Don't involve Shakespeare in our marriage. You, me and Keanu is enough."

"All I'm trying to say is that our marriage doesn't have to be real."

"Has it ever been real?" I yelled.

"Okay, you're probably wondering what's in it for you," he pointed at me with his glass of wine. "I get that."

"No, I haven't even—"

"Let me explain my offer. If you don't like it, that's fine, but I assure you we can both make a very good deal here."

## CHAPTER 9
## New Lily

"The real Lily tried to hurt a pregnant woman! What am I supposed to do with that?" I yelled. "Does it get any darker? I shouldn't be dealing with—"

"You are now the one and only Lily Rice and you're going to have to deal with it," Gabriel cut me off. He was sitting on my kitchen island and dangling his chunky calves squeezed in long white knee-socks, his black leather shoes carelessly kicking my expensive cupboards.

"Said the man dressed like a Spanish bull fighter. I'm sorry but I can barely focus when I'm looking at you in this gold outfit with these ridiculous socks. Could you change it?"

"Do you mean flip my fingers and look like a respectable Prime Minister or better…" he raised his finger, "like an angel?" I nodded. "Nope, sorry. I'm not Frederick, I'm still just a human enjoying some of heaven's perks. I still need to dress myself," he smirked.

"What's your Earth job? Is killing bulls for violent entertainment compliant with heaven's employment policy?"

"I'm not allowed to say where I work, but I don't kill anything. When you called me, I was at a splendid Spanish fiesta."

"Can you at least take your hat off?"

"Done," he said and threw his suede black hat straight at me. "Sorry, that wasn't intentional. "So, what would you like to know?"

"I've never got so far in any career to have an assistant, but I'm pretty sure that they are supposed to be consistently helpful, and you are not! You seem to avoid me!"

"Now you've got two assistants in your job. Jane is one of the best—"

"In a job, which I'm likely to lose, and for good reason!"

Gabriel crossed his hands on his chest, "You should try and defend yourself. Molly is a very troubled woman."

"Is that your expression for pain in the arse?"

"Something like that. I don't try to justify your actions, but you've got reason to hate her. Not that it's okay to hate anybody, but—"

"But throwing a chair at her? At a pregnant woman? Really?"

"Firstly, you didn't know she was pregnant. Nobody knew. She's only a few weeks pregnant and was trying to keep it a secret."

"Oh, thank heaven!" I said raising my hands in the air.

"Right now, I'm the closest piece of heaven to you, so technically you could say it looking at me," he said and took out a silver pocket flask from his red and gold jacket.

"What are you doing?"

"It's non-alcoholic Sangria, do you want some?"

I shook my head in disbelief. "It still doesn't change the fact that I used physical violence at my place of work."

"You had a nervous breakdown and that's a separate issue to deal with."

"What has Molly done to me?"

"She's never liked you and never even tried. Nathaniel was right. She's jealous of you in a very unhealthy way. Long story short, she would like to have everything you've got, and she's been more than struggling to do so in every aspect of her life. It doesn't help that her current boyfriend is a man you once dated, and he was crazy in love with you. It also doesn't help she's a few years older and going through an early midlife crisis."

"It doesn't help that I seem to have slept with every man in the bloody company, if not the whole city!"

Gabriel laughed, "That's exactly what she keeps telling everybody but it's not quite like that. You dated Romaine a few years ago, and it was only for six months. Yes, Molly was his rebound and she knew about that, but she managed to make him move on. But, he doesn't love her and was planning on breaking up until he found out about the baby."

"Well, he obviously spent too much time on *planning* while still having sex with her. I bet she got pregnant to finally convince him to marry her."

"Bingo."

"But I still don't understand why—"

"She's been plotting and scheming about how to make your life miserable since she found out about you and Romaine almost two years ago. She's been trying to get your clients by fabricating crazy stories about you gambling advance payments, sleeping with clients' husbands and so forth. Recently she's outdone herself by blackmailing you at every possible opportunity. The night before you threw the chair at her, she demanded that you convince your TV producers to put her on your show."

"What does she have on me?"

"She's been spying on you for a while, and she didn't miss the opportunity to mention it."

"She's my stalker!"

He nodded, "She said that she would tell Nate's wife about you two having an affair."

"Doesn't his wife already know about us?"

"They're officially separated, but she's got no clue about you – it could significantly harm Nate's bank accounts when it comes to their divorce. He signed a deal with Melania that for every year of their marriage he was unfaithful, she would get a million pounds."

"What? How rich or crazy... or both is this guy?"

"Crazy rich and crazy about you."

"So why has he been having an affair with me for so long instead of divorcing her?"

"You never really wanted to believe it, but he claimed he felt sorry for her. Each time he mentioned divorce she faked some physical and mental issues. She voluntarily signed herself to a private psychiatric hospital for three months just to prove it. The kids were devastated. Not to mention the pressure from his family to stick with her for the sake of the children."

"Oh god, and now I've had a breakdown that he witnessed... I don't really feel like doing any TV programmes, so I suppose I could give her mine and everybody is happy."

"Nobody wants her there. You've already tried to get her work on one of your shows. Your producers said that she was an unlikable drama queen with a terrible stage presence. She quickly came across as arrogant and know-it-all. The problem is she didn't believe them and so has continued blackmailing you..."

"Meaning?"

"She's recently threatened you with not only going to Nate's wife but also to the press," I shrugged my shoulders, thinking *Who cares*? "You're one of the most recognisable interior designers in the country! You're a celebrity. You primarily work with other woman, who are jealous of your looks. They won't want you to be near their husbands when they find out about Nate and Steven."

"Steven?"

"The man, who you met on your first night," he said matter-of-factly and jumped off the kitchen island to quickly take his shoes off and crash on my L-shaped sofa. I followed him feeling dizzy from the amount of information I had to digest.

"I wish you told me about that earlier," I snapped, while sitting on the other sofa opposite him.

"I thought it would be better for you to work some things out on your own."

I bent my head back covering my face in my hands and gasped, "What am I supposed to do now about the sociopathic Molly and my job?"

"That's what I'm not supposed to tell you."

"How convenient! I bet you have no idea yourself. I feel that any move I make will hurt somebody, including myself."

"You've got options."

"How about Nate? It looks like he's really leaving his wife and he's ready to start a life with me." Gabriel nodded with a smile glued to his face. "And he's cute."

"I can't deny that," he said excitedly.

"Hold on, you fancy him?"

Gabriel flushed and sighed, "Unfortunately for me he's not gay."

"Okay then," I said rising from the couch to go back to the kitchen area and make some coffee, "I need to start acting. I've got a job to save and a man to keep." I turned back to see Gabriel's face expression, but he was already gone.

It wasn't even a minute before the Soul Management phone started ringing.

"Hi, I've screwed up and disappeared too quickly," Gabriel laughed. "But I think, we're done for today, anyway yeah?"

"Yeah, bye Gabe," I said as I heard my phone ringing again. It took me a few seconds to realise it was my regular mobile. "Thanks, I've got another call to take."

I saw an unknown number and hesitated whether I should answer or not, but my curiosity won. "Good morning," I said carefully, stopping myself at the last minute from saying *Lily Rice speaking*. Whoever was calling should know who I was.

"I don't think it's going to be *good* for either of us," said a woman on the other side.

"I don't understand. Are you calling about the bomb you planted at my house?" I laughed.

"No, but how do you know I'd been considering it?" she said seriously.

"A bomb?" I swallowed hard. I had some serious enemies out there in the wild. *I need a bodyguard!*

"That's right," she said calmly.

"Look," I said and cleared my throat to start more confidently, "Are you with Molly? I just want to say that whatever twisted games you're playing, I'm going to put a stop to it very soon."

"I'm not the one who's playing at anything," she kept her voice calm. "I don't know who Molly is. I'm just another broken woman, who is calling you out of politeness to tell you I know everything, so you don't have to hide anymore."

I stood still. "You're his wife, aren't you?"

"Correct," she said, and we both went completely silent for a moment. She had thrown a bomb after all. "I'm not going to make the divorce more difficult. I'm going to take what's mine including the affair money and start fresh. I'm only thirty-five – I have a whole life ahead of me."

"I'm sorry. I never meant to hurt you," I said with a breaking voice.

"That's all right. If not you, Nate would find somebody else. I can't force him to love me. I wish you all the best and—"

"I know you don't wish me well but that's okay," I said feeling totally stupid.

"And I admire that you love him so much that you've already given up so much for him. I still love him, but I wouldn't do that for any man."

She was obviously playing me, but my curiosity skyrocketed and I had to ask, "Give up what?"

"Being a mother."

"Excuse me?" I yelled. "We've already talked about that and we both want to have children someday." Gabriel had told me, and he wouldn't have lied.

"Well, I wish you all the best, but from what I've found out about you online and from..." she paused, "you don't sound like a woman who takes chances. Vasectomy reversal doesn't bring much hope," she said in a sweet, innocent voice.

## CHAPTER 10
## *New Selina*

"Here you are," my mother-in-law from hell was standing above my bed, her hands on her hips, lips pursed, and huge dark eyebrows frowned in an angry bird expression. I quickly glanced at her from under my duvet, which I was now holding all the way up to my nose, trying to cover my naked body. She was wearing a vivid green two-piece costume with a flower brooch over her heart. If she had been wearing a matching green hat, somebody would have taken her for a younger version of the Queen of England. "Exactly what I thought. It's two o'clock in the afternoon, the sun is high and you're still in bed! Move your lazy arse and come downstairs because we've got a lot to talk about."

"If you want me to go anywhere, you need to leave my bedroom. I've got nothing but a pair of skimpy pants on," I said yawning.

"Are you one of those people who sleep naked?" she said taking her arms from her hips to cross them over her big breasts, which were testing the buttons of her jacket.

"Exactly, it's healthy for your skin. You should try."

"Leo bought you three pairs of tartan pyjamas for Christmas," she said and paused giving me an impatient stare. "Have you been sleeping with somebody else? Have you been cheating on my son?"

Even if I was, he wouldn't mind, but I couldn't tell her that. Before I managed to say anything, she was already looking into my closet and under the bed, opening my curtains and checking the balcony and beach. "Well, I can see some footsteps in the sand…"

"Relax, even if I wanted to, I have no energy to be unfaithful," I yawned again. I slept terribly last night and then Leo gave me a lift to the airport so I could catch a very early flight back to New York. I drank so much caffeine on my way down here that I'm not even sure whether I was driving the car myself."

"The car," she shouted with her forefinger high in the air. "That's the next thing we need to talk about!"

"Can you please give me ten minutes so I can get dressed and see you downstairs?"

She gave a loud snort and reluctantly headed down. After the sleepless night and the journey home I had a pulsating headache. I went to the bathroom cabinet to get some painkillers. Looking at my tired reflection in the mirrored cabinet, I wondered whether agreeing to Leo's deal was the right decision. I negotiated some pretty good terms for myself, and I was sure the devastated and shocked Selina wouldn't have been able to push for them the way I did – but was it a decision that would save somebody from burning in Hell, or rather push them through its gates? Unless, the point was, I was going to Heaven for saving Leo from his living hell if everybody suddenly found out. I still had some time to change my mind, but the clock was ticking – as soon as I got to the Hamptons I read a message from my husband saying that his lawyer was preparing the paperwork for our deal. *I needed to speak to Basil*, but I also needed to kneel down above the toilet and throw up – it was all too much for me.

"Are you coming downstairs?" Leona materialised at my bathroom door. The whole concept of privacy was alien to this woman. "Have you been drinking?"

"Could you make me some black tea?" I said rising from the floor and wiping my face with my hand.

"Fine, your old mother-in-law with her one hand in plaster will make you a cup of tea," she was speaking louder and louder. "Even if you were the one who put my hand in plaster."

Maybe Selina had broken Leona's hand. I wouldn't be surprised if she had a nervous breakdown. Leona was as much a bully as Molly. They both had the ability to awaken the worst instincts in their victims. Neither would stop until somebody got seriously hurt.

"I made you a glass of water. It's the best cure for a hangover," Leona was sitting behind my kitchen table, with two glasses in front of her.

"You can't really MAKE a glass of water," I snapped and switched the kettle on.

"I was just worried that I could get electrocuted while making tea. Each time I see you in this house, some accidents happen. First my hand, then you tried to suffocate me with the flour."

"That's why I'm not going to drive you anymore. I think it's too risky. I'm also starting to believe that I'm bad luck for you. Besides, I need some space. Some space from you Leona. I want you to give me your key back, and if you're not prepared to do it, I'm going to change the locks," I said categorically. It was one of the terms I negotiated with Leo – his mother had to be gone from my life.

"Don't speak to me like that young lady! I should've recorded that because my son is not going to believe his wife is so... so..." her face was getting redder and redder. In her vivid green costume she looked like a Giant Lime. I started fantasizing about squeezing her into a gin.

"So stupid not to set any boundaries earlier? I strongly agree," I said calmly and sat down on a chair on the other side of the table. I leaned back, one hand fiddling with the handle of my mug, another hanging over the back of the chair. I crossed my naked legs and felt like a cigarette. I only smoked on special occasions, and this felt like one of them.

"And what are you wearing? Those clothes are completely disrespectful."

"I think Leo's shirt is perfectly fine for this event, but don't worry about my wardrobe I've already taken care of it and I'm going to continue..." *With the assistance of your son's credit card* I wanted to add, but I stopped myself at the very last minute. People say how great it is to spend your own hard-earned money, but having been on both sides of the argument – I felt equally uplifted spending my husband's hard earned money.

"I know! I've seen all the designer clothes in the spare bedroom!"

*Unbelievable, she had already gone through my stuff!*

"You're so outrageously intrusive!"

"How dare you speak to me like that? How dare you throw away my son's money? You've got a whole wardrobe of clothes. You also don't need to fly to Washington. You could have taken a train. And I saw you've leased yourself a car! A brand-new Tesla!"

"I have, indeed. The public transport here is rubbish like in most of America. I need a car and I'm going to buy one soon."

"You can always go back to England if you don't like it here!" she leaned across the table pointing her finger at me.

"It's what you would like, isn't it? I'm not good enough for your son, is that what you're saying?" She was too shocked to respond. "No woman will ever be good enough for him, and guess what? I'll tell you a little secret..." I stopped myself at the very last minute. I'd made a deal with Leo and now more than ever I was sure I was going to sign up to it.

"What were you going to tell me?" she asked through clenched teeth, sitting straight on her chair and biting her lower lip like a child. Was she trying to stop herself crying?

"I'm not going anywhere," I said leaning across the table and looking straight into her eyes. "I'm not going anywhere, but you will. I'm going to get you an Uber, and then..." I crossed my arms on my chest, "I just don't care. Get yourself a driver and get the hell out of my life."

---

**18 Hours Earlier**

"A deal? Is that what our marriage is for you – a deal?" I placed a half glass of champagne on the table and went to get some water with ice from an impressive ice cube dispenser in the fridge door.

"Look, you know that I love you," he said, and I laughed while slowly walking back to the lounge area. I sat again on the sofa with my legs on the coffee table. "I don't mean romantically, but I've always loved you and still do."

"Am I like a sister to you?" I laughed, not sure whether my head was spinning from the champagne or all the revelations descending on me like Niagara Falls.

"You're my family Selina. You're one of the most important people in my life. You're a wonderful person and I hate myself for not being able to give you what you really deserve. If only I wasn't gay—"

"Fine, I get it," I snapped. "Or I don't. You prevented me from being really loved. For all those years I've been living a lie. My life is an illusion, A JOKE." I yelled with all the strength I had in my lungs. "What else do you want from me?"

Leo moved to the end of the sofa, his bum touching its edge, elbows resting on his knees, half of his face hidden in his palms. "I'm sorry," he said with tears in his eyes – I couldn't tell whether the tears were real or not, but I didn't care.

"I gave you almost a decade of my life and somehow it's still not enough."

"I tried. I did try to love you, to fix myself."

"There's nothing to fix! You should've married Keanu or another man instead of making all our lives so miserable!"

"My father would never have agreed," he said meekly, his hands now holding the edge of the sofa, eyes cast down.

"Don't you think that your parents shouldn't dictate your love life? By the way your mother's been way out of line. Yesterday she—"

"I know, we can change it if you decide to stay with me," he said in a begging voice and then poured himself more champagne and stood up next to the fireplace.

"Be careful, there are some bits of the broken vase on the floor. I don't mind you hurting yourself, but there's been enough drama tonight and I don't like seeing blood."

"My cleaner will deal with that tomorrow," he said and walked away to stand at the back of the sofa, looking at my shopping with disapproval.

"Of course," I gave him a forced smile.

"You'll get a cleaner in the Hamptons and—"

"Leo, but why? What's the reason you want to continue living this lie?"

He bit his lower lip, "It's gone too far. What do you think the voters will say when they find out I've been lying to them the whole time?"

I nodded. "You might lose some people but you might also gain others."

"Probably not enough to win the election. The public already trust car sellers more than politicians..."

"That makes sense," I said but he ignored me.

"I've been doing so well in the recent polls. The country is not ready for a gay president and his First Gentleman, who is half-Hawaiian and half-Mexican, as well as our children from a surrogate mother."

"Oh my god! Is this all about getting kids out of me so you can form a perfect stereotypical presidential family?"

"Listen to me..." he rested his elbows on his knees and put his hands together like at prayer, "we both want children. You're already in your thirties and maybe you haven't had a chance to think about it yet, but it takes time to find the right person to be a parent to your offspring. I'm gay and..." he hesitated, "I can't imagine a better mother to my children."

"What about Keanu? Have you asked him about his opinion? Or is he just a temporary lover? Friends with benefits kind of relationship?"

"I've been with the same man since high-school," he said proudly, realising too late what a faux pas he had just committed.

"That would mean that when you met me you were already with him."

"I ran away from the US to forget about him."

"But why?"

"My father is a... I think Keanu is right – my father is a homophobe," he said gasping. "I should have realised it earlier, but I've been blaming myself and I wanted to make him proud. He's done so much so I can be where I am now."

"Where are you now Leo? In a fake marriage, lying to the whole world about who you are just to become president?"

"To be fair it doesn't make me an exceptional candidate for president," he laughed nervously.

"Probably not, but you've still got time to change it."

"There are some people in my party, who would never approve of it and I need all the approval I can get to win."

"Let me get this straight, you're seeking approval of those who would condemn you if they found out you're gay."

"I'll be in a much better position to have some influence in the world when I win."

"Really?" I snapped. "Or will you just be forced to make up more and more lies to cover the old ones? How long would you like to continue this whole farce?"

"Depends. If I win, four to eight years."

I laughed loudly. "Okay, I'm done here. You're not taking any more of my youth. I actually can't believe that for a split second I was seriously considering making a deal with you."

"Really Selina?" he straightened up and crossed his hands like his mother did. "We signed a prenup so if you want the divorce, fine, but you'll get hardly anything. I haven't earned that much after we got married, my parents gave me the Hampton house just before."

"How convenient! Knowing Leona, I'm sure it was pure coincidence."

"And yes, I own the D.C. house now—"

"You said you were renting. Just more lies."

"My father has bought it for me recently and if I remember correctly in our prenup it states that everything that I get from my family cannot be shared with you should we split," he said with a smug face. "You'll have to stop writing and start looking for a day job and a new daddy for your children."

"You're disgusting! You're a disgusting little pig!" I shouted and stood up, barely stopping myself from throwing my glass at him. I used to think Molly was bad and pushed me to the edge of a nervous breakdown, but this family was even worse.

"Okay, I phrased it badly. Please, sit down and listen," he made a gesture with his right hand for me to sit, but I didn't even twitch. "All I meant is that I can make your life easier. If you decide to stay with me and stick to my plan..." he was talking fast, afraid I could leave any minute, "I'll pay you a certain amount of money for every year of our marriage from now on, let's say two hundred thousand bucks a year. You'll get the whole deal on paper from my lawyer. I'll also pay you monthly so you don't have to work and you can focus solely on your writing. You'll be able to have children and not worry about cleaning, cooking or even driving them to school. I'll get you a nanny, a housekeeper and a driver, even if we don't get as far as the White House."

"Keep talking," I said.

"Is that not enough? Okay, I'll move the Earth to get you a book deal and to be honest if I win – it's not going to be difficult to shake the world. Of course, on your side you'll have to sign that you're not going to write about us or anything that could affect my reputation, but—"

"No memoir then."

"I thought you liked writing fiction," he pursed his lips and frowned his eyebrows.

"I do and I'm ready to stick to it."

"Your last book was pretty good so I'm confident we'll sell your novels. I'll have contacts."

"Your mother is getting out of our life. She can't just walk into our house whenever she wishes."

He paused and took a deep breath, "Okay. When I'm not there she has to call you first."

"No, I don't want to see her at all when you're not there. I didn't marry your mother and I'm not signing the deal with her but with you."

"Fine," he said reluctantly. "I'll try to keep her busy."

"I'd rather get a restraining order," I snapped.

"Okay, okay. I'll deal with my mother," he said irritated.

"And I also want to see it all in writing, otherwise there's no deal."

"Of course," he murmured. "I'll ask dad to take her out more. They should spend more time together. As she doesn't work, she could come and live in D.C. She could still be close to Emily and Faith, New York isn't—"

"About that..." I stopped to take a deep breath.

"What? You don't want my sisters to speak to you? I thought you liked Faith, and Emily... she's just too stressed now with her career and being a mum."

"Leo, you might want to sit down for this one."

"Nobody is dead or ill?" he asked scared.

"Your parents..." I cleared my throat, "they're getting divorced."

---

## 18 Hours Later

"I'll get the hell out of your life if that's really your wish," Leona said in a breaking voice. "But first..." she paused looking like she was trying to stop herself from bursting into tears. "I came here to ask you why you told Leo about Emil and me getting divorced? He's already called the girls and they're all very upset. I told you, I wanted to save them the misery."

"They're adults, you can't save them from everything Leona."

"When you become a mother, you'll understand... You'll know how it feels to want to save your children from any misery in their world."

"They would find out anyway and Leo would never forgive me for knowing first and not telling him."

"Oh, the man would forgive you for anything. He always defends you," she said and added whispering, "even when you don't deserve it."

"I'm glad to hear it."

"I wanted them to find out during the divorce party. It would be the best way to tell them – to show them that everything is still all right and—"

"And keep the orchestra playing while the ship is sinking?"

Leona gave me a long silent stare before she exploded like a firework, "You had no right to do this. How dare you? Who do you think you are that you can come to this family and decide what's best for everybody?" She stood up so abruptly that she accidentally pushed over her chair. At least, I wanted to believe it was accidental. She switched from angry to furious, and I wasn't sure whether she was really foaming at the mouth or it was just my imagination.

"I can at least decide what's best for me and my husband," I said confidently, looking straight into her narrowed eyes.

"You better change your attitude or you're going to deeply regret it," she snorted and put her right forefinger in the air.

"Is that a threat?"

"Interpret it as you like."

"Right," I whispered, picking up her purse and mobile from the table and handing them to her.

Her lips and hands were trembling like jelly. I didn't want to push her out in such a state, but she wasn't exactly innocent. "You'll regret it," she yelled and chucked her purse at me. It flew over the table and hit me on the lips.

I licked my lower lip, now pulsating and swollen, tasting some blood. "It's time for you to leave," I said decisively.

She picked up her purse with drops of my blood on the buckle and without looking at me or even a word of apology she trod towards the door.

# CHAPTER 11
## New Lily

"How can I help you today?" asked a wide-shouldered woman. She was sitting behind a large counter, between two other members of staff, all dressed in dark suits and white shirts.

"My luggage has been lost." *Why would I be at the lost luggage point otherwise?*

"Can I see your ticket? Which flight were you on?" she asked with an annoyingly fake smile glued to her face.

"London Heathrow," I passed her my passport with a baggage label stuck on the back. She pulled it off impatiently and practically threw the passport back at me.

"You'll need to fill in some details," she spoke English in a strong French accent. "Oh, I've run out... Please, give me a minute and I'll print some more forms." As soon as she said it, she headed towards a lift located conveniently at the right side of the counter.

I gasped, thinking, *I should have taken the train. Who cares that flying was cheaper? Having so many zeros on my account, I could have gone business class anyway, well... next time.*

"I told you not to buy the uber-expensive pram. It's so flashy that it looks pricey from a mile. I bet someone stole it!" I heard a man's voice, and while pretending to scroll through my phone I kept listening.

"Really? When I bought it, you said it looked cheap and tacky! And I bet that they just left it at the airport because you wrapped it in that stupid protective clingfilm," said a woman in a high-pitched voice.

"Because it's so expensive. You could've bought a car for that."

"Junior deserves the best," she said sulkily.

"There are no other flights tonight from Heathrow, but the pram should come on the very first flight in the morning..." said a man behind the counter.

"Here you are," the broad-shouldered woman passed me one sheet of paper, still warm from the printer. She looked so proud of herself, as if she had made some uber-extra-effort to get it for me.

I started filling in my details when in the corner of my eye I saw a tall man leaning against the same counter and writing down his details. His wife must have gone with Junior and he was too focused on the paperwork to notice me, so I glanced at him secretly a couple of times. *What a body! What a face!* It was like I had been struck by lightning. My breath quickened, my heart jumped in my chest like it had been electrocuted. *Is Lily – am I somehow destined to fall for married men?* The man suddenly turned his head towards me and put his pen down, giving me a friendly smile. I smiled back feeling like my face was reddening and I couldn't do anything about it.

"How long are you going to stay in Paris?" the hot guy was asked by the woman behind the counter, but he said nothing and kept staring straight at me. "How long are you going to stay in Paris?" repeated the woman before I realised the question was aimed to me.

"Not very long. I've got another flight in three days."

"So, you're back to London in three days," she said, typing at the same time.

"No, I'm not going back there anytime soon," I snapped as if she was party to my exile. She raised her eyebrows. "I'm taking a well-deserved holiday," I smiled.

"I'm not being nosy. I'm asking because sometimes it might take longer than three days to get your luggage back with you and—"

"Afterwards, I'm going to Andalusia," I said, but she kept looking at me in anticipation, "It's in Spain. I'll be there for at least a week, and then—"

"If we don't get your luggage to you by then—"

"I won't get it at all?"

"*Non, non.* We'll be in touch."

"Wonderful," I said passing her the completed questionnaire and feeling my phone vibrating in my handbag. Another thing I was regretting, as well as not taking the train, was not packing more into my hand luggage. All I had was my coat, a guidebook I got at the airport and perfumes I bought during the flight.

I saw the handsome brunet walking away after handing over his forms, and so, to stop staring at him I reached reluctantly for my phone knowing already who was calling me.

"Are you calling me to keep talking about your wife trying to get between us?" I answered the phone only because I was angry and had nobody else to shout at. "She didn't have to try anything. Whether you realise it or not, she was right there between us the whole time we were together! And it was you who chose to humiliate her by not leaving earlier."

"Fair enough," he said, sounding like somebody had just beaten him up. "I just want you to know I love you and I didn't mean to lie to you."

"So, what did you MEAN Nathaniel?" I said while walking into the arrivals hall. Nobody was waiting for me, not even a taxi driver.

"I've already spoken to my doctor, who was quite optimistic about a vasectomy reversal. I want to have family with you."

"Okay, so are you ready to use a sperm bank if your... your machinery refuses to work again?" I said loudly, feeling confident nobody would hear me in the middle of the noisy crowd of meetings and greetings, but I was wrong.

"That's so harsh," a young man with a green backpack hissed at me. "Men are under so much pressure right now..."

"Look, Nate," I gasped. "I need to go. It's late. They've lost my luggage and I still need to buy a few things before I get to the hotel."

"Where are you staying? Why don't you ask them to get you everything you need? I'm sure you booked a five star."

"Sometimes people can't offer us exactly what we need, and it might not even be their fault."

"Oh, for god's sake Lily, we've been great for two years. I'm finally getting divorced. Give me your address and I'll be there Friday evening so we can talk in person."

"I won't be here Friday evening. I'm on health leave until further notice and I'm going... Anyway, Susana hasn't told you yet?"

"She's barely speaking to me after my wife told her about you and me having..." he hesitated, "about us being in a relationship. Maybe we both should move to the New York office."

"I'm not going anywhere. I've spoken to my lawyer. Molly has been harassing me and somebody has to finally put an end to it."

"I agree but you're not thinking about going to court, are you? It would seriously affect the reputation of the company and you can still make partner."

"I can't tell you more at the moment."

"So, are you back on Friday? What time?"

"Look, I've just started this journey and I don't have any space to include you in my itinerary."

---

It looked like I was running away, but the truth was Lily had asked me *Up There* to take a break and relax somewhere on the beach. You can't ignore somebody's last wish – and technically she was dead – although it could be open to interpretation on many different levels. Paris was at least two hours' drive from a beach but first I needed to do something for the inner-me, who had missed her birthday with her mother. If the accident and my brief visit to the Other Side had already taught me something – it was not putting off anything to a distant future. I wasn't planning on visiting Versailles because I was afraid of becoming overly sentimental – and to be honest, because Gabriel suddenly appeared at my doorstep to advise me against it. "If you want to be back to your previous body, that's not the right route. You've got Lily's life to put on the right track. Let her take care of yours."

"Fine, but I'm still going to Paris. I miss the city. When I lived in England, I used to go to France a couple of times a year. I can't wait to spend a few days there. It won't make any difference. I've got a year—"

"You don't have to explain yourself to me, it's your life that depends on the success or failure of the project. Although, I wouldn't mind getting promoted."

The only other thing I couldn't wait for was the jacuzzi and king-sized bed, which I had booked as a package deal with my flight.

"I'm really sorry but we've been having some problems with our reservation system and we've overbooked your room," said a male receptionist pursing his lips and trying to sound compassionate. He was wearing a sleek black jacket with a white shirt and dark tie.

"The airlines have lost my luggage, and now this," I threw my hands in the air in a powerless gesture. "What are you proposing?" I sighed.

He looked clearly relieved that I wasn't going to make a big issue out of it. "We've got a superior suite booked in our partner hotel, which is also five stars. We could offer you the room free of charge for three nights. One of our drivers can take you there immediately."

"Okay, how far is it?"

"There's a bit of traffic tonight so it might be half an hour. But don't worry Madam, our cars are very comfortable, fully equipped with ionizing air-conditioning and—"

"Could you write down the address here?" I passed him my phone open on Google maps. He was reluctant to take it, but he had no choice – I wasn't going to believe that a man in his forties and working at the reception of a five-star hotel couldn't type on a smartphone. "It's next to the Palace of Versailles. No way, it's too far," I snapped thinking that now I was acting more like the real Lily.

"I understand," he said calmly, but his nose started jumping in small nervous ticks. "Would you like to take a seat in our restaurant downstairs and have a three-course meal on the house? In the meantime, I'll find you better located accommodation."

"I might have a better offer, although the lady should have her dinner on the house of course," I heard a soft male voice behind my back. "I've just heard about the double-booking and I think that the hotel outside the city would suit me better," said the man, putting his magnetic card on the marble counter in front of me – when I looked at my benefactor I practically fossilised. *Junior's dad?*

"That's very kind of you. Thank you," I said in utter stupor. "It might be a better place for Junior. Fresh air, more greenery," I whispered.

"*Magnifique!*" the receptionist clapped his hands. "I'll give them a call and arrange your transport, *Monsieur*," he said and immediately grabbed the phone lying in front of him.

The man had a boyish face with messy hair, but he must have been in his late thirties. His white linen shirt was tucked into his smart, although a bit creased, navy shorts. On one arm he had the newest version of the smartwatch I wanted to get for myself, and on the other he was wearing a yellow silicon bracelet promoting a charity. "How long are you staying here?" he suddenly interrupted me scrutinizing his appearance.

"Three days," I replied putting my hair behind my ears. "How about you?"

"A week. Could I invite you for dinner tomorrow night?"

"It's very kind of you," I said, which sounded more like a question and he laughed. "But I don't date married men, or men in any kind of relationships."

"Oh, that's very..." he paused and scratched his forehead, "very moral of you I suppose."

"Yeah," I bit my lower lip.

"Everything is arranged," said the receptionist, while passing Junior's dad some paperwork and asking him to sign it.

"We can't stay here any longer," a woman dressed in a short loose khaki dress was shouting and walking towards us. "This place is completely unsuitable for children."

"And why is that?" I asked intrigued, thinking that I was probably doing Junior's parents a favour by swapping hotels with them – and a double favour to Junior's mummy by not dating her hubby. *Oh my god,* I thought suddenly, *he wanted to invite me for dinner with his family to thank me for taking their expensive but unsuitable for a child room! I've already become so arrogant and vain – and I've only spent a week in this body! I look pretty good, but it doesn't mean I have to be everybody's type...*

"First of all, we've got a room on the top floor and our pushchair doesn't fit in the lift, and it's not a double pushchair, it's a standard size one! Then the bath is too big and too deep and—"

"Madam, I'm sorry but you didn't inform us you'd be arriving with a baby, and we don't have any baby-friendly rooms available at the moment. I can assure you the lift is a standard size for a city centre hotel."

"But our pram is practically a double one," a man said calmly, holding a baby boy in his arms. They both appeared from behind the magnificent pram.

"Wow, is your child heir to a throne?" asked not-Junior's-dad-anymore, and I tried not to laugh. I glanced at the two brunettes, they were dressed similarly as if they had shopped together – but Junior's dad had milky stains all over his shirt and dark circles around his eyes.

The gold and red velvet pushchair standing next to the lift really looked like a king's carriage. I'd seen nothing like it my entire life, and I'd spent time in Manhattan and the Hamptons surrounded by some of the richest people in the world.

"Yeah, it's exactly what he is and that's why I'm not going to let him stay in some plebs accommodation. Sort it out darling," she said bossily to her husband, as she took the baby from his arms and walked away.

"I'm sorry for my wife. She's been like this since she gave birth to our son and Junior is almost nine months now. Today we also lost our pram at the airport. Somebody tried to steal it, and I know it looks terrible, but it comes from a limited collection and its value is increasing. I actually hoped we lost it and our insurance would give us the money back."

"I understand…" said the receptionist before immediately correcting himself, "no, I actually don't understand, but today is your lucky day and you can get a room in our partner hotel just next to the Palace of Versailles – I bet your wife will like it," he smirked, and the real Junior's dad went completely red. "We can charge you exactly the same price that you've already paid."

"So, I guess I'm staying here tonight," said not-Junior's dad.

"I would be ever so grateful," mumbled the receptionist.

"Could I only ask for one thing? Could I swap the room I booked with the lady here?" the receptionist looked confused. *What the hell is wrong with his room?* "Could I get the room that the family refused, and the lady could get the room I was about to have only ten minutes ago and then—"

"Of course," the receptionist interrupted him looking impatient. I wouldn't be surprised if he applied to work in a hostel after dealing with us.

"I'm sure she'll be very happy, and I just don't like the interiors anymore," he smiled.

"I understand, *Monsieur.*"

*Have I got something to say?* I thought, before deciding to avoid another issue. All I wanted was to have a bath.

## CHAPTER 12
## New Selina

The divorce cake had six silver and ivory layers, each one decorated with hundreds of edible pearls, and a few that were apparently real. Everybody was excited about finding a real pearl, but for this rich crowd gathered in one of the most splendid Hampton's mansions it was more like a hunt for a four-leaf clover, rather than an opportunity to pay their bills.

"I've never seen such a smart and classy divorce party," said a woman in her sixties, wobbling on her legs to my left. In one hand she was holding her high heels, while in the other she was fiddling with the stem of an empty wine glass – emptied numerous times by the same Botox-inflated lips. "I got divorced ten years ago and I had no party. I admire their optimism. They think that their lives are going to suddenly transform by signing some papers, but nothing will really change that much. They'll still have kids together. Practically in lifestyle he's always been a visitor at their house, now he's just formally a guest. Since I can remember, she's always been one of those impossible to please women, long before she even got married. He—"

"Maybe! But let's just enjoy the party and try not to destroy one of the happiest days in their life," snapped a young girl, who suddenly turned to us – probably at the end of her patience, waiting for the new divorcees to give their speeches and cut the enormous cake for a hundred and fifty guests. The girl had long pinkish hair, which was the only thing that was covering her Hampton-tanned back in a skimpy white dress with no bra. "By any chance, have either of you managed to smuggle a phone in? It's so Insta-story-worthy," she gasped.

"Nope, I handed mine in at the entrance like everybody else," I said and added with a smirk, "I miss *him* already." Pink-head opened her mouth to say something, but at that very moment everybody started clapping and cheering. She turned her head towards the indoor pool where on an island in the middle, built especially for the occasion, stood the just-un-hitched couple. She was wearing a two sizes too small black bikini, which she must have gotten before her boob-job, and he was proudly showing off his toned and waxed stomach in orange lowcut swimming shorts. This moment heralded the inevitable end to *the smart and classy* part of this divorce party.

"I can't believe that my parents…" Leo suddenly appeared putting his hands on my bare shoulders. Since I had found out he wasn't into women, I stopped flinching each time he touched me. I also stopped feeling guilty each time it crossed my mind he was "cute" or "sexy". It didn't matter – Lily or Selina, Selina or Lily – neither of us would ever compete with the beautiful Keanu.

"Don't tell me your parents are going to cut their divorce cake half-naked on a Robinson Crusoe raft."

"I've done a few of these parties recently in D.C. and I don't think it's a standard procedure. Bonnie and Clarence are famous for their spectacular events. You should've gone with me to one of the parties that they did in the city," he said, and bent to my ear to add whispering, although I doubt anybody would hear him in the middle of the cheering crowd, "Clarence knows some scriptwriters from LA, we need to make sure you mingle with them enough. Would you like to try some scriptwriting?"

"Sure," I said flatly, wondering how many people socialised with Bonnie and Clarence for the exact same reason – to get something out of them, as if free invites to million dollars parties weren't enough. "Do you know who designed the interiors of this house?" I shouted to Leo, but the guests were so loud he couldn't hear me anymore.

I raised myself on my toes to see Bonnie sliding a long sword-like gold knife through all six layers of the cake. The knife hit the small round table and the ceiling opened with gold serpentines and balloons, as we were nearly deafened by fanfare music. I looked again at the cake and noticed thick blood-red filling slowly spilling out on the table and dropping on the island's artificial grass.

"The cake was designed by Luisa Sanfiore and hand made by Betty Pie..." started the newly single woman with nostalgia painted all over her round and lightly freckled face, "...and it represents our marriage," she said and cleared her throat that was squeezed by emotions. "It was beautiful and classy on the outside but bleeding on the inside," she shouted and grabbed a piece of the cake with her bare hands. She took one bite of the cake and moaned. "The filling is made of cherry vodka! You seriously need to try it. Let's get this party started," she screamed from her lungs and quickly smudged the rest of her piece all over Clarence's face. He was so bewildered that I doubted it was in the script. She grabbed another bit of the cake, but before she could do anything with it, her ex-hubby pushed her into the pool. The cake she was holding landed on a guest standing in the first row. The crowd was cheering while Bonnie swam towards the island, grabbed Clarence's leg and dragged him under the water. Several guests stripped themselves to their underwear and jumped into the pool, all of them, just like the divorcees, were in their early thirties and had fit tanned bodies that wouldn't miss an opportunity to shine. In the meantime, a dozen waiters wearing only black swimming shorts and red bowties started walking up and down a narrow wooden bridge connecting the living room with the island and serving cake to the guests.

I took two plates of cake, slid one slice next to the other and gave back the emptied plate to an astounded waiter. I suppose he was used to women refusing anything containing sugar, rather than taking double portions. I needed to stop my rumbling stomach. All the canapes that they had previously offered to me were too sophisticated for my palate, which made me wonder whose taste buds I was currently utilising – Lily's or Selina's. I greedily shovelled the cake into my hungry mouth, standing next to Leo who was talking politics to a very stiff couple. I sneaked away from the discussion unnoticed. I was more interested in the house interior. Whoever designed it did a good job and I was about to give myself a private tour.

The heated and illuminated pool was stretching throughout the whole length of the ground floor and flowing outside, underneath floor-to-ceiling steel-framed windows. None of the guests playing in the water dared to dive under the large shield of glass – it would destroy their expensive hair and make-up. I walked outside. I was holding a glass of Sauvignon blanc, my long pastel blue dress sweeping a set of marble stairs, and my loose long dark hair tickling my back. The pool was chasing the horizon in the vast garden and reflecting the moonlight, while garden lights were twinkling on its surface like stars. I walked along the pool next to a perfectly straight line of sunbeds, soaking up the atmosphere of the mesmerizing surroundings. I had read the divorce-party plan and knew that the tranquilly of the place was soon to be broken by a live band and fireworks display. I walked as far as I could without taking off my stilettoes and sat down on one of the sunbeds facing the sea. I was breathing in the air with my eyes closed and listening to the sound of the waves, when suddenly somebody decided to put an end to my meditation.

"Sorry to interrupt you, but putting a glass on the ground in the darkness is dangerous," upon hearing the male voice I jumped to my feet. I hadn't heard anybody coming. "You don't want any of these people here filing a lawsuit against the lovely divorced couple to milk some money out of their already-divided pockets," the man continued with a wide smile, his hands resting on his hips. I thought I had seen him before, but I couldn't decide where and in what circumstances.

"Is that what you would do?" I asked irritated, looking at the puddle around his bare wet feet created by his soaked red swimming shorts.

"I wouldn't but I'm sure somebody here would employ me to do it."

*God*, I thought, *is he really that concerned about the glass or is he just looking for an excuse to brag about himself as a lawyer?*

"How about you just keep your clothes and shoes on for the rest of the night, instead of parading naked and causing a danger to yourself and all these other people?"

"What danger am I to other people?" he asked intrigued.

"Well, I would start with the wet floor," I snapped. My thought principally focused on drunk girls tripping and falling into the pool after seeing his body, not that I would tell him and boost his ego even more.

"Fancy a swim?" he asked cheerfully.

"No, thank you," I sighed. "The pool is very tempting, but maybe on a different occasion." *I would be right in that pool if I wasn't about to become the wife of the next president of the United States.*

"There won't be another time... well, at least not for me. I'm friends with Clarence, and Bonnie is taking the house, but I guess you're—"

"I'm not friends with either, I mean... I'm not particularly close to either of them. Leo, my..." I hesitated. I had a hot guy standing in front of me and what? Was I supposed to tell him I had a husband? Fair enough if it was a real one, but practically speaking he was my business partner in disguise. "We've got many mutual friends. They probably felt like they had to invite me back."

He frowned his eyebrows, "Have you and Leo had your own divorce party? Strange, I thought—"

"No, not quite," I snapped. *Damn it,* I thought gutted, *how am I supposed to have a boyfriend while being in a fake relationship with one of the most public people in the world? How come it didn't cross my mind when I was signing the deal? Money! It always clouds judgment – it's like persistent fog on a high mountain.*

"Leo would invite me to yours, and I've heard nothing about it," he said smirking, clearly taking pleasure in digging into the topic.

"I didn't know you're such good friends, or are you one of those I-am-invited-everywhere people?" I said in one breath before it suddenly hit me I should've been more careful when talking to unknown people, especially those who act familiar.

"Since I've been trying to redirect my career I get significantly less invites in my post box. I suppose I'm not useful enough to socialise with," he smiled and looked into the distance with nostalgia, which didn't quite suit his current look as a frivolous party-boy.

"And why is that?" I asked deciding to sit down again. My stilettoed feet were killing me and wearing them for so long was a hazard for myself. I would take them off, but I had: *#hot-guy-is-speaking-to-me* and

*#the-wife-of-the-future-president-needs-to-stay-classy* flashing in front of my face like billboards on Times Square. He took a seat on a sunbed next to me, rested his elbows on his knees and... *Hold on a sec! Is he sleeping with Leo too? Is Leo cheating on beautiful Keanu? It would at least explain him joking about our divorce!*

"Practically speaking I'm currently unemployed," he chuckled. I didn't understand what was so funny about it. "I've been unemployed for the last three months... That's the first time I've said the word *unemployed* out loud."

"Congratulations?"

"Even Leo's Hampton party invites stopped. He must've found out about my job, I mean the lack of."

"I don't think so," I said defensively, but I had no idea whether the man had lost value in my husband's eyes as soon as he got fired, or it was just a coincidence. Everything Leo did revolved around his career so it would make perfect sense. The man lost networking-value and probably wasn't able to contribute much to Leo's campaign. I was glad to find out I wasn't speaking to Leo's lover – while I wasn't the Selina who fell in love with him, I still found the reality of being his fake wife deeply unsettling and brutal. Was it a growing solidarity with his real wife? "He spends so much time in D.C. now," I defended Leo like an exemplary wife would do.

"Thank you for trying to make me feel better," he said and rolled his lips. "Since I stopped working, many people..." The first fireworks exploded above us. I leant closer to him, but I couldn't hear anything he was saying even when he started shouting, and within seconds a mass of people flooded the garden as if they had just been released from the underground. Some jumped straight into the pool, while others were spreading around the grounds like ants. I saw Leo strolling slowly in our direction.

"It's getting cold, I'd better go back to the heated pool," I heard the hot guy saying as the fireworks went quiet for a moment. He was rubbing his arms with his hands, shaking and chattering with his teeth. His *cold-play* was so exaggerated, almost theatrical. His skin was perfectly smooth without a single goosebump. "It was nice talking to you, Selina," he waved and jogged back to the pool.

"Your dress is wet where your knees were touching James' legs," Leo snapped.

"Have you dragged me inside of the house to tell me THAT? Everybody is outside, I don't understand why you're playing the jealous husband right now?" I said calmly, although I was fuming inside.

We were standing in a marble and steel kitchen that was divided from the living area by the river-like pool. On the other side there was only some waiting staff frantically tiding up empty glasses and hoovering the floor, which was covered with bits of food, flower petals and dead balloons. There was no way they could hear us – even if they were standing quietly on the other side of the pool and they were trying to listen to us – we were separated from them by two loud waterfalls. The water fell from round holes in the ceiling straight into the pool. The position of the waterfalls between the kitchen island and the sofas must have been to prevent cooking sounds being heard in the living area. It was a clever idea, but they looked too much like showers to me. I felt like jumping under one of them and shampooing my hair.

"I'm not playing," he snapped.

"Really?" I giggled.

"All guest bathrooms downstairs have hairdryers on the wall. Go and dry your dress," he said bossily.

"It's not really that wet," I said shouting through the sound of hoovering, the fireworks and the waterfalls. "I don't even know why I'm explaining myself. Why are you acting like this?"

"James has always been so flirty with you," he said through gritted teeth.

"And why would you care now? I'm not the one who lied that I was in love with you, while the entire time I was fucking my high-school sweetheart. I'm not the one who deprived you of the chance of true love!" I shouted tearfully. I was furious with Leo. I was furious with Nathan – for him I was the *beautiful Keanu,* while he was probably letting his wife live under the illusion there was still hope for them.

"The guy is suspicious, that's all. I don't trust him."

"Can you at least explain to me why? If you expect me to avoid him, I should—"

"Fine," he cut me off while vividly gesticulating with his hands in the air. "I don't believe he decided to quit his job just like that. Apparently, he did something significant and needed to go quiet for a bit."

I laughed, "Don't you think you're being paranoid? You sound like he is the damn Godfather. He looks like a guy who makes money advertising boxer shorts!"

"Rumour has it, he represented a mafia boss in a divorce, and left the wife with nothing. He's done similar to so many ex-wives in this country."

"Divorced? Has he—"

"Don't tell me you didn't recognise him in the swimming shorts? It was dark outside but even I could spot him at a distance."

"Except that you're totally obsessed with him!"

"The man has no morals."

"Is that why you stopped inviting him to your Hampton parties or because he isn't useful to you anymore?" I asked with hands on my hips, "Why did you invite him to anything if he's so dodgy?"

"What?" Leo looked completely confused. "No use to me?"

"He thinks you stopped sending him invites because he lost his job and without that he was no longer useful."

"Is that what he told you?" Leo put his right hand on the marble kitchen island like he needed to support himself from falling.

"More or less."

"He never made it to any of my Hampton parties so why would he ever care?" He asked baffled.

"Not even one? So why have you kept inviting him? I don't get it."

"That's why I stopped, and I even told you about it a few weeks ago. It was when I picked up the parcel that he signed for us."

"Oh!" I exclaimed. *Eureka!* "But you still invited him—"

"I did because I like to keep my enemies close!" I nodded in understanding, although I was still miles away from comprehending what was wrong with James the Neighbour. I gave up on getting the truth about James from Leo. He was getting irritated, and it wouldn't be wise to poke my Cash Cow. "Fair enough," I said calmly.

"I don't expect you to live in celibacy, but I need you to be careful. All the other man needs to know is that you're having an affair. Under no circumstances should you tell him the truth. I'll ask my lawyer to specify that in our deal. There are other men out there for you. Not him," he said pointing his finger at the steel windows. I looked from there at James drinking in the pool with some giggling girls, who kept touching and throwing their long hair in all possible directions. *Just a pretty party boy like many!*

## CHAPTER 13

## New Lily

I commenced my first Parisian evening by taking a bath infused with organic rose oil and real rose petals. I immersed myself in the warm water up to my chin, switched on a French radio with some soothing music and spent almost an hour watching candles playing shadows on the bathroom's marble walls. When the water cooled down, I released the plug and got out of the tub to examine the contents of a white basket sitting on a long dark green basin cabinet. It was staffed with luxurious full-sized French cosmetics. I got almost dizzy from smelling body lotions, scrubs and face creams. Before my nose was completely smell-confused and lost any scent-judgment, I rubbed my whole body with almond cream and went to have dinner in bed. I greedily put a spoon into a large fruit bowl, prepared for at least two people, and had all kinds of berries with the whipped cream I had found in the room's fridge. Feeling full but wishing to indulge, I opened a box of Belgian chocolates, which were lying invitingly on a table in the lounge. Funny thing, I booked the hotel so quickly, based on its five-star reviews that I'd completely missed I had a suite with such a big lounge! I always associated surprise with something bad, but my life was changing, and I was just starting to come to terms with the idea that unexpected could be amazing. I fell asleep wrapped in Egyptian cotton, one hand reassuringly inside the box of chocolate.

After twelve hours of undisturbed sleep, I woke up to the hotel phone ringing like a fire alarm.

"Hello," I said half-comatose.

"It's Louis," I heard a man saying cheerfully.

"I'm sorry but it's early and I've just—"

"Early?" he laughed. "You've just missed breakfast downstairs. I was hoping to see you there. I had a full English at eight, then I updated myself on yesterday's news by reading today's newspaper..." he said laughing. I never understood how people could get themselves in such a good mood early in the morning, I also never understood how anybody could enjoy a full English breakfast – all the fat would slow my brain even further and only prolong the time I needed to wake up.

"Look Louis, I think you've got the wrong number," I said yawning.

He burst out laughing. *Seriously, is he drunk or on drugs?* I thought not understanding his great mood. "Liam, not Louis, and I'm sure it's the correct number. I probably shouldn't confess, but I successfully bribed the receptionist to give me your name and number. First clue, I'm a guy who doesn't date married women or those who are in any kind of relationship."

"Oh my!" I exclaimed, finally getting myself to a sitting position. Now I was one hundred percent awake, and with one hand movement I managed to tip the box of chocolates upside down so the contents landed on my white bedding. I couldn't resist and stuffed my cheeks with two large truffles, saying through a full mouth, "Not-Junior's dad?"

"Why would you change your voice to pretend you're not Lily if you recognise me?"

The truffles melted in my mouth leaving me with an amazing velvety texture and appetite for more. "Sorry, I've just had some chocolate."

"You must be hungry. It's eleven, but don't worry, with the deal you've got you can have an a la carte breakfast whenever. They just won't do a full English after ten."

"Wow," I said cheerfully. "I'm not into bacon and sausages in the morning, although I admit it's getting quite late... Anyway, I'm impressed with this hotel. An a la carte breakfast after eleven? It's an expensive room, but I didn't expect fresh bouquets of flowers everywhere, bowls of fruit, cosmetic baskets, the latest magazines and beauty vouchers."

"No way!" he snapped. I wasn't sure whether he was slightly irritated, or I was imagining it.

"What? You don't have them in your room? Sorry. I must have got the deluxe package without realising it," I sighed.

"Unbelievable!"

"What?"

"Oh, never mind," he said more gently, and I had the feeling that some of his words before were aimed at somebody else who was currently with him. "See you in the downstairs foyer in fifteen minutes?"

I thought immediately about using the hair and make-up vouchers I found in the bathroom basket, but my stomach couldn't wait that long. "Twenty," I said and put the phone down.

*Why didn't I brush him off to enjoy my breakfast alone?* I thought, while looking in the bathroom mirror. *I could do my hair and make-up and then meet up with him for lunch or dinner! But why would I even care?*

"Because he's not married unlike any other boyfriend you've had in the last ten years?" I heard the voice behind my back and screamed. "Gabriel? What the hell?" I didn't move, looking straight into the mirror and seeing my assistant sitting on the bath with his legs crossed, one of his feet making circles in the air. He was wearing red and white stripy socks and brown loafers with a large buckle at the front. "Can you read my mind? It's freaky! I didn't sign up for that!"

He laughed, "Nope, you signed up for worse."

I turned to face him, feeling grateful that at least I'd dressed before he arrived, and then another scary thought came to my mind, "Does it mean you can see me all the time?"

"Chill," he said with a smile that wasn't even thinking about leaving his lips. "You said it all out loud, you were thinking that you were thinking it but in reality—"

"Do I do that often? Think out loud without realising it?"

"Only when you're alone and deep in your thoughts."

"Do you want me to date him?" I asked feeling I needed to stop obsessing about what Gabriel knew about me or what my secrets were, if I was even allowed to have any. "I could probably do it for the sake of the experiment. Liam is good looking and keen as mustard."

"I'm impressed at how easily you got into Lily's shoes," he said nodding his head and rubbing his chin. "I want you to do what YOU want to do. Don't overanalyse. Listen to your heart and try to do the right thing."

"Yeah, that's like saying eat anything you like but stay slim."

"All I'm saying is – don't use anybody simply to forget about Nate. If you like Liam, great. If not, move on. You probably need to practice dating."

"I thought Lily was constantly practicing."

"Nah, she tends to get straight into relationships."

---

"Good morning, where can I have an a la carte breakfast?" I asked a young female receptionist. I was five minutes early and wasn't going to wait for Liam. I thought he would find me, and if not – I would have some much-appreciated time for myself.

"At the restaurant on the roof terrace," she informed me matter-of-factly, "but it's only for the guests who booked luxurious suites," she bit her lower lip and made an I-am-sorry face expression.

*No surprise*, I thought, *she's wondering how I can even afford the hotel. Maybe they've got some single rooms without a window in the basement, which is where she thinks I spent last night.* I had no other clothes than the same set I wore for my flight, which was a pair of coffee-stained jeans and a pastel pink jumper – comfortable, but slightly stretched around my neck and hips. I bet my predecessor used to only wear it around the house. *But should she really judge a book by its cover?*

"I've got one of those, it's room five hundred and eleven," I smiled, happy I could rub it in her judgy nose. She looked at me in disbelief, but I passed her my room card that she quickly slid through a card reader next to the computer's keyboard.

"Oh!" she said and paused for a minute to read whatever notes she discovered on her screen. "Anna and Liam Malone. I'm sorry for misunderstanding Mrs Malone. There are so many people asking about a late a la carte breakfast and I have to send most of them away."

"No problem," I said coldly. "But I'm Lily Rice. I swapped rooms last night with Liam. I also don't remember him being here with his wife. Are you sure—"

"He isn't married," I heard a voice behind my back and tensed.

The receptionist gave me a smirk a la *I've heard that so many times before.*

"Your marriage is your business," I snapped, and turned back to the woman, "How can I get to the roof terrace?"

"Take one of the lifts on the right..." she hesitated, looking at Liam, "when you're ordering your breakfast, use the name Anna Malone, otherwise they might get confused. Let me know when you've finished, so I can contact the person on shift last night and correct the information."

---

"Honestly, you don't have to explain yourself. I'm grateful for the suite with all the unexpected perks," I said to Liam sitting in front of me at the roof terrace restaurant. "I'm sorry I didn't realise earlier that all the extras were yours..." We were both sipping our coffees, while I was waiting with a rumbling stomach for some specialty omelettes and hot buns. We were the only people sitting there and enjoying the view of the Champs-Elysées. The weather was stunning. Most hotel guests must have already gone on their sightseeing trips or were working in the city. I wasn't going to waste my time on any more married men, no matter how good-looking and tempting they were. I couldn't wait to spend a few days in one of the most romantic cities in the world completely on my own. *Just me, myself and I,* I was thinking joyfully.

"Anna is not my wife. The trip, the hotel, the luxurious suite – everything was supposed to be a surprise for her because..." his voice started breaking, "I was planning to propose, but before it happened, I found out she had an affair with a friend of mine – a married friend of mine," he finished just as my omelettes arrived.

"Would you like to have a glass of prosecco or perhaps Moët?" our waiter asked, his intuition was right – the couple having a late breakfast in the capital of love and soaking up the sunshine were far from thrilled.

"Not for me," Liam said, and I shook my head. "I'm not even upset anymore, *c'est la vie!* I'm glad I found out before I wasted any time organising our wedding in St Lucia."

"It's good that you seem to have moved on and use the holiday for yourself," I said, thinking I wouldn't go on a proposal-holiday alone.

"I couldn't let her ruin everything, and it would be a shame to waste it, but then I got here, and I thought – do I really want to spend the night in a suite so carefully prepared for our proposal?"

"I'm glad I could help," I said, so seriously it made him smile. "If you ever want to use something from my cosmetic basket, my basket is your basket," I said, and we both burst out laughing. "Talking about baskets, I'll need to go shopping somewhere. I have nothing to wear," just as I said it my phone rang. "Excuse me for a second, my luggage must be on its way." I wiped my lips with a white cotton napkin and left the table to take the conversation at the terrace's glass barrier.

"Hello," I picked up cheerfully.

"Hi Lily, it's Ally," a woman said, and I froze in anticipation. "Ally, your lawyer. Sorry, am I speaking to Lily Rice?"

"Yes, yes. It's me."

"You sound nervous, have you already heard the news?"

"I'm in Paris. I was just getting out of the metro, and I thought I was at the wrong station... Anyway... No, I haven't heard any news."

"Molly is missing."

"Missing like she left a goodbye letter or missing like she missed a few days at work?" I said picking food from between my two front teeth.

"It's serious. Nobody knows where she is."

"I've never been good friends with Molly, so why do you think I might know where she went? I mean, thank you for telling me, but I'm afraid I can't help."

"What makes you think she ran away?" If Ally hadn't suspected me of having anything to do with Molly disappearance before, now I'd made her suspicious. "Lily? Are you still there? I'm asking you as a friend, not your lawyer."

"Oh, come on! What else would it be? Oh, wait a second, I know! She's actually a drug queen who's been abducted by the mafia because she started stealing their customers?"

"Maybe when I tell you that she left her mobile in her flat, and the police have already listened to your voicemail, you won't think it's so funny." At first, I couldn't remember even calling Molly, but then it struck me what I had said. I felt a flow of heat going through my body. "It's not that funny now, is it? The police won't think it's funny either, especially when the person goes missing exactly a day later. Why would you even speak to her instead of leaving it to me?"

"She left me some nasty voicemails too!"

"But she didn't attack you with a chair."

"At least it's obvious now she's only been pretending to be pregnant."

"How do you know that?"

"Jane texted me about Molly trying to fake a miscarriage and Romain leaving her. She's a crazy bitch so I wasn't really that surprised."

"I hope you're not going to use the word "crazy" if you get interviewed. Say emotionally vulnerable or unstable – that's what her ex-boyfriend told the police."

"Finally, people are starting to realise she's the problem, not me," I gasped.

"I wouldn't go that far yet. You need to be careful – you've got a strong personality. When it comes to fighting professionally, people consider you a predator. Romaine said that Molly admired you, that she wanted to be like you, but she was also afraid of you."

"Afraid of me?"

"You're very powerful in the designer circles. You can pull all the right strings if you want somebody to succeed or…"

"Or what?"

"Or fail."

"What are you trying to say? That I've been the one bullying her?"

"No, but some people might think so, and I want you to be

prepared for every scenario. Everybody talks about the successful designers you made through your show. You can create or kill dreams."

"People tend to exaggerate."

"I agree, but we need to be prepared. I've read all the emails and texts that you received from Molly over the last two years. I'm on it, but you need to help me and behave. Better to say nothing instead of saying something stupid."

I sighed heavily, "Fine."

"Let's hope they find her alive."

## CHAPTER 14
## *New Selina*

"Where's the newly divorced couple?" said a young skinny girl, dressed all in black standing in the middle of the dance floor and nervously turning her head. "They were supposed to be smashing their wedding photo frame right now," she looked at her bulky watch gleaming fluorescent green in the darkness. "They really need to do it before the last dance."

"Just thinking about safety, wouldn't it be better to smash anything on the dance floor after everybody has stopped dancing?" I asked baffled.

"We've put the photo in a white cotton bag, and they won't be jumping on it with bare feet," she snapped and rolled her eyes like I had just said the stupidest thing ever.

"Right," I murmured and waved to Leo standing next to a bar in his parents' living room. The bar made of glass and dark heavy wood looked very unassuming during the day. It came to life at night when it was illuminated by a warm orange light revealing a collection of the most sophisticated liqueurs from around the world. Leo waved back to me with no intention of moving anywhere, so I trod in my stilettoes across the whole dancefloor and lounge to ask where the hell his father was. The party organiser was annoying, but she also looked very stressed, and

I had enough mercy in me to try and help her. The truth was, I also had nothing better to do.

"No idea. I saw my father speaking to Emily just a few minutes ago, but as far as I know they don't intend to smash any photos. I see no reason why my father would still like to do that when my mother is not even here. After he turned the party into Ariana's birthday, it would be poor taste to jump on my mother's photo with his lover. It would be savage."

"Yeah, I don't suspect Emil would do anything like that," I said looking at a woman in a green silky suit rushing towards us.

"Sarah, I'm glad to see you," said Leo. He didn't even know how glad I was that he had told me the woman's name. "One of your assistants told my wife something about smashing the—"

"I'm really sorry for her," Sarah was so tall in her heels that she was talking to me and Leo from above. "We should never let our intern work such an important event. She's just back from LA today, still jetlagged and keeps forgetting things."

*Maybe the problem is you've worked her into the ground.*

"That's fine," said Leo, clearly not caring about any hiccups related to this odd party. "Even I have a problem with this being Ariana's sixtieth, and you specialise in divorce parties."

"We organise different events, but yes – divorce parties are our specialty," she said proudly. "We've never had a request like this, but we've tried our best."

"You've done a good job," I said just to say something.

"Thank you." I got the feeling Sarah was perfect for divorce events. She looked like a person who never smiled, a smirk was the most you could ask for. "Some things were very difficult to change last minute. It was a blessing that Leona and Emil went for a very conventional looking cake, we didn't have to change anything but the topper."

Leo laughed, "Don't tell Ariana about that. Dad keeps telling her the cake was specially designed for her birthday."

"By the way she looks fantastic for her age. I'm actually jealous! I don't think I'm going to look that great in twelve years', and that's despite the best efforts of my plastic surgeon and relentless dieting," Sarah said while staring at Ariana walking back to the living room and eagerly chatting to some guests – her hips swaying in a red fitted dress, long diamond earrings dangling above her bare and tanned arms, and long fingers squeezing her gold clutch bag.

Ariana was slim and fit, that was apparently thanks to many holidays she spent hiking in the Alps but, somehow, she still managed to keep her curvy bum and breasts. *Provided that they are both real*, I thought suspiciously. She looked healthier and more glowing than many women who were two decades younger. She responded to never-ending compliments by saying that her magic elixir was *true love*. Each time she said it with Emil around, it sent him over the moon, making a small bald spot at the top of his head bright red. Emily, the older of Leo's two sisters, kept whispering to everybody that Ariana's had many *true loves* and their father wasn't going to be the last.

"I don't know," said Faith the day before the party. She was the youngest of Emil and Leona's children, and she seemed to be the most likeable of the whole family. "Obviously, I'll never like her, but we need to give her some credit," she said unexpectedly wisely for a eighteen year old talking about her father's lover. "Yes, she divorced three husbands but she's sixty and she got married for the first time when she was only twenty-three. By the time I'm twenty-three I'll probably have like… at least five boyfriends."

Ariana did appear to be confident and experienced. She didn't look like a woman who was prepared to compromise on her love life to avoid being alone. She wasn't a thirty-year-old floozie, who was using Emil for his money. Leona painted the picture of Emil's lover as she wanted her to be. It must have hit her hard that her husband's lover was a rich and successful travel photographer, a couple of years older than Emil. If that wasn't enough, Ariana was beautiful, not simply through age but through dedicated effort. Leona had hoped that her friends and children wouldn't know the truth of her replacement, at least not for a while. Unfortunately to her despair, Emil, for whom reputation was a prize in itself and the sign of a successful life – suddenly decided to introduce Ariana to everybody. The same man who virtually forced his son into a sham marriage decided to shamelessly parade his lover around the entire Hamptons, Manhattan and Washington D.C., before he was even divorced. Poor Leona was so embarrassed that she packed her bags and went away to live in a mountain cabin in Canada for a couple of weeks. Emil was initially thrilled with her unexpected departure, that was until he received a phone call from his lawyer saying that Leona hadn't signed any divorce papers. When Leona left a letter informing him that she didn't want the divorce party, the thrifty and business-minded Emil couldn't waste the thirty percent deposit that he had already paid Sarah for the event. Leona's stunt backfired because he had his one and True Love to impress. Leona had always organised the family's parties and with Sarah's help she had prepared an impressive event with fireworks, stand-up comedy shows and two live bands that were supposed to play till dawn. Ariana was in seventh heaven.

---

"There you are my darling," Ariana said and planted a passionate kiss on Emil's lips while her right hand wandered around his hips and finally squeezed his bum. Emil jumped but looked very content. She did it despite two of his children and his daughter-in-law standing just next to him staring at them. "Have any of you seen Emily?"

We all shook our heads. Emily seemed to detest Ariana with all her heart and, as Leo said, when his sister had made up her mind about somebody it was impossible to change her opinion. That was why we were surprised that Ariana, who normally avoided Emily, was now asking about her. None of us said a word for a while. We were standing in front of the garden fireplace watching wooden logs slowly disappearing behind the glass. The last few guests had gone ten minutes ago and everybody except Ariana was showing tiredness – hunched backs, red eyes, eyelids involuntarily sliding down, and mouth open to yawn more often than to speak. It was just after five in the morning, and the golden sun was breaking through the darkness. I felt the wind on my face, which normally would help me to wake up, but after such a long night and the sound of waves and seagulls, it was inviting me to sleep. I looked around – Emil was holding Ariana with his right arm around her shoulders, but his eyes were distant. Was he thinking about Leona? Leo and Faith were standing with their arms crossed, staring at the fire with sad and nostalgic eyes. Their family as they had known it was over.

"Why have you been asking about Emily?" I interrupted the silence just as everybody bar Ariana looked like they were going to jump into the fire.

"I met her in the bathroom upstairs. She looked very distressed. That's all."

I didn't trust her. I was sure she was hiding something. At that very moment Emily slowly walked out on the terrace with bare feet, her hands shaking, face covered with tears and smudged mascara, "Mum is gone."

"Come here darling," Emil said with his trembling voice, and immediately pushed Ariana away to offer his outstretched arm to his daughter, but Emily didn't move an inch. "I know you find this situation difficult, but you're still our children and nothing will ever change between us. We're still a family, just a... Faith, how did you describe family like us? A patchwork?" Faith looked at him questionably like she had no idea what he was talking about.

"You've all been having fun not giving a damn about mum when she's been gone the whole time!" Emily was shouting hysterically.

"Darling, please calm down. Your mum is a grown-up woman who decided to go on vacation without consulting any of us. She left us all the same letter, saying she was going to Canada with Patricia. Whether we like that or not we should respect her and give her some space. It doesn't mean, however, that we need to put our lives on hold and wait for her till god knows when."

"No, you don't understand! I hadn't heard from mum for the last few days—"

"She said... I mean, she wrote, that she wouldn't have any reception in her cabin and she'd have to go down to a village to be able to call us," Leo explained calmly.

"And you didn't think even for a split of a second it was weird? Mum never wanted to even hear about glamping, but would go to Canada to sit in a wood with a high-school friend, who she last saw in Montreal five years ago!"

"Your mum has changed darling," Emil walked to his daughter and tried to hug her, but she pushed him away.

"I found Patricia on Facebook. It's true that she's got a cabin in a national park," Emily was looking into the distance and speaking flatly as if everything she was saying didn't directly concern her. "She met mum in Toronto, where she now lives with her family. She couldn't go anywhere with her because she has a full-time job and other commitments so..." she swallowed hard and continued, "so she offered to give mum the key to her cabin and bizarrely mum took it. She went there alone. When I couldn't get in touch with her, I called Patricia. The very next morning she drove to the cabin with her husband. The moment I called her she said she knew something was wrong. Apparently, mum was nervous and acting odd, not like Leona who always managed to keep her emotions in check outside of the family."

"Oh, my god, a suicide..." Ariana murmured, and all eyes turned on her.

Only Emily, a moment ago hysterical and now weirdly calm, didn't stand paralysed and agape, but kept talking, "I've spoken to Patricia. When they arrived the door to the cabin was closed but not locked. They found mum's phone, car keys and wallet on a table. Her luggage wasn't unpacked, the bed looked unused. They searched the house and the area around, quickly spotting their boat floating in the middle of the lake. The local search and rescue team has already spent a few hours searching the lake and..." her voice started suddenly breaking, tears flooding her cheeks."

"No!" Faith screamed. She furiously kicked a rattan chair, and curled up on the floor, her head hidden in her hands. Leo and Emil were standing petrified like they didn't understand anything.

"They haven't found a body, but the lake is so vast..." she didn't finish, but this time she did let her father hold her.

## CHAPTER 15

## New Lily

"Like most monuments it looks the best from a distance, at night and ideally reflected in water," Liam said, his head twisted to the right as far as his neck and arms could go. "You get too close to it in daylight, and you wonder what all the fuss is about."

"So just like most things in life," I mumbled with my mouth full of crème brûlée.

"Anything more specific than that?" he rested both elbows on the table, looking at me with curiosity.

I thought about the Woodhouses. The first time I met them, they seemed to be such a perfect family. Immaculately dressed, strolling along their lit pool in the Hamptons, holding glasses of expensive wine, nibbling canapés from trays carried by waiters and chatting to everybody. They seemed to be so important and always had something to say worth knowing. Well, all that glistens is not gold. The caring mother turned out to be a possessive (if not possessed) woman, treating any female who dared to get close to her son as a tiger stealing a little birdie from her nest. The driven and ambitious father turned out to be a man obsessed with power, a man who would walk over anybody to get what he wanted. And Leo? The independent, opinionated, well-rounded, worldly American student was just a puppet in his family's hands. I wondered how much of Lily's life was what it seemed to be on the outside. Career-wise Lily was doing great, but her personal life was out of control and pervading the professional one. Was she happy? What does she want? Was Molly's jealousy justified?

"Sir, would you like me to move you so you can both watch the Eiffel Tower?" Our waiter put an end to my contemplation, pointing out a table next to a window.

"I'm fine here thanks," Liam said without any note of appreciation, leaving the waiter with the uncomfortable feeling that he had just interrupted something important.

"It's actually weird that the best table is empty," I said, surprised I'd only just realised it. "Somebody must've missed their cruise."

"Perhaps," Liam mumbled and practically dived into his large glass of red wine, taking a long sip.

"No... You didn't..." he gave me a questioning look, pretending he had no idea what I was talking about. "You booked that table to propose to her."

"No, of course not," he said flatly. He wasn't a good liar, which had its benefits. "And even if I did, why would it matter? It would be a shame to waste such an exclusive cruise on the Seine, one that had to be booked months ahead."

"True," I nodded, wondering what his ex was like. It was odd to think I'd taken her place, but did she still want it?

"Now I think that our table, although ten times cheaper, is a much better option. Look at all those people crowding around that one to get the best selfie. I wouldn't like them putting their elbows in my back, looking at my plate, or breathing on me."

"Well, it's not expensive because it's the best, but because it's the most desirable."

"Like most things in life," he smiled, now more relaxed.

"I wish you had been honest with me. And just to be clear, if I find a ring at the bottom of my crème brûlée, I'm keeping it?"

"I've already returned it."

"What a relief."

"*Excusez-moi*, Jean," Liam waved to our waiter, who reluctantly returned to our table.

"Could we have another bottle of the same wine?"

"Of course, sir."

"*Merci*. Oh, and thank you for offering us the table next to the window, I really appreciate it. The thing is, I booked that one to propose to my girlfriend... my ex-girlfriend..."

Jean looked at me terrified, and quickly turned to Liam, "Of course, I understand."

"But now that my girlfriend has slept with my best friend and I've met this beautiful woman, I thought it would be inappropriate to take the same table. I want to build new memories," he was saying it all without a hint of embarrassment. "And Lily deserves better, I don't want her to think she's a rebound."

"Liam," I tried to stop him.

"I'll bring the Merlot," Jean used the moment to sneak out and didn't return. Another waiter brought us the wine. I wondered what Jean told him.

"What? You wanted me to be totally honest with you," he smirked.

"Shouldn't you stick to water from now on?"

"I'm sorry if I embarrassed you. That wasn't my intention. All I wanted was to demonstrate that you don't really want me to be entirely honest with you, especially at the beginning of..."

"Beginning of what?"

"We've just met, right? Do you really want to listen to my entire life story? I would rather enjoy the here and now with you."

"Fair enough," I said, letting him take another sip of wine in silence before adding, "but how can I know *who you are* without knowing *how you got here*?"

The engines roared and our boat started slowly moving away from the Eiffel Tower. The view was still mesmerizing, but none of the people surrounding us cared anymore. They went back to their seats, getting completely lost in their food and conversation. Did I really need to know *his story*? We were attracted to each other. We were both free and single, and Heaven probably didn't care in the slightest whether I slept with him or not. It wasn't going to be an earth-shattering experience that would change Lily's life. He was just a fling or was I trying to convince myself?

## CHAPTER 16
# New Selina

"I know my mother," Leo said matter-of-factly, sitting on a wooden stool with his long legs tightly wrapped around it like he was afraid it could slip from under his arse. He was wearing a white shirt, grey jacket and a pair of navy trousers, all the clothes were still warm from Juana's iron. "The last thing she'd have wanted – would be for me to stop." He took a deep breath, "To stop when we've gone so far with our campaign. She wouldn't have wanted me to let down all the people who count on me."

"Okay, stop!" Emily shouted. "Are you seriously going to talk about your campaign just five days after our mother is declared missing? Because now you sound like you're using this to score a few more points with your potential electorate."

"Emily, what you've just said is despicable," her father said outraged. "You're in pain like all of us, but it doesn't justify you being so mean to your brother."

"Oh, right. Despicable me!" she scoffed. "We shouldn't do it at all. It's our family drama, not the whole country's. I don't feel like sharing anything with anybody out there."

"Do you prefer people to make up their own stories?" Since Leona disappeared, Faith had started acting like the older sister. She was also more emotionally stable, but she did take a whole pile of tranquillizers, which Emily persistently refused.

Reluctantly I eventually agreed to some Xanax at the suggestion of our personal doctor. I was very comfortable with manufactured drama, but the real-life version was more of a challenge for me than I'd expected. Watching how devastated Emily was and how much she wanted to be left alone was twisting even my pretty resilient stomach. Not to mention, I also had to actively participate in this awful show.

A couple of hours before Leo was put on the ridiculous stool, one of the female producers said that we needed to make the viewers feel our grief – as if it was their own family member missing.

"Do you mean that you expect us to make people weep in front of the TV so you can increase your viewership?" Emily asked flatly with her arms across her chest.

"When the Woodhouse Family drama goes viral, we've got a better chance of finding mum," Faith said adjusting the mike on her chest. I glanced at her little black dress decorated only with a string of white pearls and her freshly styled blond hair put into a high ponytail. She looked smarter and more dignified than Emily, who was wearing a white T-shirt and a pair of light blue jeggings, having refused to change. She couldn't care less about her appearance – like every normal person, she was distraught at losing her mother.

"Darling, we have to be realistic. I'm afraid—" Emil started, but Leo cut him off.

"Dad, please." He jumped down from the stool and walked towards the rest of us gathered in front of the fireplace at my in-laws' Hampton villa. "They haven't found a body," he said, his voice cracking at the last word. "Yes, I know the lake is large, but I know my mother. She wouldn't kill herself."

"Bingo!" A woman in heavy black glasses and with a smart ginger bob suddenly stopped talking to her assistant and rushed toward us. She was talking to a family, who had lost their mother and wife, but she was clapping her hands, smiling and shouting *bingo*. What was wrong with that woman? Leo said her TV program was the best – but really – the best in what? Being completely immune to anybody's tragedy? "That's what you should start with Leo," she said, "you know your mother, she would never kill herself. Then in the second part you can say again that you know your mother wouldn't have wanted you to stop your campaign."

Leo nodded. "Don't you think it would better if I sat down on a sofa? We're filming in our house. It would look more natural."

"Good point," she rubbed her long thin chin. "You'll all sit on the sofa and hold each other's hands while Leo is speaking. You Leo – you need to stay calm and coherent so keep looking straight at the camera, no matter what's going on to your left or right. The rest of you – you can cry if you want to."

"Thank you for your permission Diana," Emily snapped looking like she wanted to slap Diana's face.

"I protest," said Faith with disgust painted all over her face. "Leo has sweaty hands when he's nervous. I'm not holding hands."

Emil gasped putting his right hand on his chest.

"Dad, are you all right?" Leo asked.

"Fine, absolutely fine. I just need a glass of water," he said looking pale.

*If he kicks the bucket while they're filming, Diana the bitch will be ecstatic! She'll probably get promoted three levels!*

"Can you leave us alone for fifteen minutes?" Leo stood on his toes and shouted to the whole crew. More than twenty people started leaving the room. There was a certain relief painted over all their faces. The temperature inside had been rising and I bet they preferred to stand outside in the scorching heat than suffocate inside from Diana's demands and the heavy atmosphere.

"Five minutes, okay, guys?" Diana said.

"Half an hour," snapped Emily.

Diana opened her mouth to say something, but Leo didn't let her, "As my sister said we need half an hour."

A few minutes later the living room was filled with nothing but painful silence. We were all physically and emotionally exhausted. None of us had a decent sleep or a full meal since we found out about Leona. I couldn't tell whether they really believed she was alive or they were just lying to themselves as they couldn't stand the horrifying truth. I didn't have much hope for a happy ending – it's been five days...

"Thank you, my darling," Emil said to Faith who brought him a glass of water and a chocolate cookie. "Thank you but I'll need something stronger. Would you be so kind and pass me a glass of whisky on the rocks and my Cuban cigars?" She obediently moved straight towards the bar. I had the feeling Emil used it on a regular basis even when there was no party at the house.

"Dad, you're not going to smoke inside," his older daughter snapped. "My children spend time in this house, their lungs still haven't developed and nicotine stays on the upholstery and the furniture. I sent you a link to an article but obviously you never read it."

"Fine, I'll go outside."

"You're not going anywhere. Diana will be here in like…" Leo paused to look at his watch through his tired red eyes, it took him a few long seconds before he could count the time, "in twenty-five minutes! We need a plan of action," he said pressing his palms against each other so hard his fingers and knuckles went white.

"I personally don't care what you're going to say," Emily was fiddling with her tiny stud earrings and looking outside the window at Diana chastising one of her assistants.

"I've got a feeling the kidnappers might want something more than just money," Leo said mysteriously.

Emil took a large sip of whisky, "Son, we haven't heard from anybody for five days. Nobody would spend five days with your mother without saying anything, unless they've already sold her to other kidnappers."

"Dad!" Emily looked at him agape.

"I'm certain we will hear from them soon," Leo was saying while walking nervously around the room with his forefinger pointed in the air. "I didn't want to worry any of you, but I've received numerous threats. There are people out there who want me to stop my campaign. They're afraid I can win."

"You're paranoid," Faith said. "God knows what will happen when you're the president." She was sitting on the sofa, her arms hunched, neck bent against her chest and fingers strolling on her phone.

"How can you check your Instagram at such a moment?" Emily

exploded. She stood behind the sofa looking down at Faith and trying to see her screen.

"It relaxes me. Dad has his whisky on the rocks, Leo likes to walk, you prefer to shout at everybody, Selina just stands quietly processing everything, and I've got my Insta." Faith turned back to look straight at Emily, "*Capeesh?*" Her older sister put her hands up and walked away to sit on the floor next to an armchair, where Emil was drinking his second whisky and massaging his temples.

"They'll ask for money and try to influence my campaign, if not completely ruin it. It won't just be about money, it's also political."

"Mum was right," Emily sighed. "Men in this family think it's always about them. The world must revolve around their ego – if not them, the Earth wouldn't even see the point of moving around the Sun. What for, eh?"

"They'll call, I know it. The only question is whether I should act like I have no idea about anything or rather I should be more suggestive, I mean—" The doorbell rang and everybody looked alert at the hallway. "That's it! That must be a package or a letter from them!"

"Mr Woodhouse, it's Keanu Rodriguez," Juana, who only the day before got promoted from an occasional cleaner to a full-time maid was doing surprisingly well in her new role. She stood on the doorstep of the living room in a black dress with a white apron. Considering her outfit was bought from an online sex shop – the clothing looked okay despite being two sizes too small. Emil insisted that as long as the eyes of all of America were on us, the Woodhouse family had to have a maid. He had never had a maid or even a regular cleaner while his wife was bringing up three children, but he immediately employed one when his wife went missing, and the children didn't live with him anymore. "Would you like me to let him in or are you too busy right now? He says it's important."

Emil stopped massaging his temples and frowned his bushy eyebrows, or rather one very long bushy eyebrow running along the top of his nose, "Keanu Rodriguez? Leo, isn't Keanu Rod-something the GAY? Your high-school friend, who one day turned out to be gay? That gay politician from the opposition?" He stood up, one hand rested on his left hip, another holding the glass of whisky close to his chest.

Leo was struggling to breathe steadily, his face was white, his hands started shaking. If it wasn't for Faith, who decided to respond first, Leo might have even fainted. "Dad, it would be enough if you just said *gay* once. We love you, but you need to do something with your narrow mindedness. We must weed the angry homophobe out of you at the first opportunity, after we've found mum."

Emil's face reddened. "How can you speak like that to your father? It's all your mother's fault. You're the youngest, we tried over ten years for you and then… She completely spoiled you!"

"Enough!" Emily screamed.

"What would you like me to say to Mr Rodriguez?" Juana said meekly.

"Let him in," I snapped, and everybody looked at me surprised. "What? There are witnesses outside, I think beautiful Keanu is safe with us. Emil won't burn him at the stake!"

"Beautiful?" Emily smirked. "To be honest I've always fancied him too."

"So, should I go now?" Juana whispered.

"No," said Emil. "Although, I wouldn't be surprised if he, his whole party, came up with the idea of kidnapping my wife. Not because he's gay but—"

"Let him in Juana," I said decisively and turned to Emil, "I'm sorry Emil but it might be better if you keep your opinions to yourself, at least for the time being."

Keanu walked into the room carrying a large pink box. "I know nothing is able to soothe your pain, but I thought that the least I could do is bring you some food. Everybody has to eat. This is dessert," he said putting the box on a glass coffee table in front of the sofa. Juana walked into the room soon after him holding an even larger box, smelling of Indian food."

"And what makes you think that while we're grieving we would like to try your ethnic food?"

"I'm not Indian Mr Woodhouse," Keanu said calmly. "I've spent a lot of time in your home – enough to know that it's one of the favourite meals of your children. Then—"

"Nobody is grieving. Mum…" Emily was speaking through her tears, "is still alive."

"She is," said Leo and rushed to wrap his arms around his sister.

Juana put the box on the floor and walked away full of relief that she'd heard the phone ringing.

"Well, I just wanted to show some support. When we were still at high-school and my beloved grandmother passed away, Leona and Leo were very supportive and I'll never forget it."

"It's the police, who shall I pass the phone to? Mr Woodhouse?"

Emil swallowed hard and looked at his son in anticipation, "It hasn't been good between me and your mum, I shouldn't—"

"Coward," I snapped and pulled the phone out of Juana's hand.

"Mrs Selina Woodhouse speaking," I said confidently.

"It's detective Dylan Grayson. We've got some news about your mother," the policeman said and paused, I wasn't going to correct him. "A body has been found and we need a member of the family to identify it."

## CHAPTER 17
## New Lily

Dear Lily,
The last two days with you have been amazing...
And totally unexpected!
It didn't even cross my mind I could meet anybody so quickly... I came to Paris to be alone and give myself time to reflect on life — what I really want, where I'm going, and who I am. Thank you for being part of it! I really appreciate last night's conversation. You gave me so much to think about! Thank you for being so motivating and inspiring — for awakening in me a zest for life, this new "joie de vivre".
I want to see you again... but first I need closure on some unfinished business. I want you to get to know the NEW ME, and I need time to get there.
In the near future I might change my phone number, but I've got yours and I promise I'll be in touch as soon as I can.

*Please forgive me for leaving this way. I'll be thinking about you.*
*Love*
*Liam xoxo*

"Seriously?" I screamed and let myself collapse on the bed – Liam's bed. I was wearing his designer blue shirt and boxer shorts. How desperate was he to sneak out like that from his own hotel suite? He wasn't supposed to leave the hotel for another few days. He didn't even bother to take his shirt and pants! It was easier for him to say goodbye to his clothes than me. I cringed at the thought of his fiancée-not-to-be giving him the shirt. *Utter waste of time. Two days out of three-hundred-and-sixty-five totally wasted on a random dude! You're doing great Selina, or Lily, or whoever you are now!* "Gabriel where are you? Yoohoo?" I said in a singing voice, with not much hope for a response.

I didn't have to wait long. The door to the en-suite flew open, "How are you doing?" Gabriel stood in front of the bed, wearing only a fluffy white robe. "Sorry for my outfit, but FYI I've got swimming shorts underneath. I've been in the spa downstairs. It's fab, just fab!"

I frowned, "How long have you been in the bathroom?"

"As I said I've been in the spa, but I often use the trick with the door instead of just materializing out of thin air. People seem to be less freaked out."

"Oh... Glad to know you're having fun on the job."

He blushed, "I'm always here to help, but you didn't seem to need me. You were very busy."

"Busy wasting precious time."

"It's not for me to judge," he said seriously. "I've seen Liam in the spa a few times. I can't really blame you," he said, blushing again. *Oh, my!*

"Was he there alone?" I asked before I could bite my tongue and stop wasting more time on that man.

"Oh well, he was flirting with a couple of women, but nothing meaningful."

"Yes, he's good at that," I gasped. "Gabriel, I don't really understand what I'm supposed to be doing here."

"Don't worry. Most people don't – even those who haven't died and switched lives. It's just being human. You spend ages trying to work out your route—"

"And then get hit by a car and realise how much time you wasted mulling over every single move, instead of just going forward, getting lost, finding yourself again, trying new avenues..."

"Something like that," he smiled. "Your questions need to be more direct."

"Okay, should I go back to London?"

"Not that specific," he said apologetically.

Before I managed to come up with another question, my phone rang. "It says *sister*. What's her name?"

"Emma," he said cheerfully, finally being able to offer me some help.

"I'll call her back later."

"Take it. She might be more useful than me."

I nodded and reluctantly reached for the phone, lying on a mahogany bedside cabinet. "Hi," I said, but it was too late. She'd already hung up.

"Call her back," Gabriel said, his arms crossed, his eyes fixed on me.

I felt sick to my stomach. What was I about to tell her? Lily told me to have a break from the family, but Gabriel was adamant I needed to talk to her. She answered after one ring. "Lily! Finally!"

"I'm sorry, I was in the shower."

"For a week?"

"Yeah, I'm at a spa hotel," I said nonchalantly. Gabriel smiled at me approvingly and disappeared.

"Glad you're having fun sis," she said sarcastically. Wasn't I allowed? Did I need her permission?

"Well, I'm glad you're glad."

"Lily are you okay?" she asked with a hint of worry in her voice.

"Things could definitely be better, but I'm working on it. I'm taking a long-deserved holiday and—"

"Nathaniel called us last night. We all worry about you," she cut me off.

"He's got your number?"

"You listed me on your emergency contacts at work."

"There's no emergency," I cried.

"First you shock the entire family by exposing your affair with a married man. Second, you dump him a week later without explanation."

"I see you had a good chat about poor, lost and confused Lily on the verge of a nervous breakdown. What else did he tell you?"

"Not much, really." I'd never seen the woman in my life, but I could tell she was lying.

Determined not to lose any more time I went straight down to business, "Nothing about Molly?"

"The co-worker who's gone missing?" I didn't answer. What game was she playing? "He mentioned you never liked her so you probably wouldn't miss her."

"Was he trying to be funny, or what? The woman might be dead. Anything could have happened to her."

"Oh, I didn't get that impression from him. He inferred that after the conflict between you and Molly escalated, she just went away to have a break. Just like you did."

"Interesting. So why did he call you?"

"He's desperate to get you back."

"And since when are you so eager to help a married man reconcile with his lover?"

She sighed, "I actually like him. Apparently, his marriage has been dead for a long while."

"Shame, his wife was blissfully unaware of it. Don't you need to get divorced to kill your marriage?"

"Nate said his wife knew about Molly, knew about you, and still wasn't interested in divorce."

"Sorry, did you just say *Molly*?"

"You don't have to pretend anything to me. I know Molly had an affair with Nate before..." she cleared her throat, "...before you did. He said that when he saw you for the very first time it was like a lightning bolt."

"How romantic," I scoffed. "Hold on. He said he was with Molly?" *What the hell?*

"He sounded very upset and nostalgic. I do believe he loves you. He said that when you joined the company, his relationship with Molly was already—"

"Dead?"

"Yes. How do you... Sorry, you've been together long enough to have talked about it. I just don't understand why... how she could still work there? I couldn't look at my ex every single day with his new girlfriend."

"Don't ask me, I don't understand the woman. I don't get any of this."

"Nate says she's a very determined woman, who won't miss an opportunity to take revenge. Apparently, she spent months targeting your ex..." Emma was talking enthusiastically. "Romain. She was only interested in him because she knew how much you cared about him and how much he broke your heart. She did her research."

*Is this soap opera going to be my life for another year?*

"It must have been more than revenge. They've been together for a couple of years. She talked about getting engaged and—"

"Do you know that Romain left her after she faked the pregnancy? He was about to break up with her anyway, even before that..."

"It's funny how they all are *about to* leave their wives, girlfriends, but somehow they never get the courage to do so. Poor little souls."

"You're so cynical today."

"Emma, why are you calling me?"

"Come back home and talk to him. Talk to me, mum..."

"Does she still want to talk to her rotten apple?"

"She'll get over it. I'm sure she will love Nate."

"Even if he chose not to have children with me?"

"What?"

"Did Nate tell you he'd had a vasectomy?"

"We didn't get that personal," she said, now less enthusiastic about him.

"From what you're saying it got really personal."

"Well, I've got a few friends who can do vasectomy reversal."

"I'm not sure that's the kind of help he's expecting from you, but I'm glad you bonded. I said you would love him," I giggled, more irritated than amused.

"Lily, please..." she kept talking, but I wasn't listening. Somebody was persistently knocking at my door.

"Look I need to go. I need to open the door."

"Oh my god, you've already slept with somebody else! Lily! Really?"

"Goodbye Emma. I'll speak to you soon," I said and disconnected, shouting to the person behind the door, "A minute, I'm coming."

I briefly considered changing my clothes, but the knocking on the door was getting louder and it was probably only room service. I threw my duvet aside and slowly put my feet on the super soft carpet.

"Liam, open the bloody door! I know you're there!"

*No way! My own life has enough drama* I thought, so I strolled to a round table to get some leftovers from last night's room service. There was a piece of chocolate cake and a vegetarian pizza, both still good to eat. I sat down on a chair, my right leg folded under my bum, when I heard the click of a hotel room card. "I don't remember calling you Gabriel."

"What the fuck?" a woman in a tight white dress said standing in front of me, her arms crossed, her eyes piercing me viciously. "Of all the women in the world!"

## CHAPTER 18
# New Selina

*All I ever wanted from her was to leave me alone, that's all. To let me live my life my way, and for her to lead an equally happy and unrestrained life – separate to mine. I would never wish she killed herself or... was murdered. The police said the body they'd found was first suffocated and then dropped in the lake. They estimated she was killed a week ago...* I thought, with my hands under my bum as I was sitting anxiously on a grey plastic chair. Emily with her husband Owen and Faith couldn't stay still, they were walking along a dark corridor and breathing heavily. Each time a door opened it made me jump, and them freeze. Every word echoed off the empty concrete walls – the walls, which I felt were closing on me and slowly suffocating my throat. The tension was painful and with every passing minute getting more unbearable.

A door opened with a swing, far more powerful and louder than any other. "That's not mum," Leo said, and I felt I could breathe easily again. He leant against a wall and slowly let himself slide down to sit on the cold concrete floor of the morgue, which was located just outside of Toronto. I was about to sit next to him, but he suddenly stood up and ran towards a toilet.

"He always throws up when he's stressed," said Emil dismissively.

He was the only other person who went with Leo to identify the woman's body, and he didn't look half as distressed as his son. Owen rushed after Leo to the men's bathroom. Emily and Faith threw themselves into each other arms and started weeping loudly. "Don't look at me like that," Emil whispered to me, "Of course I'm relieved. We might have our differences, but I didn't want to see my ex-wife like that," he said pointing at the door.

"You're still not divorced," I stood closer to him whispering.

"That's true," he nodded. "Trust me, I have prayed for the last twenty-four hours that the woman in there wasn't Leona," he whispered through his squeezed throat, "but I don't want my children to have false hope. Their mother is not coming back, and the sooner they face that awful truth and move on, the better for them."

---

"There was something unsettling about her. I just couldn't work out what it was. To be honest I didn't spend that much time talking with her..." Patricia was sitting on the opposite side of a table in Tim Hortons, her eyes welling up each time she said *Leona*. We had a box of doughnuts lying between us for the last twenty minutes, but neither of us even touched one. We were just sipping our vanilla lattes while trying to make something meaningful from the snatches of information we knew. Had Leona really been acting weird, or were we just making this all up to somehow justify her disappearance?

"As you probably know, I've never had a particularly good relationship with Leona. At best she just tolerated me. If she'd been going through something difficult, she would've never told me. I wanted to see you because from what you were saying on the phone you two used to be good friends – much better than her whole family had suspected. Nobody knew that you regularly spoke... but actually the more time I spend in this family, the more I think nobody really knows my mother-in-law."

Patricia nodded and reached for one of the doughnuts, "I know your stomach must be squeezed, but we should eat something. I need to be at work in less than an hour and I'll probably be working till midnight. We've got an important deadline to meet tomorrow, and I'll be lucky if I don't have to sleep at my office," she gave me a faint smile. Patricia liked to emphasise at every possible opportunity how busy her job was and how little time she had left for anything else. Was it true or was she looking for an excuse to suddenly leave if I started asking inconvenient questions? She was perfectly nice and caring but at the same time she appeared to be cagey and defensive. Was it because I was meeting her alone without Leona's kids or Emil? It wasn't my fault none of them considered Patricia a reliable source of information. Leo and Emil suddenly had to be in D.C, Emily and Owen missed their children like never before, and Faith had to study for her exams not to let her mother down. I on the other hand had nothing more important to do. It was also one of the undeniable plus sides of being a writer – I had time to talk to people, and most importantly to listen to what they were saying.

When I called Patricia she picked up after one ring, like she had been waiting for somebody from the Woodhouse family to get in touch with her. She quickly invited me for dinner at her house. I'd only just managed to find her house on google maps before she called me back apologising that she wouldn't be able to get home on time. "I've completely mixed the days up. If it was tomorrow, I'm free, but today I'll be working A LOT. Such a shame you've got your flight home booked tomorrow. Anyway, would you like to see me somewhere in the city? I work in the centre and there's a great doughnut shop just around the corner," she said enthusiastically, as if she had also completely forgotten that Leona's children or children-law weren't five anymore.

Patricia slowly chewed a doughnut with pink icing, sipping her coffee in between mouthfuls, her left hand was tightly wrapped around the paper cup and lightly shaking. She was in her mid-fifties, married to the same man for over twenty years, two kids and a house in one of the most expensive neighbourhoods of Toronto. She was still pretty and slimmer than most women in their thirties. Her delicate rounded face framed with a golden bob placed her somewhere between late forties and very early fifties. The white blazer she combined with light blue jeggings and pink stilettoes could deceive many she was a decade younger. She was speaking slowly and confidently, weighing every word.

She wasn't the kind of woman who would have a glass of Prosecco and blab out her whole life story. She was the kind of woman who was very aware that words carried meaning, and she used them in a very deliberate and careful manner.

"Do you think she killed herself?" I started with the big guns. Time was running out, and I had the feeling I couldn't count on any breakthrough in the discussion unless I approached her directly.

"I didn't see any signs that she was capable of doing something like that," Patricia said flatly. "She wouldn't do it to her children, she loved them too much."

"You said *loved*, so you think she's dead?"

She raised her eyes from the table and looked straight at me, "Don't you?"

"There is no body," I shrugged.

"Of course, of course. There's still hope. I'm sorry."

"That's okay," I cast my eyes down and reached for a doughnut with chocolate topping. "Has she got any enemies?"

"Why do you think that I know more than you and your husband?"

"Well, we know nothing, so the bar-of-knowing isn't particularly high. I've personally spent more time arguing with her or responding to annoying comments than talking with her about anything meaningful."

"She cared about you more than you think," she said, so confidently that it struck me. *She can't be serious.* "I remember when she called me once... no, I really shouldn't be telling you."

"You think she's dead, so if she's already up there," I pointed at the ceiling, "she doesn't care or will find the mercy to forgive you." *Trust me, I'm speaking from my own experience,* I wanted to add, but stopped myself at the last moment.

"Leona was very worried about you when you had that false pregnancy," she said practically whispering, guilty of betraying her best friend.

"I had what?" I said loudly through a full mouth, bits of doughnut started falling out – I coughed some of them into my right hand. In the corner of my eye, I noticed two teenagers stuffing their faces in mini doughnuts and staring at me with fascination. *How much have they heard?*

"Nobody judges you Selina. Both Leona and I had a long history with pregnancy, me with my first child and her with her third. I appreciate it's a very sensitive topic and I regret even mentioning it. I just wanted to assure you that she cared about you like a third daughter."

"I find that very hard to believe. Everything she did and said spoke exactly the opposite."

"She could..." she paused and gave me a fearful look, "I mean she CAN be tough on those who she loves, and sometimes she tells the truth when she should stay quiet, but you've always been important to her. She talks fondly about you and worries about you."

"Has she also mentioned my writing career?"

Patricia gasped heavily, "She has, she appreciates how hard it is to break through in any artistic industry. Leona is a very talented dancer and—"

"I've never seen her dancing," I snapped, quickly regretting I couldn't take my words back. *I had only known her for a few weeks before she disappeared!*

"I think that's because it still hurts that she gave up on a dancing career."

"Why would she have done that?"

"The usual – pressure from every possible direction. First her parents insisted on her getting a solid education and giving up her *hobby*. She proved them wrong – she graduated as an accountant, while also being a professional ballroom dancing champion, but in the meantime... she met Emil and then Leo was born," the way she said *Emil* spoke for itself – if she could have advised young Leona on her love life, she would have told her to run away as fast as she could from Mr Woodhouse.

"Let me guess, he believed that women were best around the kitchen."

"He believed that his career, or whatever he was doing, was far more important than Leona's *hobby*. He was a politician so how on earth could her *little hobby* even vaguely compare to his noble service to society?" Patricia said with a comically deep voice and rolled her eyes. We both laughed. "Ironically, at the beginning of their marriage – she was making more money than Emil. She got a very good job at a large accountancy firm while still on maternity leave. She was working from home when for most people it was still unthinkable."

"Has she never doubted her decision to stay at home and not use her degree or dancing skills?"

"She wanted to have a big family and Emil convinced her that she was the one who needed to compromise. She never said she regretted her decision, but she mentioned a few times she missed having something that was entirely of her own."

"And after all those years he left her for a woman who has practically devoted her life to her career."

"There is actually one thing that changed in her," Patricia was saying while staring at the people queueing at the counter and drooling over the displayed food. "She suddenly started analysing her life more than ever. She's asked a lot of *ifs* in reference to her past. She's been wondering whether she could still do something with her life or whether it was all too late for her. I just hope she didn't decide it was the latter."

## CHAPTER 19
# New Lily

I'd seen her before. I definitely had, but who was she? I recognized her good-looking face, large but perfectly plucked eyebrows and brusque manner. *Gabriel, where are you when I need you the most!*

"You really can't miss an opportunity! I should've trusted Molly"

"I haven't slept with anybody," I got my voice back just in time to defend myself. "And I don't know..." *No, I know who you are! Oh, no!*

"I got my key at reception. I paid for this room. No, I paid for the most expensive suite in the hotel, and he swapped it with you! He knows how to get into a woman's pants. It hasn't even been a week since he left me."

"Naomi, I'm so sorry..." I said, still standing next to the table with leftovers from last night. How was she going to believe I didn't sleep with him? There was an empty bottle of rosé upside down in a silver bucket! There was a piece of chocolate cake and pizza – shouting loud and clear we were hungry after having sex! *Christ, I'm also wearing his clothes!*

"Don't be," she sighed and waved her right hand nonchalantly. She didn't look anymore like a woman on the verge of a breakdown. She looked like a woman who was just about to get married! She had on silver strappy stilettoes, a white sleeveless dress cut just below her slim knees and dense blonde hair put into a bun with a fresh white flower on one side.

"I know you're not going to believe me, but I... we haven't done anything. We spent the night talking about work. Air got trapped in a bathroom sink and water exploded on my drees. That's why he gave me—"

She smirked, "Lily please, have at least a trace of respect for me. It's none of my business anymore. If not you, it would be somebody else. And you..." she hesitated, "it looks like you didn't know who he is. He used us both."

*Finally, a piece of good news. I might have spent the night with my client's boyfriend, but I hadn't known he was HER boyfriend. Besides, she slept with his best mate! How dare she judge Liam or me?*

"I should probably go to my room."

"Are you not in your room?" she asked, maliciousness painted all over her face. She still cared. Of course, she did.

"I'm sorry for whatever happened between you two," I said confidently. I wasn't going to be everybody's victim. Enough was enough. "I'm not going to change my room again, not halfway through my holiday. If you don't want me to design your house anymore I totally understand. I'll speak to Nathaniel and make sure you get your deposit back." I walked towards the bathroom to get my dress – it should be dry by now.

"Do you still speak to Nathaniel?"

"What do you mean?" I asked, stopping at the bathroom door.

"No problems in paradise? Was Liam your rebound? Because I'm pretty sure you were his."

"I don't talk about my private life with my clients. Nathaniel and I get on very well in our professional environment. As I said, it's probably better you find a different designer."

"I would ask Molly, who apparently is second best in your office, but she's missing. Honestly, in your company people are as interesting as their designs."

I shut the door to the bathroom to change, but it didn't discourage her from talking, "It may be my fault Liam almost left me at the altar, but he also isn't a saint. Him coming here – you know – it was far from accidental." I was dressed and ready to leave the en-suite, but I couldn't move after what she said. He lied to me. They were about to get married. He had already proposed, and she said yes. Paris was their honeymoon – I was slowly processing the information.

"Naomi, why are you even here after what he's done to you?" I shouted through the door, looking at my reflection in the mirror. The sleepless night was talking its toll on my face. *I need to finally use the spa facilities, and Gabriel!* She didn't answer so I slowly opened the door to see her sitting at the table and staring blankly at the wine bucket. I felt sorry for her. If I was about to save myself, I needed to be a better person than Lily. But was she really that bad, or like me now, she just happened to always be in the wrong places at the wrong time? I sat on a chair opposite Naomi. "Maybe you and Liam will somehow work it out," I said, not believing a word I was saying. If I learned something about Liam during the last two days, it was that he wasn't going to forget what she did. Forgive yes, eventually, but not forget.

"Who was I kidding? I hoped that if I pitched up here and apologised to him, we would throw ourselves into each other's arms and... I'm so stupid. I even thought we could have a small impromptu wedding – just as he wanted."

*Liam, how could you do this to me? First you run away, and now THIS!*

"Well, he's on his way to London. Probably to see you," I forced myself to smile. I was lying. I wasn't a better person than Lily, but I was suffocating in the room. I couldn't stand the pressure.

"Do you think so?" she sounded so hopeful.

I nodded. "I'm sorry to leave you like this, but I've got a meeting in the city," I kept lying. "Even on holiday, I can't completely stop working."

"Could we have dinner together?"

*What? Is she not going to chase him to the airport? She would rather have dinner with ME?* I was highly suspicious she was planning on poisoning me. "Sorry, I really can't today, and I'm sure you want to go back to London tonight."

"Why would I? Because of Liam?" she chortled. "I'm not going to chase that man around the world. I'm done," she said categorically. "I need to focus on my business and renovating the house. I wanted to talk with you about some new designs I've got in mind. I hope you haven't devoted yourself too much to my last idea. Now that Liam is gone, I need some changes. I'm back to my natural hair colour and my original plan to decorate my villa like the Palace of Versailles. We could go there tomorrow." Suddenly she was beaming with joy and enthusiasm.

"Actually, we've got a designer, who specialises in royal-style," I made it up. What did she really want from me?

"No, I want you," she smiled. "Only you Lil. Don't even try to talk me out of it. If you resign you'll have to pay me. Besides, you don't want Susana to be even more pissed off with you."

Was that a threat?

I took a deep breath, "Lunch tomorrow?"

"Perfect." Her smug face was so irritating I wished I had slept with her fiancé, instead of having a pyjama party and listening to how Naomi (who he called Anna) ruined his career. She didn't really ruin anything, and he should have been more strong-minded, but from what he said – she was the last person to support his goals. Liam was an architect, who dreamed about designing iconic city buildings. He spent months unsuccessfully trying to win contracts for city projects around the world. The competition was fierce, and he didn't have any connections. Naomi kept pressuring him to stick to designing houses for wealthy people, and as an ex-top model she had enough rich friends to fill up her boyfriend's schedule until he retired. Although thrilled with a steady income, Liam was frustrated at the complete lack of time to fight for his dreams. When he didn't work, he had to constantly socialise, networking for potential clients. Naomi loved attending and throwing splendid parties, Liam less so.

"Now, when I've finally left Anna, I have time to do what I want," he said with a bitter smile, as we were stuffing our faces with pizza and sipping rosé. "My calendar is completely clear, and phone silent. As soon as they found out about us, they cancelled all my projects. I kept some deposits, but nothing that lets me live the same lifestyle."

"When one door closes, another opens," I was trying to keep his spirits up. "What are you going to do now?"

"My parents have a company. They're both research psychologists.

They've recently lost an assistant, so I'm going to help them. They pay well, and I've got some savings. In the meantime, I'll try to win a contract for another city project."

---

When I left the room a stone dropped off my chest. What was worse than getting involved with a married guy? Getting involved with a guy who has a crazy ex-fiancée. I walked fast to the lift, jumping and looking back over my shoulder each time I heard a door opening. After I got to my room, I turned the locks and put a chain on my door. *Shit, she knows which room is mine! She booked it! Even if I meet with her for lunch tomorrow, I have to change hotels. I'm not going to be able to sleep here.*

I grabbed my phone to order room service. Coffee and croissants were what I needed, and I wasn't going to risk meeting Naomi downstairs.

*No, no, no, no...* One missed phone call from Naomi, seven from Nate, and fifteen from my assistant Jane. All made early in the morning, when I was still fast asleep, and Liam was sneaking out of his room. Jane was the only one who left me a voicemail:

 "Hi, it's Jane. I hope you're all right. Two things," she gasped, "Naomi went to Paris to see her fiancé, and while she's there she would like to meet with you. I told her you were on leave, but she was adamant she needed to see you personally, pronto. She's got some ideas to show you. Apparently, it can't wait because it needs some vintage furniture that is selling fast and must be ordered asap... I haven't promised her anything, but stand by because the woman is ready to hire a private investigator to find you! Rumour has it, her fiancé left her for another woman just before their wedding. He left her with the entire cost of the wedding, can you believe it? I don't like that woman, but what he did... what a bastard! Now, she needs to redirect her thoughts, as she said, on something else and guess what? She's going to be an even bigger pain in the arse for us. I'm available twenty-four seven on my private phone. Please call me back if there's something I can do. Oh, have you already heard that Molly was kidnapped? I bet you did, it's all over the news. I can't believe it. Nate and Susan are considering paying a million pounds ransom. Jeff says they can take it off the tax. I would never think it's possible, but well... we learn our whole life."

## CHAPTER 20
## *New Selina*

Dressed in a long beige trench coat and equipped with a rainbow pride umbrella, I sneaked around the large car park of a VIP fitness club in the Hamptons. The umbrella belonged to Faith, who bought it during a gay parade in Europe and it was the only one I could find at Leona's house. No matter how I maneuvered its handle, one of my trainers was absolutely soaked. It was pouring rain and didn't look like it was about to stop anytime soon. I glanced at my watch, Claudia should've already been here after her classes – unless I looked at the wrong schedule or she decided to stay for a gym session afterwards. All I knew was that she was definitely inside, and at some point, she would have to go the whole length of the car park to get to her white Land Rover, the number plate of which I had clandestinely written down after our first brief meeting.

---

Claudia Newman was one of Leona's closest neighbours, but by no means could they wave to each other from their driveways – the entrance to Claudia's mansion was half a mile from Leona's. Claudia and her husband were well established real estate developers with offices in Manhattan and developments all over the East Coast from Florida to Boston. Their Hampton house was their weekend and holiday oasis, the rest of the time the only people on their property were a maid, a gardener and a dog-walker for the Newman's two Bernardines.

"Is there something more that I should know about them?" I asked Basil as we were both sitting on the beach in the evening, facing a calm sea reflecting the full moon.

"I don't think so," he said, clearly thinking about something else. He was drawing in the sand with a stick and didn't seem to be particularly present. We sat for a while in silence before he spoke again, "The dog-walker's name is Gloria and she's also their part time dog-sitter. She's in her late twenties and often walks the dogs on the beach in front of your mother-in-law's house. Worth speaking to her when you've got a chance."

I called Basil as soon as Leo left for D.C. and I had to stay completely alone at his parents' house. The emptiness of the seven thousand square feet house was now creeping me out and I regretted that I had agreed to temporarily move here. There was Juana, but she spent only a couple of hours a day at the house. Two weeks after Leona went missing, Juana's work hours got significantly reduced. The rest of the time Leo and Emil carefully instructed me to say in a Spanish accent, "This is the Woodhouse estate, Juana speaking," whenever I picked up the phone. The landline might have been bugged and Emil seemed to be afraid that the kidnappers might call demanding a ransom, then somebody listening to the tape would know the Woodhouses were picking up their own landline. I didn't think anybody would call to demand anything, but each time the phone rang and Juana wasn't there I picked up with a trembling heart. I was so happy to hear the frequent scam phone callers.

"You know, don't you?" I asked Basil. He was looking in the distance and chewing the same stick that only a moment ago was stuck in the sand – I guessed he couldn't get sick. He nodded without looking at me.

"What was her reaction after she arrived *Up There*?"

Basil laughed, "You won't trick me Selina. Many have tried and nobody has succeeded so far. If you want to know whether Leona is dead or alive, you need to work it out for yourself."

"Well, it was worth trying," I said sulkily. "You know I won't tell them the truth."

"I have no idea, I can't control you or predict what you would do."

It turned out I was also unpredictable to myself. Leona's disappearance had been bothering me since I met Patricia. I felt an obligation to continue my investigation – even if it was purely for my own peace of mind. I decided not to involve anybody from the Woodhouse family, and I started by checking Leona's diary. The two names that were the most prevalent in her notes were Claudia and Pam. The second was easy to find as Pamela Goodrich kept calling every couple of days asking for an update on the search for Leona. She cried each time she said Leona's name, sent us chocolate and flowers with handwritten notes and looked actively for her best friend through social media. Claudia was initially a mystery. I asked Faith, and she had never heard of any Claudia. Both Emily and Leo suggested she just might've been Leona's beautician or hairdresser.

"Mum doesn't have many friends in the Hamptons. She's always been busy with the family and when she does socialise it's with dad's friends who mainly live in D.C.," Leo said. "I don't think she's got any enemies. I'm telling you, if somebody kidnapped her it's because of my campaign."

"You're right," I said only to stop the discussion and disconnect.

Basil hadn't answered my calls for a couple of days, I guessed he wanted me to find out who Claudia was on my own. I moved to Leona's house so at least I had an excuse to engage with the neighbours. I drove slowly up and down their street trying to spot somebody to talk to. I told people I was temporarily living at my mother-in-law's house so they wouldn't be afraid somebody broke onto the estate when they saw the lights on. The neighbours generally gave me dismissive or suspicious looks. Most couldn't care less and barely expressed any emotions, until I eventually spotted a white Land Rover with both its front doors wide open and two people standing next to a high metal gate. The man was clearly annoyed, treading on the spot with his arms crossed, while a woman was talking loudly on her phone. I parked on the street behind them, so I was blocking their way out if they suddenly wanted to leave.

"Everything ok? Do you need some help?" I asked forcing myself to smile.

"We're fantastic, thank you," snapped the man. It was a chilly and windy evening, and he was standing only in his T-shirt and a pair of shorts.

The woman put the phone into her orange Birkin bag and smiled at me without showing her teeth. "We're okay, thank you," she said and quickly turned to the man, "The gate is broken. Charlie is driving down to open it."

"Do you live here?"

"Why are you asking?" the man narrowed his eyes giving me a suspicious look. "Is this some sort of interview for *house burglary ltd*? If so, please smile to the camera," he pointed at two cameras hanging on the trees above the gate.

"I'm actually here to tell you that I now live at Leona Woodhouse's estate. I'm her daughter-in-law. I wanted to tell you, so you don't think somebody broke into the house," I was speaking quickly, sensing I didn't have much time before Charlie arrived to open the gate and my not-so-eager interlocutors disappeared behind it.

"Selina!" the woman exclaimed. "Of course, now I recognise you from Leona's photos. I'm sorry to hear about the accident. I was about to speak to your family, but I didn't want to bother you at such a difficult time. I truly can't imagine what you're all going through," she was talking with her hand pressed to her chest. "Please forgive my husband. We're just back from the airport, after a long flight from Hawaii. We're so exhausted and we can't get into the house."

"I understand. Everybody would lose their temper in such a difficult moment," I said and smirked to the man.

"It was nice to meet you Mrs Woodhouse and my condolences," the man was getting more and more impatient. He slid his chubby fingers through his dense black hair. I wondered whether it was a wig or they were dyed. "Let us know if you ever need anything, but remember that we don't reside here most of our time. We're very busy."

"Actually, Leona is missing, not dead."

"Of course," the woman said compassionately.

"Now if you'll excuse us," he said and jumped in the Land Rover's driver seat, the gate started moving.

"Richard, you're not going to drive. You've drunk a bottle of wine on the plane and—."

"Don't be silly. I can drive as drunk as I want on my estate. It's only half a mile to the house," he shouted from inside the car through an open window. "Claudia, are you getting in or are you going to walk?"

"Claudia," I whispered and we stood there for a moment staring at each other

"I can't talk right now, but I've got my Zumba classes every Saturday and Sunday morning at the gym in East Hamptons. Meet me there," she said lowering her voice.

"Which gym?" I whispered now aware that she clearly didn't want her husband to hear us.

"The most expensive one."

---

Women were leaving the gym in small groups of three or four, all holding umbrellas, jumping across puddles and running straight to their massive cars. They had perfectly coiffured hair and full make-up. In their fashionable fitness outfits and with designer gym bags, they could have easily been employed to advertise the very VIP gym. Ten minutes passed since I saw the last gym fashionista passing me in a hurry and nearly hitting me with her bag, but there was still no sign of Claudia. New cars started arriving with more people determined to sweat in the gym before nine o'clock on a Saturday morning. I reached for my phone to call a taxi, go home and have a warm bath when I heard a familiar voice calling me from behind my back, "Selina? I would never expect to find you here."

"Well, people change. Good morning, James."

"Wasn't it you who said once how you didn't understand people driving just to close themselves in another box, in order to run like a hamster on a treadmill?"

*Of course, sounds like the old Selina! No wonder my belly is so annoyingly sticking out, marking its existence in every tight dress. I should sign myself to this gym.*

"Maybe, I don't remember. I'm sorry, I'd love to have a longer chat with you but I'm super busy."

He smiled at me with disbelief, "What about some coffee and cake? It's the best that I can think of in weather like this."

"Aren't you afraid of all those extra calories?" I asked eying him from head to toe. A friend of mine would say he was like a piece of cake himself. Tall and well-built, even in a dark blue hoodie and jeans he looked strikingly hot. *Maybe Leo didn't want me to speak to him, because he himself secretly fancied James.*

"I don't have sugar-phobia like most people, who visit this place. What about Frank's coffee shop? They've got a fireplace. You could dry your shoes."

Being extra cautious meant not driving to the gym in Leona's Tesla, but that also resulted in getting wet, cold and potentially ill. "Do you have a car?" I asked suddenly enlightened. Taxis in East Hampton were expensive and often took a long time.

"Yep, I'm a happy car owner," he said proudly, teasing me as he knew exactly where I was going with it.

"Did you park nearby?" I looked around but quickly realised I didn't even know what car he drove. I remember it was large and blue but that was it.

"I parked right here," he took out a key from the pocket of his jeans. "Would you like to test drive my car in the rain?" he pointed the fob towards a Volvo SUV just next to me. *Fantastic, now it looks like I'm stalking him!*

"Oh, is this your car? I didn't know. I've been waiting for Claudia," I said before I managed to bite my tongue. *You aren't supposed to know that!*

"Claudia? She's now in yoga. She runs there straight after Zumba, and yoga lasts at least an hour and a half."

*Another reason to leave!* "You're very well informed."

"I do Zumba, don't look at me so surprised!"

"I'm more impressed than surprised. I'd love to see that," I said, again regretting I didn't bite my tongue in time.

"I bet you do! So, do the other girls. That's why they pay me to be there."

"They do what?"

"If you promise to keep my secret, I'll tell you all about it while we're driving to the coffee shop."

"You've got me, I can't miss this," I said relieved at the thought I was about to sit in a warm car.

I folded my umbrella and literally threw myself on the front seat, which did turn out to be heated. I had never appreciated so much the pleasure of a warm ass. "It's a great car," I said contentedly.

"I was serious. Would you like to drive it on the way back?"

"What makes you think that I would want to test drive your car?"

"Are you going to keep Leona's car? I love her Tesla, I'd even been thinking about getting one before..." he stopped to quickly correct himself, "only a few months ago. Do you really want to keep her car? I would find it a bit spooky."

"Leona might be alive, you know?" I said not sure whether I really believed it, and he gave me a merciful look. "But I agree, it looks weird. I'm living in her house, driving her car."

"I won't start freaking out until I see you wearing her bright pencil skirts with matching blazer. That would be a little odd," he laughed. "I'm sorry, I shouldn't have—"

"That's okay. We never even liked each other, but despite that I still feel a need to know how and why... It's been over two weeks. There is no body and it's not like there are sharks in that lake."

"The lake is huge, it takes time, but... I get it. I would like to know. That's why you've been looking for Claudia?"

"Yeah." *How does he know so much? Leo might be right, I need to be careful with this guy.* "You sound like you know many people in the Hamptons."

"Everybody needs a lawyer at some point in their life, and I guess people trust me."

Everybody *except Leo Woodhouse, but he's full of dangerous secrets himself.*

James and I sat opposite each other on two leather sofas, which were sideways to a huge stone fireplace with logs loudly crackling behind thick glass. The fire was warming up our cheeks and showing our faces in a favourable warm soft light. I slowly sipped my mulled wine with orange and cloves, while James was sitting with both hands entangled around his second mug of cherry hot chocolate.

As I was studying the drinks menu with wide eyes, James offered an explanation, "This place is famous for warming drinks. The Hamptons might be a seaside resort, but it can be freezing here. This place is run by a couple from Europe, who apparently got annoyed by the omnipresent drinks with ice."

"I'm well aware of the local temperatures James," I smiled in a friendly manner. "I live here too."

"You moved here only a year ago, and you probably still believe that all the chilly and rainy days are exceptional," he smiled sympathetically. "In New York at least you can warm yourself from the hot steam blowing on the sidewalk."

The coffee shop was selling branded goodies and accessories with Frank Muller's logo, ranging from mugs, cushions and coffee beans to socks and skimpy underwear. I bought a bottle of Irish cream liqueur and a pair of woolly socks, which I put on immediately before making myself comfortable on the sofa, my knees bent to one side, resting on a knitted cushion, and feet folded under my body.

"I normally don't drink at half past nine in the morning but..."

"I don't judge you," he said with a wide smile, his cheek pushed to their limits. "So, what do you do Selina?"

*He seems to know so much about me and my family but he has never asked about my job?*

"What do I do about what?" I asked confidently. Before he smiled again, he narrowed his eyes and gave me an inquisitive look. "What do I do to look so young?"

"Yep, that's exactly what I meant," he pointed his finger at me.

"Well, I can give you the name of the face mask I'm using, but I think the crucial thing is that I don't have to work."

"Right, Leo! You married well!"

"I don't know how well but—"

"Ouch!" he exclaimed joyfully, while fidgeting on the sofa and fiddling with strings from his hoodie.

"I'm Leo's copywriter," I said thinking it wasn't really that far from the truth. He was too stingy to pay anybody to write or correct his speeches.

"So, you must share his views."

I deliberately ignored his last statement. It wasn't like I really knew what Leo believed, or which of his loudly announced beliefs were carefully picked and tailored by his father so Leo would become their party's leader. "I'm also a novelist."

"That's amazing. I would love to read your book... or books? What have you written?"

"I have a couple of completed novels in my drawer, waiting for the right agent to take me on."

"Good luck then," he said raising his mug to clink with mine. "What are they about?"

*That reminds me, I haven't had time to finish reading any of the books! I haven't reviewed any corrections from my proof-reader or sent them to any agent! O sole mio!*

"Psychological thrillers with strong love plots." *Based on the first few chapters, it's a crime plus some thoughts on life – all spiced up by an emotional heartbreak and a falling in love – I can't be too far from the truth.* "How about you? If I understood correctly, you're working at the gym. What exactly are you doing?"

"I'm a gym influencer."

"Does it make me old and out-of-date when I say I've never heard of a gym influencer. I'm intrigued..."

"I'm paid to take part in the gym and fitness classes. I do everything from Zumba and belly dancing to yoga and Pilates. My role is to always keep the pace, dress well and look happy and enthusiastic."

"Hold on, instead of paying for the classes, they're paying you to attend them?"

"That's correct."

"*Dios mios!* Really? They're paying you to look hot, so you attract more women to come to the classes!" I shouted a bit too loud and his cheeks flushed red.

"Yeah, that's the embarrassing part of the job that I don't normally mention," he laughed. "They also expect me to attract a new market of customers…" he cleared his throat, "more men". My boss thinks I can break the stereotype that fitness classes are mainly for women. She claims that men can be more reliable clients as they don't skip the classes because of periods or pregnancy. I personally don't agree, but it's her argument. Men skip the gym for more trivial issues like staying on their couch to watch sport."

"It only shows how much women love other women… Is it a temporary job?"

"One of my jobs at the moment. I'm also working with a friend of mine on an App. I don't want to talk much about it yet, it's still in its infancy."

"A start-up?"

"I guess you can call it that."

"You're not going to go back to being the number one divorce lawyer in Manhattan?"

His eyes sparkled, "I see somebody's done her research."

"Don't flatter yourself. I'm just nosy."

"I wouldn't dare. You're beautiful, but as a married woman out of reach."

*Is he openly flirting or making fun of me?*

"You probably divorced so many people that you don't believe in marriage anymore."

"It certainly has some influence on how I perceive marriage and…" he took a deep breath, "and people in general. Quite often it gets nasty, even when you think you're dealing with the most civilised of civilised people on the planet," he said nodding his head and looking nostalgically at the fireplace.

"How about your love life?"

"My what?" he sat up surprised. "Indeed, you're nosy," he said raising his voice and leaning back on the sofa. "It's complicated."

"That's the part I've got no doubt about," I said still staring at him in anticipation. *Did you think you had the monopoly on asking personal questions or throwing in the air comments about me being beautiful but unavailable?*

"I've never been married, divorced or separated," he said carefully weighing every word, "and I've survived like that for nearly thirty-eight years."

"My congratulations?"

"No, it's not what I aspired to... it's just the way everything has worked out for me."

"Okay," I nodded.

"Not that I feel like I need to explain myself, but I used to work a lot – some would say too much, but I had no choice if I wanted to succeed. I also travelled a lot. My clients were all around the world, and it wasn't unusual for them to pay me an insane amount of money to follow them. I always tried to warn every woman what my situation was. Initially they all said they understood, but sooner or later they always became unhappy."

"Does that mean you can finally be happy now when you've stopped being..." James seemed not to listen, instead he was staring at my wet cotton handbag that I had put on the table between us hoping that the warmth of the fire would dry it. *I need at least one proper handbag, this one is pathetic, it looks like a beach bag!* My phone was vibrating and ringing loudly in a plastic washbag at the bottom – I put it there when it started raining and I was still hoping for Claudia to turn up. I reluctantly took it out to see Claudia's name flashing on the screen. I pressed *decline*. I didn't want James to get involved. She immediately sent me a message:

> Sorry I didn't show up. I'll explain later. I saw u driving away with James Hudson. Hope you didn't tell him about our meeting and if you did, find a way to erase it from his memory! Can u come to my house Fri evening?

*Where did she get my number from? Erase from his memory, how am I supposed to do that? Is she inferring that I sleep with him? That could help! No, it's not what she means... Erasing memory... Erasing... Wait! Talking about erasing! It's already erased! There is no history on my laptop at all! Just like it was never used.*

## CHAPTER 21
## New Lily

An old-fashioned landline phone in my room kept ringing like a fire alarm. It paused for a minute and then rang again. I was lying on my back looking at the ceiling, arms and legs spread wide on the king-size bed, thoughts racing through my brain like a roller-coaster. I finally picked up the phone, but only to put it on the bedside cabinet.

"Lily Rice? Madame, are you there? I've got a very important message for you," I could still hear a woman at the other end. *My bad, I should have hung up!*

"Yes, how can I help you?" I asked, but she went quiet on the other side. Obviously, it wasn't what the person was expecting to hear. "Hello?"

"Sorry, it's normally me who asks that question. It's Amelie from the reception desk. Sorry to disturb you, but I've got a very distressed gentleman sitting in our foyer. He says he needs to speak to you. His name is Nathaniel Tusk."

"Are you allowed to tell random people I'm staying at this hotel?" I snapped.

"The man has been inferring that..." she hesitated, and then continued whispering, "that you might not be well. That you might be a threat to yourself. I'm sorry, I just... he said I would have you on my conscience if I didn't check up on you. I'm so glad you answered because he almost convinced me to send one of our staff to your room."

"I'm perfectly fine."

"I'm glad to hear it. Can I direct the man to your room?"

"No," I snapped. *Can everybody just leave me alone?*

"I understand," she said disappointed. "So..."

"Would you mind telling him that I'll reach him on his mobile?"

"Sure," she sighed with relief.

Nathaniel, Naomi, Susana... All these people were so suffocating. They didn't take *no* for an answer, acting like the entire world owed them. I thought Leona was intense, but that was only one person to get rid of. How was I supposed to set myself free from a whole bunch of annoying people? *Organise a teambuilding trip, put them all on the same bus and push it off the cliff?* I thought, smiling to myself – I found the idea very soothing.

"Lily, thank you for calling," Nate sounded concerned, but I was pretty sure it was all for show. He was still in the foyer with the anxious receptionist watching him. "I've been so worried—"

"Please leave the hotel, so you don't have to pretend. You made quite a show. What do you want?"

"I've been worried."

"You're acting like a stalker. Do I need to get a restraining order, or what?"

"Oh, I'm sorry but after Molly was kidnapped, I've been terrified that the woman who I love might also become a target for the same kidnappers!"

"You can't be serious?"

"I think it has something to do with our company. Susana and I suspect at least a couple of customers."

"Customers?"

"More like M-A-F-I-A!" He spelled out quietly.

I swallowed hard. "But why?"

"Why? Why? I don't know *why*. Is it not what they do for a living?" he was shouting, while breathing loudly. Where was he going? Upstairs to see me or leaving the hotel? I heard in the background some road noises with a horn blowing and I gasped with relief.

"Well, can you get me a bodyguard? If that's a company matter, I'm pretty sure you could take it off the tax bill?"

"What?" he asked irritated. "We're an interior design company, I doubt that bodyguard services can be written off. But maybe you as a TV celeb—"

"I'll check with my accountant. Would you like to see me later for dinner?"

"Of course. That's why I'm here darling. I know the perfect romantic restaurant—"

"I thought I'm in danger and we need to be careful."

"It's a public place but—"

"No, I've got two tickets for a cruise on the Seine. They've got the most fabulous chef, and the atmosphere is equal to none."

"Ok, I'm in," he said cheerfully.

"I need to go, but I'll send you all the details within the hour."

I didn't have an idea yet what I was about to do with my new life, but one thing was certain – with or without Molly, I couldn't work for Nate and Susana. How could anybody function in such a toxic environment where no one was allowed to have a private life? Although, on reflection getting involved with a boss made the distinction between personal and professional much more difficult to maintain. Was my predecessor particularly strong-minded? Was she one of those people who seem to never care about what was going on around them – and just did their job? It couldn't be the case. People like that don't throw chairs at co-workers, at least not in front of everybody. If she had any sense in her, she would have been better off *accidentally* tripping Molly up so she fell on her face and knocked her teeth out.

The problem was I couldn't just quit without a solid plan. I had a mortgage to pay and from what Gabriel told me – if I left the company, my contract prevented me opening my own design business in the UK for a year. I could buy myself out of the clause for a million pounds – a crazy sum, considering it would only allow me to legally start my business. Besides, what could I – New Lily – start? Her skills didn't automatically pass on to me! The Soul Management program needed some serious adjustment and more consideration. As the first souls taking part in the program, we definitely had it harder than our successors.

Quitting wasn't an option, not yet. I just needed some time to put together a plan of action, but it did seem a bit mission impossible. As I got off the call with Nate, I already had three messages from Naomi and two from my new mother. Only one required immediate reply:

> Hi Naomi. Would you like to have dinner with me this afternoon? I've got two VIP tickets for a cruise on the Seine. You will love it.

> No, thank you. I have a flight to catch straight after. I'll book us a table in the city.

> Have to stay low key after Molly got kidnapped. Will explain later. The boat doesn't move so you can leave whenever you want, you'll be fine.

I stopped typing, thinking, lies, lies, lies ...

## CHAPTER 22
## *New Selina*

When James dropped me home in the late afternoon, Faith was already waiting for me in the kitchen. It was her family home, but I still found it surprising how often during the last couple of weeks everybody just arrived and left without giving me any notice. It made me feel like I was their housekeeper. I had the alarm on during the night and I kept a heavy glass sculpture under my bed. I didn't believe for a moment that Leona being missing was an accident. *Unless that angry steam from her ears rocked her boat too much. Maybe she was drunk!* I didn't feel safe in the house. *Has nobody ever thought I could hurt them if I was surprised by an unexpected visit?* I thought, looking at Faith sitting on a bench laid with cushions in the kitchen's bay windows. She was polishing off her father's whisky and staring at the churning sea. I felt sorry for her, but I'd be much happier if we could take the conversation to my house, at least I'd have a degree of control over what she was allowed or not allowed to do. Also, I had no whiskey. I had a feeling that her unrestrained *whisky-ing* was going to end up in the downstairs toilet, and Juana wasn't coming until Tuesday.

I had called Leo early in the morning before going to see Claudia at the gym. I asked whether I could go back to our house in Southampton, but it wasn't even an option. He and his father had already contracted renovations of the house. It was also my house, but again nobody thought about sharing the news with me in advance! Emil was planning on moving there with Ariana. There! To my house! I wanted to say that everybody has *moved on* surprisingly quickly, but I bit my tongue at the last minute. It was stamped and sealed, if Leona ever came back, I was going to be living with her!

"Have you eaten?"

Faith looked at me from under her heavy-coated eyelashes. She looked more tired than upset. "I've had half of the cake that was in the fridge. I hope you don't mind."

I ordered the cherry-chocolate cake especially for Pamela Goodrich, who was visiting on Sunday, but with Faith in the house I would have to call it off anyway. That reminded me, I also had to call off James, who planned to pop round *whenever most convenient*, which in reality would mean when Pam was gone. How am I supposed to run my Leona investigation when I had no privacy at all? "No, of course not. I wasn't going to eat the whole cake, anyway. I live alone."

"That's what I thought. Besides, the last thing you need is sugar."

"Oh, thank you for being so critical of my body, that's exactly what I need right now," I snapped as I took off my coat and started undoing the laces of my trainers.

"I'm not talking about your weight, you look fine – for thirty-something. I don't want to preach, but you shouldn't have much sugar when you're trying for a baby."

"Since when have you known so much about getting pregnant?"

"I'm following a few pregnant women, and a few who're actively trying to—"

"Following? Like spying?" I raised my eyebrows. I was tired, cold and not in the mood for guessing.

"Seriously Selina, you need to make friends with social media if you ever want to achieve anything in this world."

"Of course," I murmured. "I knew what you meant, I just wasn't sure why you would be following anybody who's pregnant. Oh my god, are you—?"

"No! The women just happen to be some of the best paid influencers in America. They're absolute gurus when it comes to managing their profiles."

"That's truly wonderful," I walked towards the bay window and almost slipped just in front of Faith, the warm woolly socks I bought in Frank's café weren't designed to be worn on tiled floors. She giggled like a teenager, which was exactly who she was, and that annoyed me even more. How was I supposed to know how to handle drunk teenagers who had lost a parent? I felt completely powerless. She was being malicious and mean, but I couldn't even get angry with her, she was suffering.

"You must've drunk more than me," she smirked. With one swipe of my right hand I took away her half-drunk glass of whisky. She clearly didn't expect that as she stared at me in silence the entire time I was pouring the contents of the glass into the sink and preparing us both strong coffees.

"It'll make you feel better," I handed her a large mug of coffee with frothed milk at the top. The smile faded from her face and despite the heavy make-up she was wearing, she now looked like a little girl. She pulled her legs towards her chest and made some space for me on the bench. She was dressed in a bright yellow oversized jumper and black jeggings. "I thought you were taking extra classes on Saturdays to be better prepared for your final exams."

"I'm not going to college. I've made my decision so save yourself some time and don't even try to convince me otherwise."

"You know what's best for you," I said, and she looked at me astounded. "I just thought that's what you wanted."

"It was for a brief moment, but it's mainly what my parents wanted for me. Mum isn't here anymore," her voice cracked, "and dad would rather have me marry a politician than become one. He'll be annoyed initially, but he'll get over it very quickly thinking how much money he can save on me going straight to work. Ariana wants her next wedding to be the most splendid of all and dad is so crazy in love with her he'll pay for it."

"How long have they known each other? Isn't it too soon to be getting married?" I regretted asking the question as it reminded Faith about her father having an affair with Ariana rather than – as he wanted everybody to believe – dating her after splitting up with Leona. She shrugged her shoulders. "Anyway, more importantly what do you want to do?"

"I've already been working for a couple of years," she rolled her eyes. "But now it looks like I'm not too far away from earning some serious money. I've even been thinking about employing a few people to work on my profile seven days a week. Yeah, I know it's demanding, but they can work from home and most of us spend a few hours on the Internet every day, so at least they would be doing something meaningful with that time, right?" Faith was speaking enthusiastically. "I've just put an advert up for an unpaid internship and had a great response."

"Sorry, I'm not sure I understand correctly. Are you talking about your blog?"

"Emily has her blog. Don't get me wrong, she's doing fine but it won't make her an independent woman. I'm an Instagram influencer."

"Can you do it in your free time and still study?"

"I knew sooner or later you'd start judging me. Look – you, mum and Emily all went to university, and for what? Higher education is massively overrated. You all became housewives, even if it wasn't your intention. And I know that you all have your hobbies, you write novels, Emily—"

I wasn't going to argue about me being a housewife with a hobby. It would be pointless. "You could be the exception in the family. You could get your degree and do something with it!"

"Sounds idealistic and naive. It's utopia in its clearest form. You spend years studying and when you finally graduate with your masters, you're already in your mid-twenties. That's the time when from a biological point of view, you should start procreating, especially if you want to have more than one child. That's also the time when you should start working full-time and climb your career ladder. It's only a matter of time before you conclude that you can't bring the two together, unless you agree to give your kids away to an orphanage-style childcare or accept that when you return to work from your maternity leave, you're going to be starting all over again, just older, fatter, more frustrated and worn-out. And don't get me even started on how many women get molested in their work place."

"Jesus Christ! Are you even listening to what you're saying?"

"You're in your thirties, you should know better by now. Whether you want to believe it or not, you can make your own choices, but the world out there is still very brutal for women."

"So what are you suggesting? Shall we all just give up before we've started?"

"I suggest being more creative and not following in the footsteps of our mothers and older sisters. History doesn't have to repeat. By the age of twenty-five I'm going to be a financially independent woman, which will give me some options... Currently I've got five million followers and the number is growing. I need to give them some time, some respect – otherwise they'll go somewhere else."

"Where? To the library? Or to build a spaceship?" I scoffed and she immediately chastised me with her eyes. She didn't look like Leona at all, but she had her piercing disapproving eyes, which gave me shivers. "Of course," I murmured. "Well, it's admirable you got yourself so many followers. How did you manage to do it?" *Or how many times did you show your boobs?*

She lowered her eyes. *Here we are, she must have shown her boobs, arse, and god knows what else...* She cleared her throat and spoke confidently, "Actually no... I'm going to tell you. You'll find out anyway, and I've got nothing to be ashamed of. I've been running my Instagram profile for the last two years, but a week ago I also launched my first Vlog talking about my mother going missing. I used to have fifty thousand followers, now I've got five million."

I choked on the last sip of coffee. "You must be so proud of yourself." *And if Leona is somewhere out there still alive, it'll probably kill her! What a family!*

"I'm actually very proud," Faith said while slowly raising herself from the bench. "I'm also prepared that some people might not like it," she stood on her toes and stretched her hands up in the air, "but I've read a few online guides on how to deal with haters and I think I'm well prepared."

I didn't ask any more questions, I had enough to process after this discussion with my sister-in-law. "Would you like to have a bath? Or I could make us some dinner."

"No, thanks. I'm going to sleep at Jeremy's, his parents are in Tokyo on a business trip. He should be at home by now," she said, just as I was thinking that I wouldn't mind somebody staying with me in the house.

"Oh, I hoped for a girl's night in."

"Sorry to let you down. I wouldn't be able to fall asleep here anyway. I feel like my mother's spirit is in the house. It's spooky."

*Tell me about it!* "You and Jeremy," I smiled. "Since when have you been dating?"

"Oh no, it's just sex," she said flippantly, moved her hands and involuntarily pushing some cushions from the bench onto the floor. She started walking across the kitchen when I spotted a pink envelope lying on the tiles just next to the bay window. *It must have been hidden under the cushions!* I quickly picked it up recognising Leona's writing with big, rounded letters saying: To my baby boy, Leo. Not without some guilt, I didn't say anything to Faith and put it into the back pocket of my jeans.

Faith was adamant that she would call herself a taxi and there was no need for me to give her a lift. Just as she ordered her cab, the bell rang.

"Are you expecting somebody?" she smirked.

"I don't think so," I said seeing a familiar red raincoat through the glass panel next to the main door. I saw it only a few hours ago drying in Frank's café. *Why now?*

"Don't worry, I don't expect you to live in celibacy while Leo spends so much time in D.C."

"Faith!"

"What?"

My anger quickly made some space for curiosity, "Do you think Leo has somebody?"

"Nah, he's a workaholic."

"Right, and I'm just a housewife."

"Exactly! The naughtiest type of all," she said deadpan and opened the door to let James in. "Sex is good for blood pressure and it's the best way to release endorphins."

---

Faith threw a quick *hi* to James and before he had a chance to respond she was already running to the taxi parked in front of the house. As soon as she threw herself on its back seat, the black jeep with privacy windows drove away with a squeal.

"Wow, I've never seen a taxi arrive here so quickly," I said to James. "Sorry, please come in," I said to him as he walked into the hallway holding my mobile. *What the hell! Because of Faith's unexpected visit, I haven't even noticed I lost it! Damn it! Could he read my messages?*

He immediately read the panic in my eyes, "Don't worry I'm good with computers, but I can't get into your phone without the password."

I forced a silly laugh, "I hadn't even thought about it. I'm just surprised I lost it without noticing."

"Look," he said still holding my phone tightly in his right hand, "I'm only here to give you the phone back, don't feel any pressure to invite me in. Are we still seeing each other tomorrow?"

I found myself lonely and anxious in the big house. The thunderstorm was coming and as much as I didn't want James to drive in the bad weather, I also didn't want to watch alone how the vast empty rooms in the house were illuminated by lightning, and its floors were shaken by thunder. "Actually... if you don't have any plans, we could... could we..." I felt uncomfortable asking him for another favour. Giving me a lift, bringing my phone, and now *this* – which we really planned on Sunday.

"Sure, we can recover the deleted history on your computer tonight. It normally doesn't take much time."

"Only if you've got no plans. I know it's your Saturday evening."

"I had no other plans except crashing on the sofa with a glass of wine."

"Perfect, nothing we can't do here afterwards," I said without much thought and started walking through the long hallway to the kitchen. *What are you talking about you stupid woman? Drinking wine with him? Getting comfy with him on one of Leona's sofas? Knowing her, she probably bugged them! What is he going to think about you now?*

"Sounds like a plan," I heard his cheerful voice. *Of course, now he feels invited! Is it a date?* "Do you feel like a take-away? Or I could cook something for us."

*Food! I have nothing to eat except the half-eaten cherry chocolate cake!*

I stood in front of the fridge, both hands holding its double door, my nostrils filled with chocolate-cherry aroma, and my face feeling the cold breeze. *Exactly, what I need right now, to cool down! Breathe in and out, in and out...*

"Are you okay?" James stood just behind me, I felt the warmth of his body on my back, his breath on my neck.

I turned to him leaving the fridge still open, "Fine, I'm perfectly fine. Except I forgot to do the shopping."

"Hmm..." he stood in front of the fridge with his hands on his hips. "You've got eggs, milk, maple syrup. Have you got any flour?" He finally closed the fridge as it demanded by loudly beeping and flashing a tiny red light.

I opened the door to the pantry on the opposite side of the kitchen. It was better equipped than I had suspected. It had tinned tomatoes and pretty much all kinds of food that could be put in a can – it looked like Leona was prepared for a catastrophe, or at least hard Brexit. There were several types of flour, cereals, rice, dried fruits, spare maple syrups and plenty of other things, mostly unopened.

"I've got flour!" I shouted out with such enthusiasm that James laughed out loud.

"Then we're saved! As long as you like pancakes!"

"I love them." *I just never had enough time to master a pancake recipe. First of all because I wouldn't stand that long in the kitchen above a hot pan to make something only for myself. Second, it's a standard breakfast when a man tries to impress me after a first night together; or when Nate wants to apologise for being an arse the previous night. I guess Selina has more reasons to learn how to make pancakes, or does she?*

James dived into the pantry, rubbing his hands and eying the three walls filled with wooden shelves, all bending from the weight of tinned food. "Red beans, chickpeas, tomatoes, sweet potatoes, red onion... hmmm... I could make you a Mexican veg chilli."

"Fantastic. Make yourself at home!"

I helped him find a large non-stick pan with a lid and other necessary utensils. Many looked like they had been barely used, I wonder whether Leona never cooked, or she had recently undertaken a massive turn-over in kitchen utensils. James rolled the sleeves of his grey T-shirt and started chopping onions. I sat down on a high stool resting my elbows on the marble island and watching what he was doing.

"Do you cook a lot?"

"Most days. I often make a few portions at the same time and freeze them for later."

"I wish I was that organised," I sighed. My eyes started stinging from the onions, I needed to move away for a moment. "Would you like a glass of wine?"

He gazed at me, the corners of his lips were slightly moving up and down like he was fighting his urge to smile. "I'm driving. Unless you're offering me one of Leona's spare bedrooms," he said flatly and poured some oil onto the pan. The induction hob beeped loudly, as loud as an alarm in my head. I didn't mean it to be such a loaded question.

"Sure, there are like six guest bedrooms here. I could also call you a taxi. I'll text Faith, her cab was here in less than a minute."

James frowned his eyebrows, "Are you talking about that black jeep?"

"Yeah, why? Is something wrong with that company?"

"Generally, everything is wrong when it comes to Richard Moon," he murmured while energetically stirring the pan.

"Richard Moon?"

He immediately stared at me surprised, "Claudia's husband. You were waiting for her today."

"Of course, of course. I thought her surname was Newman."

"She kept her maiden name," the way he said it indicated it was common Hamptons' knowledge.

"I'm terrible with names."

"Or you meet so many people at all those parties here that you've stopped caring."

"But what about Richard? And why would Faith tell me she called a taxi if Richard picked her up?"

"No idea, although…" he stopped abruptly and changed the topic, "I hate their slogans. I just don't get it – they earn so much money, but they can't get anything better than: *Buy with us, you'll be over the Moon,* or, *You'll love your house to the Moon and back.*"

I realised I was still standing in the middle of the kitchen, so I walked towards a small wine fridge under the counter and grabbed the very first bottle of white wine I saw. I found two glasses in the cupboard above and put them on the island where James was gradually making a complete mess. I poured a full glass for him and a half for me.

"Thank you," he quickly took a sip. "At least I can always say I told you that because I drank too much," he took another sip, "as opposed to just being another Hampton's gossiper," he giggled nervously. "Although you probably know anyway from your husband."

"We've barely talked in the last couple of weeks. He works hard on his campaign and is impatiently waiting for the kidnapper to call. He's convinced his mother was abducted."

"I'm not so sure. There's no body, but Leona is probably dead, and at least some of the family is coming to terms with it. I've heard Emil initiated the life insurance claim."

"He did what? Does he get anything?"

"I'm not his lawyer, but I think so."

"Is your friend his lawyer? Do you know he's getting something?"

"I haven't said anything," his cheeks went red, and he helped himself to more wine.

"What a bastard! He leaves her for another woman. As soon as she is missing, he uses her for money... It couldn't have happened if they were already divorced."

"A lot of money."

"But where's Richard Moon in all of this?"

"Faith might get a good sum too actually, Leona's children will get more than Emil. Maybe she's thinking about buying a house for herself or simply investing."

"I don't think so. Both her and Emily are devastated. I don't think they have even started thinking about the insurance money."

"I've learned in my job that you can't make assumptions about other people. We only know others as much as they want us to know."

"What if Leona killed herself?"

"What makes you think she would?" he asked curiously like it had never even crossed his mind.

"She was pretty unhappy. She considered the divorce her failure. She cared deeply about public opinion, and he humiliated her. Maybe she was in a dark place, severely depressed and none of us saw it," as I was talking the envelope in the back pocket of my jeans felt heavier and heavier.

"There's no proof of suicide. We'll probably never know."

"But if she did kill herself, would they still get the money?"

"Selina, they're also your family, but you always talk about them like it's you and them," I couldn't find the right words to comment. *I'm just on a contract here but nobody can know it.* I shrugged. "Normally an insurance policy will pay when somebody has been murdered, but not when people kill themselves."

## CHAPTER 23

## *New Lily*

I felt like a mobile call centre. If I wanted to answer every single call, I wouldn't have moved from my hotel room, and leaving the hotel was my top priority. I believed that Naomi bumped into me accidentally, but even if not, I'd spent a night with her fiancé, so I couldn't exactly blame her. But Nate? Did he track my mobile through an app? Did Jane tell him? Or maybe Lily always stayed in the same hotel? That wouldn't be so weird, it was the highest rated hotel in Paris. *Well, another reason to leave early, god knows who else I could meet here,* I thought as I put my phone on silent and shoveled it into my handbag. On the bright side, with my hold luggage still missing, I was travelling light, and I didn't have to worry about losing anything. Also, with Liam clearly having no intention of continuing our friendship, I wasn't tempted to glance every five minutes at my phone. *What a wonderful lightness of being* I thought, shutting the door to the suite, only slightly regretting I couldn't enjoy it longer.

I was sitting in the departure hall of Paris Charles de Gaulle Airport, chewing an energy bar, when a man in a tight navy suit and a smile glued to his face sat down on a plastic chair opposite me. Of all the empty seats around us he had to choose that one. It was three in the afternoon, morning flights had already departed, but it was still too early for the evening business flights.

"Nice dress," he started chatting me up in English with a distinctive Spanish or Italian accent. "Have you also left the expo early?" he asked, his feet crossed, and hands wrapped around a shiny silver laptop.

"No," I lightly shook my head. I wasn't in the mood for chitchat, no matter how good-looking the guy was. I might have been overdressed for a flight, but I had no bag for my new red dress, the one I had bought for the cruise on the Seine with Liam. I'd binned the clothes, which I flew to Paris in as it was time to start making decisions and getting rid of unnecessary ballast. That decision, however, proved to be a little hasty.

"Okay, I understand," he said, smile not fading from his face.

I gasped, "I came here for a friends' wedding, but the groom departed prematurely so I'm going home early."

"Ouch!" he frowned. I felt a slight satisfaction that I had managed to wipe his smile away. "How's the bride?"

"Oh, she's fine. She is actually relieved." The stranger looked at me baffled, just as I started enjoying my story. "It turned out she had an affair." His eyes widened. "Most guests stayed for the party, but I thought I could use the unexpected time off for a small holiday."

"Where are you going now?"

"Malaga."

"Me too!" he said enthusiastically. "I was annoyed the flight was delayed. I left a trade show early just to catch this particular flight, but..." he smiled again, "maybe it was meant to be."

*Definitely it wasn't meant to be!*

"Where are you staying?"

"I haven't decided yet. I thought it would be fun to stroll around the city and pick a hotel last minute."

"Adventurous," he nodded. "Not many people would have the courage to do it."

"Courage? I thought it's safe there."

"Yes," he laughed but many people would panic that they might not find a room on time and end up..." he hesitated. "You don't look like you would be happy to sleep in a cheap hostel.

"Aren't tapas bars open twenty-four-seven?"

He gave me a wide smile, "Maybe some. Look, I live there so I could give you some ideas on where to stay, where to eat... I'm going out tomorrow night with a group of friends for dinner. Would you like to join us?"

"That's very kind of you, but I'm not even sure whether Malaga is my final destination. I was thinking about renting a car and looking somewhere further down the coast."

"Have you ever been to Marbella?"

I hesitated. *Selina has never been to Marbella, but Lily?* "Yes, but a while ago."

"I'm trying to buy a holiday house there and one of my friends who will be at the dinner tomorrow is an estate agent. I don't want to pester you, but—"

"But if I wanted to buy a house..." I laughed. "Who knows what the future brings."

"Exactly," he said, just as his phone started ringing. He looked at the screen and hesitated, "I need to take it. It's my boss." He picked up the phone, and while speaking to a Jose, passed me his business card. The man, whose name was Miguel, was an executive buyer for El Corte Inglés, the largest department store in Spain.

*"No wonder, he can get a second home in Marbella, but hold on..."* I thought and smiled to myself. I realised too late that Miguel might take my reply as a YES to his invite, *"I can afford a house on the Costa del Sol. My own house, just for me... even just for a year! Who said I have to have a tough time trying to convert Lily into a decent woman?"*

He was speaking loudly in Spanish and vividly gesticulating, occasionally bursting into laughter. I glanced at the screens above my head, the flight to Malaga was another thirty minutes delayed. I reached for my mobile. I didn't feel like strolling purposelessly around the airport, I was too tired for that. *Luckily*, I had a bunch of messages and a long list of voicemails to go through. I put on wireless headphones and clicked on a voicemail from Nathan:

 I'm super pissed with you... I went all the way to Paris to speak to you Lily – to you! About us, about work, about what happened to Molly. I thought we could talk it through like two adults. I know I let you down, but don't I deserve a chance to explain myself? For god's sake, you've never expressed any desire to have kids... Anyway, Naomi missed her flight. She knows you lied, and is currently trying to rearrange her return flight.... I'm drinking wine alone and thinking about you... All things considered, I'm impressed at how you planned it – how you got rid of me and her at the same time. Give me a call, or better yet just come back home. You can't run forever. Love you.

I ignored all the many messages from Naomi. Miguel was still chatting in front of me, I didn't want to risk him hearing a woman screaming at me. I pressed on a voicemail from Jane:

> Lily, can you give me a ring? Your clients keep asking about you and I don't know what to tell them. You never said how long you were taking off. Please get in touch. Also, on Molly. Nathaniel and Susana, after a meeting with their accountant and lawyer, agreed to pay the ransom. Molly will probably take sick leave so she won't be around for a while, but more importantly nobody will think her disappearance had something to do with you...

*Something to do with me? Like I killed her or what?*
The next voicemail was from an unknown number:

> Good afternoon. It's Amelie from the Parisian Pearl Hotel. A delivery man brought your lost luggage. He said he had been trying to reach you on the mobile you gave them at the airport, but you hadn't been answering. You haven't checked out of the hotel, but I'm starting to worry because I also can't get in touch with you. If I don't hear from you, I'm going to send somebody soon to your

room to check whether you're all right. I really hope you're well...

*Thank you Nate!* I thought irritated and pressed the number to call her back, not carrying anymore about what Miguel thinks of me if he happens to listen to my conversation.

"Hello, it's Lily Rice. I've got your message about my luggage. I had to leave the hotel early."

"That's not a problem. Our reception desk is open twenty-four hours. I'll let Rosalie know you'll pick it up later. Thank you for calling. I was worried."

"No, sorry. You've misunderstood me. I've already left for the airport."

"But there are still some clothes on your bed," she said surprised, sounding almost offended as if I was lying to her. *I should've put them in the bin!*

"How do you know? I presume it's not normal for cleaning ladies to report to reception on the state of my bed."

"I'm sorry Madam..." she started in a more official tone, "I couldn't reach you. The delivery man also couldn't get through..."

"Have you mixed up working in a hotel with a kindergarten?"

"I'm sorry," I heard her taking a deep breath, "it was only last week that a man killed himself in one of our suites. It happened during my shift."

"Jesus!" I said loudly, and Miguel glanced at me. Was he still on the phone with his boss, or only pretending so he could overhear my conversation? I bet it was the latter.

"Then your friend arrived today, and he was so worried."

"Okay, now I understand," I said gently. "Could you send me the bag by courier?"

"Of course, let me grab a pen and I'll write down your address."

"Actually... I'll send you the address in a day or two when I get there."

"There?"

*Oh, heaven! The harder I try to defend myself as a mentally stable woman, the more I fail. But do I really have to explain myself to a random woman?* "I'm going to be travelling so I just need to think about where you should send my luggage, so I don't miss it again."

"Of course," she didn't sound convinced. "Or would you like me to give it to your friend? He's already offered."

"Which friend?" I asked, trying to remove the rising panic in my voice.

"Nathaniel Tusk."

"He offered?"

"I'm sorry I called him when one of our housekeepers found your clothes in the room, but we couldn't reach you."

"I'm sorry," I started, fuming with anger, "but could you please stop contacting Nathaniel regarding my person? I've got a restraining order against him," I snapped. The woman went silent. Miguel looked at me with a mixture of fear and mercy. "I feel sorry for the man who killed himself on your shift, but you need to respect my privacy, otherwise I'll have to speak to your boss... Yes, thank you. I will. Goodbye," I said, while staring at Miguel, who was not going anywhere, despite the fact our flight had just started boarding.

"Look, I don't need to know your name or your story, but if you ever need any help, you've got my card. That friend of mine I mentioned can also help you with a rental. He can offer you a whole range of properties, from the most luxurious ones just on the beach front to the very affordable and discreet in beautiful hidden villages."

"Thank you," I said, feeling guilty that I had a go at the poor girl from the hotel, particularly after she dealt with that customer's suicide. Miguel must have concluded I was running away from an abusive partner.

I felt even more guilty when I left the arrivals hall without any luggage, and Miguel chased me to a taxi offering a pre-paid sim card, "Just if you didn't have roaming, and you know... not everybody speaks English here, so if you had a problem—"

"No, no, I'm fine," I was trying to explain, baffled, but he wouldn't have any of it.

"My car is parked at the long-stay, or..." he hesitated..."do you need some cash for a taxi? They're not good here with cards."

"I'm fine," I laughed, embarrassed. "I've got plenty of cash. Thank you so much," I said, getting into my Uber.

"We're perfectly fine with credit cards and English here," said my Uber driver.

"I'm sure you are," I smiled.

"He thought that..." I stopped half-sentence. I didn't need to explain myself to everybody. "He was just being nice."

"Do you know who he is?"

"A nice guy," I shrugged.

The driver, a middle-aged bald man with large glasses, laughed and glanced at the front mirror to see my reaction, "He's one of the richest guys on the Costa del Sol. I would let him pay. If he can afford a five percent stake in El Corte Ingles, he can pay for your cab."

"I can afford my taxi fare."

"Normally, girls chase him, not the other way around. I would marry him, and I'm not even into blokes," he said, making himself laugh.

## CHAPTER 24
## New Selina

I was lying in a guest bedroom and staring at the ceiling, hands alongside my body, eyes set on a non-working fan. A bedside lamp with an oversized round white shade was switched on, casting a shadow on a wall covered with family pictures from the times when Leo, Emily and Faith were still little. When I moved in, I immediately took down all of the photos with Leona, wrapped them in sheets and hid them under the bed. I couldn't fall asleep with her looking at me. Like all six guest bedrooms in the house, this one was modestly decorated with light blue and gold cushions and old-fashioned flowery curtains. There wasn't much personality in the room, it reminded me of a medium range B&B in England. I thought that if I was going to stay here any longer – which seemed likely given Emil and Ariana would be in my old house I hadn't much choice – I needed to at least redecorate this bedroom and turn one of the rooms with a sea view into a study.

Normally after drinking half a bottle of wine, having a large dinner, and going to bed at midnight, I would be fast asleep within a few minutes, but with James sleeping on the other side of the corridor, I was barely able to lie still. I didn't regret inviting him in. It was my best night since I had landed myself *the position* in this body, but undeniably he was making my life situation even more complicated. I had a gut feeling that the reason why Leo wanted me to avoid James was exactly the reason why I needed to get to know him better. The Woodhouse family was still one big mystery to me, and James seemed to know a lot about all the richest and most influential people in the Hamptons. From what I gathered we had never been close neighbours, but he was easy to talk to and treated me like an old friend. Was he interested in me? As an ex-divorce lawyer who hardly believed in marriage, he wouldn't be particularly bothered with my marital status. Or did he have another agenda – if so, what could it be? He seemed to be on my side, but didn't have a single good word for the rest of the Woodhouse family. He didn't heavily criticize them, but he was good at planting persuasive doubts about them and their friends.

"How well do you know Richard?" I asked when we were sitting at the oval table in the kitchen finishing the meal he'd prepared.

"A friend of mine represented several clients who sued his company. The last case I remember was about some residents of a luxurious apartment block in Chicago, who weren't allowed to use most facilities in their building like the swimming pool, sauna and gym. Apparently after seventy percent of the flats had been sold, Richard and Claudia decided that to sell the most expensive apartments they needed to make the facilities more luxurious and exclusive. So they changed the policy and limited access to the facilities only to those who owned apartments larger than a thousand square feet."

"Outrageous. I hope your friend won?"

"The people got some compensation, but the amount was laughable considering how much they paid for their apartments. The facilities weren't guaranteed in their leases but a courtesy of the company. Long story short, Richard just keeps throwing money until he achieves the desired result. She is a very good lawyer, that friend of mine," he said blushing and took a glass of wine, "but she had no chance with the sharks Richard employed and his unlimited budget."

"She... were you dating her?"

"Nah," he blushed again.

"I'm not buying that, but you don't have to tell me."

He gasped, "Four years. We moved in together, got engaged, planned our wedding and..." he paused and started fiddling with the stem of his wine glass. It felt like talking about her was tormenting him, but I waited patiently. *He knows so much about my family, I deserve to know more about him.* He took our plates and continued his story while walking to the dishwasher, "One evening she got back late from work, I was taking a bath. She let herself in to the bathroom, still wearing her winter coat and hat. The moment I saw her, I knew something was off. I practically convinced myself somebody must've died," he forced himself to smile while packing the rest of the food into plastic containers for me to freeze. "I'm not trying to be poetic, but it was our relationship that died. She closed the toilet seat with disgust, I thought she would comment on me always leaving it open, but this time she said nothing. She sat down on the toilet with her legs crossed, hands holding her knees – and just like that she said she couldn't do it anymore. She had slept with somebody. She wasn't pregnant or in love with the guy, but she didn't want to be with me either. I think I would have felt better, or at least less shocked if she had tried to drown me in that bath."

"It would be more shocking, unless you're trying to say she's that badass."

James was leaning at the white porcelain sink, drying his hands with a pink kitchen towel and looking into the distance, "I was so occupied with my work that I had no idea how my own fiancée felt about us. I didn't notice when she stopped loving me. I didn't notice she was depressed and had to seek a therapist for help. I had no idea she had problems at work and with her family."

"Not that I'm trying to justify you, but couldn't she just tell you?"

"She did, but it wasn't until she left I realised how much she had already told me."

"Was she the reason you quit being a lawyer?"

He energetically took the cherry-chocolate cake from the fridge and started cutting it with the precision of a chef into perfectly even thin slices. Once he had put the slices on our plates, he licked his fingers and looked straight into my eyes, "That's a story for another dinner."

*Is there going to be another dinner? Why would Leona kill herself? Does he fancy me? How long did she plan it for? Should I tell Leo first or just give him the letter? It wasn't a good idea for James to stay. Will they still pursue the insurance money?* I was wriggling in bed for over an hour not being able to sleep a wink. *There are some herbal pills in Leona's ensuite bathroom, just what I need!* I threw my duvet away and tiptoed towards the door – despite my best efforts to be quiet, the old wooden floor was cracking loudly under my feet. I slowly turned the doorknob and lightly pushed the door. I stood still in the hallway – the door to James' bedroom was half ajar, his bed empty, and a bedside lamp on. *Is he looking for something in the house?* I didn't move for a while, listening for any suspicious noises until I finally heard some sounds coming from the kitchen and ran downstairs.

---

"Sorry I woke you," James was standing in front of the kitchen island, a pile of paper towels in both hands, vigorously wiping red wine he had spilt all over the marble. "The bottle just slipped out of my hands. I've been punished for helping myself to your wine. I couldn't sleep so I thought a glass of red would help."

"The same here," I sighed. "I was actually going to get some herbal pills before I noticed the door to your bedroom was open," I sat on the highchair opposite James, the kitchen island between us, as well as my fake husband and the ghost of my mother-in-law stubbornly standing in our way...

"So pills or glass of wine? I wouldn't try both."

"Wine, but white for me."

James grabbed two new bottles from the wine fridge and put them in front of me. I glanced at him and laughed out loud, he looked hilarious in Christmas pyjamas that had a massive reindeer's head on the long-sleeve T-shirt. The last thing I wanted was for him to sleep naked under the same roof as me. "What if the fire alarm suddenly went off? Will you run outside naked?" I had asked as he reluctantly accepted the brand-new pyjamas set, which I had found in a storage cabinet on the first floor. It was where Leona stashed piles of Christmas presents and decorations she bought almost a year ahead in January sales. I knew Leo would hate the present – those pyjamas could seriously impact his sex life with Keanu. What was Leona thinking when she bought it?

"I'm glad I can make you laugh. Admit it, you only gave me these hideous pyjamas so you can laugh at me. I bet your mother-in-law bought it for Leo, and you don't want to see him in this."

"Are you warm, comfy and decent?" I asked and laughed when he pressed on the reindeer's nose and it played a Christmas jingle.

"You've also got yourself a pair of comfy pyjamas. Let me guess, last year's present from Leona?" Of course, it was. I wouldn't normally wear a tartan flannel shirt and baggy tartan trousers, but I wanted something covering most of my body – and for that it was unexpectedly perfect. I had even kept my bra on underneath.

"Looking at her current Christmas stash, I'm sure she must've bought it at least two years ago. God, it's so sad she won't see another Christmas," tears rolled down my cheeks, which James noticed before I managed to wipe them. *Too much wine, too many memories,* I thought and quickly blew my nose into a piece of paper towel, which was completely soaked in red wine. "I always have so much hope for Christmas, but somehow it always manages to disappoint. I don't remember a single good one in my entire adult life," now Lily was talking, and it was too late to take the words back. *Oops!* James was staring at me with his full attention and a childlike curiosity. I had to come up with something, pronto! Luckily, I remembered what Basil told me about Selina's relationship with Leona. "Whenever Leo and me planned to spend Christmas in England, my mother-in-law would start a crusade against the idea at least four months in advance. She would point out all her health issues and throw casually, 'You know, it could be my last Christmas.' She insisted on driving us to the airport and cried her eyes out like we were going to permanently live in the Arctic circle. She always called us in the middle of our Christmas dinner saying she had something incredibly important to say. If I didn't pick up the phone, she would call my mum's mobile and then her landline. Once she even called my mother's neighbours, don't even ask me how she got their number. Mrs Goldsmith ended up knocking on our door to find out if we were all alive and alright."

"She sounds like a mother-in-law from hell."

"Bless her," I said mercifully, "We shouldn't talk about her like that."

"Why?"

"Because it's probably where the poor soul is now," I said without much thought. My brain was actually projecting Lily's Christmases. All those festive dinners during which my family were persistently nagging me about studying medicine or finding a husband and getting pregnant. Last year I said I would go skiing with some friends. In reality, there was only one friend, Nathan, and he didn't even show up to my home-cooked dinner on the twenty sixth, he couldn't give me just Boxing Day. I understood his children were more important, but understanding didn't change how rubbish I felt. I ate alone and spent the whole evening working.

"I've got an idea," James was nodding enthusiastically. Let's have Christmas now. A Christmas pyjama party! There's enough in the cupboard to make it happen. I've even found some mincemeat so I can bake you mince pies."

"Mincemeat?" That was rather thoughtful of her, the tradition of Americans having mince pies for Christmas died a long time ago.

"What else is in there?" as soon as I asked the question James started walking out of the kitchen and climbing up the stairs. He was definitely feeling at home. Leo and the rest of the family wouldn't like it, but it was their fault, they were constantly away leaving me alone in this empty house. *Well, not empty anymore.*

"Extra-long luxurious tinsel, handmade baubles from Poland..." James was passing me brand new boxes with sale stickers, and I was putting them on the floor outside the storage closet. When he finished, the hallway on the first floor looked like somebody had just moved in. We put our hands on our hips, glanced at the boxes, exchanged looks and suddenly the craziness started.

In a flash James was wearing reindeer antlers and star-shaped glasses, while I got a Santa hat and glasses shaped into gingerbread men. There was so much of the luxurious gold tinsel that we managed to wrap it over all the stairs' railings, two large paintings, throw it carelessly around the entire ground floor and use the rest for our Hawaiian style Christmas necklaces. James then untangled some Christmas lights and hung them on the curtain rails in the kitchen-diner. I cut and peeled oranges for mulled wine, while he made mince pies. Afterwards we sat down around the large kitchen table drinking the wine and doing some Christmas colouring books, while waiting for the pastries to bake.

"The only thing we're missing here are the scented candles we left upstairs. Let me get some," he said and stopped colouring to go upstairs. I had a sip of wine and followed him. I was loving every minute spent with him, except, I constantly had at the back of my head the thought that I couldn't entirely trust him and it wouldn't be wise to let him search through the house on his own.

"I'm sure I saw some spruce candles up here," for the fifth time that evening James was standing inside the storage room and scrutinizing its contents. There was not much left except several boxes of Christmas cards and some old stuff haphazardly packed into large cardboard boxes. James' eyes stopped on one of them, "Have they already boxed her clothes to give away?" he raised his eyebrows in disbelief.

I moved inside the storage, "What are you talking about? Nobody has packed anything!"

"Are you sure?" he opened one of the six boxes tucked under the lowest shelf of the storage. I asked him to move so I could look inside. I couldn't believe my eyes and I had the feeling James didn't believe me either when I said nobody packed Leona's wardrobe. I checked other boxes too. All contained perfectly ironed skirts and blazers, mostly with heavy flowery patterns and vivid colours. All in Leona's size! James was staring at me like I owed him an explanation, but I had nothing to say – I had no idea what was going on. I rushed into Leona's bedroom, and he followed me.

I ran straight into her walk-in wardrobe. "There are still some clothes here. It's a very large closet just for clothes."

"Forgetting about it being half empty, don't you think it's weird there isn't a single Leona-style outfit?"

I nodded. The wardrobe was full of fashionable skirts, blouses and jumpers. There were some designer jeans and shirts I had never seen Leona wearing, as well as several strapless ball dresses and coats I wouldn't mind for myself. Some clothes still had labels, I turned a few to see that they were all two sizes smaller than Leona's. "Maybe she bought them to motivate herself into losing weight, but never managed to do it. She wouldn't be the first woman who's done it," I shrugged.

James wasn't convinced with my explanation. We both were tipsy but his detective side was stronger than mine. "If you say so. But... something just doesn't quite add up."

"What are you suggesting? I haven't seen anybody packing her clothes or bringing new ones to her wardrobe."

"You also said the family just lets themselves in when you're not here... What's Ariana's size?"

"I have no idea, but I can ask her next time I see her. She'll love that."

He rolled his eyes, "But realistically? Two sizes down from Leona?"

"She might be... I've still got some of my stuff in my old house, where she lives now so I can go and check." He looked at me with disbelief. "Emil and Ariana moved into my house, and Leo and I live here. It's what Leo and Emil decided. I didn't have much to say and have only just found out." His eyes widened. "I guess it would look weird or rather inappropriate for Emil to move into the family house with his new girlfriend just after his wife died in some mysterious circumstances."

"You said she might be alive."

"Jesus, James! Stop interrogating me."

"I'm sorry, I was just curious. I'm sorry if I overstepped, I didn't mean—"

"Fine, I don't understand much of what has recently been going on, but if I let myself think too much, I feel like I might go crazy." I'd had enough thinking about Leona and luckily the mince pies came to my rescue as the oven began beeping so loudly we couldn't ignore it.

James served the hot mince pies with warm custard. We switched on some Christmas songs and sat like that in silence for a while. *Another brilliant Christmas* I thought. *Maybe I'm doomed to never have a happy one.*

"Where did you spend last Christmas? In England?" he asked all of a sudden.

"Here, so this year we're going to my mum's," I said and at that very moment I realised that I would have to make up some excuses for Leo so he could spend Christmas with Keanu, while I would go to Oxford on my own. Life is too short to be forced into doing something we don't enjoy, even if it's not entirely my life. "It's two o'clock, are you sleepy?"

"Not particularly," he smiled, "but we can call it a night if you want."

"I was thinking whether you could retrieve the history on my laptop. I've lost some links that I need to use again."

"No problem. Bring your computer, and I'll heat up some more custard."

"I feel like I've already gained a few pounds tonight, but well it's Christmas."

When I got back, James was again going through my larder. It was like he couldn't resist checking and sniffing around the house. "Are you looking for something?"

"Icing sugar, we don't have much custard."

"I don't need any, the pies are great on their own," I said while putting the laptop on the table and plugging it in.

"It won't be long," he said as he quickly typed on the keyboard, his eyes wandering across the screen. I sat next to him to make sure he wasn't scanning the contents of my laptop to send to himself. If I had any life motto since I became Selina, it was *Trust no one*. "Done," he said contentedly, however instead of handing the laptop back to me, he couldn't help looking at my newly found history.

Initially stunned I got my voice back after a couple of seconds, "What? Don't look at me like that? If I had something to hide I certainly wouldn't be asking you for help. As I said, I've been doing extensive research for my book."

"Fair enough," he said and moved his lips dangerously close to mine. I might have been drunk, but not that drunk to sabotage my deal with Leo. *What was I thinking when I invited him in, asked for help, and then let him cook me a romantic dinner? Phew, we'd already spent Christmas together, and it didn't feel any less real than all the other Christmases I'd had throughout my adult life.*

## CHAPTER 25
## *New Lily*

Malaga-Costa del Sol Airport was actually a couple of miles closer to the beach promenade in Torremolinos than to the city centre of Malaga. I asked my Uber driver to drop me next to the first busy street bar that attracted my attention. I had paella with a glass of sangria, and did exactly what I'd said I would do to Miguel. I walked along the promenade looking for a suitable hotel to spend my first night on Costa del Sol. It was nine in the evening, and the place was rammed with tourists, happy and relaxed, slowly strolling along the beach. A light warm breeze was smoothing my long loose hair to the left, stroking my naked arms and calming me down. Waves crashing against the shore, loud music coming from crowded bars and restaurants, along with people talking and laughing were all melting into one pleasant sound. There was something addictive in the atmosphere of the place. The sky full of stars harmonized with the colourful lights along the promenade – the cheesiest neon signs seemed to perfectly complement the smartly lit palm trees. Or was it me looking at the world through a pair of rose-tinted glasses? The mix of Sangria, sea air and the feeling of freedom also had its stake in my perception of the surrounding world.

I took a room with a sea view in a large five-star hotel with three pools and five restaurants. I booked it for a week and paid upfront. It was glamorous and too big to receive random phone calls from receptionists. With the shops not closing at least till midnight, I even found enough time to get two bikinis, a few summer dresses, a pile of shorts, T-shirts, sandals and flip flops. I was so tired when I got back to my room that I threw all the shopping bags in the middle of the floor, lay on the bed in my red dress and immediately fell asleep.

At nine in the morning, I was woken up by a cleaning lady knocking on my door. I raised myself up to stretch before answering. I bent at the knees and moved my arms in front of me like in an extended dog pose during yoga classes. Just as I said, "no need to come in," a lady was already standing in my door and apologizing. She said something about a tough night and foreign girls drinking too much. One glance at me and she already knew I was a drunky who would never find time to learn another language. One glance at myself in the bathroom mirror, and I knew why anybody would make such an assumption. If messy tangled hair, make-up smeared around my lips and eyes, and both bra straps hanging loosely on the side of my arms weren't enough, I was wearing two completely different shoes. I vaguely remembered trying on one of my new sandals before collapsing on the bed – the memory was so vague I thought it was a dream.

I took a long shower and put on a new fitted pink dress with a blue bikini underneath. Wow, clothes looked so good on me! *Hopefully, the real Lily will do with my body what she's done with hers,* I thought sighing, when my phone rang.

"Hi Jane," I said cheerfully, happy with my look and grand escape to Costa del Sol.

"Thank god, you answered," she was shouting over the hustle and bustle of a busy street. "I left the office to try you again. Nate and Susana are giving me such a hard time. They don't believe you won't pick up, even from me!"

"Is Nate already back?" I asked, smirking to myself.

"No, but he called from the airport in Paris. He said that if you got fired, they would also fire me so I should try harder."

"Okay, nobody is firing anybody. Let me handle it," I said confidently, having no idea how I was going to handle anything! "And if I go, I'll employ you in my new company."

"Don't you have to pay them a whooping million pounds to—"

"Everything is negotiable," I kept bluffing. "Look, I need to be offline for a week. I still have loads of unused leave. Can you put two weeks off for me? After that I can start taking on clients again. Tell them that I'm in hospital for minor surgery. Nothing to worry about but I'm not well enough to work from a hospital bed."

"Okay I can do it. A week, including today."

"No, no... Two weeks."

"Susana gave me an order that if you try to take more than a week you have to speak to her."

"Fine," I snapped. "A week, but don't give me any client appointment inside two weeks."

"What about Naomi?"

"Especially Naomi. No Naomi for two weeks."

"Done."

---

I relaxed completely for six days, only opening my work phone on the seventh day of my holiday. It's a known truth that people are more innovative when they rest. Who knows, maybe the world would be a better place if its creators just relaxed for six days and then pulled up their sleeves and did the whole job in one day?

I switched on my phone, and ignored all the missed calls and messages, grabbed a business card and got straight down to business before somebody could change my mind. And that somebody was most likely to be me!

"Hi Miguel, it's Lily Rice."

"I'm sorry but I don't know any Lily," he said with a sleepy voice. It was Sunday morning, I should have waited at least a couple of hours, if not till Monday, but I really didn't have much time after my week's break.

"We met at the airport in Paris a week ago. I don't think I told you my name."

"Of course," he said enthusiastically. "How are you doing? I've been thinking about you."

"I've had a great holiday in Torremolinos, which sadly is coming to the end."

"Oh, I wish you called earlier," I could hear disappointment in his voice.

"But now I'm ready to buy a house here."

"Wow," he said and went silent.

"I'd been thinking about it long before I met you."

"Oh," he laughed. "I convinced myself I'm super persuasive. Some people have said I should switch from buying to selling."

"I can definitely send you a letter of recommendation… I'm calling because you mentioned that your friend is—"

"An estate agent," he finished for me enthusiastically. "He doesn't normally work on Sunday but if he doesn't have any other plans, we could definitely arrange something."

"That would be amazing. If I find something that I like, I can buy it with cash next week," I said to add a little extra motivation for his friend to change his plans for today.

## CHAPTER 26
# *New Selina*

I woke up at midday with an awful headache and only two things on my mind – water and painkillers. Luckily, Leona's bathroom cabinet was well equipped with every medicine you could think of which didn't require a prescription. *I just need to get there, and I'll be fine. Just a few meters, you can do it,* I was thinking while slowly lifting my body to the standing position. I finally pulled myself together and walked onto the landing, I stood up on my toes, stretched my hands towards the ceiling and rubbed my eyes. Then I rubbed them again and again. "What the hell?" Something was wrong. Something was missing. "Oh heaven!" I screamed and covered my mouth with both hands. "What the hell happened to the stairs' railing?"

"Neither hell nor heaven, we're still here on earth!" I heard a male voice speaking from downstairs and I flinched. *James, of course, it wasn't just a dream, he really did spend the night in my house.* "Don't worry, I'll bring my tools and fix it later."

I carefully walked down the stairs, sliding my right hand along the wall as there was no railing to hold. The railing was lying on the hallway floor, wrapped in gold tinsel, cracked in two places, white gloss paint chipped all over it. "I don't remember how it happened," I rubbed my forehead trying to bring back some memories from the previous night.

The last thing I could recall was James trying to kiss me, then me jumping to my feet and running into the hallway. He followed, apologised and made me dance with him to a Christmas song I could still hear in my head.

"We took our dancing too far. We shouldn't have slid down the rail, it's too old and fragile. It didn't take my weight."

"If the railing looks like that, how are you? I don't see you've got anything broken, but are you all right?"

"I'm bruised like an old apple, but it will teach me a lesson," he said vividly, gesticulating with a red plastic brush in his right hand. He was shaved, refreshed and smelled of coffee and mince pies. Unlike me he had already changed and even the yesterday clothes he had on looked brand new on him. "I heard you moving upstairs and made you some coffee."

"Give me a minute so I can clean my teeth and get some painkillers."

I sat on Leona's bed to wait for the pills to kick in, my back resting against its wooden headboard, legs stretched out on the gold and silver bedspread, my eyelids drooping against my will. And then I suddenly remembered. My whole body flinched, I felt blood rushing through my veins. I quickly opened my eyes and looked at the portrait of Leona hanging in front of me. She had a severe face expression with furrowed brow and pursed lips. Her hair was put into a high bun, hands were crossed under her chest, pushing her large boobs up. She was wearing a light blue cardigan, buttoned all the way up to her neck, which was squeezed by a white collar. *How even for a minute could she think she looked pretty like that? Or was she just trying to spread fear? Why would she put such a portrait in front of her own bed?* I took the painting off the wall and saw some marks on the wallpaper that had been left from two smaller pictures. I put the picture back up and rested against the wall. *Oh Selina, what have you done? Was she worth it? She was incredibly annoying, but seriously? A hitman? If you were really going to do something like that, wouldn't it have been better to burn the laptop instead of just removing its history? That's so amateurish! What other traces have you left?* I was thinking frantically. *The letter! Have you forged it!?* It used English spelling, which I thought was a bit weird but who would get obsessed about a few words spelt in British rather than American English, *while reading somebody's goodbye letter? Inhale and exhale, maybe it was only research for a book. The book, I need to read it. James needs to go, and I need to read the book. Oh god, how much does he remember from last night? What will he make of my computer history?*

"Selina, are you ok?" James was shouting from downstairs.

"I'll be there in a minute."

When I made it downstairs the kitchen was perfectly clean, and the Christmas decorations were squeezed in a big cardboard box next to the fridge. James was waiting for me with toast, coffee and a big glass of orange juice. Between us on the table lay a newspaper, brand new and untouched. I glanced at its front page, there was a large article about climate change and its effect on the Hamptons, and a small piece about Leona Woodhouse still being missing without a trace. *Yes, still without a trace. All traces are on my computer, and in this letter! I need to get rid of everything incriminating me! Or maybe Heaven wants me to turn myself in? No way, I'm not sitting in jail for something I haven't done – or I can't remember doing! Over my dead body! Or hopefully not so dead yet!*

"You're not feeling well," he was looking at me sympathetically. "We drank quite a lot last night." I nodded and gulped down the whole glass of juice. Then I switched to coffee while James went to the fridge to bring me more juice, "Before I forget, you've got a voicemail from Pamela Goodrich."

"Voicemail, where?" *Has he still got my mobile?*

"I gave you back your phone last night, don't you remember?" he laughed while clearly reading my mind. "She called the landline."

*People still use a landline?*

"What did she say?" I tried to sound casual.

"You need to listen to it again. I was doing something in the kitchen when the phone rang in the hallway. She said you were planning to see her today."

"I'm not in the mood. I'll have to call her and rearrange."

James put in front of me another full glass of juice and sat down on his chair looking curious, "Do you think she might know something about Leona that could help you find her?"

"Oh, no, no, no... If the whole Woodhouse family doesn't have a clue, I doubt Pam would know anything helpful," I quickly lied, but he didn't look convinced. "She's been ever so nice to us since Leona went missing. Every few days she sends me her delicious pies and cookies. She's been posting info about Leona all over social media."

"Does she need to do it? The whole country knows that the mother of the senator who's running for president went missing. God, Leona was famous even before that. Her husband ran for president a decade ago. Emil might not have won but he was close, and she was very involved in his campaign."

*Emil? Considering his worldview – along with his empathy to missing loved ones and those of different sexual orientation – thank god he didn't win!*

"It's not the point whether we need her help or not, she tries and that's what counts."

"Of course," he sounded apologetic.

"I just wanted to thank her for her support, so I invited her for coffee and cake," I felt like I needed to make it clear I was meeting Pam strictly socially.

"The cake we had last night?" he laughed. "Well, at least I'm leaving you with some mince pies. I'm sure she won't know it's Christmas food in England."

"I'm not seeing her today," I was trying not to sound irritated, but I wasn't particularly successful. "I should call her—" before I finished the doorbell rang.

"Speak of the devil," he slowly raised himself from the chair. "I'm not going to interrupt you two."

"But—"

"She said she would be here at one, so you didn't have time to call it off anyway."

"I wish you at least told me that so I'd be dressed!" I looked at my Christmas pyjamas and tried not to panic.

"Do you want me to make her some coffee and entertain her for ten minutes?"

"And tell her what?"

"That you're taking a shower upstairs," he said innocently.

"Have you lost your mind? You're leaving via the back door," I shouted and ran to open the kitchen door. After he'd disappeared I made sure the door was locked in case he forgot something, and I pulled the curtains across.

---

The bell rang again, and I had no other choice but to go and open the door. She knew I was in. The car was outside and all the lights were on.

"Good morning Pamela," I said while opening the front door to an immaculate looking lady in her early sixties. She was dressed up like for tea at the Ritz – under a light beige coat she was wearing a white polo neck, probably cashmere, a black pearl necklace and a burgundy pencil skirt. She had very subtle tights, gold shoes with a red sole and a small matching gold handbag. "Please, come in. I'm sorry for the way I look."

She waved her right hand in front of her handsome face. It was one of those faces that despite several noticeable wrinkles still managed to keep youth in its features, it had a freshness and energy of someone mid-twenties. I thought I wouldn't mind looking like her in my sixties. "Don't worry darling, you're grieving."

*Oh my! You've also assumed Leona is dead... not that you're wrong, but you haven't even seen the goodbye letter and my search history! Hold on, Selina might have forged the letter, but what about the packed clothes?*

"Leona might be alive," I was fiddling with my hair and suddenly noticed that some of them were sticky and glued together. *Yuck!* They smelled of mulled wine. "Would you mind if I pop upstairs to change?" I asked trying to sound guilty and embarrassed, while actually I was angry with myself for inviting James and forgetting about Pamela.

Pam threw her bag on a console table in the hallway. I held my breath for a second as her gold clutch landed right next to a large silver vase. Thankfully, she seemed not to notice that the flowers, which she had sent to *the Woodhouse family* only a few days ago, were rapidly becoming dry sticks. I wished I put them in water. Even mulled wine would have been better than the air and dust filling the vase. She slowly took her coat off and hung it on a hook in the hallway, "Don't worry my dear, do whatever you need to do, and I'll make myself some coffee. I know where everything is, I've spent plenty of time in this house," she sighed, looking more nostalgic than sad.

I took a quick shower and went back downstairs dressed in oversized dungarees and a tight red T-shirt with long sleeves. I couldn't find anything else that wasn't currently in a dirty laundry bin or an ironing basket. "I know, I look like I'm going to paint the house."

"You look gorgeous darling," she said in a soft motherly voice and gave me a faint smile. She was sitting on the bench, in the same bay window where I had found Faith the day before. She was sipping a hot drink that was steaming her glasses, legs crossed, a newspaper on her lap. "But the house needs some DIY," she looked at me disapprovingly. "Drinking and partying heavily might temporarily mute the pain, but it won't solve any problems."

"I wasn't actually—"

She abruptly put her left hand up to stop me from talking and let the newspaper slide on the floor, "You don't have to explain yourself my child. I'm only saying."

"I've already found somebody who will fix the railing."

Pam's face suddenly lightened, "So you've already met the new local carpenter? He's such a delicious looking boy. Just don't think about sleeping with him," she wagged her finger at me, "although his babies, he would make such beautiful little babies," she sighed.

"Delicious?" I laughed. "A boy? How old is he?"

"Early thirties. He's got his own company. Apparently, he quit his job as a hedge fund manager and decided to do what he loves the most! Paul Jones, isn't he the one you found?"

I shook my head, "Never heard of him."

"So do you mean Ricardo? I wouldn't bother. He used to be good but now—"

"A friend of mine knows somebody in the city who's going to be here next week," I lied. Suddenly I knew why she got on so well with Leona. They were equally bossy, nosy and irritating.

"Okay, but I always say that we should try and support local businesses. I'll leave you Paul's number. I'm sure he'll be happy to help."

"Thank you," I said through gritted teeth.

"How have you been doing?" Before I had a chance to take a breath and reply Pam was already replying for me. "I know it's tough for you, but you'll get through it, I promise. Despite what everybody is saying, I always knew you two loved each other. She treated you like her own child, and you argued like most mothers and daughters do. The friction between you two is only because you're so much alike."

I furrowed my brow, "Are we?"

"Of course," she screeched. "You're both stubborn, when you believe in something you stick to your guns like mad and…" she paused, her eyes wandered to the ceiling, "you're both opinionated, introverted, extremely private and very caring when it comes to those who you love."

"I don't know about extremely private. As far as I know Leona told quite a few people about my false pregnancy," I snapped.

"Oh yeah," she waved her right hand dismissively. "But that was the whole point of that, wasn't it? She lied to everybody so you wouldn't mess with her anymore."

"I'm afraid I don't understand. False pregnancy is practically an illness – you have real symptoms like morning sickness—"

"Oh, please stop it. I'm sixty years old, and I'm not stupid. Leona was really hurt that you lied to her about your pregnancy, only so she would piss off with her baby-talking. She called all her best friends telling them she would be a grandmother again. Then the very next day she found out from Leo it was a lie. I agree that she shouldn't tell anybody before the end of your first trimester, but she was so excited, you can't blame her for being proud and happy," she was speaking quickly and emotionally, for a moment I had a feeling Leona's ghost was in Pam's body and talking through her. "When she found out the truth she was devastated, and she made up an excuse to her friends telling them you had a fake pregnancy. Yes, I know everything, but it doesn't mean that everybody knows it. I was one of her best friends, if not the best one. She liked Claudia and Patricia, but deep in her heart she knew she couldn't confide in them as much as in me."

*So the good news is I probably didn't kill Leona because: I was a frustrated writer with no career on the horizon, desperate to get pregnant, stuck in a marriage with a guy who was never there for me, and constantly poked and verbally abused by my mother-in-law. I didn't have any false pregnancies or mental issues. I lied to Leona, I knew how to fight back and how to make her angry. However, the bad news is I still might have killed her just because she was pissing me off, which certainly won't stand well in court!*

"Pam..." I started seriously but again she cut me off.

"Leona loved you and I know she would want me to look after you when she's gone. Your mother is far away in England, Leo has a very demanding job and while you're still living in the Hamptons, I want you to know that I'm here for you. If you ever need any advice or anything—"

"Thank you, that's very sweet of you."

"My daughter went through in-vitro herself, so if you want I can support you every step of the way..." I wasn't sure whether my "want" or "not want" would have any impact on what Pam would do anyway.

*Poor Selina! Poor ME right now! These women together were like a broken pop-up toy – you shoot, or rather shut up Leona, and then Pamela pops up!*

"Pam, I won't lie. I wanted to see you because..." I raised my voice so as not to let her interrupt me again, but she did anyway somehow.

"Darling, have you eaten anything? Sit down and I'll make you scrambled eggs."

I sat down obediently. I was a bit hungry and if it was the only way to finally ask her some questions, I would eat most things. "Pam, I think you agree Leona's death remains mysterious. It's been over two weeks and they still haven't found her body. It's a big lake, I know, but on the other hand there's a large search and rescue team going through the lake every day and they're looking for a senator's mother.... Of course, who she is doesn't make her any more important than any other people but still..."

"I know what you mean. It seems suspicious," Pam was whipping the eggs before throwing them on the pan. I had noticed Leona doing this once for Leo, who didn't like any running white in his scrambled eggs. "I think it's just how our brains work, we're still in a stage of denial. If there's any chance she's alive, we want to believe it's possible. It's natural."

"I'm more worried, and I might be absolutely wrong, but..."

"What is it my darling?" she turned to look at me while stirring the eggs in the pan.

I took a deep breath, "What if Leona wanted to disappear? Emil leaving her after so many years... It must've come as such a shock. I think she may even have forgiven him the affair, but a divorce? She was definitely not expecting that. Besides she's a very proud woman who cares what people say."

Pam didn't say anything for a while until she put a plate with eggs and toast in front of me and sat down, eyes fixed on her shaking hands that she put flat on the table. "I also thought about that. I even blamed myself for not noticing she was so depressed."

"So you must've noticed that there was something different about her just before she went missing."

"I did, but it wasn't quite what I'd expected. She didn't seem upset about Emil filing for divorce. She acted like nothing significant had happened. Actually, she didn't seem to care about most things, which wasn't like her."

"Self-denial or was she planning to get away?" I was more thinking out loud than asking Pam a question.

"Then, maybe a week before she went to Canada, she called me, sounding like she had already had a glass of wine. She didn't dwell on the time she wasted on Emil, because as she said, he gave her three wonderful children. But she asked a lot of *what ifs*. She started questioning her life choices, in particular the lifestyle she was leading after kids."

"Was it about being a professional dancer?"

"Yes," she said and looked at me surprised, "you see, you knew each other so well. She only told you that because she trusted you." I kept silent on the fact I had found it out from Patricia. "She even questioned the clothes she was wearing. I told her she was famous for her bright costumes, the style suited her – the pencil skirts and buttoned jackets were really her. It would be weird if she suddenly started wearing jeans and T-shirts," Pam laughed. "I can't imagine."

"People have a right to want something different, they've got a right to change. They're just clothes, they didn't identify any traits of her character," I felt sudden solidarity with Leona, but I was annoyed with myself that I upset Pam, who might suddenly shut down. "I'm sorry, I didn't mean to be rude. As you said, I'm grieving, which sometimes makes me angry."

"That's okay," she smiled faintly but I knew it wasn't okay. I had a strong feeling Pam wasn't the type who would quickly forget about me criticising her.

"So, she appeared to be fine with Emil leaving her, stopped caring about everyday issues, was nostalgic about her past and considering making some changes including her wardrobe," I was summing up all the facts more for myself than Pam.

"I couldn't sum it up better. You still haven't touched your meal."

"Of course," I quickly shovelled the eggs and toast into my mouth.

Pam got lost in her thoughts before saying quietly, "Who knows, maybe she reached a conclusion that it was too late for any changes and her life was already defined."

"Did she say anything like that?"

"She said – but at the time I didn't pick up on it – she said that she didn't want to deal with the consequences of her choices for the rest of her life."

"Did she say anything that would indicate she was saying goodbye to you? Did she give you any advice for the future? A note? A last email?"

"A goodbye letter? No. Although, I wouldn't be surprised to find out she had some letters prepared in case she died."

"Right. So you're saying there might be some letters."

Pam looked at me inquisitively, her eyes narrowed, lips pursed. "Did you find a letter? Was it addressed to you?"

I felt she could see right through me. I'd brought it on myself! "To Leo," I whispered. Pam gasped and covered her face with her palms. "But we can't be sure she wrote it before she went missing, right? She might've done it ages ago, right? The letter is very generic, it says she loved him and would look after him from heaven."

"Leona was very spiritual and religious, so it sounds like her! Can I see the letter?"

"I think Leo should read it first."

"He hasn't read it yet?" she asked practically outraged.

"I only found it yesterday and I haven't had a chance yet to tell him about it. The envelope wasn't sealed so... I didn't mean to be nosy, but I had to know. Leo thinks she's still alive."

"Let me see the letter, I'll be able to tell whether it's real or somebody left it as a joke."

"Why would anybody joke about this?"

"The Woodhouse family are like celebrities, and there are some nasty people out there. Somebody could've sent the letter as a joke. Does it have an address or just a name?"

"I need to check," I said and left my chair reluctantly.

As I was leaving the kitchen, from the corner of my eyes I saw Pam shaking. She stood up, grabbed a TV remote and switched on the TV. It was like she couldn't stand her own thoughts and had to mute them with a roaring TV.

I was about to take my first step on the stairs when I suddenly stood still listening to Leo leaving me a voice message on the phone in the hallway. I didn't even hear it ringing! It went straight to voicemail. "Selina, for fuck's sake pick up your mobile or landline, anything! What's going on with you? I told you! My mother was kidnapped! They're demanding half a million dollars! I'm worried about you! I don't want you to be next!"

## CHAPTER 27
## New Lily

"If they're prepared to knock fifty K off the price, I'll take it today." I said, making Miguel's and his friend Pablo's jaws drop. "Maybe ask for eighty K down first, so they can raise it to fifty," I smiled, realizing too late that I was preaching to an estate agent.

"Are you sure that—" Miguel started, but Pablo elbowed him gently, obviously he needed to be more loyal to his friend than a woman who he'd just met.

"I like it. It needs some work but mostly cosmetic. As an interior designer I love an opportunity to make it mine," I said as if I was reciting from a script for a real estate drama.

"I'll call them right now," said Pablo, and rushed outside through a bifold door to stand with his back to us on a terrace, nearly as large as the one Leona had in the Hamptons. He stood still, looking into the distance with his phone glued to his right ear. The villa was on a hill, twenty minutes' walk from the coast, and had a breath-taking sea view, unobstructed by any high buildings, which was hard to get in this part of the city. Now, with the sun going down, I couldn't take my eyes away from the orange and yellow sky, the sun reflecting in the dark sea – a vista only disturbed by palm trees and beach parasols moving in the gentle breeze. Was I buying Selina's dreams?

"Well, it's pricey but you're paying for the view I suppose. You know that you could get a villa like this in Torremolinos for almost half of the price, and closer to the shore?" Miguel said, staring at me with curiosity. We were standing on a shiny white tiled floor in a spacious living room with an open plan kitchen, the sun throwing across the floor shadows of palm trees from the garden.

"There's a good piece of land around. Maybe I could get planning permission to extend it."

"You do think like an interior designer all the time," he smiled. "But beyond the job, you're still one big mystery to me. After seeing twelve houses and spending not more than ten minutes in each of them, I thought you were just having fun. I wanted to call it off before seeing house number thirteen, but I didn't know how. Pablo had faith in you, and it turns out he was right. And now..." he eyed me up and down. I was wearing a long sleeveless emerald-green dress with a deep V-neck decolletage, fitted at the top and loosely wrapping my hips. I bought it only a few hours before, while waiting for Pablo and Miguel. If I was about to convince them to show me properties worth a million euros, I needed to look like a million euros.

"And now?"

"I'm sort of disappointed that you really want to buy a house. I thought that it might have been an excuse to see me," he smiled, blushing.

"Well, I'm a very busy person so I often like to kill two birds with one stone," I said, and eyed him up and down.

"I'm flattered, not many women are prepared to buy a million-euro house just to spend time with me."

"Not many men jump into a suit on a Sunday as soon as I call them."

"Oh this," he laughed and adjusted his burnt-orange tie. His dark navy suit and light blue shirt looked like they were tailored for him, or was it just the advantage of being a tall and well-proportioned man? "I dressed for a divorce party this afternoon. I hoped that you could join me after we saw a couple of properties, but it has probably finished by now. Cristina needs to catch her flight to Buenos Aires, where her new boyfriend lives, and Benjamin is going tomorrow to his fiancée in San Sebastian."

"Right," I nodded. "Have you been to many of those?"

"A few," he cast his eyes down. "I'm thirty-nine and it seems to be the golden age for divorce parties."

"Okay," I nodded, glancing at his fingers in search of a mark after a wedding ring.

He noticed it, and smiled bitterly, "I took mine off two years ago. I've been on the market for a while now, looking for a better offer. I keep readvertising."

"Well, that reminds me that I need to sign a prenup if I ever decide to get married."

"Just casually throwing it out there?"

"Thinking out loud," I laughed.

"I'll do the same when I buy my villa in Marbella."

"Absolutely, you don't want anybody to marry you just for a house on a beach."

He frowned his eyebrows, "Sometimes I feel that maybe there's something wrong with me and I've got unrealistic expectations. If I keep being too picky, I'll eventually have to play that house-on-the-beach card too."

I laughed, "Then you could always get your lawyer to create a more complex deal. Like, she gets a bigger stake in the house for every year of marriage, and nothing if she is unfaithful."

"What are you laughing at?" Pablo said with a stone-cold face as he walked back through the terrace door. "Well, I don't have good news."

"Get something in Marbella. Honestly, this place is overpriced," Miguel said enthusiastically.

"I don't have good news. I've got great news. They immediately accepted the eighty-thousand-less offer! My congratulations!" Pablo exclaimed, finally letting his emotions out. They didn't want to lose a cash buyer!"

*Maybe, I should've asked for a better discount!* I thought, feeling butterflies in my stomach. But, it was just money, and if nothing else Lily had plenty of cash.

"Fantastic, I'll call my lawyer tonight and send her all the paperwork. When can I move in?" I clasped my hands.

"If everything goes smoothly, two weeks is realistic."

*I'll need to find another hotel, or I could go travelling. The accident and switching lives with Lily was like winning a lottery!*

---

## 16 Hours Later

I heard a ring and felt sick to my stomach. I was taking quick, short breaths, while tapping the fingers of my left hand on a glass desk in my hotel room. By the time he finally answered, my brain – deprived of a decent amount of oxygen – started shutting down. *Pull yourself together, woman!*

"Lil, hon, are you there?" Nate asked gently, and when I took a deep breath in, thinking that it was one massive misunderstanding, he crashed my hopes immediately, "I was expecting your call. If nothing else, money always talks."

"Sweet," I snapped. "You've blocked my salary!"

"You overestimate my power. I tried to stop the board from doing it, but after the incident with Molly and considering that she's still missing, there was nothing I could do. I'm sorry Lily, you can't keep running away... and anyway, it's not like you. You always want to confront every single problem face on. I don't understand—"

"Hold on, didn't you pay the ransom for Molly?"

"We did, but we haven't heard anything since. We won't be able to claim the tax back if they don't release her."

"Tax? Is that what you're worried about most?"

"And my job! It was ME who suggested paying the money! It was ME because it looks bad on you that she is missing, just after you threw a chair at her and started threatening her with all those messages. They'll eventually find out about our affair, my wife is blackmailing me, so I'll probably become a suspect too! If I lose this job, I won't even be able to afford a divorce lawyer!"

"Okay, okay, I get it."

"Do you? Because if you did, you would be here right now."

*I can't because I'm buying a villa on the Costa del Sol!*

"I needed a break."

"Lily, please come back home. We can talk everything through and try to get out of this together. You know I'm going to support you, no matter what... I don't even know where you are right now. Please, let me help."

"I need to go, but I'll speak to you soon."

"Where do you need to go?"

"I promise, I'll be in touch soon. Thank you for supporting me," I said formally, and disconnected. *Did he really convince the company to pay the ransom for Molly in an act of desperation to save me? He'd said that mafia was involved, but now suddenly I'm the suspect?*

---

Ally answered after one ring, which took me by surprise, considering it was Monday morning and she was a highly successful lawyer. I almost hoped she would be too busy, and I could just carry on introducing more of my spontaneous ideas into Lily's life.

"They blocked my salary," I said tearfully, slowly realising that the way I approached this whole new life wasn't benefiting anybody in the universe.

"Lily, you need to come back home. I knew something happened and was just about to ring you. An Italian lawyer called me an hour ago saying the payment for your villa in Tuscany didn't go through."

*Villa in Tuscany? She almost bought a house abroad! I'm not miles away from what she wants!*

"Too many things happened," I gasped, turning on a swivel chair to look out of my open balcony window. The beach was slowly filling up with people carrying bags stuffed with towels and sun creams.

"But now as your friend, not your lawyer, I'm impressed you can rely on one wage to pay for a property in Tuscany!"

"They blocked my wage, AND they blocked my account. I've called the bank, and they said I typed the wrong password in too many times, which I don't even remember doing. But now, I'm in and it's all working fine, just with significantly less zeros than I was expecting to see."

"You don't even remember typing in a wrong password? Okay, now you're worrying me. Where are you?"

"In Spain... Look, I can see the payment for the villa went through just now," *Whooping million and a half pounds! Now I know why I'm broke!* I was thinking, while scanning my monthly expenses. They were way more than most people could earn in a year or two.

"I suppose it's a good thing. You would have to pay a high penalty if you tried to pull out of the offer last minute. You can always use your magic by doing a total internal make-over and sell it at a profit. I can give you a contact for a local estate agent who deals with luxurious properties. One benefit of not sharing the house with Nate."

"I'm not going to share anything with him."

"I mean, you would have over seven hundred thousand pounds in your pocket if you shared the purchase with him so—"

"That's not the point I was making. Why do you think I'm going to sell it? Can they really freeze my salary?"

"They can fire you if they want. First, the act of violence. Now, you don't cooperate when it comes to Molly's case. It doesn't look good."

"Do you know that Nate and Susana apparently paid the ransom, but Molly hasn't been released yet?"

"Yes, I follow the news," she snapped. "They could also use it against you. You hated her. You needed money and found a way."

"Seriously? That's crazy! She went missing before they stopped my salary."

"You wouldn't believe how crazy people get when they act in desperation... I would tell you to expect it if you spoke to me earlier. As I said, we need to be prepared for every bomb that they throw at us."

"I understand," I said resigned.

"When will I see you?"

"I better get started with packing. I'll be in touch. Thank you Ally," I disconnected before she said her goodbyes, because that was exactly the moment when an idea popped in my head. I've been pushing too long against the stream to give up now. Maybe there was a different shore waiting for me.

## CHAPTER 28
## New Selina

"Get on the floor on your hands and knees... spread your palms..." a man in Aladdin-like khaki trousers was instructing me along with six other women and James to bend and twist our bodies in various painful poses. He had a soft calming voice, which I could listen to for hours in any language. I was concentrating on him, trying hard for my yoga poses to resemble, at least vaguely, what he was doing. His name was Ron, "Just Ron, not Ronald," he informed me when I went to introduce myself at the beginning of the class. It was one of the poshest of posh gyms in the entire country where everybody knew each other. It wasn't enough to pay an extortionate sum of money to join the VIP training club – you had to have connections, solid recommendations and get approval from other members, often extremely wealthy, and sometimes also famous. Leo was adamant that it was the only secure gym I could use in the Hamptons and being the wife of the now most popular senator in the country made its door wide open for me. Even if some members didn't approve of Leo's political views, they felt sorry for our family losing Leona and they understood how much we valued both safety and privacy. The gym had gates at the entrance that scanned my eyes and thumbs, while bodyguards strolled through and around the building, either undercover or dressed all in black, their hands on their gun belts. I thought it was a bit over the top, but it was the only way Leo would let me join a gym, so I accepted the conditions.

I glanced at the floor to ceiling mirrors and immediately thought I looked ridiculous. My leggings were digging into my bum and my sports bra was squeezing my sides so hard that my fat rolls were visible through a tight T-shirt. Even the old Selina must have made some effort to keep her weight off because during the last three weeks I put on half a stone!

"Lift your knees away from the floor, but keep them slightly bent..." Ron was demonstrating every posture with so much care and precision like his whole life depended upon it. The soft timbre in his voice was literally massaging my ears. For a brief moment I closed my eyes and almost fell over. "Selina, focus all your energy on your body movement. Don't let your thoughts wonder outside of this room. That's the key to relaxing your mind." *Easier said than done. How many people have you killed?*

I was lifting my right leg up during the downward facing dog posture when I felt like something cracked in my back and sent a painful shot all the way down to my bum cheeks. I couldn't believe how stiff this body was. I prayed silently to get out of this unscathed, without straining every muscle and dislocating my bones. I'd only agreed to yoga because James was paid for bringing new clients, and I'd expected Selina's body to be more flexible.

Relieved I survived my first yoga in Selina's body, I couldn't wait to dance off my worries during Zumba. Our instructor was Mia, a beautiful petite woman in her early forties. James said she danced for twelve years on *Dancing with the Stars* before she quit at the peak of her fame to settle in the Hamptons and have babies (two set of twins, all girls!). She had a bouncy blond bob and wore short leggings, which looked more like boxers, along with a loose vivid green tank top, exposing her lightly tanned and perfectly smooth body.

Before the music even started, Mia was talking to us while jumping from one leg to another. She was bouncing on the stage as if she was standing on a trampoline. "Hope you're having a wonderful day. If not, now is the time to get all the energy back and choose to be happy! Let's get this party started!" she shouted into the mike wrapped around her head and clapped her hands three times. The main lights suddenly went off, the disco ball hanging in the middle of the ceiling twinkled with colourful lights, and speakers played some loud music. I tried hard to follow Mia's complicated dance routine, but to my surprise I just couldn't! James and more than twenty women of all ages were moving to the rhythm like true professionals, knowing exactly what to do at each precise moment. After the first five minutes James gave me a merciful look and whispered into my ear: "Don't worry, some of these women took private classes just to follow the routine. You'll get into it, just give yourself some time."

Every song had different and elaborate choreography and my head was spinning from trying to learn them all! I was so fixated on following Mia's steps that I barely felt any rhythm or listened to the songs, let alone noticed when somebody walked into the room. A woman suddenly patted me on my shoulder and I jumped as if her hand had burnt me. I tripped and almost fell on my face. "I'm really sorry," she shouted through the music, "but somebody is waiting for you."

I turned back irritated, sweat dropping from my forehead, legs trembling from exhaustion.

*Leo? You should be in D.C..* He waved his hand so I would join him and presumably leave the class. *No way!* I shook my head. *I'm not giving up yet.*

"Hey you! Handsome stranger, come and join us!" Mia shouted, not stopping dancing even for a second. I bet she didn't recognise Leo the presidential candidate. In a plain white T-shirt and black skinny jeans, he looked so different from the earnest Leo Woodhouse who spoke so often on national TV.

Leo was only a few steps away from me, but I put my hands around my lips shaping them into a tube and screamed, "Oh, don't be shy, come and join us!" I thought it would be enough to scare him off and he would just leave with a defeated face, but I was completely wrong. He ran into the middle of the room and danced like he was a professional, confident smug face, legs and arms as flexible as if they were made of plasticine, a perfect sense of rhythm. I must have looked comical standing there with my jaw dropped to the floor, arms dangling from my body and eyes blinking fast. Thankfully nobody was interested in me because they would think it was weird that I had no idea how impressively skillful a dancer my husband of so many years was. Mia and a few other women were ogling Leo like he was a stripper – a bloody Magic Leo! – but he was too lost in the dance routine to notice that. In the meantime I was trying to pull myself together and move at least slightly faster than a woman next to me – she was in her late sixties and had her left hand in plaster.

---

"Do you go to Zumba in D.C.?"

"Seriously Selina?" As soon as we got in his car, relaxed cool Leo turned into a grump because I dragged him into the class. "Over ten years of dance classes and three national championships, and you thought I wouldn't be able to cope with Zumba in the Hamptons? Most of the moves were familiar to anyone who's ever danced professionally."

"You've got talent like your mother," I was trying to stay calm and friendly.

"We've paid the ransom today," he said flatly, both hands on the steering wheel, eyes set on the road. The large SUV looked brand new, but I didn't ask when he bought it. I wasn't his real wife, we only had a deal.

I pushed myself harder into the seat hoping it would prevent my body from shaking, and my heart from tearing my chest apart and smashing itself against the front window. "Are your PIs confident that the people really have Leona?"

He nodded, "The things that they said…" he paused, "nobody could know except my mother."

"But YOU obviously knew."

"I mean our family. Nobody except our family." He blew out his cheeks and looked like he was thinking on what I just said.

"Can you tell me what they knew?" I asked after a longer pause.

"It's irrelevant now," he snapped. "The hair they sent us – it also belongs to my mother. The DNA test came back positive."

"I don't want you to lose hope—"

"So don't!"

"Why haven't they sent you any video? Have you considered that they might..." the words couldn't go through my throat.

"Killed her and then cut her hair to blackmail us? Of course, I did. The police suggested several similar options. My mother could've been killed in an accident and whoever did it, had initially no idea who she was. When they found out, they came up with the idea of making some extra money. Or they kidnapped her, wanted to scare her but instead accidently killed her. Or we pay them, and they kill her anyway, especially if they think she could identify them. I'm well aware my mother is a very difficult woman and she could piss them off without trying too hard. Even if they've kidnapped before, she's probably the most annoying hostage they've ever had so god knows how it could go."

"Leo! She isn't that bad." *No, of course she is!*

"I know," he said tearfully. "And we needed to try."

"How much have you paid them? The whole amount?"

"What they wanted, half of a million dollars plus twenty thousand for our guy who passed them the money in the middle of the night at a car park in New Jersey."

"Wouldn't it have been wiser to give them half the amount and ask for some more evidence that they've got your mother alive?"

"I asked and they said they could send us her finger and a video of them cutting it off. Dad agreed, but the rest of the family decided to pay the full amount."

"Emil," I gasped, "charming as usual."

"Besides, that's not all they want," he paused as he parked on Leona's driveway. I only managed to touch the car doorhandle before he stopped me. "The car is bulletproof and it isn't bugged. Let's stay here."

"It's been six days since your dramatic voicemail saying that your mother had been kidnapped and you worried about me," I was speaking through gritted teeth, trying not to explode. "I've been living in the house for almost a week all by myself, and now you're telling me you won't even go inside because it's not safe enough for you? Is your life worth more than mine, is that what you're saying?"

He rolled his eyes, which annoyed me even more, but I took a couple of deep breaths and let him talk, "You've got an alarm, the house is being watched by the police. The only thing we can't be a hundred percent sure of is whether somebody is listening to your conversations."

"Thanks for telling me. But what's with the bulletproof car? I presume the windows in the house aren't bulletproof?"

"I only mention it to explain why I've got this new car."

"Why should I care? Our marriage is a business deal." He tried to hold my hand, but I jumped back putting both hands up as if he had been aiming a gun at me.

"You're still very important to me. If I wasn't gay, I would marry you."

"Well, you are gay and you still married me!"

A faint smile appeared on his face. "I want you to be the mother of my children, I think that's quite something."

"Sure. You want me to be your *baby mama* because beautiful Keanu can't deliver this one time!" he looked at me defeated not knowing what to say. "Anyway, what's next? You paid the half a million, but you said the kidnappers want something more."

"Yeah, about that..." he leaned away, which brought me some relief, rested his head on the seat and rolled his fingers through his hair, "they want me to withdraw my candidacy."

"What?"

"I suspected a political angle from the very beginning, but nobody believed me. I'd received several threatening letters months before mum was kidnapped. They arrived from different areas of the country, but all had something in common – they were threatening the safety of our family if I decided to run for president."

"Isn't it normal? I mean, freaks are everywhere, and politics always seems to have the ability to whip certain individuals into frenzy."

"That's what I thought and this is the result."

"What are you going to do?"

"I've agreed to all their terms. I haven't shown my face on media this past week. There's already some gossip about me resigning, but nothing official. They could release my mother while there's still time to win the campaign."

"You're young, you could always try again in four years. I'm sure people would understand."

"So I would give some other freak an opportunity to blackmail me again? It's not *gonna* happen."

"What does Keanu think about it?"

Leo gazed at me surprised, "Why would it matter?"

"Because he's your boyfriend and if not for all the political nonsense he would be your husband, unless there's something I'm missing here."

"No, but why does his opinion matter to you?"

"I'm just curious."

"He would like me to resign," he waved his right hand dismissively. "He works for the opposition, he would love me to have nothing to do with politics unless I join his party."

"You're making your life so damn complicated."

"Said the woman who agreed to live in a fake marriage and—"

"Don't! Don't say anything before I change my mind."

"It would be the biggest mistake of your life my darling. I'm going to make you a first lady, I'm going to make you famous—"

"Even if it means the kidnappers can kill your mother? Maybe it's not too late to change everything. You could use it as an opportunity to get out of this mess, to come out, get married to Keanu, be happy. We would get a divorce, split the assets and start again."

"Don't be silly. You're not getting anything if you walk away now," he laughed maliciously.

"I'm going to hire a bodyguard today," I snapped.

"Fine," he said calmly.

"I don't want to see you near me. If you really need to get in touch, just send me a message," I left the car. I left him with his mouth wide open.

He didn't get out of the car to follow me, he texted me a minute later, when I was already inside:

> I'm sorry. Please forgive me. I'm under a lot of pressure right now. I'll speak to you soon. Take care of yourself xxx

I rushed to the kitchen, opened the fridge and took out a smoothie I had prepared in the morning. I poured myself a glass and drank it in two big gulps. I was pouring myself a second glass when I received another message. *Seriously? If you don't stop texting me, I swear I'm going to drag you out of that bulletproof car!*

I read the message, then reread it three times.

> The balance on your Swiss account has changed. Log in to see the recent transactions…

I'd already known I had a secret Swiss account. Basil told me Selina used it for all the money she had earned before she stopped working and devoted her time to writing. Apparently, she regularly took money from her and Leo's joint account (little by little!) shifting it onto the Swiss one. Obviously, she trusted her husband! *Was she planning to divorce him? If so, why didn't she go back to work?*

I logged on with the password that I had been given by Basil. *OMG! A money transfer for a quarter of a million dollars?* I laughed hysterically and logged out. *You're fucking kidding me! Who's got the other quarter?* I wanted to scream, but then I quickly thought about the house being potentially bugged. *Jeez, this smoothie is bland, it needs some rum!*

## CHAPTER 29
## New Lily

"Wow, *tan bonita!* You look beautiful! Every time I see you, I think you couldn't look any more beautiful and each time I'm wrong." Miguel was staring at me agape. I didn't know what to do with my hands, so I was smoothing invisible folds on my gold sequin gown. His reaction was similar to a man who saw me only a couple of hours earlier trying on the same dress in one of Marbella's exclusive boutiques. After giving me a long stare, he asked if I needed a date. It wasn't my body, but I felt weirdly myself. I felt more Myself than since I'd moved with Leo to the Hamptons.

The dress was extortionately expensive, but so was the party thrown by a Spanish billionaire of Russian origin on his superyacht in Puerto Banus. One glance at the floating castle convinced me I needed to get something extraordinary to fit in. I could have just made up some excuses to Miguel, but he insisted that it would be great fun and it didn't need to be a date. Besides, a part of me wanted to get a little piece of Lily's fairy tale, and networking with the super rich could benefit my current job situation.

A couple of bodyguards, who couldn't look any more intimidating, approved Miguel's invite, but that wasn't enough. We had to go through a security check like at the airport and put our phones into lockers. The latter made me uncomfortable, but I kept telling myself I was on a yacht in a civilized country, and I was too irrelevant to become a hostage. *You're nobody for these people, Molly is a totally different story* – I kept telling myself like a mantra, even more so after a woman tripped in her stilettoes and went overboard in front of two old men who pretended not to see her fall. If I hadn't started screaming to rescue her, she would have probably drowned. She hit her head on the way down and was totally unconscious when they brought her back to the deck.

"I think I've seen enough," I said to Miguel, and waved to a waiter to take my wine and bring me some water. Being sober increased my chances of leaving the party on my own legs, alive and kicking.

"Yeah, I admit it was weird, but let's not create any false preconceptions. They really might not have seen her. Nobody pushed her."

"I'm not so sure anymore, she tripped on the guy's leg," I said, pointing with my chin at one of the old men. He took off his tuxedo jacket to cover the poor woman, still in shock that she had a second chance. The man must have been at least in his mid-sixties, his large belly accentuated by a tight white shirt was falling over a shiny black belt. He didn't look relieved. I was watching his clenched jaw and narrowed eyes, while putting words in his mouth, *Damn the bitch in gold sequins, I'll have to do it all over again.*

"My boss wanted me to do some networking, and he's a very decent guy. The fact that these people are filthy rich doesn't make them evil. It's a common misconception that—"

"Fine," I interrupted him. I met hundreds of filthy rich people through Leo and could count on the fingers of one hand those who weren't prepared to throw their best friend overboard for an extra zero on their accounts. "Can we at least move away from the edge?"

Miguel grabbed my hand like I really was in danger, and dragged me to a small table next to a lit round stage in the middle of the top deck. We both jumped in our chairs when a female singer hit her highest notes, and a pianist accompanying her played like he wanted to push the yacht underwater with just his fingers.

"Do we need to move again?" Miguel asked, his right hand pressed to his chest.

"No, they're going to have a break now," I said, watching the singer in a long red dress going down the steps from the stage.

"But the boy chorus is even louder."

"What?" I asked, but in the corner of my eyes I saw six young men, dressed all in white, heading in our direction. "How do you know? How many of these parties have you been to?"

"Just one. Do you want to see fireworks?"

"Is it always based on the same script?"

"No idea, but the last time they sang during a fireworks display, and I can see from here another superyacht preparing something on the top deck. Apparently, Octavio always tries to compete with the owner of the other yacht, so he must have some fireworks."

"A whole new world I haven't experienced yet."

"Can we go to the bow? I promise to catch you if you trip," he smirked, amused with himself, and I nodded. *I'm not important enough. Not important enough.*

Octavio and the owner of the other superyacht, whose name was Antonio, launched their *rockets*. "I've never seen anything like this," I said in awe, "and I've celebrated New Year's Eve in Sydney and New York."

"The police will soon pitch up with a fine for disturbing the peace without a permit," Miguel laughed out loud. It was the first time he had laughed in such a genuine and unrestrained way. The choir sang a well-known ballad that prevented me from hearing anything else he was saying. The night sky went bright. *Two men fighting about their position in the universe. Well, if that's the worst that they do to show their power,* I thought looking at Miguel. He stopped smiling, scrutinizing my face, and held my gaze. I felt shivers going down my spine. He lowered his head and bent it slightly to the right. I closed my eyes, felt his breath on my shoulder and his hand on my naked arm. I bent my head to the left ready to take his kiss, but instead of the touch of his warm lips on mine, I was literally swept off my feet. My arms flailed to catch hold of something. As my stomach hit the yacht's railing, I grabbed it with both hands. When I opened my eyes I saw nothing but black sea beneath me, and gasped, not being able to say a word. I was teetering on the top rail, falling forward. I took a deep breath and let out a scream from my lungs, instantly feeling two large warm hands on my waist pulling me back. I couldn't stop squeezing the cold metal railings. The person must have realized I was terrified to let go, so instead he gently put my legs back on the deck, then grabbed my waist and turned me towards him.

"Liam?" I whispered. *Have I died again?*

## CHAPTER 30
## *New Selina*

"We've already talked about it Selina. I can't tell you whether you had anything to do with Leona's disappearance. That's against the rules," Basil started losing his patience.

We were sitting on the terrace, it was approaching midnight, and the only light we had was coming from the outside fireplace. It was a chilly summer night with clouds densely covering the sky, not letting a single star shine. I was wrapped up in a soft white cashmere cardigan that probably belonged to Leona, but who knew? It was at least two sizes smaller than she normally wore and still had a label. It might have been an unwanted gift – beautiful designer outfits weren't what Leona tended to appreciate. Maybe it wasn't cheesy enough or – as another thought popped in my head – she lied to everybody about her size and so was gifted too small clothes!

Basil was dressed for safari as he had just left one in South Africa. The only thing he revealed was that a New Yorker who had swapped his life with a *Doctor Without Borders* was loving his new life and, to everybody's despair, didn't want to go back to the old one! Basil was still annoyed with him when he materialised in the middle of my living room. He insisted he needed some air so we sat on the terrace, covering our bodies from the chilly breeze and straining our eyes while looking at each other through the dark night. Nobody could see Basil, but I didn't want to have any of the garden lights on, the fireplace had to be enough – no one could know I was sitting alone outside in the middle of the night talking to myself. I brought us blankets, so Basil's bare calves stopped shaking from cold. He was dressed in a beige short-sleeve shirt, poop-brown shorts and black leather shoes with white ankle socks – it was a very tacky variation of a safari outfit.

"So, what are you suggesting? That I just sit tight and wait until the full half a million appears on my account?"

"Why half a million?" he asked naively. "Oh, is it just a random number you chose?"

"Aren't you supposed to know such things?"

He shook his head, crossed his arms and leant back on the sofa. He looked like he was about to fall asleep in a minute. "I specialise in research of the past," he yawned. "I'm not aware of everything that is going on in the present, although I still know a lot."

I pulled my blanket up to my chin and took a sip of coffee that was already cold, "Leo expressed no desire to give up on his campaign. He's staying in the game!"

"From what I know, it could literally kill his mother."

"He's been negotiating with the kidnappers all last week. They permitted him to keep going with the campaign, but in return demanded a million dollars on top of the half a million that the family had already paid."

"A million dollars or give up on being president this year. Wow! He must be really convinced he's going to win."

"That, and also the fact his father has suddenly turned out to be minted. Apparently, Emil received a large inheritance from his mother, who died five years ago but never had a chance to tell his ex-wife about it," I scoffed. "The girls have no idea about the money. He's mostly been investing in Leo's run for the presidency. An extreme case of how somebody's ambitions can affect their children. I can't help but wonder whether Leo has ever had any real influence over his career."

Basil was stroking his chin while looking at the fireplace. Suddenly he pulled out a mini tablet from under his blanket and without a word of explanation began energetically tapping on its screen and frantically reading something. "When are they going to give the money to the kidnappers?"

"I don't know exactly, but it's going to happen soon."

He put the tablet back under his blanket, as if he needed to keep it warm. "Now I'm talking as your friend, not your assistant," he said and cleared his throat. "If you get half a million on your Swiss account, then you can be sure you had something to do with it."

"No kidding," I snapped more amused than irritated.

"Otherwise, you could probably assume the two hundred and fifty thousand is an odd coincidence. There are a number of possibilities that could explain it: inheritance, tax return or even winning a lottery."

"Tax return? I'm not making any freaking money! I'm a housewife with an unfulfilled dream of becoming a writer."

Basil smiled, "You've been here months, and you still barely know who you are and what you really do," he was speaking louder and louder not letting me interrupt him, "I'm well aware Leona went missing four weeks ago and it's been really emotional *Down Here*, but you still haven't made any effort to get to know the real Selina."

"I've checked her..." I glanced at Basil's disapproving face and immediately corrected myself, "I've checked MY internet history and it doesn't look good. Then there's the money that took me completely by surprise. Either I had something to do with Leona being gone or somebody is trying to make it look like that."

"Are you not the only person who knows about the money and the history?"

"Are you trying to say I'm getting paranoid? It's possible, the family is driving me mad. As far as I'm concerned, they're all mad including me!" I threw the blanket away and strolled a couple of times around the terrace to cool down. "James was here to recover my search history, but I think he was too drunk to notice anything suspicious."

"Focus more on getting to know yourself than solving the Leona mystery," he said peacefully like a psychologist who had just listened to his patient – and ignored everything that the patient had said. "That's the only advice I can give you right now."

"Shouldn't you be less mysterious and more specific? You wouldn't last a day in any *down-to-earth* job as an assistant."

He glanced at me with a smile, rolled his blanket and walked inside the house. I followed him to the kitchen, expecting he would suddenly say something more meaningful and helpful, but he seemed not to even notice me. He poured himself a glass of water from the tap and leant against the sink. "The best assistant I've ever had was a woman called Susi," he whispered, staring at the box stuffed chaotically with Christmas decorations that I had forgotten to hide.

"What did you do before becoming an assistant for *Up There*?"

"I know what you're doing. You're trying to trick me into telling you whether I've ever been human. Well, I think I want to change my job anyway... and there's a mess *Up There* so they won't even notice I told you..." just as I thought I would explode with excitement he was again dragging out his answer. "I'll tell you, but if they remove me from the job, you can only blame yourself for being nosy. Although, you might get somebody who's more competent, involved, attentive, yeah so... Okay... so... I was a human once. Two wives, not simultaneously of course, six children, three dogs, one cat. I was a captain of a cruise ship and travelled the far corners of the world until my ship was captured by Somali pirates and... everybody survived but me."

It was not the answer I expected, although I should have assumed he must have died one way or another if he was originally human. "I'm so sorry."

"I had a good sixty years on Earth, nothing to be sorry about. Many had it worse."

"Can you somehow get in touch with your family? I've always wondered—"

"I can't tell you anything else," he made a gesture of zipping his lips and throwing away a key. "Although the management will probably insist on you forgetting some things after you return to your old life anyway – and please make sure you do return. There is more than one life waiting for you, you just have to be able to see it."

"Easier said than done," I said when a phone rang in the hallway. "It's bizarre people use their landline here so much."

"Time for me," he said and suddenly disappeared leaving only a faint green fog.

I reluctantly picked up the phone and not moving even an inch from the console table said, "Hello." The phone was so old-fashioned I almost couldn't believe it was wireless and I didn't have to stand just next to it.

"Hi Selina!" I heard a relieved male voice on the other side. "I tried your mobile five times tonight. I was just about to drive to you when I suddenly thought I should try the landline."

"Are you all right?" I asked yawning.

"I wanted to ask you exactly the same question. You haven't been answering all evening."

"It's Friday night, I could be in a club." *Plus it's not like we're in a relationship, and even if we were, do I really need to report to you and update you on every minute of my life.*

"A club? Nah... it's not you," he said, so dismissively it annoyed me.

"The fact that I normally don't go clubbing doesn't mean I'll never go. What's wrong with you people? Leona has to wear her bright costumes for like *forever*, and I should spend quiet evenings at home or dine in posh restaurants."

"Fair enough. I'm just glad you're okay."

"Well, thank you for caring but is there something I don't know? Last week Leo drove me here in a bulletproof car and refused to go inside the house."

"I just worry about you. Your mother-in-law got kidnapped, your husband is running for president and—"

"And he worries about nothing but his campaign. You're right, I'm potentially in danger because if somebody kidnaps me, I'll need to make them kill me quickly. He's not going to resign from anything to save me. I'm not even sure whether he and Emil would decide I'm worth paying the ransom for. After all, running the campaign is an expensive business."

James laughed forcefully, he knew I wasn't joking. "Listen, I'm going to the UK next week, would you like to go with me? I don't like flying on my own."

"Are you afraid of flying?"

"I would enjoy some company... your company actually. I've never been anywhere in the UK outside of London and I think I might feel a bit lost as a foreigner."

I laughed out loud, too loud for something that wasn't even funny. I was flattered but also scared that his flirting was going too far. He had just mentioned my husband, and a minute later was suggesting we fly to Europe together! "They speak the same language, you'll be fine."

"It's not the same, it's British English which is much posher. Each time I hear it, it blows my American mind. I'm often so focused on how the words sound that I don't understand what people are actually saying," he said in comical exaggerated RP.

"With that pronunciation you could easily become a new prince of something. Now after Harry's resigned, there is a vacant position."

"I'm pretty sure that's not the way it works, besides I'm more into British emigrants than royalty," he replied quickly, probably too quickly and we both went silent for a couple of long seconds. "Okay, the truth is that there is an offer – buy two business class tickets for one. I thought I could save some money while flying business. What do you say?" he said and I heard him taking a sip of something.

"I think you mixed up some offers. The buy two for one must be for the wine you're currently drinking."

"When was the last time you were in England? You said you missed your mum's birthday, and you spent yours alone with a cake that Leo sent by courier. You were supposed to go to Paris. Now you've got an amazing opportunity to make up for the lost time, see your mum, and even take the train to Paris. I'll be glad to carry your bags, such offers don't appear every day."

"Now you're talking."

"Amazing! I'm going to book our seats. Next week? Where do you normally like to sit? I prefer close to the wings, it's less bumpy."

"I haven't made any decision yet," I said matter-of-factly. "Let me think about it, at least till tomorrow morning."

"Sure. You could take your computer and write while we're away."

"How long do you think you would be there for?"

"A couple of weeks," he said and added quickly, "unless you want to stay longer."

"Two weeks is long enough, if not too long. I'll speak to you tomorrow. I've got loads to do and think about. Good night, James."

I wasn't going to consider any trips outside of the US in the near future. I had to find out as much as possible about *the new me* and keep investigating Leona's case. The only thing I wondered after the phone call was what James' true intentions were. Why would he want to go with me to England? Why now? Were we friends? Was he trying to kidnap or seduce me? Did I send him any false signals? I was leaning against the console table in the hallway and thinking about James until eventually my legs started to hurt and I realised I had spent over half an hour in the position.

I walked into the kitchen intending to nibble something and make myself a cup of hot chocolate when I suddenly saw an unusual message in the middle of the large table. I read it petrified, swallowed hard, feeling hot and shaky until I got to the last line saying *Basil*.

"You bloody scared me!" I shouted looking up at the empty white ceiling. "I appreciate your creativity, but you scared me!"

The whole table was covered with small but perfectly formed white letters made of some white powder. At first it crossed my mind it was cocaine, but when I licked my right forefinger and smudged the word *Hello*, I discovered it was just flour. No human could write with flour!

*Hello again,*
*You're right, I could be a better assistant at times. Time is running out, so I'm providing you with a little clue. You've got a second email account, which you only use for anything-related to your books. If you search through your notebooks, you'll find the right login and password. The email is not linked to your smartphone for one simple reason. You don't want to jump with excitement each time your phone beeps with an email that could be about your book, but it's just a ten percent discount to a shoe store.*
*Basil*

I didn't have to destroy the message because as soon as I read it, it turned into white dust looking like I had been rolling dough on the table. I got a couple of biscuits from the larder, gave up on making hot chocolate and ran upstairs to a guest bedroom. The floor was covered with paper boxes. I had planned to unpack them for the last month, but I had never found enough motivation to do it. *What's the point?* I was thinking each time I opened the door to the room. *I've got everything I need at the moment, and if Leona comes back, I'll need to move back to my old house. But is it really still my house?* One of the things that surprised me the most in the Woodhouse family was how easily Emil assumed that Leona was gone forever. *He must've assumed that if he made Leo and me take her house, right? And he had already unpacked and made himself cosy with Ariana in my house!*

It took me the entire evening before I finally found the precious notebook full of various logins and passwords. The funny thing was, I could easily log into the Swiss account because old Selina had saved her password on the laptop, but I had to dig out the notebook to get into her email that was only for book-related messages.

I patiently went through over twenty rejection emails from agents, all saying that unfortunately they wouldn't represent me, but I shouldn't give up because their opinion is always subjective and somebody else might think differently about my book. *Think how differently? That my book could win the next Nobel Prize or that it's not complete rubbish?* It looked like all agents were using the same copy-paste paragraphs. I imagined a poor intern or assistant spending most of their working hours changing names in the template emails. If it's true that an easy but mundane job is more dangerous to our mental health than a stressful and challenging one – the agent's assistants must have been at the top of the list for a breakdown.

I read the last message from an agent and was about to log out when I suddenly decided to check the junk email. Bingo! Over ten emails from Virginia Russel, who as I remembered from my brief visit to somewhere near Heaven, was my English mentor and proof-reader. All the emails were marked highest priority and had pretty much the same subject asking me to urgently contact Virginia. I clicked on the most recent one, which was sent a couple of days ago.

If you don't get in touch with me by Sunday evening and explain to me what's going on, I'll have no other choice but to contact the police!!!

*Okay, breath easily! I've still got two days to reply... What have I done to this woman? Artists can be over-emotional so let's not jump to conclusions too quickly.* I took a few deep breaths and started reading all the emails from Virginia in chronological order. When I finished, I grabbed my phone and with shaky hands searched for James in my contacts. He didn't answer so I left him a message, "Hi, it's Selina. I've been thinking about taking you up on your offer. Let's go to England! The only problem I have is that I need to be back in two weeks and a bit, so could we fly tomorrow or Sunday morning?"

## CHAPTER 31
## *New Lily*

"I told you I'd find you," Liam said with a self-satisfied grin as if he had just given me the best surprise ever.

Miguel didn't share Liam's enthusiasm, "You almost threw her overboard,"

"I'm really very sorry about that. I tripped and I don't even know how," he said, still grinning.

I felt tension in the air. Both men looked like they wanted to push each other into the sea.

I cleared my throat to mark my presence, "Miguel this is Liam, who I met in Paris. He was going to be at the wedding I told you about. Liam, this is—"

"I know who he is," Liam said seriously. "If not for Miguel I wouldn't be here."

"Hmm? I'm confused."

"I went into a lot of effort to get him on Octavio's guest list, but Liam never even bothered to RSVP me."

"I'm sorry mate, but I've been beyond crazy busy this last week. I RSVP'd Octavio's PR. Thanks again for all your effort to get me here. I really appreciate it," Liam said cheerfully and tapped Miguel on his back. "Drinks all evening on me!"

"Is it not a free bar?" I asked.

"It is, conveniently for our mutual friend."

"So how are you guys? I didn't know that this was a date," Liam was holding Miguel's sight but got no response.

"I didn't know that you were a run-away groom" I said, and in the corner of my eye saw Miguel trying to suppress a smile. "What I also didn't know was that your wife-to-be was Naomi, and that's a piece of information that would have been really useful."

"Lily, can you excuse me for ten minutes?" Miguel was looking for his way out. "I see Octavio is here and it might be my only chance tonight to have a word with him."

"Of course," I said. We never said it was a date, but I felt no obligation to make it clear to Liam. He left me a note on a pillow. We didn't even sleep together, and somehow, he still treated me like a one-night stand that he wanted to forget.

"Should we find a place to sit? I can explain everything."

I didn't need his explanation, but with Miguel leaving and me not knowing anybody else, I had nothing better to do. "The table next to the stage is empty."

"It's going to be loud. The screaming diva will be back soon from her break." Once again, he managed to surprise me. "I've been here before. Once. Maybe twice... Can we?"

"So where do you suggest going?"

"The floor below there are some empty guest bedrooms."

"What? I'm not going to any more bedrooms with you. I don't need any more of your exes jumping out of a wardrobe with an axe."

"Was it that bad? I shouldn't probably ask. Naomi can be harsh sometimes."

"Did she tell you we met?" He nodded, and suddenly was pushed forward to stand right in front of me, our noses almost rubbing. A tall brunet was passionately kissing an old short man in a green tuxedo, their hands flying around – threatening to hit Liam. "Fine, let's find somewhere else to talk," I said.

I started slowly realizing that there was a lot I didn't know about Liam. I probably should've known him better before staying alone with him in an empty bedroom with soundproof walls on a Russian billionaire's superyacht. "Where did you get the card to the room from?"

"Miguel and I," he cleared his throat, "we're invited for the party and a cruise tomorrow. Octavio gave us a room each."

"Nice," I nodded. "And what a coincidence that you two are friends, eh?"

He gasped heavily, "I really don't want to talk about it, but I know that I need to be honest with you."

"You don't owe me anything Liam. I had a good time with you. Nothing happened. I'm happy to move on." At least I thought I was, before I saw him again, looking in his tuxedo like a billion-dollar superyacht!

He sat on one of two uncomfortable armchairs made of metal and plastic. I bet they were designed by a well-known artist, but I wasn't the real Lily and couldn't appreciate the art. I preferred to stand, which also seemed to be a better position for an argument.

"Miguel's ex-wife is one of Naomi's close friends. They were both supermodels. That's how we met," he turned his eyes down and took a sip of wine that he had brought from upstairs. I didn't drink anything – I didn't need my life to be any more out of control. "He called me as soon as he heard I was leaving her. Miguel saw a while ago, what I was able to see only recently."

"Meaning?"

"Me and Naomi, we were more of a transaction than a relationship," he looked up staring into the distance. "We met at the beginning of her career, and when I thought I was on the path to success. We were young, ambitious, hungry for love and adventure. We literally fed each other with our energy and zest for life. We were constantly up for more, although sometimes we didn't even know what the *more* was going to be."

"And then she succeeded, and you didn't..." I saw pain painted all over his face. I might've been too bold. "Well, at least that was the way you saw it."

"That wasn't the reason. She achieved exactly what she wanted and literally a moment later quit at her peak, deciding she wanted something completely different. She had millions of plans for herself and I really didn't mind what she was doing. I didn't mind as long as she fed me with her positive energy and let me set my own goals."

"But she started planning your career."

"She said she was trying to help me, but with her money and network, she was the one calling the shots. I don't even know when I lost control over my own life and…" he paused, staring at a lamp shadow in the corner of the room.

"Look, it's really none of my business."

Liam suddenly set his eyes on me. Have I offended him? I had my own life to save. I didn't need to know his whole life story, and he felt incredibly needy.

"The worst was…" he continued, while I had the weird impression I was now a hostage forced to listen to his memories. "Absolutely the worst was that I let her control my life because it became convenient for me, and if something went wrong I had her to blame. Not that she let me blame her but…"

"I understand," I said rolling my eyes, while he wasn't looking. "Freedom means responsibility."

"No, you don't get it yet," he snapped. "Naomi didn't accidently pitch up in your room."

"No, I don't really understand why she would chase you, after you left her just before your wedding."

"She was there to see you," he said accentuating every word. "I went there to see YOU. When I spoke to you at the reception desk and swapped rooms with you, I knew exactly who you were."

"What? Have you been spying on me?" I shouted and glanced towards the doors. Were they locked?

"Naomi has been desperate to make a deal with you for the whole time you've been working on our… *her* house," I looked at him with curiosity. "We wanted to buy you out from Morgan and Tusk."

"What?"

"Naomi wouldn't even approach you without hiring a PI, and what she found out exceeded her expectations. The moment to put her plan into action was perfect. You've been bullied by Molly, arguing with

Susana and sleeping with Nathaniel. Plus they kept promising that they would make you a partner when it was never going to happen."

"How could any PI know whether I would make partner or not," I scoffed. "Nate and Susana probably didn't know it themselves either."

"The PI is brilliant. She doesn't always act legally, but she gets the information. She found a draft of a new contract for Stephen. If anybody is going to make partner, it's going to be him."

"Okay," I said, sliding the shoes off my feet and sitting in the middle of the room on a silver rug. "What do you exactly mean by buying me out?"

"Naomi would pay a million dollars to Morgan and Tusk so you could start a company with her. She would also pay you another million to leave."

"Holy cow!"

"Now she might sound like your saviour, but if you take the deal, you'll lose your identity. You'll become Naomi's puppet."

"Liam, you were about to be a part of that deal. Don't tell me you came all this way to save me?"

"I hoped to make a deal of my own with you, but I don't have a million pounds, which I found out while in Paris with you. Before I even got there, Naomi called all our mutual friends – *her* friends as I now find out – and I lost all my contracts bar the initial ten percent deposits. I know how it looks, but trust me – if you agree, you're going to make a deal with a devil."

*I'm not that thrilled with my current deal, the one I made near-Heaven, so maybe I should at least consider collaborating with 'the devil'.*

"I need to stay open to all possibilities. I just blew two million on a couple of holiday homes, and I'm not sure it was the wisest decision."

## CHAPTER 32
# New Selina

It was Saturday night, eleven twenty, and the boarding for our flight was just getting started. I felt a degree of relief knowing I would soon be onboard. Although, I wouldn't completely relax until the plane was airborne.

We were waiting inside of the air bridge when our queue suddenly stopped moving. I felt a flow of heat and my chest tightened. *What's the worst case scenario? I could become a suspect. So what? Innocent until proven guilty!* I started breathing deeply to calm myself down.

"Are you okay?" James asked, and I nodded. "It's been a long day," he put his hand on my arm and smiled gently. "I bet somebody is blocking an aisle while trying to squeeze their luggage into the overhead locker."

*The last thing I need right now is to have a panic attack, and the cabin crew insisting I go on another flight tomorrow. Breathe Selina, you're fine. Nobody knows anything except for Virginia Russel, who won't spill the beans for at least another twenty-four hours, and realistically by the time she speaks to the police it will be Monday morning, you'll be in Europe by then.*

"Would you like me to get you some water?" James asked when we were finally getting comfortable in our seats, our belts already fastened, listening to the engines spooling up and the plane's wheels rolling on the runway.

*Ten, nine... four, three, two, one... We're up in the air!* I re-directed the air vents so I could feel the pleasant cool breeze on my face, and I fell asleep. The tranquilizers that I had taken a few hours before the flight finally kicked in.

I woke up with my head resting on James' arm. He was just folding a magazine and passing a stewardess some rubbish.

"Good morning sunshine," he said cheerfully. "It's your last chance to go to the toilet, we've just started descending."

"I slept for eight hours?"

"Seven, we've hit some good winds. Anyway, I kept you something from breakfast," he pointed at his tray, "a plain croissant, pain au chocolate, natural yoghurt with muesli and orange juice."

"*Merci*," I said, and immediately immersed my teeth into the pain au chocolate, hoping that after I got something into my stomach, my head wouldn't feel so thick anymore.

"Ladies and gentlemen, I've got some good news," said the captain, "despite the fact we've arrived early, we don't have to wait for a slot to land and should be on the ground in fifteen minutes. The weather in Paris is very pleasant..."

---

"I'm glad we're in Paris," James said, as we sat on a roof terrace of one of the best Parisian hotels. It was midday, the weather was glorious with its cloudless sky and a delicate summer breeze. We were enjoying a view of the Champs-Elysées, while having a three course brunch prepared by a well-known chef.

"Me too," I replied shortly, regretting I couldn't tell him the whole story. I was just glad I left America, and I would be equally happy dining with him in Denmark, Berlin or Buenos Aires. "You're right, connecting flights are tiring and so often they lose your luggage."

"But I was surprised you didn't want to wait for a direct flight till Sunday. I didn't say anything because I was afraid you could change your mind if we waited any longer."

"That was exactly why I needed you to get the flights pronto. I've had so many doubts. I shouldn't really leave the family right now. But I also felt like being spontaneous and finally doing something for myself. I can't help anybody when I feel depressed."

"It was what I thought, and..." he started sheepishly. "I've got a surprise, and I hope you won't kill me..." When he said the word *kill* I got an awful feeling in the pit of my stomach and for a second I thought I would throw up. "Are you okay? You don't look happy, but there's no problem... I can rearrange everything again."

"That's not it. A piece of olive got stuck in my throat, but I'm fine. What's the surprise?" I smiled forcefully. I thought briefly about clapping my hands with excitement, but it would look too staged.

"I've booked our flights to London for Tuesday evening. It's only a day and a half later than we planned," he said looking all tense. "I've never been to Paris before and—"

"Okay," I whispered.

"Okay? Cool!" he smiled. "I'm going to pay for your room, the hotel is pricey, and it was all my idea."

"Thank you, but I don't think you should. By the way, you're doing great for someone unemployed. In fact, we're both doing fine for two unemployed people," I said, and we laughed.

"I've saved a lot from the times I was working, and I should be able to launch my start-up soon... Anyway, you said you knew Paris well, so you're welcome to become our tour guide."

"I can't wait." *Long live Google maps! And a special thank you to my dear parents who made me learn French; and Heaven for not taking the skill away the moment I became Selina!*

"Fantastic. I wouldn't mind seeing Versailles."

"Let me quickly change into some lighter clothes, and I'll see you in the hallway in an hour?"

"Do you need an hour to change?"

"I'm thinking about a power nap and straightening my hair," I lied. *I need to make a phone call! Now!*

"Hi Selina," I heard a cold voice on the other side. "I have max ten minutes. I tried to call you several times last night, but each time your phone went to voicemail."

"I was on a plane..." I hesitated, "I'm in Europe," I said lowering my voice as if Virginia Russel could hear me. *What the heck*, I thought, *If the police want to track me down, they'll easily find out I flew to France.*

"That would explain it, I tried like five times," Claudia said pretentiously, wasting precious seconds that would all add up and fill our ten minutes' slot.

Aware of the passing time, I still couldn't help defending myself, "I was available on the phone till midnight."

"And what time do you think I can talk to you without Richard being around and eavesdropping? He doesn't go to bed till one, and recently it's been even later as he's had some trouble sleeping."

"Claudia, please tell me everything you can about Leona's disappearance," I said matter-of-factly. I'd been waiting to speak to her for the last four weeks.

"I don't know what happened to her," she said defensively and for a moment I had a feeling Richard was around.

"But you obviously know something, and you think I should know that too."

"Leona is my best friend and I'm afraid something bad has already happened to her or is going to happen very soon."

*Oh, sweet Jesus, no kidding. Is that all you've got to say?*

"I need some details," I was rushing her. "As far as we know she's been kidnapped."

"I've got some reasons to doubt that she'll ever be released."

"And it's because?" My blood was boiling in my veins. *Tell me something that I don't already know!*

"Oh, just a gut feeling."

"You said you've got some reasons to—"

"All I know for sure is that Emil didn't leave Leona, he didn't ask her for a divorce. She did."

"The result is still the same. She did the right thing, he had an affair."

"No, he didn't."

"Are you saying she asked him for the divorce because SHE met somebody else?"

"No, she wasn't having an affair. She also didn't suddenly discover Tinder in her late fifties hoping to have some *swinging sixties* that would make up for all the dull years with her husband. She wanted to end her marriage with Emil because she was unhappy with him. That's it."

"Well, maybe that's what Leona told you. She's a very proud woman who cares deeply about other people's opinions."

"So does Emil. He confessed to Richard one night that Leona was leaving him, and he couldn't convince her otherwise. He made Richard promised he wouldn't tell anybody how humiliated and devasted he was. I know her well, and when she makes her mind up—"

"But why would she lie that Emil had an affair?"

"Neither of them talked about their divorce beyond the fact it was happening. Neither of them confirmed or denied anything. They let people talk and literally add to their own story anything they wanted. Between the two of us, I think Leona agreed to keep silent about why she was leaving Emil, so she would end up with the bigger house in the Hamptons and more money on her account. Otherwise, Emil would have nothing to lose and he can be vicious."

"Do you know that Emil moved into our house and made me and Leo take the bigger house that was supposed to be Leona's after the divorce?"

"I thought you were living there only temporarily to look after the house and be there if she suddenly reappeared."

"Initially I thought so too. Many decisions in this family seem to be made by Emil and Leo without the consent of anybody else," I said, then went silent, trying to put two and two together and guess why Claudia thought that Leona leaving her husband was so important to the whole story. "What about Ariana? Did Emil really meet her after Leona left him?"

"Richard said they met almost a year ago and they immediately liked each other. However, she was shamelessly flirting with him, and wanted more, while he just enjoyed chatting to her."

"Do you really believe it? Emil is a male chauvinist, he doesn't just enjoy chatting to women, and as far as I know Ariana is not an I-make-you-a-three-course-dinner type of a woman."

"Maybe. Maybe... but all I'm saying is that there was no affair. Ariana is well-known in the political circles as a respected and trustworthy photographer. It wasn't difficult for Emil to get her number and call her when Leona left him and he felt lonely. She's a beautiful woman, no wonder he reached out to her."

"Wonderful, so Emil is good as gold and—"

"The fact that he didn't cheat on Leona doesn't make him a good husband. If you think so, you don't put the bar high enough," she was irritated enough for me to think Leona wasn't the only one having troubles in her marriage. "Emil's first loves are politics and money, so you can imagine what sort of person he is. If they got divorced, Leona would get half of the money from his inheritance that he had already invested in some properties without her knowledge." I immediately thought about Leo's Washington house, which he also hadn't bothered to inform me about. It runs in the family.

"Are you saying Emil got rid of—"

"I'm not insinuating anything," she raised her voice. "I'm only making you aware of some facts. You're the only one in this family who wanted to talk to me so I'm trying to help you," she said sulkily. "Besides, you're the only one who can look at the whole situation both from the inside and the outside perspective. Sorry to say, but I've always thought they never really accepted you as a full member of the family."

"It's all right. You're not saying anything I haven't managed to notice myself. On numerous occasions Leona tried to show there was no place for me in the family."

"I think she actually accepted you the most, at least she cared about you. I know she can be difficult at times but—"

"What else can you tell me?" I looked at my watch, we had already talked for fifteen minutes, but she either didn't realise it or the ten minutes time limit was only a figure of speech.

"Ariana has had three husbands and apparently now she's insisting on tying the knot with Emil," she sounded outraged. "Richard told me, that Emil told him that, Ariana told him..." the call was breaking up and I couldn't hear anything else.

"Claudia, are you still there? Claudia?" I was panicking. She probably had nothing ground-breaking to tell me but, because I suddenly couldn't hear her, I felt like her words could change my life. *Oh, please Claudia, please tell me I had nothing to do with Leona's disappearance!* "Claudia, are you there? If Richard is there, say you'll see me tomorrow."

I almost gave up and pressed disconnect when I heard a rustle on the other side and then Claudia shouting, "I had to drive away because Richard was back and knocking on my window."

"Window?"

"I'm talking to you from my car," she said irritated as if her calling me from her car was obvious. "Now, I'm driving to a supermarket, I can't drive home empty-handed."

"I heard nothing that you said about Ariana."

"Ariana... oh yeah, she seems to be desperate to marry Emil. She told him that it shouldn't matter that they had only been dating for a month, because they'd really known each other for a year. She said that considering their age, there was nothing to wait for. They understand each other and..." she paused.

"And?"

"Nothing important," she sighed, "fine, I'll tell you. Apparently, their sex life is wonderful. She had some job done on her, you know... ehhh her lady parts," she said singing, "and she convinced him to have a penis enlargement."

"Wow!" I burst out laughing. "That's really a game changer. Now if they release Leona, she'll go and hide anyway."

"It's not funny at all. Richard hired a PI and he discovered Ariana went bankrupt a few months ago. She left all her three ex-husbands with nothing. She's got a very good divorce lawyer, James-something. She always hires the same one. Her second ex-husband told our PI that he felt like Ariana would happily have flayed him like a bear and use his skin as a rug if she only could."

"Do you think she had something to do with Leona—"

"I don't think anything. I'm only telling you that... Fuck, holy fuck! It's the last thing I need now!" as she was shouting I was having some doubts whether I could trust the woman, she felt a bit unstable, maybe drunk or over-using some prescribed meds...

"I'm not going to tell anybody what you told me."

"No! I've just driven into a Porsche and the owner is furious and... " she paused, "And also strikingly handsome. Fuck, I haven't renewed my car insurance and I've already had a glass of wine!"

"Oh, Claudia."

"I didn't intend to drive! It's all... Never mind, I'm rich and it certainly can be handled with money. Need to go. Remember, I didn't imply anything, just stating facts that you should know," she said and disconnected me.

## CHAPTER 33
## *New Lily*

"This one is to the front door. This is the back gate..." Pablo was waving in front of my nose a bunch of keys on a keyring with a logo of his company. "My congratulations," he gave me a wide smile. "If you have any more questions, don't hesitate to call. And if you ever want to get yourself another house on the Costa del Sol, or anywhere in Spain, I'm available twenty-four-seven including Christmas Day," he laughed and gave me a wink. No wonder he was so excited – obviously Miguel couldn't keep his mouth shut and had told him about me also cash buying the villa in Tuscany. He'd overheard my vivid conversation with Liam when he walked me off the yacht.

"Here you are! I've been looking everywhere for you," Miguel said flatly, conveniently just as I had stopped arguing with Liam and was about to walk away.

I wondered how much he had heard, but now reading from Pablo's behaviour probably everything. He was looking at me hopefully, thinking he had finally found his cash cow.

"Thank you so much for organizing it so quickly. I'm so glad I can move this week, finally settle and start working."

"I can recommend a great moving company."

"Oh no, I'm fine," I said glancing at my small hand luggage that I'd shovelled under a kitchen bar table. The bag looked tiny when put between four highchairs cushioned with green velvet and gold buttons.

"Don't tell me you're going to buy all new furniture? If so, speak to Miguel, I'm sure he can give you a good discount at El Corte Inglés."

"I will," I said only to brush him off.

"Miguel is a good guy, and he really likes you. Since his divorce, many people have tried to set him up, but he has never liked anybody enough to move to a second date, until..." he hesitated and eyed me up and down, "until he met you."

"Maybe you should stop trying to set him up. I'm sure he's perfectly capable of finding love himself and he looks like a guy who knows what he wants."

"I couldn't agree more... Well, I hope to see you soon then. Will you be at Miguel's housewarming party next week?"

"I think so," I said, thinking how much I didn't like when people tried to set me up. Although Leo was my own choice and it didn't go that well. After Pablo left me alone in the villa, I had a bittersweet feeling about the new home and it reminded me of my wedding day. As soon as we were through our first dance, Leo rushed to comfort his heartbroken best friend Keanu. He was a good guy, but seriously? It was our wedding! Couldn't he wait one day to break some upsetting news to Leo? I spent the entire evening dancing with my girlfriends under a gigantic gazebo in Leona's garden, wondering whether it was a one-off event or I was never going to be first in Leo's life. I had this gut feeling my happiness wasn't going to last – and now I felt the same about my new purchase.

I popped the cork off some champagne that Pablo had left me, poured myself a full glass, spraying my little black Gucci dress in the process. "Dry cleaners, another expense," I mumbled to myself, switched off all the lights and moved to the terrace. My heart skipped a beat, the sun going down over the Torremolinos beach – surely it was better than spending an evening with any man. I took a sip of the champagne, and *speaking about men*, my doorbell played a soothing melody heralding Liam's appearance.

"I'm coming," I shouted, while going back through the terrace door, nearly falling on my face on the polished floor. I took my stilettoes off and opened the front door, one hand holding a glass, another the shoes. "Gabriel?"

"You've been so deeply in your thoughts that I was afraid to scare you if I just appeared out of the blue."

"I don't remember calling you, and…" I glanced at my watch, "Liam is going to be here anytime soon."

"I gave us a bit more time by puncturing a tire on his car."

"Oh, how sweet of you! Please, come in then and enjoy a cup of tea – meanwhile Liam is sweating somewhere waiting for a road service."

"He's fine. He paid for the best rental car insurance."

"Good for him. Please sit down… yyy… I've forgotten I don't have any chairs or tea." Gabriel's eyes shined in the darkness. He clicked his fingers, and we were suddenly sitting on a large cream corner sofa. "Can I keep it?" I asked, putting the shoes and the glass on the floor.

He nodded, "My housewarming present. I noticed you've got bags of candles and cushions in the boot of your car, which by the way I locked for you. Girl, you've got yourself nothing practical, and the house only comes with ten different types of glasses!"

"You locked my boot? I thought you were not allowed to physically interfere?"

"I've recently gained a few extra permissions and we're in the process of modifying some rules for the Soul Management programme."

"Does it enable appearing without notice?"

Gabriel nodded, crossing his legs and spreading his arms on the back of the sofa. It was heavenly soft. I closed my eyes, but he wouldn't let me sleep. "How's your Bermuda account?" he asked sharply, accusation in his voice.

"I haven't spent everything. I've estimated that I've got enough to pay my bills for almost a year and I'm mortgage free."

"Really?"

"I mean here and in Tuscany. And, if you mean my apartment in London, I've just rented it for a year, furnished. Emma helped me," I smiled, suddenly feeling clever and organized. *Yes, you've got it girl!*

"And what's your plan? You're not going to sell this house tomorrow at profit just because you walked its floors. You're not that famous, and from what I can see, the TV company broke their contract with you."

"I'm temporarily suspended. Somebody spread gossip that I wanted to hurt Molly. I bet she's lying somewhere on an exotic island, plotting and scheming about how to take me down."

"She doesn't have to do anything. You're sinking your own boat by drilling bigger and bigger holes in the hull."

"You trusted me enough to give me this life without having to follow any script, why are you coming now preaching at me? I've got it all under control."

"I'm glad you follow your heart and your instincts. That you're fearless," he said, now his voice was smooth and gentle. "I'm glad you dream big and you're ready for revolution, but having said so, success also requires a certain amount of reason."

"Are you calling me stupid and reckless?"

"I only ask you to slow down and maybe for a while use the sideroads."

"It's just money. Are you even supposed to care about materialistic goods in Heaven? Don't you think Lily would be a better person with less resources? I've always thought money brings freedom, but she seems to be a prisoner to everything she's got. No wonder she's had a nervous breakdown. These people..."

"And what?" he scoffed. "Do you think that when you clear her account and run away from *these* people, you're going to make her happy?"

"Not quite."

"Oh Selina. I know you haven't asked for it, but I'm going to give you a clue. There are things that you need to drop immediately. Things you should run away from as fast as you can... but for the rest of the time you must learn how to manage what you've got and handle your demons – both the external and internal."

"Noted. You see..." I gasped. "If I just had the courage to..." I stopped to take a breath, trying to suppress tears already rolling down my cheek. I wished I just dropped some... I just ran away from—"

"I know," he interrupted me. "But that's Selina's life. Lily's life is the only one you've got now," he said decisively, looking straight into my eyes. "And one more thing. After I'm gone, check your Bermuda account again."

## CHAPTER 34
## New Selina

"I've got enough of the whole whodunnit theatrics. If it was me who had Leona killed or kidnapped, I deserve to know," I said and stomped my feet like a petulant schoolgirl.

Basil was lying on my hotel bed smirking, his legs crossed, and arms spread behind his head, "I think we can both agree that getting angry, stomping your feet and saying that *enough is enough* won't really solve any problem. You can't make any Selina-exit until you at least attempt some positive changes… That's the deal."

"What are you talking about?"

"You're so focused on your own drama that you've got no idea what's going on in the world right now. Never mind," he was murmuring to himself. "Only a minute ago, you were telling me that Emil or Ariana – if not both of them – had something to do with Leona's disappearance."

"I wanted to see your reaction. I hoped your face would give me a clue, but you're doing incredibly well – somehow whatever I say, your face remains as expressionless as if it's been filled with Botox from your neck to the top of your forehead. Life is so unfair," I said sulkily. "I've got a cute and keen American guy waiting for me downstairs to take him around one of the most romantic cities in the world, but at the same time I've also got a fake husband and potentially life in prison."

"Well, your marriage is very real in a legal sense," he said, as he left the bed and walked to my room fridge that was hidden in a desk, on which I was sitting. He opened it and helped himself to a bottle of a fizzy orange drink. "Don't worry within a few minutes the drink will be replaced with another one."

"Whatever, I'm happy to pay for the entire contents of this fridge if you could just be a little bit helpful. Sometimes I get the feeling that you're having fun instead of working."

"What makes you think you could hurt your mother-in-law? Except the obvious facts that you had a motive as she had been torturing you, and the two hundred and fifty thousand dollars," he smiled and walked back to the king-sized bed with flowery bedding, which Leona would have certainly loved.

"Virginia Russel is convinced that—"

"Oh, right. I just wanted to make sure you read her emails and it wasn't something else. I need to be careful, I've been in trouble in the past for guiding people too much."

"Well, I'm definitely not one of those people. First, I thought she was exaggerating, she's an artist, right?"

"I don't know anything about her doing anything creative. She lectures English at one of the best universities in the UK, she corrects papers, provides guidance. Her gramma is flawless, but to call her an artist?"

"Anyway, she wasn't exaggerating at all, she might even have been downplaying the whole situation in her first emails. I read my book. I read it from cover to cover on Saturday night and if somebody had to decide whether I was guilty or not based on that book…" I put my face in my hands.

"It's just a book, don't you dramatize a little?"

I jumped to my feet and walked towards a balcony glass door. I felt like my chest was tightening and the room was closing on me. I needed to see there was another world out there, except just Basil and me trapped inside four walls. "If you think I dramatize, you haven't read this book or you're playing me again," I said while looking through the window, trying to breathe steadily. "I've checked the computer. Old Selina put the last sentence in this book three months before Leona went missing. It tells a story of a very frustrated thirty-something woman, who is unhappy in her marriage and having trouble getting pregnant. If that's not enough to make her sad and angry with the whole world, she's also an unsuccessful writer, desperately trying to get her first novel published while she's constantly getting only copy-paste rejection emails. If that's not enough..." I started walking around the room, waving my finger in front of me, "her husband is only a guest in their large empty house, but her mother-in-law pops by every day to bully her. Finally, after getting more and more frustrated and lonely the woman, whose name is Brenda, gets drunk, switches on the computer and hires a hitman to get rid of her mother-in-law – as it's the only problem she's able to solve. She pays money the same night by PayPal and goes to bed. When she wakes up she doesn't remember what she's done. She wasn't only drunk but also took some pills... There are other suspects like an unfaithful husband, an odd acting father-in-law, and a peculiar neighbour..."

"Okay, you've convinced me," for the first time this evening Basil's face showed some expression – it was a mixture of terror and surprise. "I've read Virginia's emails, not the whole book."

"The only thing I don't understand is why Selina would incriminate herself. It doesn't make sense..." I said, looking at Basil frowning his eyebrows. I knew he had some idea, but he wouldn't tell me.

"Unless?" he looked impatient, waiting for me to utter his thoughts out loud.

"She's crazy," I said and by studying his face that was becoming gradually more expressive I guessed it wasn't what he had in mind. "Frustrated in her marriage, depressed by not being able to get pregnant, carrying around her unfulfilled dream of being a writer, furious with her mother-in-law. First, she wrote about it to vent, but it turned out not to be enough to release her emotions. Then one day Leona did or said something that was like pouring salt on a wound and Selina drank too much, googled a hitman..." Basil couldn't help himself, he was shaking his head. "No, you're right..."

"I haven't said anything," he said smirking. "I mean, it doesn't make sense. She wouldn't write about getting drunk and hiring a hitman and then doing it – that's not spontaneous... Maybe it was all carefully planned or..."

"Somebody like Emil or Ariana wanted to get rid of Leona and they're framing me now. It wouldn't be so hard to find my book, it was just lying on a shelf. The book might've actually inspired somebody. It gave them a perfect suspect! And if it's Emil, he's just paying the ransom to himself. Two hundred and fifty thousand is a small price to pay when he won't have to share his wealth with his ex-wife. Although, it would mean she's really dead... God, I never thought I would say it, but her being alive would make my life so much easier."

Basil chuckled, "Be careful what you wish for. Have you checked whether you've received more money on the Swiss account? They've recently paid the kidnappers again, haven't they?"

"Not more money," I gasped. "But why would they make up such an unrealistic demand like asking Leo to quit his campaign? His father is obsessed with it. Although, in this way it sounds more realistic and once again makes them less suspicious... Aaaa!" I shouted walking around the room. "I'm going crazy... What I need right now is a romantic date in Paris."

"Remember you're married."

I shrugged, "Difficult to forget – as it's also difficult to forget my husband is gay and I'm his cover-up. Selina deserves some happiness! Now if you'll excuse me, I need to get ready because James is waiting."

Basil disappeared leaving a pink fog. I wondered for a moment whether the colour of the fog could mean something as it changed each time, or if it was more of a gimmick, a special effect. I read the messages on my phone and realised I'd completely lost sense of time.

> 1:05

> Text me when you're leaving your room. See you soon

> 1:15

> I don't want to pressure you but it's been exactly an hour and twenty minutes. Will you be ready anytime soon? xx

> 1:30

> I think it's more than just a power nap. I'm going to have a swim in the spa downstairs and will have my phone in a locker. When you're ready, I guess you could ask somebody from the spa to go and grab me See you later xx

I glanced at an alarm clock, it was 1:45. I should let him enjoy the spa and we could grab some lunch later. I felt guilty for ignoring him, but equally I had a good excuse – arranging the last-minute flight across the Atlantic was pretty exhausting, both physically and mentally, and there was also jetlag on top of it. I was sure he would forgive me.

I switched on some TV and started getting ready. I liked to listen to something in the background while brushing my hair and putting on make-up. I flicked through a few channels until I found something more interesting than commercials or telemarketing. Basil was right, I had no idea about my surrounding world anymore – but there were some merits to it – if they suddenly announced that Earth was about to get hit by a gigantic meteorite and there was nothing to do to save us, I could spend my last hours blissfully immersed in my own dramas. I threw the remote on the bed and fiddled with my hair in front of a large mirror next to the main door, not being able to decide whether I would look better in straight or curly hair, whether I should put them up or down and whether to use some hairspray or leave them all natural. *Every-freaking-day equals so many dilemmas!*

"We've got breaking news from Washington D.C." I suddenly heard a man speaking in a deep and alarming voice that made me immediately turned my head to the large TV screen, hanging above the desk. "Leona Woodhouse, mother of the senator Leo Woodhouse, went missing almost five weeks ago. For the last two weeks she's been believed to be kidnapped. Initially, her kidnappers demanded half a million dollars and for senator Woodhouse to resign from running his presidential campaign. However, when they received the money, they changed their mind. They demanded a further million dollars ransom. The desperate family has been prepared to do anything to save their beloved mother, grandmother, mother-in-law and wife. They paid the million dollars three days ago, but Mrs Woodhouse wasn't released. Today the family received an anonymous letter saying..." the stumpy journalist was dressed in a dark suit, in one hand he was holding an umbrella, and in the other had a note that he was now reading, 'Thank you for the money. We assure you that it will be well-spent. Sorry about Leona, but we had no other choice.' The family is devastated and ask for privacy so they can grieve in peace."

## CHAPTER 35
## *New Lily*

"I'll take the cushions and blankets," Gabriel grabbed four completely full but light paper bags from El Corte Inglés and Zara Home. "I still don't understand why you would buy all this when you don't even have a sofa," he rolled his eyes.

"I was going to buy a sofa, but there was nothing that caught my eye," I said and held my breath, the bags with candles were so heavy I couldn't talk and walk. I put them on my new cobbled driveway. "Would you mind?"

"No," he said categorically. "I've got a bad back."

"Seriously?"

"No, but I don't like lifting," he shrugged. "You somehow managed to put it all in your car, yeah? You can't just shop for everything and then expect an angel to carry it in for you."

"I thought you're not an angel."

"Technically I am a..." he paused, crossing his feet in snazzy colorful trainers. He was still holding my bags high in the air, his elbows bent and resting on his slim hips squeezed into dark blue joggers. "You're the closest to an angel you've ever been."

"And translating that into human language?"

He sighed, "I'm the first assistant to one of the most senior Guardians *Up There*."

"So... technically he's in charge of my life."

"*She*. You're in charge of the life you've got, we're looking after you. Besides, she manages a hundred Souls of which I'm responsible only for a dozen, so I provide you with a more personalised care... But maybe this guy will help you carry the candles, frames and other tat."

"Which guy?" I asked before noticing a masculine figure emerging from the darkness behind Gabriel's back and walking towards us. "Whoever you are, you seem to have eyes in the back of your head."

"On that note, I see *you. I see you*, New Lily Rice," he pointed his finger at me, just before he disappeared into thin air, and it was then I could see clearly that the man coming my way wasn't the one I'd expected.

"Nate?"

"I'm sorry to disappoint you," he said smiling gently, hands in the pockets of his blue jeans. He had a smart navy blazer, but I noticed that the white T-shirt he was wearing underneath was stained."

"My plane went into unexpected turbulence, and a stewardess spilled some wine on me."

"Yours? Like a private jet?"

"When I found out where you were, I couldn't wait till tomorrow to catch a regular flight."

"Company expenses?" I smirked.

"Will you invite me inside?"

"Will you help me with these bags?"

"Sure," he said, grabbing the heavier bags then groaning.

"Are you ok?"

"Something just cracked in my back."

"Really? Weren't you supposed to be like the fittest man in Morgan and Tusk?"

"No, not really but I could still use a massage," he smirked, but the smile quickly faded from his face when I chastised him with a look.

"Call Donald. He still might have my slot available."

"The woman who's renting your apartment employs him on Mondays."

"Good knowledge," I said surprised, pushing open the front door with bags stuffed with cushions. "Do I even need to ask how you found out where I live, or should I just call Jane right away and tell her she's fired?"

Nathaniel glanced around my living room with an open plan kitchen and whistled. "I'm impressed. And the view is stunning."

"Put the bags anywhere," I said as he suddenly seemed to forget about the weight on his arms.

"But it's finished to such a high standard that I'm dying to see what you're going to do with it to make a profit."

"Excuse me?" I asked stunned and took the bags from his hands.

"Isn't your plan to flip houses?"

"Emma, how could you? I can't believe it! I can't even trust my own sister!"

At that moment I expected to see his smug face, but instead, he stood in front of me, put my head into his palms and whispered, "You can still trust me. I'm not going to let you down ever again." He kept looking straight into my eyes as if he was trying to examine the deepest corners of my soul. Like he knew I wasn't the Lily, who once loved him. Like he could see right through me. Like he could see the new Lily could also fall for him.

I touched a strand of his dense dark hair that was falling on his forehead and combed it up with my fingers. "I'm not going to *let* you let me down," I whispered, my lips touching his right ear, "Never ever again."

He slowly moved away, a mixture of pain and confusion painted all over his handsome face – wide jaw, dark shiny piercing eyes and long neck sprayed with strong oaky perfumes.

"You have no idea how much I missed you. I hope that one day you let me see again not only the strong woman you most certainly are, but also the most vulnerable and sensitive parts of you." I crossed my hands on my chest, not knowing what to say or do. He threw me off guard. "You look glamorous even when you're not expecting anybody," he gave me a bitter-sweet smile.

"So, there is still something you don't know," I kept whispering, like I had lost all my strength. There was something in his eyes and voice that was crying for me to surrender. I didn't want to fight anymore. I didn't want to run away. Not from him.

He smoothed his hair. "Can I sit down?" he looked at Gabriel's sofa.

"Sure. Don't you have any luggage?"

"Nope. I flew by private jet, and I hoped that you would be able to offer me at least a toothbrush."

"Nate, I don't have a single spoon or bar of soap," I laughed, suddenly realizing how unprepared I was for the move. When I moved into Leo's house, everything was already there. If we didn't get something as a wedding gift, my mother-in-law had looked after the smallest details, including napkins and three types of salad bowls. She wasn't all bad – at least at the beginning of our marriage.

"I saw a twenty-four-seven supermarket on my way here. We could go shopping," he said questioningly. "I rented a Land Rover," he got suddenly enthusiastic, "I'm pretty sure the *supermercado* will have some inflatable beds. They were actually advertising loads of camping stuff and—"

"How about you get yourself a room in a hotel and I'm going to look after myself?"

He glanced at the open bottle of champagne on the kitchen counter, "You can't drink and drive. Unless you're expecting somebody."

*Liam! They can't see each other! Nate must know Naomi's run-away husband! That's the last thing I need right now! It's going to be a disaster!* I was thinking, while frantically walking towards the granite counter. I grabbed my phone. It was a bit sticky from the champagne, which I'd accidently poured everywhere. A couple of missed calls and one voicemail were already waiting for me.

"Excuse me, I need to listen to this," I headed straight outside onto the terrace, avoiding Nate's eyes.

 "Hi! It's me, Liam. Based on our last conversation, you might actually be glad at what I'm going to tell you,"

I heard him sighing.

> "I'm not going to make it tonight. Believe it or not, I've had a flat tire – twice! I won't take your time by going into details, I'm sure you've got loads to unpack, but could I meet you tomorrow night? I'll bring dinner. Please let me know. I really want to see you again..."

I wasn't glad, but I was certainly relieved. At least I didn't have to try to step out of my own body (again!) to get rid of Nathaniel, who was now sitting on my new couch and staring at me angelically. He took his blazer off and made himself comfortable by putting his legs up and stretching them on the sofa, his back resting against the armrest and right hand squeezed around one of the cushions I'd bought. I didn't realize that I'd stood for so long on the terrace – staring at the sea and mulling over how I felt about Nate and Liam – that he had time to unpack all the shopping bags. Not only that, but he also ordered two large pizzas, two pieces of Tiramisu, freshly squeezed lemonade and a bottle of Italian wine.

"Sorry, I've completely lost all sense of time," I said sitting on the sofa, while Nate was handing me a piece of vegetarian pizza on a paper plate and the wine in a plastic cup. I felt like we were a happy couple, who had just bought the house together.

"You've got loads on your mind," he said, touching my hair and slowly moving them from over my left arm to the back of my shoulders.

"Don't," I flinched and moved an inch away from him. It was only to demonstrate we weren't at that stage yet – the stage of touching each other. *Yet? Are we ever going to kiss? Why am I even thinking about him? About undressing him. About putting my hand under his stained T-shirt. That's not my... but it could be. He shouldn't. I shouldn't.*

"Lily, please speak to me," he said beggingly, and for the first time I saw him as somebody who might also be hurt. "Is it really about the vasectomy? I should have never made that decision on my own. I thought it was what you wanted, but I should've talked to you first before... I spoke to Emma. It's reversible but not always successful. If you tell me that you really want to have a child and I can't, we could use a sperm donor. Anything to make you happy."

"What?" I almost choked on my pizza.

"Also, I might've even frozen some of my stuff, just in case," he laughed nervously.

"Seriously?" I asked, and he nodded. "Oh, that's a total game changer. We can finally be together," I clasped my hands. "Because it was all about your sperm being easily available to me, and nothing to do with you hiding something important from me or lying to my face. Even your wife knew!"

"I paid for it from our joint account," he said blushing. "It was an honest mistake."

I burst out laughing. "What else have you paid for from your joint account?"

"Look," he took a deep breath, put his legs back on the floor and straightened his posture. "I always got the impression you weren't interested in being a mother. You hated your family constantly pestering you about getting married and having a child. I thought it was what you wanted. That we were *enough*. We were together only because we wanted to be. No strings, just love. I always wanted you for *you*, not for making babies, sorting out my laundry or cooking dinner. I thought it made us special – we can easily live without each other, but we don't want to."

Just like that he said everything that I ever wanted to hear from Leo. But he wasn't Leo, and that was even better, which suddenly hit me like lightning. If I managed to get back to my previous life, I wasn't going to hear it from my husband, and that was okay. It was okay because I didn't care anymore. I wanted the man with a soft timber voice and big dark eyes, who was sitting right in front of me. *Maybe good girls go to Heaven, but bad girls go wherever they want*, I thought putting my hands under his stained T-shirt.

## CHAPTER 36
# New Selina

I switched off the TV and chucked the remote on the bed. The silence in the room was soon broken by the sound of my phone. I glanced at its screen, it was Leo. I stood next to the desk completely petrified, afraid to make a move, my heart pounding in my chest, my hands shaking like jelly. *Has Virginia Russel already informed the police? She must've heard the news! I bet she's been glued to the TV since she found out about Leona.* The phone stopped ringing, I felt better, but still scared to do anything more than just try to breath steadily. The screen flashed with a message:

> Watch the news. Mum is not coming back…
> A journalist might be able to find you in England. Don't speak to anybody and ask your mother to do the same.

I called him back, not even knowing what I wanted to say. What was the most appropriate thing to say to somebody who had just discovered his mother was murdered? He'd lost his mother, lost his hope and I needed to be there for him; whether our marriage was pretend or not I was still a member of the family.

"I'm sure they killed her because she kept threatening them. I know my mother, she wouldn't just sit there quietly waiting for the kidnappers to take the money and release her. She would threaten them with her status, that they would be tortured on a deserted island or sent to the worst prison in the world, never seeing daylight again. She was the mother of the future president of the United States, wasn't she?" It turned out I didn't have to say anything, he just wanted me to listen. "I'm not saying it's her fault, but I just wish she would shut up sometimes. My father always said that opening her mouth would kill her one day and look what happened…" with every passing minute he was angrier and angrier, and I wasn't really that surprised – anger is easier than sadness, it gives you the strength to keep going, unlike sadness that just makes you feel powerless.

"I'm so sorry Leo. I can't believe it's all happening. I still hope she—"

"Stop, she's not coming back and the sooner the whole family can accept that, the sooner we can deal with our grief and get our lives back," he said matter-of-factly.

"What are you going to do now?" I asked sheepishly.

"I'm not going to lose my chance to be president if that's what you're asking. It's clearly what the kidnappers would want and now I'm not going to give them it. The polls say I might win. I can't waste such an opportunity," he sounded angry again.

*It looks like somebody is desperate to move on without letting himself grieve*, I thought while sitting with one leg on the desk. "Of course, do whatever you need to do," I sighed. *Maybe it's what he needs right now, to keep working and being busy all the time.*

"Look Selina, send your mum my regards and please don't tell her anything beyond what she can find out on the news."

"Of course."

"Take her to Paris as you planned a few months ago. Celebrate your birthdays. The journalists are more likely to look for you in England than in France. Use the credit card to our joint account and have fun. As long as you keep a low profile, nobody will look for you in Paris."

"And you don't think it will look weird that your wife is not with you when your mother—"

"Nobody knows you're not here, and if you're not going to tell them, nobody will. When it comes to the funeral," his voice started breaking for the first time, but he swallowed hard and his voice rapidly returned emotionless, "we're not planning anything yet. We hope that the police can still find the body. It's especially important for Emily and Faith, I don't think that they'll get any closure until that happens."

"How are they?"

"They're doing fine, me and my father can't give them as much time as they need, but I've already found them some great therapists."

"That's good, but they also need family," I said it so silently I wasn't even sure he heard me.

"Did I say I wouldn't be there for them?" he exploded, and I took the phone away from my ear for a second. "I only said that I can't be with them twenty-four seven. They get it, they want me to win and I'm going to do it for them and for mum."

"Of course."

"I have to go."

"Leo, just one question."

"What?" he gasped impatiently.

"How do they know where to look for Leona? They didn't know before, but they—"

"On the video that we received from the kidnappers a detective spotted a pack of cigarettes on the floor. When he zoomed in, he saw the package had the warning 'fumar mata'."

"Mexico? How did they even cross the border? She was in Canada. Patricia met her there a couple of days before she went missing."

"I was surprised too, but the detective said that based on his experience we should trust no one, even Patricia. He's got some more evidence she was kept hostage in Mexico. I'm seeing him tomorrow, so I'll know more then."

"Leo..."

"I've got an important meeting in five minutes."

"Could you send me the video?"

When I finally made it to the spa at three o 'clock, James looked so relaxed that I suspected he was grateful I was late. His spa visit was a blessing for at least one other reason – he hadn't seen any news as his phone was in a locker. *If I could only make him stay off-line for a bit longer, I might be able to avoid talking about Leona.* I was thinking, when my stomach rumbled loudly.

"Time to eat? I've heard the hotel restaurant has a great chef," he stood in front of me with a wide smile, his fingers running energetically through his damp and messy hair. "I don't use a hairdryer, it's bad for my hair," he said seriously, and made a gesture of throwing his head back, as if he had forgotten how short his hair was.

"Really?"

"No," he laughed. "I didn't want to queue to use it. I can do it in my room."

I couldn't let that happen. We would have to go through the foyer where there was a TV switched on full volume broadcasting Leona's death. I wasn't ready to talk about it! "Let's go out. Your hair will sun dry before we get to a restaurant." He nodded approvingly. "I know a nice place fifteen, maybe twenty minutes away." I lied, searching frantically on my phone for a nearby well-reviewed restaurant.

Also, after the conversation with Leo, I needed to get some fresh air and... a pair of decent shoes if I was going to stay in the city much longer. Leo asked me to keep a low profile, but my scruffy trainers and well-used pumps were so strikingly unfashionable they would attract unnecessary attention.

I successfully managed to drag James through a hotel side door, avoiding the foyer, and convinced him to some speedy-shopping. I felt a pinch of guilt shopping when Leona had just been announced dead, but I convinced myself I couldn't do anything about it. She had hated me. Her son had Keanu to comfort him. And Leona was already *Up There* and I had zero influence on her further journey. If her final destination wasn't up to her taste – she only had herself to blame.

James raised his eyebrows in response to my desperate hunt for some heels, but he patiently accompanied me and offered his advice in several upscale boutiques on the Champs-Elysées. Every time a shop assistant glanced at my trainers with disgust, I rushed with an explanation that my luggage had been lost. At least I had a few sets of decent clothes that I had bought in D.C., while visiting Leo, and I had given them to the laundry as soon as we made it to the hotel. I put on a fitted pastel yellow dress with a thin white belt, a matching yellow hat and... navy trainers, which I finally replaced in a third shop with a pair of pastel grey stilettoes.

I examined the shoes in a floor to ceiling mirror, "They're so comfortable."

"They're so high!" James exclaimed. "Do you know how many women die every year because of high heels? Think about the European cobbled pavements."

The shop assistant looked at him mercifully, "Of all the male arguments against buying a pair of shoes in our boutique, yours is the most sophisticated. Clever, clever..." she was nodding. "You're trying to use fear to save yourself some money."

"It's not my money," James said defensively.

The shop assistant was a six-foot-tall woman in her late forties with a universally beautiful face, spoiled only by too big glasses and too *inflated* lips. Her flawless figure was well-presented in fitted white trousers and a white blazer with nothing but a bra underneath. She was wearing gold sandals with small heels that allowed her eyes to be the same height as James'. She was looking sternly at him, clearly having mastered her man-intimidation skills to perfection while working in this shop. "Of course, of course," she said with a smirk. "I haven't said you're a Scrooge or that you count every penny that your wife or girl-friend spends... You're just thrifty and it's a good quality, but..." she raised her finger, "the shoes don't cost as much as a Lamborghini and they don't depreciate. They come from a limited collection and will be worth even more next season."

"How much?" James looked taken aback.

"How much will they be worth next year? I would expect at least thirty percent more," the woman said without hesitation.

James laughed, "If that was true, you would have a long queue of serious investors."

"And that's exactly what our customers are doing, they're investing."

"Why don't you buy yourself a few pairs if you can make so much money so quickly?"

I felt like the air was getting thicker and thicker in the shop and I needed to react pronto. "It sounds like a good investment compared to my money just lying on my account. I'll buy three pairs. I'll take the grey one," I quickly glanced at my feet, "and the same shoes in dusty pink and black. I don't need the boxes, thank you."

"You're not serious," James whispered.

"Seven thousand five hundred Euros," the shop assistant said with a smug face.

---

"Why would you give the woman the satisfaction of thinking I was your penny-pincher husband, who lost the stupid shoe argument in front of her?" James was almost shouting, while walking fast on the Champs-Elysées with his hands tucked into his blue chinos. "Although you don't have to be a penny-pincher to think twice about getting a pair of shoes for two and a half thousand euros, do you? Anyway, you know I couldn't care less how much money you spent on the stupid shoes. It's not my money. Why would I care what you do with Leo's money?"

"Excuse me?" I shouted.

"What?" he stopped to look at me.

"His money? I'm his wife for god's sake! Yes, I haven't worked recently, but really?"

"That's not what I meant," he took his hands out of his pockets and put them up in a defensive gesture.

"That's exactly what you meant. Well, if I'm a kept woman, I choose to be a well-dressed kept woman. No matter whether I quietly polish the floors at home wearing well-worn granny pumps, or whether I run around Paris ostentatiously showing my feet in designer stilettoes, people will talk and will be annoyed that I somehow don't deserve what I've got. Bah! I will never fully own anything as everything is always given to me – the lazy arse, the lady of leisure, the gold-digger – given to me on a sparkling gold tray provided by a poor hard-working husband, who I exploit. All I do is get up in the morning, spray myself in expensive perfumes and wait for my donkey-tired hubby to get back from work."

James rubbed his head probably regretting he had caused a volcanic eruption. "I've never said anything like that, you're twisting my words," he whispered. "The woman was bluffing, the shoes are no investment. She would literally say anything to sell you a pair of shoes."

"And you think I'm so stupid I didn't know that?" I put my hands on my hips while from the corner of my eyes I noticed people passing and staring at us. I lowered my voice trying to avoid causing a scene.

"No," he said meekly. "I wanted to stop you from compulsive shopping…"

"Oh, you tried to save me," I said slowly, preparing to fire more words like with a machine gun, "Why is it – that when you're a woman everybody feels entitled to question your choices? As if you already didn't have enough doubts about what's best for you and your family. Everybody keeps bombarding you with supposedly better alternatives, as if you had no idea they even existed. All the advice you've never asked for! Everybody knows how you should live your life, as if theirs was exactly the same and they had already lived it in a hundred different ways."

"I totally agree," James was fiddling with the sleeves of his jumper, which he'd thrown over his shoulders immediately creating the image of a respected golf club member.

"Why should I explain to anybody that I took some time off to finally kick off my writing and finish a novel or two? Is it really so demoralizing that I don't have a baby crawling at my feet? And even if I had one, I would just be killing my career to become a dull and dumb housewife! Oh dear god, how do I dare to think I can be anything more than average? Because obviously I must be thinking I'm truly extra-fucking-ordinary if I quit one job for another that is bringing in no money… I shouldn't be relying on my husband's income because that's HIS money and it's repulsive to even think I could spend it for things other than groceries he needs or toilet bleach," James' serious face suddenly became more relaxed and his shoulders shook with laughter, while I realised, I was practically quoting Selina's book. "Do I exclusively own the floor I'm polishing? Nobody would say so, as nobody would say that only a woman has children because she gave birth and spends twenty-four-seven with them!"

"Wow, I've never heard such a brilliant defence for the purchase of three pairs of shoes. I think it would have easily stood up in court. The judge would probably ask why you only spent seven and a half thousand." James was now laughing while I was still shaking from my sudden explosion of anger.

One of the biggest advantages of Lily's lifestyle was that she was running a one-person household, which meant nobody ever questioned her expenditure, no matter how compulsive or ridiculous they were. I missed the old life, but for the first time I felt a genuine need to save Selina. A few tears rolled down my cheeks that was purely a stress relief action and had nothing to do with me being upset, but obviously James read it otherwise. He tried to touch my cheek, but I pushed his hand away, cleared my throat and took my phone out of my handbag, which now looked cheap above my new stilettoes, "On the way back I'm going to get a handbag, but now..." I zoomed out on google maps, "we're only five minutes away from that restaurant."

"Brilliant," he said enthusiastically. "I'm really sorry. I don't even know why I said it..."

"It's fine... I mean it wasn't fine, but the topic is closed."

"I also understand that you finally feel free without Leona patronizing you about your lifestyle and shopping choices," he said casually. Was he inferring in any way that I got rid of my mother-in-law to be able to spend the family fortune on shoes without her antagonizing me, or was I getting paranoid?

"It has nothing to do with Leona. You can't even imagine how much I would like her to return home safe and sound. It would solve so many of my problems."

"I always thought she was your biggest problem."

I stopped and looked at him in disbelief. He was right, but why would he say it? She was dead, and even if he still didn't know that, she was at least a missing person! "But it doesn't mean I wanted something bad to happen to her."

"I didn't say that," he said innocently. "But you were always upset with her. God, it's how we met, don't you remember?"

I was still staring at him blankly. "We met by the pool during the divorce party of the..." I couldn't remember the name of the couple.

"So you really don't remember. A few months before the divorce party, you ran out of your house crying, while Leona was standing on your doorstep and shouting. All I could hear was her calling you repeatedly an English bitch. I was just getting out of my car when I saw you running bare feet towards the main road. I asked Leona what happened, but she slammed the front door so hard, I thought it would split in two. I jumped back in the car to look for you. It was dark and you looked really vulnerable. Now you remember?" I shook my head. "I thought you had a glass of wine, now I would say a bottle. As I said, it was dark outside and I was wearing a suit – I look different in a suit," he smiled. "Anyway, I found you sitting on the doorstep of a closed café, looking into the distance and breathing heavily. You told me your mother-in-law was a bully and you had no idea how to get rid of her. I drove you home. Of course, first I rang the doorbell to check whether Leona was still there. She wasn't, so you asked me to go inside and check whether she wasn't hiding anywhere. First, I found it amusing and then rather..." he hesitated.

"Sad, ridiculous, scary, disturbing? Well, I probably drank too much, that's it."

"You quickly fell asleep on a couch, and I left. I always thought you were embarrassed, and you pretended not to remember, although there was nothing to be embarrassed about..."

"I don't remember, sorry," I said flippantly like I didn't have a care in the world and started walking again. "English bitch," I mumbled to myself, "there was literally nothing she liked about me, even me being English was somehow a problem for her."

"Well, that's one thing I might actually understand," he said without a trace of humour or irony.

"What do you mean?"

"Leona was sent to a boarding school in England..."

I was frantically thinking whether Leo could have ever mentioned that to me or if it was just another secret in the Woodhouse family. "I heard that she spent some time in the UK," I lied, "but a boarding school? I thought her parents weren't particularly wealthy and private school has always been expensive in my country."

"Her family was poor," he said boldly, "but her aunt married rich, they had no children and she suggested she would help her niece. She spent years in a girl's boarding school somewhere in Oxfordshire."

"Makes sense. Leona is a victim of her cold upbringing! Deprived of love with her parents living abroad! I guess she also had a complex about being a poor American girl. Well, at least I know why..."

James laughed, "Nothing could be further from the truth. Apparently, she maintained at school that her father was a wealthy film producer. Everybody wanted to be her friend. There was no Internet, so who could have known she was pulling their legs?"

"Pulling legs? Knowing Leona, it was a well calculated lie aimed to bring her fame and prestige. But you said you understood why she didn't like English people..."

"Because one English man broke her heart. *The first cut is the deepest*, isn't it?

"Yeah, she's a very empathetic and sensitive soul," I snarled.

"Maybe she used to be."

"Are you defending her? And wait a second, how do you know any of this?"

He hesitated, "Ok, it's too late. Now I have to tell you." He smiled, "My mother is friends with Claudia Newman, and Claudia is not good at keeping secrets.

*Claudia? She told me not to tell James anything about us talking about Leona! Difficult to tell who's worse at not keeping secrets!*

"What's Leona's love story?" I said pushing open the door to the restaurant, finding it completely full of people gathered around a stylish bar and sitting on windowsills. A nervous-looking waiter welcomed us with a forced smile and a *Bonjour* pronounced through his gritted teeth. "We booked for half past four today," I said rapidly in English feeling his tension.

He glanced at his watch, "There must be a mistake, we're fully booked at the moment," he said in a perfect English accent.

"We're only five minutes late," I said raising my voice.

"We're fully booked by a group of students from the Sorbonne."

"That's right, we're from the Sorbonne," James said confidently, while the waiter looked at him with disbelief. "We're Erasmus exchange students."

"You're not. They're all second year students."

"Who said that I have to be twenty to study in the second year?" James looked genuinely irritated.

The waiter gasped, "Look guys, maybe you're less than thirty and in the programme, that's not for me to judge, but..." he gasped again, "I can't believe that I'm even explaining this to you right now. I was an Erasmus student a few years ago. It's only for EU students, and you're clearly—"

"England is still in Europe," James snapped.

"I know, I'm English," he rolled his eyes. "You have an American accent. I've actually been learning a New York accent for my new audition."

"Good luck and sorry to bother you," I grabbed James' elbow and dragged him outside of the restaurant before they called security.

"What? It's your favourite restaurant. We've gone so far to get here and soon we're off to England."

I couldn't say I had found it on Trip Advisor, had never been there before and didn't really care about eating there. "As you were talking to him, I realised I must have booked a partner restaurant on the other side of the city. Besides I appreciate the effort but..." I took a deep breath. "I might need to stay here for a bit longer. Leona is gone forever."

---

"What else do you know about Leona's teenage heartbreak? I wonder how much it affected her." I asked, after a long moment of silence as James and I were just staring across the Seine River with the moon reflecting on its surface. We were sitting outside a wine bar, which we found while strolling along the river, after having a quick one-course dinner. The food was delicious, but we had to rush it because our table had been booked for six. Now we were drinking rose, listening to light music and contemplating life. We had more to digest than French steaks with classic gratin Dauphinois – the latest news about Leona also shook James. I suppose it's difficult to believe one of your neighbours could have been abducted and then killed. James seemed not to hear my question. I energetically took the bottle of wine from our ice bucket and poured myself the last half a glass. He quickly ordered a second bottle of the same rose and some local mineral water that tasted just like Paris tap water, offensively metallic.

Just when I thought he didn't want to reveal anymore from Leona's life, as if gossiping about dead people was inappropriate, he suddenly broke the silence, "I don't know that much." I kept looking at him in anticipation. "She fell in love with somebody from a local boarding school for boys. I'm not exactly sure how they met. I think he was a friend of her best friend's brother. They went out for most of their senior year. Leona was planning on staying in England and going to a university in London, but her mother and aunt had some serious disagreement and her mother convinced her she needed to go back to America."

"That's it? Well, I suppose there was no Internet."

"The boyfriend had a very rich family and they supported his plans to study at one of the Ivy League universities. The problem was that his parents found out Leona had lied to everybody about her wealth and her father being a well-known producer. They threatened to cut him off if he continued the relationship and they insisted on him studying in Europe. He chose his family and their money. Apparently, he tried to get in touch with her a few years later, but Leona was already married to Emil and pregnant with Leo."

"Wow, your mum told you all of that? You said she got it from Claudia Newman?"

"Well, she didn't tell me everything, I eavesdropped a conversation she had with Claudia," he smiled. "It was a while ago... God, I can't believe she's really dead."

"Neither do I. Such a tragic end. Such a sad love story. Interesting whether she kept wondering to the end *what if...* because if what you're saying about her not liking me for being English is true, she must have still missed him. I bet if they had a chance to be together they would have broken up anyway, it was just a first love, a high-school love... Unfulfilled love is always the most perfect and romantic..."

"I wouldn't trivialise it like that."

"Okay, what's her name?"

"Whose name?" he took a sip of the water and screwed his face. "Definitely comes from the tap."

"I know it does. When I tasted it, I realised the glass bottle must have been open before the waiter brought it. We won't tip them," I smiled. "What's her name?"

"Stop interrogating me," he laughed and poured us a full glass of wine each. "In high school I used to fall in love every couple of months with a different girl. I met my first serious girlfriend at uni."

"And how long did that last?"

"A year and a bit. It was ages ago. Why would it matter?"

"I don't know, I guess I just wanted to change the topic and you're rather mysterious when it comes to your private life."

"I'm not mysterious, there's just not that much to say. I've fallen out of love the same number of times I've fallen in love... Interesting whether the man forgot about Leona."

"Now, you're changing the topic to avoid talking about yourself," I laughed.

"No kidding. What would you say if we go for a walk?"

"I'm all in," I took a gulp of wine and waved at the waiter. "Could we get the bill please?"

The waiter took so long that we drunk another glass of wine waiting, but we barely spoke to each other. I wanted to get to know James, but I was too tired to grill him about his love life.

"The tap water cost twelve euros. No way I'm paying that much," James said to the waiter.

"I'll get my manager," the waiter said with an emotionless face expression. He had a short ponytail that was moving energetically as he was walking away with our bill.

The manager was a stumpy woman in her forties, she looked like she was a trained bodybuilder. "The water doesn't come from tap."

"So why does it taste like tap water?" James asked patiently. "Would you like to try it?" He offered her his half-drunk water, and I chortled.

"No, thank you."

"We can still consider the whole event a genuine mistake. Please get yourself a glass and try our water," this time he pointed at the half-empty bottle of water.

"You need to pay sir," she said with her hands on her hips.

"I'll pay when you bring me the mineral water I paid for," he said with a smug face.

She gasped heavily. "You're on holiday. I don't have time for this. You pay or I call the police."

"Please do, we'll wait here."

She murmured something in French. "No, you'll run away."

"Trust me. I'm not going to go anywhere until the police arrives and tries the water. Besides, I'm so kind that I tell you now to expect a food standards agency visit in the next few weeks. If I was you, I would order more bottles of the mineral water for your menu. You see, I'm nice. I'm telling you all this instead of bitching about your place on TripAdvisor and surprising you with an inspection."

Now she looked seriously pissed. "Fifty euro for the wine. The water is on the house."

James threw a fifty-euro banknote on the table and smiled with satisfaction, "Great idea, you should call it *house water*."

We walked for a few minutes before any of us said anything, "Well... that was a spectacle. I was afraid you would make me run away just to make the point of not paying for tap water. I think many people would let it go to avoid the confrontation."

"Would you?"

"I don't know... maybe..."

"I think it's nasty. If they don't make enough money, there are other ways than deceiving people."

"I agree... And coming back to Leona, did Claudia mention the name of the boy?"

"Are you still thinking about that?"

"Not until now. I just thought I really didn't know who she was."

*Would she argue about the water or obediently pay and later write a nasty review online? Or would she run away not even paying for the wine?*

"We don't know who many people are," he said while looking into the distance with nostalgia. "Often we're absolutely convinced we know somebody well, but it's just our brain playing tricks on us – we place people in all these "good" or "bad", "nice" or "nasty" drawers so we can get some peace. Once our world is systemised, we can peacefully fall asleep and stop reflecting on it. And everything the person does just confirms our label."

*What is your story James? Who are you? Why are you here?*

## CHAPTER 37
## New Lily

It was the closest thing to heaven that I could imagine. Fresh warm breeze, carrying the smell of the sea and helping me wake up. My eyes were slowly adjusting to the increasing dose of sunshine – the golden horizon turning gradually into a light blue sky, perfectly smooth and unobstructed by a single cloud. I bent my knees and pulled them closer to my chest, while sitting on the heated terrace tiles and wearing only Nate's T-shirt. Next to my feet, on paper plates with a logo of a local café, there lay – still warm and barely touched – almond croissants and churros with thick dense hot chocolate served in an ice-cream cup. After a good night's sleep in the most perfectly shaped arms and having a shower resembling a cascading waterfall, I felt a sudden surge of hunger. I grabbed the biggest of the churros, dipped it in the chocolate and took a bite like my whole existence depended on it. I closed my eyes and moaned. There was only one thing missing. "Coffee," I whispered to myself, climbing to my feet. Nate had left our coffees on the kitchen counter. Before he went to enjoy his shower, he drank his double espresso in literally one gulp. I'd been hungrier for the view and the sunrise.

By the time I took my first sip, my vanilla latte was already cold, but who needed hot drinks with the glorious Spanish weather. On my way back to the terrace, I couldn't help glancing at Nate's phone that he'd left on the sofa, squeezed between the armrest and a large cushion. I could still hear the shower running upstairs. It was so tempting, so irresistible. Like looking at churros fully dipped in chocolate when you had your last meal twelve hours ago. I sat down on the sofa, slowly sliding my hand across the whole length of one of its soft velvet cushions. I flinched when the tips of my fingers finally touched the phone – it was like it electrocuted me. Did it have a special electric shock function for unwelcome nosey little fingers or was it my conscience? I touched it again and nothing happened, except my heartbeat raised and my breath sped up.

*Nothing! What was I expecting? That he would have a pile of messages flashing on his screen from his other lovers? A wife laughing at me for being so naïve and thinking that he would ever leave her for me? Stephen saying thank you for making him a partner before me?*

The shower suddenly stopped running, and the phone beeped with a message from Susana:

> Have you found her? Don't let your feelings cloud your judgment. She did it! It was her! Do what's necessary to get it out of her and bring her here!

I was about to put the phone where I found it, when its screened flashed with another message from Susana:

> Record everything that she's saying. Make her drunk. Use your puppy eyes! Whatever it takes! Call me as soon as you know something.

My forefinger landed on her name almost involuntarily. I heard a ring. Another ring. She picked up.

"Nate!" she screamed both surprised and excited. "Have you got something?"

*I killed him, I have his body decomposing in my bath and guess what I am going to do with you next if you don't leave me alone Susana?* The response was rumbling in my head, but I couldn't pull myself together to make a sound.

"Are you there?" Susana was shouting. "Nate? Are you there?" She couldn't endure the tension, which brought me a little bit of satisfaction.

I pressed disconnect, but it was too late. Nathaniel was already walking down the stairs, his wet hair sticking out in every direction and naked chest that looked like it was from a Calvin Klein advert. "Have you been speaking to my wife again?" he asked amused.

"No. To Susana."

The cocky confidence left Nate's face. He stood petrified in the middle of the living room, "Susana?"

"Yeap," I said nonchalantly. "The house is crying for some more soft furnishings. I don't like the echo here, and Susana's name bouncing off its white walls is particularly distressing for me."

## CHAPTER 38
## *New Selina*

"His name is Edward Hastings. At the time, his family lived in Oxford. Later, he moved with his wife to Windsor – although I don't know which wife – might be the third one. Why do you need all this information?" Claudia suddenly got irritated. "For god's sake, Leona is dead! May she rest in peace," she gasped, and loudly blew her nose.

"I'm sorry, I didn't mean to upset you."

"Who told you about Edward?"

"Leona," I lied without hesitation. "She told me about him ages ago during one of those rare occasions when she drank too much wine and got sentimental."

"And you skilfully took advantage of the moment to interrogate her on her love life," she snorted.

"She asked me about Facebook and how it worked. She wanted to find him. She said it was out of curiosity."

"When did it happen?"

"Oh, I don't remember exactly," I paused and started humming, pretending I was looking for the answer.

"It must've been a year ago," she said. "We also tried to find him on Facebook, but with no luck... Although, there was this one man, who looked like a teenage-him. I wouldn't be surprised if he called his son Edward. He was very narcissistic and loved everything about himself."

"Did she stop looking?"

"No, she didn't," Claudia said reluctantly. "Why is it so important? You don't think he would have kidnapped her? Not that she would mind, I think it was her fantasy but—"

"I'm not sure whether I want to know her fantasies," I cut her off.

"So what? Do you think Edward's wife killed Leona after she finally found him? It crossed my mind, but I can't go to the police and tell them Leona looked for her high school sweetheart, she would have never forgiven me. She cares deeply about her reputation and would probably prefer her killer to get away with murder rather than—"

"Jesus, really? I don't think she was so fixated on what other people thought! Hold on a minute," I exclaimed excited. "You said you found him."

"Fine, we did. I warned her not to open old wounds, but you know Leona. She wouldn't listen so…"

"Wait a minute, I'm completely naked," I shouted.

"Okay, but you know I can't see you darling," Claudia giggled. "Oh god, I knew you would be traumatised hearing about her death. Deep in your heart you loved each other."

"No, no… Somebody is knocking on my door, give me a second and please don't disconnect."

James kept knocking on the door, so I quickly undressed to my underwear and wrapped myself in an oversized hotel robe, so he didn't catch me lying. I opened the door a crack and spoke to him while pressing the phone to my chest. "Sorry, I've got an important phone call. Can I call you later?"

"Is it Leo?" he whispered, and the smile faded from his face.

"No," I said decisively and slowly shut the door on him.

"Was it a man?" Claudia sounded very curious. "Well, I don't want to interrupt you and I'm not going to ask anything. A good lover is the best remedy for all worries, including getting older. I can tell you a secret – the man whose car I drove into… oh, he's absolutely worth every risk I'm taking to sleep with him."

"That's wonderful, but what about Edward?"

"You know what? When you want something you're just like Leona. She hired a PI and it turned out he's got a few social media accounts but all with different names. That's why we couldn't find him."

"What are the names?"

"No idea, Leona had them written down somewhere. They also should be in the report she received from the PI."

"Can you get hold of the report?"

"Are you crazy? The police will be searching her house! And by the way, where are you?"

"Back in America," I continued lying. "What did she discover about Edward?"

"He's had three wives, but judging by the speed he was going, he might be on wife number four by now," she scoffed. The first marriage was the longest and lasted over twenty years. He married a girl from the boarding school which Leona attended. In his late forties he divorced her for a twenty-years younger Instagram influencer. He left his first family everything, but their three-bedroom apartment in Paris, which he moved into with the floozie. They eloped to Las Vegas, but as soon as she put every piece of his home on Insta, she filed for divorce. Then Edward fell in love with a woman his own age, Felicity, who had a modeling agency, and they tied the knot a couple of years later. Long story short, he had an affair with a model at his wife's company. Felicity quickly found out, emptied his bank account and asked for divorce. When last we checked he had moved into a one bed studio."

"Leona must feel lucky it didn't work out with him!"

"Or he's never forgotten about Leona!"

"Maybe," I said unconvinced. "It looks like some people never grow up and get wiser," I murmured, but Claudia heard everything.

"Who are you talking about? Leona? Rest her soul."

"I meant Edward. Is he still in Paris on the hunt for wife number four?"

"Nope, he moved somewhere else in Europe."

"He's very mobile. What does he do for living? Is he a male escort?"

"Close."

"Really?" I squeaked.

"He's a commercial pilot. Last time we checked he was flying for a business jet company."

"Nice. Is he still handsome?"

"Why? Are you interested?" I didn't reply. Claudia was like a ticking bomb. I never knew what would make her explode with anger. "Yes, he looks good, and by good, I don't mean good for his age, but good like Kevin Costner in his late fifties."

"After you said that, I can't not ask you this question – where does he live?"

When I expected her to get more irritated, she laughed. "The town is called something like Marella."

"Marella?" I asked wondering. "Do you mean Marbella?"

"Exactly!"

"In Spain!"

"Yeah, Leona said it was a Little Mexico in Europe."

"What?" I burst out laughing. *Even after her death, the woman doesn't stop offending people.*

"They speak Spanish but yes I know, it's a totally different country," she said, and I imagined her rolling her ignorant eyes.

"Exactly, it's not Mexico," I said slowly. "It's Spain!"

"Okay, okay, I get your point."

"Thank you. You have no idea how much you've helped me."

## CHAPTER 39
## *New Lily*

Nate tightened a superhero beach towel around his waist and sat down on the sofa. It was one of the least ridiculous towels that we had found last night in the *supermercado*.

"Let me explain from the beginning," he started, while spreading his hands out like during a work meeting.

"I'll definitely let you." I sat down on the other side of the L-shape sofa, trying to distance myself from him.

"A few days ago our office was searched by the police. If you'd gotten in touch with me," he was trying to supress irritation in his voice, "you would have known by now."

"If you hadn't lied to me—"

"Okay, okay," he cut me off. "They took all our laptops and gave them back forty-eight hours later. We had nothing to work on and lost a couple of new clients. But that's not the most important part. They found something on Susana's computer," he sighed, and put his face into his palms. I stayed quiet, trying to be patient. If he was making up the story, I wasn't going to guide him with questions. But, there was something in his eyes and voice that made me believe him. *Now I might be an easy target with my feelings getting in the way of reason, and he knows that.*

"Nate," I rushed him.

"She removed her history, but their IT guy retrieved it. "She had searched for a serial killer, top ten musts of successful kidnapping, getting rid of a body and framing somebody for murder."

"That's lucky," I said before I managed to bite my tongue.

"What?" he blinked his eyes and shook his head in disbelief.

I couldn't ask for a better ending. Just like that I was going to get rid of Molly and Susana. Of course, I wanted Molly to be alive but traumatized enough to never go back to work for Morgan and Tusk. "Sometimes it takes years to solve such cases. I bet they didn't expect to have all the answers so quickly."

"No. They didn't but..." he took a deep breath, "the real lucky one is Susana. She was adamant that she didn't have the laptop on the day the searches were made."

"Everybody in their right mind would start making excuses. Has she got a good lawyer yet?"

"Our guards dug out the CCTV recording of the day the searches were made, and it showed you carrying Susana's laptop out of the office. She took leave that day, and let you borrow her computer after you claimed that one of your design programs had failed."

"Does anybody really think I would be so stupid to play it like that? If I ever wanted to kill Molly and frame somebody else for murder, I would come up with a better idea," I scoffed. Lily couldn't be so amateurish! The Soul Management project had some serious flaws. How could I know whether Susana was lying or not? My body wasn't carrying Lily's soul that day!

"I believe you. I do, but all the evidence is currently against you. You need to go back to London and meet with Ally. Think about a good alibi. Oh, it would be so much easier if you were a thriller writer."

*It would be. For once my profession would turn out to be useful!*

"I can always start writing a book. Many people do it without telling anybody."

"Right, and at the same time they throw chairs at people who then go missing."

"True."

"You need something better, like your nephew borrowed the laptop from you."

I laughed out loud, "Nate, don't ever try to frame anybody with murder." He didn't look even a little bit amused. "How can you be so sure it wasn't me? Weren't you afraid to fall asleep next to me last night? Nobody knows where you are…"

"I know you well enough."

"Yeah?" *I'm not so sure about it.*

"You wouldn't deprive yourself of the pleasure of destroying her in public, which prevents any kind of murder."

"So why haven't I done it yet?" I asked, and it was the first time I saw his preconceptions were slowly falling apart. We were staring at each other intensely, when the doorbell rang.

"Have you ordered anything?"

"Not as far as I remember."

"It would be fun to go clothes shopping in town later. You've got great taste," he said cheerfully. I didn't share his enthusiasm. True, I needed some clothes, but I couldn't waste hours hunting for some pretty outfits. I was a murder suspect. On the edge of bankruptcy. On the verge of a nervous breakdown. Still sleeping with somebody else's husband. Still clueless on how to manage my afterlife challenge.

I didn't hesitate long before going to open the door, wearing only a black thong and Nate's T-shirt was the least of my problems. Besides, I was sure a delivery guy in this area must have seen plenty of people in bikinis. I pressed on the doorknob, glancing at my feet that were carrying some tiny bits of churros. *Also, probably nothing unusual in this area.*

"You didn't have to dress up for me," Liam said with a mischievous smile.

"Shit," I whispered, but loud enough for him and Nate to hear me.

"I know. I'm sixteen hours late. But before you tell me that you could've expected that from the guy who missed his own wedding, let me explain myself. Although, this is the worst part… I don't think you're going to believe what happened," Liam said, while trying to get inside, but I wasn't moving even an inch, still holding the door.

"Liam Malone," I heard Nate behind my back, and before I had a chance to react, he put his left hand on my waist. His right hand was preventing his superhero towel from sliding down to his ankles. "I know you and Naomi don't speak much these days but after having a few turbulent discussions we reached an agreement. So, I see no reason why you would still bother Lily."

"I'm here privately," Liam snapped. "I had two flat tires last night, my engine failed. My phone is dead. Could you please let me in, so I can at least charge my phone and have a glass of water? My Uber is already gone, and I have no way of calling another one."

I opened the door, letting him and Nate eye each other like a bull and matador in a ring, before they sat on the opposite sides of the sofa – Nate wrapped in the silly towel, and Liam with his jeans stained with, knowing his last night history, motor oil.

Nate suddenly jumped off the sofa like it was burning his arse, "I'll go and get my trousers, but you can keep my T-shirt Lily," he said looking at Liam.

Liam completely ignored him. "Can I use your charger?"

"Of—"

"Oh," Nate interrupted me, stopping halfway to the stairs, "I hope you're not here to hire Lily behind my back." Both of us, baffled, said nothing which gave Nate more ammunition to support his new theory, "You must know she's currently suspended and has no right to continue any projects for Morgan and Tusk. Naomi doesn't want to hire anybody else, so she agreed we would keep your... her... deposit and wait until Lily is back to work. I hope..." he raised his forefinger in a preaching gesture, "you're not trying to hire her behind the company's back. Lily is not allowed to offer her services as an individual. Unless she wants to buy herself out for a million pounds."

I swallowed hard, "Understood, Nate. Now, you can go and get dressed."

Liam gave me a questioning look, and he didn't even try to whisper when Nate disappeared somewhere at the top of the stairs, "Why would you be with this guy?"

I didn't have an answer for it.

## CHAPTER 40
## New Selina

"Of course, I'll go there with you if that's really what you want," James said looking at me suspiciously. I got a feeling that, like Claudia, he was thinking I was going slowly insane after my mother-in-law was killed. He walked to a round table and pointed at two armchairs in his room, like he was expecting us to have a longer chat. Only two days ago I wasn't even sure whether I wanted to fly with him to England, and now I was with him in France asking him to go to Spain. I followed him, thinking how sexy he looked in a white hotel robe and with his wet messy hair, but I didn't take a seat. "Would you like me to order a breakfast to the room?" he asked, probably hoping I'd change my mind somewhere between polishing off a croissant and stuffing my face with a bowl of fruit.

"No thank you, I'm not particularly hungry," I lied thinking I needed to grab a quick breakfast downstairs instead of staring at him in the dressing gown and wondering how he looked underneath it. "I've already rented a car and it will be ready within a couple of hours. I suggest we go through Avignon and Barcelona, it's two hours longer than going via Bordeaux and Madrid but I've done part of the route in the past."

"A car? How long does it take to drive from here to south Spain? I've heard good things about your low-cost airlines in Europe, or we could even go by train."

"Just over twenty hours. After all that's happened, I'll feel safer going by car," I said matter-of-factly. It was Monday morning, and my clock was ticking. I hadn't got in touch with Virginia Russel by Sunday night. If she still hadn't reported me to the police, it was only a matter of time – a very short amount of time. I couldn't tell James that at some point while we were on our way to Marbella I was going to become the primary suspect in my mother-in-law's murder investigation; and all because of a stupid book I'd written.

"I understand, but you'll be travelling with me the whole time. I can protect you," he said, while straightening his posture with his chin up and chest out.

I didn't ask whether he had something important to do in London and how much time he could give me. It was almost weird he was so eager to accompany me wherever I was going, but I was afraid that if I raised any questions, he could suddenly change his mind and I would be left alone. "Okay," I sighed. I was nervously looking for a lie closest to the truth. "I don't want to use public transport because I should be in D.C. right now with the family. Leo knows I'm here. He asked me to keep a low profile in Paris and not to cross the border to the UK as they're not in Schengen. I don't need anybody to see my passport."

"Didn't you have to show your passport to rent the car?"

"No."

He frowned his eyebrows, "What car have you rented?"

"A white Land Rover. White cars are good with heat."

"A Land Rover? Where did you hire that from without ID? Driving a stolen car will definitely draw attention to us!"

"I bought the car with cash. It's used. I'll sell it before going back to America."

"Why do I feel I shouldn't ask any more questions?" he rubbed his forehead and for a short moment I felt nervous he would back out.

"I'll tell you everything while we're driving." *Maybe not exactly everything but still more than I have told anybody else.*

"I could use a beach holiday, but are you sure you want to go there right now?" I nodded. "All right then. I'll get dressed, pack and meet you in the foyer."

---

As we drove around Paris, James suddenly switched off the radio and glanced at me, "We've been driving for over an hour. Can you finally tell me why we're going to Marbella? I've already committed to the journey. I promise I'm not going to run away." He better not be going anywhere. I needed him more than I initially assumed. I bought the car, but I had forgotten to pack my driving licence. *On the other hand*, I thought, *if I become a missing person and they find me, nobody is going to care whether I've got a license or not – I'm going to be a murder suspect!*

"I thought that while we're here in Europe, I could take the opportunity and go to see an old friend."

"Just like that?"

"Yeah, why not be spontaneous sometimes?"

"Except it's like me flying back to New York to see my family in the Hamptons and suddenly the very next day driving to Key West to see a friend."

"Sort of, is it so weird?"

"Selina, what's going on? I promise I'll drive you all the way there, but don't you think you owe me a little bit of explanation?"

I took a bite of a *pain au chocolate* that we had bought in a drive-through café and washed it down with cappuccino from a paper cup before I was ready to speak, "Have I told you that the police suspects Leona was kept hostage in Mexico?"

"I don't remember but it's all over the news."

"Well, I think it all happened in Spain." James gave me such a long stare that he almost drove into a car in front of us. "Keep your eyes on the road," I shouted.

"What makes you think they kept her in Spain?"

"A gut feeling and a little coincidence."

"I'm more interested in the latter. The last time I had a gut feeling it didn't turn out well," he said nervously. "I had a gut feeling it would be nice to fly to London with you, and here we are – going to Spain to search for some gangsters who somehow managed to smuggle a US senator's mother to Europe."

"Have you heard about Edward Hastings?"

"No, I don't… wait a minute, what? Isn't he Leona's boyfriend? The boyfriend?" James shouted while abruptly slowing down at the last minute, so we didn't drive into a bus.

"Can you stop somewhere before you crash and ruin my whole plan?"

"There's nowhere to stop, I'm fine," he snapped. "What has he got to do with Leona's murder?"

"He's currently living in Marbella, and the police has no idea where Leona is, except that they noticed a pack of cigarettes saying *fumar mata* on the video that the kidnappers sent to the Woodhouse family."

"The Woodhouse family," he murmured.

"What?"

"Again you refer to them as if they weren't your family."

"Well, it's how I feel most of the time," I snapped.

"If you really think that he could've had something to do with her disappearance, which for the record I think is ridiculous, why don't you tell the police?"

"Because they'll think exactly what you've just said, that I'm being ridiculous."

"So, you thought that instead we could drive all the way there, meet him in person and ask, 'Mr Hastings have you or have you not kidnapped my mother-in-law, took a million bucks for releasing her and then killed her anyway? Hm?' You know what? It makes perfect sense. I wouldn't come up with a better plan, not in a million years."

"I can drive you to the airport and I'll go alone. I mean it," I said decisively.

"No."

"No?"

"No! You don't have a driving licence and you're now in a vulnerable place. You've just found out your mother-in-law was murdered. I'm not leaving you anywhere alone. I just don't understand why you don't want to see your mum in England instead of searching for Leona's abductors. You didn't even like her."

I was about to tell him about the book and Virginia Russel, but the words were stuck in my throat. I had this gut feeling that it would be too much for him – one thing too many, that would stop him for good from going with me to meet Edward.

## CHAPTER 41
# New Lily

"Are you sure it's a good idea?" Liam was sitting in my rented car and fiddling with his seatbelt.

I nodded, "Buckle up, the first few turns on the way down are bumpy."

"Nate will be pissed. I don't want to get you in any trouble."

I put my foot down and the car lurched forward, "I need to buy my own car."

"Are you sure it's the car?" he asked with a smirk. I got used to using automatic cars in America, and whenever I went back to the UK I always rented one. Tough luck, I didn't have time to hunt for the perfect car and preferred to compromise on the manual gear than size. I was planning to fill the boot and back seats with various knickknacks that could add some value to the house. The knickknacks wouldn't do the job on their own, but when carefully chosen by Lily Rice – the host and judge of the most popular interior design show in the country – they could become a dealbreaker for increasing the value of any property. "But coming back to Nate—" Liam interrupted my daydreaming.

"He doesn't get to decide to whom I talk to. Quite frankly I don't care what he's thinking right now, and you also shouldn't." I glanced at my naked legs and Nate's T-shirt, "He's not going to chase us bare-chested."

"So, you don't care what he's thinking but you still slept with him," he said slowly, as he was processing the earthshattering discovery.

"Did you come all the way here to preach? Do you always sleep with people because you care deeply about what they're thinking? Because you want nothing more than to be wrapped around by their wonderful thoughts?" I snapped and he went quiet until we made it to the promenade. To his surprise, I jumped out of the car in my skimpy outfit and headed straight to the first shop I could find to get a pair of shorts.

"How come you don't have any clothes? First you lost your luggage—"

"The airline lost my luggage. Then I had to leave the hotel in Paris pronto. Then..." I hesitated. *Should I tell him that I spent a couple of nights in Miguel's house because I got my moving day wrong? He's not going to believe that Miguel just left me his key and went on a business trip. Aaa...Why do I even care what he thinks about me?* "Then I got my moving day wrong, having already checked out of the hotel... but a friend of mine was kind enough to offer me a stay in her villa... I mean apartment. He... She gave me her key, but I shut myself out on the very last day. Luckily, I had my phone with me. I'll pick up my stuff when she's back."

"You're very absent-minded for a successful businesswoman."

"I'm more of an artist than a businesswoman," I shrugged. "And normally my assistant, Jane, looks after me." I wondered how absent-minded he would be if he suddenly had to navigate somebody else's life – using his soul and a borrowed mind.

---

"The shorts look perfect on you," he said, looking impatiently at me trying on the seventh pair of very similar jean shorts, just in different colours.

"Nah, I'll try on the blue dress."

"Lily, what's the plan? Are you using me as your shopping buddy so later you can impress Nate? I would like to take you for lunch. I'm starving, and I thought we could talk."

"Fine. I'll just pay for the dress and get ready in the car."

He laughed, "So you're not going to buy any of the hundreds of shorts that you've just tried, but you're going to pay over three hundred euros for the dress—"

"No need. Everything looks good on me," I said, thinking out loud. Lily could wear anything with her body. *My body,* I thought smiling to myself.

"I can't deny but... you sound just like Naomi."

"Am I your type then?" I asked, typing my pin number.

"Would you like to be *my type*?"

"Not sure," I turned to meet his eyes, while a shop assistant was packing my new dress into a large paper bag and printing a receipt.

He caught my eye for a few long seconds before saying, "Well, I still think it's better to break up just before the wedding than get stuck in a bad marriage."

*I couldn't agree more*, I thought, thinking about Leo. But, were we really such a bad marriage or was his mother destroying our relationship? Or, did we let her rip us apart, because it was easier to blame her than accept the fact that neither of us cared enough? She was the only tangible obstacle; the rest took place in our minds. We didn't seem to know anymore what we wanted from each other. Did we want anything at all? Why did I never ask when I still could?

"*Gracias.*" I took the bag from a young pretty woman standing behind the counter. She gave me a wide forced smile. I couldn't tell whether I was imagining it, or her eyes were full of sadness. She looked like she was trapped in the shop, in the job, in her life. She might have been one of the freest people in the world, but couldn't realise it – couldn't realise that she could do practically anything. When I was in my early twenties, I had this constant tingly itchy feeling that I had to work out where the rest of my life was going. I wish I could go back there and scream into my ears *"no, you don't have to,"* banging cymbals together between every word. *Just take the next corner and see what's out there. Then take it from there and keep moving forward, never be afraid to change direction.*

"Liam, what do you really want from me?" I was standing on the beach promenade, facing him and looking intensely into his eyes. The light blue sleeveless dress was moving swiftly with the wind and stroking the whole length of my legs. Was I a bit intimidating? Maybe. But he didn't seem to mind.

"The thing is... I don't really know," he whispered, raising the corners of his lips, and narrowing his eyes.

"You're confusing me. You act... you look... you sound like..." I paused, seeing his eyes widening and giving me a questioning look. Old Selina would stop and give herself an answer, but now the New Me was talking, "What am I to you? An open business deal or...?"

"Or?" he arched his eyebrows with anticipation.

"You seem to care what I think, feel and have to say."

"I care deeply what you think, and all I want is to be wrapped in your wonderful thoughts," he laughed, wrapping his arms around his shoulders. "Does it have to be mutually exclusive? There are so many people who are married and run a business together."

"Says the man who just ran away at the altar from his business partner to a woman who had an affair with her married boss."

"You can put it like that or..."

"Is there any other way?"

Liam looked at the beach where a group of carefree teenagers were preparing for a volleyball game, "We both lost one set but that doesn't mean the game is over..." he moved his eyes to me, "Look, when I saw you in the hotel in Paris, I didn't plan anything. I knew who you were and yes – I'm not going to lie – it crossed my mind, I could make a deal with you without Naomi, but ultimately, I don't have a million quid, so I think I'll pass," he gave me a big beaming smile.

"And if you had..."

"I'm trying a different career now, which gives me enough time and resource to contemplate what I really want to achieve in architecture. I need to find my own voice before I invite anybody else to work with me."

"Fair enough." I was surprised, if not slightly disappointed, he wasn't suddenly interested in doing business with me. *Or, was this his new strategy?* "Why did you want to see me if you're not going to compete with Naomi to make me your partner? You didn't come all the way here to tell me this personally, did you? You're very good at writing letters."

"Luck had it, I've found a great research job here, on Costa del Sol... I spend plenty of time on a boat which allows me to think..." he yawned. Was he into the job so little that even talking about it made him bored? I thought, smiling to myself. "Long story short, I'm keeping an eye on this big fish... and I've got so much data to gather that I'm going be here for a while."

"Well, sounds great to me. I would also like to stay here for a while, but it all depends on..." *Whether I get arrested or not. Whether I can take a break from my London job without paying them bloody millions. How could anybody be so stupid to sign such a deal? Whether I'm not bankrupt before I complete my house project...*

"I get it. You don't have to explain. All I want is to get to know you, and I hope you let me."

"What if I want to work with Naomi?"

"I'm not going to try to stop you. You know what's best for you." Even if he didn't mean it, he gave me a green light to use his ex-fiancée as my life raft. Was she my *get out of jail free card*, or was I only going to change my keeper? Was it worth it, even if I was about to ruin my chances with Liam? I didn't know him, why was it so hard to let him go?

"Why does everything need to be so complicated?" I groaned and started walking towards the beach.

We passed the volleyball team and found an empty spot on the sand right next to the water. Liam stretched his legs forward and bent back supporting himself on his elbows. I hunched my back, crossed my legs and started fiddling with the bottom of my dress, staring into the rays of sunshine playing gently on the calm sea.

"I know that at first sight it might look too messy or complicated..." Liam broke the silence between us, "But since I met you, I've had this feeling that I would regret giving up on you... And I'm sorry for leaving without a word, but I needed to close the previous chapter of my life to be able to write a new story. I couldn't tell you at the time, but I still had to move out from Naomi. You gave me the strength and energy to say my final goodbye. I'm sorry I didn't tell you the truth, but how could I? Where would I have even started? Hey, I've just left my fiancée a few weeks before our wedding."

"Who knows. Maybe..." I was saying, still looking into the distance, watching two yachts sailing next to each other, "Maybe we didn't lose our first sets. We just did our warm-up session and learnt what not to do."

## CHAPTER 42
## *New Selina*

I knocked on a heavy wooden door using its lion's head knocker. It made a loud noise, but I felt like my heart thumping in my chest was even louder. Nobody opened the door, which wasn't that surprising considering it was an early Thursday afternoon. Even if Edward was at home – and provided it was still his home – he could have been enjoying a siesta. Outside the white painted house it was scorching hot. I was wearing just a strapless light blue dress with a pair of sandals, but I couldn't stop dreaming about jumping into a pool. *The house doesn't look like it has a pool,* I thought while taking a couple of steps back and looking up, *unless it's on the roof terrace.* I couldn't see what was on top of the house because of plants in large colourful pots lined up along its flat roof. *What if the pots are there to be thrown at unwelcome visitors,* I thought, standing closer to the door and knocking again. Nothing. The dark green wooden shutters were closed, and if that was not enough to make the house secure in the middle of Marbella's old town centre, the windows at the ground floor also had black metal bars.

"I don't want to say *I told you so,* but I told you that it was unlikely Edward would be at home just when you wanted to see him. He might not live here anymore, or he might be flying to Costa Rica right now…"

"Or digging a hole for Leona's body in the woods," I snapped.

"For example," he said with a nervous giggle.

"You think I'm going crazy, but I tell you what—" I didn't finish because a bald man with a dense grey beard waved to us and shouted something in English. He was standing outside a hat shop, a couple of houses away from Edward's home. It looked like he was just closing for siesta.

"Excuse me?" James shouted back to him.

"Are you looking for somebody?" The man asked in English, walking in our direction. He was tall and notably well-built for somebody who was likely in his mid-sixties.

"Edward Hastings," I said.

The man looked at me suspiciously, "You're not one of his children, are you?"

James laughed nervously. He was obviously amused by the idea that posh boarding-schooled Edward could have been indeed a frivolous womaniser with kids all over the world.

"No, just friends of the family. We're on a vacation to the Costa del Sol and thought we could personally give Edward an invite to our wedding," I said, surprised with myself that the lie so easily popped into my head. Was the real Selina a good liar?

James was wearing a pair of large sunglasses, but I could see his eyebrows were moving higher and higher above them.

The man rubbed his left ear. I thought he must do it a lot because he had so much hair in his ears that it surely tickled. "Congratulations. You look young so I guess it's a first wedding for both of you."

James grabbed a bit of his linen shirt between his fingers and stretched it forward as if it was squeezing his chest. "First and hopefully the last," he said calmly. "Are you married yourself?"

The man laughed. "Not anymore. My ex-wife and I dreamed about settling in Spain since we got married in our twenties. But when we finally moved here after we retired, we quickly found out we didn't like each other anymore. However, we both stayed in Spain. I live here, and my ex is in Estepona."

"Do you know when Edward will be home?" I said matter-of-factly.

I was sure he had loads of interesting stories to tell us, but I didn't have time to lose.

He opened his mouth to respond, but the heavy door with the lion's head knocker suddenly opened with a swing. A woman's figure stood in the darkness staring at us. I swear her eyes shone like those of a wolf in the middle of the night. "Hola, que tal?" she asked and took a couple of steps forward. Now when she was standing on the doorstep, we saw a handsome woman in her early seventies with a blond bob and strong red lipstick. She was dressed in a casual cotton skirt reaching her slim knees and a loose top.

"Oh, I didn't know you were at home," the man said in English. His cheeks were blushing. "I've just been having a nice conversation with your friends. They've got a surprise for you," he blinked.

"I can tell," she snapped, and the man slowly walked away holding his head down and eyes glued to the pavement.

"At my age shouldn't I finally become invisible for men? Sometimes I wish I was," she rolled her eyes. "Please, come in. I've just made some tortilla for lunch," she smiled invitingly but sternly.

We followed her, walking barefoot, through a long dark corridor. James glanced at me and made a face. *Is he thinking what I'm thinking? Is she Edward's newest girlfriend?*

"If he really killed Leona, should we even be here?" he whispered just before we reached a spacious light kitchen that opened to a garden full of pink flowers, and with a three-layer lion fountain in the centre.

"Please, sit down," she pointed at a long table with chairs on one side and a bench on the other. The kitchen had dark blue cupboards with colourful mosaic tiles. It was huge and took up most of the downstairs. The house had a traditional look, but I could tell from my experience it was expensively renovated. *Was Edward going to stay here longer?*

"You've got a beautiful kitchen, have you decorated it yourself?" I asked and took a seat on the bench.

"When my son bought the house it was in a terrible state inside, like nobody had done anything here for a hundred years. He employed an interior design company from London. It was Morgan and Tusk or Tusk and Morgan," she said and my heart started beating faster. "I love the result but the bill that he received..." she put her lips into a peck and whistled. "It was beyond ridiculous."

"Then, I won't ask how much he paid," James laughed.

"Don't because it elevates my blood pressure. What would you like to drink? I've got coffee, tea—"

"Coffee with some milk and no sugar, would be great, thank you," I said interrupting her.

"The same for me, please."

"So, are you here to see my son?" she asked while preparing our coffees from a beautiful steel coffee machine that my company pushed on our customers to ensure it got ten percent of the sale from the Swiss brand. I was surprised at how many people went for it considering its price, although it looked more like a piece of art than anything functional.

"If your son is Edward Hastings, yes," I said and noticed that my hands had started trembling. I quickly put them under the table, resting them on my knees until they calmed down.

She slowly put the coffees in front of us, while examining our looks. I had a feeling somebody had pressed slow mode on a movie. Her eyes created more tension than I could stand. I was torn between wanting to run away and dying to ask more questions.

"Is Edward your son?" James repeated.

"Yes, I'm looking after his house while he's away." When I looked at her again, she looked older than I initially thought, but her impeccable hair, make-up and slim waist were making her look at least ten years younger.

"Oh," I said. "For how long if I may ask. I really hoped to see him."

"He left a month ago and should be back in a few weeks. Edward took a job in Asia to temporally fly for a local airline. He needs to recover the money that he's lost on all his divorces," she gasped. "My son is so passionate about women and still so naïve."

"Well, love can make you blind," James said with a beaming smile, "that's why I signed a prenup with my wife-to-be."

"How lovely," she said flatly. "So, you're getting married," she glanced at my left hand. I still had a noticeable mark on my finger, where only a couple of days ago my wedding band was pressed tightly against the engagement ring.

I took a deep breath, "I'm Selina Woodhouse, and…" I hesitated, "this is James, my bodyguard."

"I'm Sophia," the woman said with a slight tremble in her voice. She sat down on a chair in front of us. "Are you from *the* Woodhouse family then?"

I nodded. "My mother-in-law was kidnapped and subsequently killed. Her abductors are still at large. I've managed to obtain some information that Leona was in Spain shortly after she disappeared. The only reason I can see why she flew all the way here was to see your son. I don't say he had something to do with her disappearance, but he might've been one of the last few people who saw her just before she got kidnapped. You must understand why I would like to talk to him."

"Why is Leona's son not with you?"

"My husband is grieving," I said decisively. "I wanted to save him more pain."

"I see," she said meekly. "My son and Leona were together, but it was ages ago."

"Well, you were determined to put an end to their relationship because my mother-in-law wasn't wealthy and posh enough for your son," I said in an exaggeratedly posh English accent, which Sophia either successfully eliminated from her own pronunciation or never had.

"It wasn't quite like that," she said and immediately stood up to bring herself a glass of water. "I told you that my son is passionate about women," she sighed. "It's been probably long enough so I can tell you the truth. I wanted to save Leona some disappointment."

"Have you ever wondered *what if* you just let them be together? He would have been…" I paused trying to find the most accurate words, "less confused and wouldn't have married three times." I couldn't suppress my irritation, when I should have controlled myself the most. James elbowed me gently, and when it didn't stop me from talking, he gave me a stronger kick under the table.

"No," Sophia said sternly. "While he was with Leona, he made another girl pregnant. He was in tears when he told me about it, but not because he regretted being unfaithful to Leona, but because he had unprotected sex with a few other girls and was terrified they could also be pregnant."

"Wasn't he like eighteen then?" James asked.

"He was but you see... we sent him to a strict male boarding school. Effectively the place was like a monastery, except none of these boys had any intention of becoming a vicar. We didn't talk much about sex, at least not enough. Girls seem to receive far more advice on sex. I guess because they are the ones who can get pregnant," she covered her face with her hands.

"Did he make anybody else pregnant?" I asked bluntly.

"Not as far as I'm concerned, at least no other children have knocked on his door to this day, but if his high-school girlfriend can knock on his door after so many years, anything could happen."

"What happened to the girl who got pregnant and the child?"

"Her parents and I..." she hesitated, looking embarrassed, "we initially wanted the child to be adopted, but Dona – the girl was much more mature than my son, and had just turned eighteen so the choice belonged to her. She moved with her family to Paris, where they had a second home, and she brought up her baby girl there. Her name is Nina. Edward has tried to build a relationship with her since she turned ten with some success."

"That's why he moved to Paris and was determined to stay there. It wasn't about other women," I was thinking out loud.

"He often went to Paris on his own as his first wife hated that he had another child. It was how he met his second wife and," she rolled her eyes, "and also wife number three... I've been at all the weddings. I'm his mother and I need to support him no matter what, but each time I saw him at the altar, I had a feeling the bride wasn't the woman for my son."

"A feeling? Like the one when you met Leona?" James snapped.

"I told you that I was trying to protect her."

"If you'd had nothing against her, you would have let your son continue the relationship. Would you really care that he didn't deserve the woman?" James smirked. James once mentioned his mother was a difficult woman who didn't like any of his girlfriends. Was he angry with Sophia or was he really talking about his own mother?

Sophia looked at me intensively, "Leona was your mother-in-law so you're more likely to understand what I'm going to say now." I nodded involuntarily. "My son was weak. I knew he wouldn't have been able to keep his secret from Leona, and she wasn't a woman who would let it go so easily. She would have left him anyway, except that in this scenario the whole boarding school... phi!" she hit the table with her fist with such a strength that both me and James leant back on the bench, "the whole town would have known my son was an unfaithful son of a bitch, who had promised one girl marriage and made another girl pregnant."

"Pregnant is the key word here," I said. "You wanted to keep the pregnancy a secret. What a shame for such a perfect family."

"I admit it was part of the reason but—"

"Have you seen Leona recently?" James bent on the table while spreading his elbows and looking straight into her eyes. "You said his ex-girlfriend had recently knocked on Edward's door."

"Did I say it was Leona?" she smirked, which made James irritated, his jaw clenched, eyes narrowed.

"I know she was here, so you'll either tell us the truth, or next time it will be the police that knocks on your door. They're not likely to be as nice as we are now," I said.

"I'm not afraid of you," she said confidently, moving her chin up and pursing her lips. "You also don't seem to be particularly nice at the moment."

"Selina has been through a lot recently, she's afraid for her own life."

*You don't even suspect how much,* I thought.

Sophia looked at me more understandably, if not even with some mercy, "I understand but I don't think I'll be able to help you. Leona was here a couple of months ago to see my son..."

"And then he left a month ago..." James murmured.

"It has nothing to do with her. As I've already told you, he needed to temporarily relocate to make some decent money."

"Why was she here?" I asked.

"It was funny actually," Sophia genuinely laughed. "She surprised him, and me even more! Finding us in Spain after so many years! As she was a wealthy woman she could afford the best PIs, but I never thought she would've bothered."

"You were here when she arrived?" James asked impatiently.

"Not quite, but I wanted to surprise my son on his birthday. I've got a spare key to the house, so I walked into the kitchen on a Saturday morning to see..." she paused blushing, "my son having sex with Leona on the very table we're sitting at."

James leant back.

Sophia laughed, "I had it repainted as soon as Edward went to Asia, otherwise I wouldn't be able to have my breakfast here."

"That's why she wanted the divorce. One of them was unfaithful. But it wasn't Emil."

"She told my son that her marriage was over anyway."

"So, they reconnected after all. Leona wanted to divorce Emil, move to Marbella and start with Edward all over again," I said, frantically thinking that finally something made sense. But *then Emil found out and killed her, and Edward ran away because he knew he was in danger.*

"No," Sophia shook her head. "And this time, I had nothing to do with it," she said raising her hands in a defensive gesture. "I even booked myself into a hotel to stay away from them."

"I bet," James laughed.

"Fine, I did what every good mother would do for her son. I stayed in a hotel for three nights calling Edward every day to check up on him until he asked me to go back to England and give him some space," Sophia still looked hurt. "I did what he asked me to. He called a week later when it was all over."

"What was over?" I asked puzzled.

"Leona had fun with him and then went back to her old life," she said with satisfaction, *I-knew-it-would-happen* painted all over her face.

"Obviously Edward had a terrible time," I said.

Sophia gasped, "She told him that the sparkle wasn't there anymore, but she was glad to see him – well, not only SEE. She didn't want to wonder *what if* for the rest of her life. Edward was heartbroken again."

"Makes sense, although my mother-in-law had changed a lot since high-school, and I saw Edward on the Internet... It's nice to think it wasn't all about looks."

"I thought she looked good," Sophia said almost offended for Leona.

"Of course, she looked good for a woman her age," James tried to rescue the situation.

"I searched for her online ten years ago – just to see how she was doing..." Sophia looked like she regretted mentioning it, but it was already too late, James was staring at her with his eyes wide open, "and quite frankly, I thought she'd let herself go. I blamed it on being a mother of three and a full-time housewife. I read somewhere that her Emil was obsessed with his career and quite traditional when it came to the woman's role..."

"Furniture or lampshades can be *traditional*. Outfits can be *traditional*. Festivals can be *traditional*. Making your wife into a house slave has nothing to do with tradition. Some men are just old-fashioned backward pricks," I snapped.

"I couldn't phrase it any better! That is exactly why I'm a happily divorced woman," she said proudly.

"Right," James started fiddling on the bench like something was tickling his arse. "About Leona. I suppose you don't have any photos with her from that period?"

Sophia initially shook her head but quickly raised her forefinger, "Ha! Edward sent me one, let me get my phone," she said and left us in the kitchen. "Don't touch anything," she shouted climbing stairs to the second floor.

"Do you think she saw Leona?" James asked, and I shrugged my shoulders.

"Oh yes, of course..." we heard Sophia walking down the stairs. She entered the kitchen forcefully laughing into her phone. "I know darling, I know. You're a wonderful mother and you're doing great. That's why I'm trying to protect you from making some bad choices. It's not worth it. You're not one of those mothers who are ready to compromise the wellbeing and the future of their child just to have it a little bit easier. Mhh... Of course, I do understand you can't sleep at night but trust me, other people have it worse," she paused and frowned her eyebrows. "Look, I've got some guests here, I'll call you later... Oh, right. Later you're going for a run... Lovely. Of course, it's very important to shed the extra kilos, but just for your own good don't promise yourself too much – your hips will be wider after childbirth and there's nothing you can do about it. You're a mother now, you've got more important issues on your mind than squeezing yourself into your old jeans. Mhh... Sure. Bye, bye, take care," she sang cheerfully into the phone despite having an angry face. She sat down and forced a little smile to me and James.

"It sounded like something important. We can wait," James said and this time I kicked him under the table.

"It is indeed, but I need some more time to reason with my daughter-in-law. It's about my grandson."

"Edward's son?" I asked intrigued.

"No," she shook her head and looked into the distance thinking. I was pretty sure that Edward was the only child when Leona was with him.

"So how old is your grandson?"

"Three months," she sighed and seeing our surprised faces added, "I had Edward when I was twenty-one, and Andrew when I was forty-one. Nina, Edward's oldest daughter is one year older than Andrew."

"It happens sometimes," I said.

"You wouldn't believe it, but my daughter-in-law wants to use formula milk for one feed in the evening, apparently it helps babies to sleep better."

"I've heard about it too," James said, and I kicked him on his ankle. Of course, Sophia was another mother-in-law from hell, but we needed to solidarize with her in the name of the greater good.

"That's absolutely terrible," I said with understanding. "Could we see Leona's photo now?"

Sophia jabbed her finger on the screen of her smartphone and passed it to me saying, "I think she looks really good."

"It's not her," I said disappointed, and passed the phone to James.

"No," he said rolling his lips, "although..." he scrutinized the photo again, "she's just like Leona but younger, slimmer with better hair and make-up. That's the only photo you've got?"

"Scroll to the right, there's actually another that Edward sent me."

I looked over James' arm. Edward was sitting in front of a round table, with two long lit candles and a bunch of flowers stuck in a round glass vase. He was wearing a dark grey jacket with white shirt underneath and embracing a woman with beautiful long blonde hair, falling naturally over both breasts. She was dressed in a tight red sleeveless dress that exposed her sleek arms and stressed her flat stomach. I couldn't see her legs, but the woman was wearing clothes at least four sizes smaller than my mother-in-law. She had subtle make-up with a strong red lipstick, large diamond studs and a matching diamond bracelet that I had seen once on Leona's dressing table. "It's her," I whispered. "It's her but not like her... When did you get the photo?" I asked but quickly looked up to see the date at the top of the screen. "Two months ago."

"I told you, she was here two months ago," Sophia sounded almost offended I didn't believe her before.

I exchanged glances with James, both baffled, frantically looking for some answers.

"I understand the hair. She finally released them from the silly bun. The make-up is just make-up, but how could she lose so much weight and then gain it so quickly? Yo-yo effect?" James was staring at me while rubbing his chin.

"I told you she looked good. Maybe you didn't see her that often or pay much attention to her?" she asked accusingly. "Don't get me wrong but the mother-in-law tends to be invisible for the daughter-in-law."

"Leona was making herself strikingly visible and present," I snapped and added more gently, "may she rest in peace."

I was still looking at Leona-not-Leona when Sophia's phone suddenly rung and made me jump. The screen showed Andrew Hastings' name and face. He looked similar to Edward, only younger and with lighter hair.

"Can I have my phone?"

"Of course," I said and passed it to her.

"Hello my darling. I'm glad you're finally calling to hear how your mother is," she smiled. "You haven't called me much recently, so I've been wondering whether I've said or done something wrong. I'm pretty sure I haven't but you know me, I can't stop worrying... Yes, I talked to your lovely wife today... No! I would have never said anything like that. The compromising on your son's future and wellbeing wasn't in any relation to the formula milk – don't be silly, it's just milk," she forced herself to laugh out loud. "I'm really sorry she took it the wrong way. Amélie is now very stressed and tired so don't get annoyed with her that she totally misunderstood me. Besides, her English is really good but she's French, you have to understand things like that will happen sometimes... I love you darling, but I've got guests and need to go..."

"Wow," I said.

"Don't judge me, I must allow myself a little victory from time to time," Sophia snapped. "Long term, she won anyway – she's got my son."

"No need for any more explanation," I said, feeling my blood boiling in my veins.

"It's time for us," I stood up and looked at James who was still sitting, "unless James has more questions."

James seemed to ignore my comment, but he stood up and followed me to leave. We were halfway down the long dark corridor when a key turned in the front door. Sophia immediately passed us and ran towards the door, but it was too late – Edward walked inside.

## CHAPTER 43
## New Lily

I dropped Liam off at his rented apartment and was back to my villa by the late afternoon. I hoped that by then Nate's car wouldn't be there. I had left him without a word of explanation and no T-shirt. I hadn't taken my mobile and had driven away with another man. It wouldn't be unreasonable to think, he would stop trying and furiously storm out of the house. Wishful thinking. I switched off the engine, rested my head back on the seat and closed my eyes. A few deep breaths in the quiet sanctuary of this car – it was exactly what I needed to be able to confront the demons of a past that wasn't quite mine.

I turned the key in the lock and pushed the door, which slammed hard against an unexpected obstacle. *What the hell? I didn't have any furniture in the living room. Nate wouldn't move the sofa, would he?* I pushed the door again, this time slower. It easily gave way, but I stood still, listening to the sound of something rolling on the tiled floor.

"Welcome home honey," Nate was standing in front of the granite counter, dressed in a light blue shirt and wiping wine glasses with a kitchen towel.

"Oh, have you been shopping?" I asked, but before he answered, my eyes landed on three large plastic suitcases, which I had left at Miguel's. I swallowed hard. *This is not happening!*

Nate stopped wiping one of the glasses, spread his hands on the counter, squeezing a kitchen towel under his right palm and smirked, "It turned out I didn't have to. I like the Spanish lover of yours more than Naomi's ex. He's a keeper. He brought you a whole pile of different glasses, plates, designer cutlery, pots and pans. Also, a coffee machine and a toaster. He said he would pop back at some point to cook you dinner. We had a good chat. Such a shame he needed to go back to work." I was listening to all of it, not able to make a move, staring at his shirt that looked somehow familiar. Nate immediately noticed, which brought an even wider smile to his smug face, "Nice, isn't it? Two-ply, a hundred and eighty threads."

Suddenly I was able to shake the amazement off my face, and my stupor gave way to anger, "I knew you'd like it. I bought it for you, but after..." *After we split up? Did we officially split up?*

That was clearly not what Nate was expecting to hear, "Oh, really?" I nodded. "Miguel asked whether it was mine. Apparently, you were sleeping in it and he thought it was Liam's."

"He asked about the shirt?" That man wasn't a keeper. He was as nosey as Leona Woodhouse.

"To make him more honest I might have told him I was your brother."

"You might? Hmmm... You *might* not want to speak to me like you did in front of Liam or lie to my friends to manipulate them into telling you something. Because it *might* not end the way you want."

"I'm sorry," he raised his hands in a defensive gesture. "I was jealous. First Liam. Then Miguel. I know you struggle being on your own, always looking for a rebound, but..." he hesitated, "I thought you would be more bothered about Molly and your career falling apart not to waste your time on two different men within a few weeks. Should I expect more of your rebound boys in the next twenty-four hours?"

"Said the man who's still married."

"Officially separated and preparing for divorce."

"Since 1990," I snapped, "and six lovers ago... It would be nice if you managed to close the project before you *officially* retire or... die."

Nate made a face like a petulant teenager, "Miguel said you should be careful with Liam."

"Another jealous man talking. Has he said why?"

"He's not exactly the sweet innocent man that he seems to be."

"I obviously assumed that."

"Fine, do whatever you want. But I'm not interested in an open relationship. Also, I've lost interest in trying to defend you in front of the board, when you can't even be bothered to pitch up at the office! I'm not going to make a fool of myself anymore. A fool who thinks with his dick and lost the last trace of his professionalism for a pretty woman."

"Is that what I am to you?" I scoffed, but he didn't answer. He didn't even look at me as he was storming out of my house. *Be careful what you wish for*, I thought. *Maybe he's not the baddie here. I do seem to sabotage all good things in Lily's life.*

## CHAPTER 44
# New Selina

"Selina Woodhouse?" Edward knew immediately who I was, but somehow he still managed to look like he had seen a ghost. He leant so far back that for a moment I thought he would lose his balance, fall back and hit his head. I was relieved when at the last minute he pulled himself back upright. I didn't want to be accused of another murder. He was holding his right hand on his chest and breathing heavily. "God, you scared me. I didn't expect any guests."

"How do you know Leona's daughter-in-law?" his mother asked, putting her hands on her hips and frowning her overly plucked eyebrows. "Never mind, we had a lovely chat, but sadly they've got a flight to catch."

"Oh well. My mother is a very good source of information irrespective of the topic, so I'm sure she's been able to tell you more than I would," Edward giggled, his breath smelt of whiskey and chocolate. He leant against a wall in the hallway to take off his funky red trainers. He was dressed in a pair of narrow white shorts and a white Polo T-shirt with a green jumper thrown casually over his shoulders. I suddenly noticed a tennis racket sticking out of his soft leather bag, which he had put next to the front door.

"Interesting," I said spreading my feet on the floor and crossing my hands in front of my chest. "According to your mother you're now in Asia."

"Actually, I was very close to taking that job," he said while putting his trainers into a narrow shoe cupboard of a Norwegian design, which I knew Susana had offered literally everybody to get her twenty percent commission. "I backed off at the very last minute because of the distance. I didn't want to leave my loved ones for so long. I've missed enough in my life."

"I understand," James said.

"I don't," I snapped and turned to Sophia," why did you lie to us?"

"My son is grieving, I only wanted to protect him."

"I'll be fine," he said, his voice breaking and tears rolling from his eyes – the view took me by surprise. Was he pretending to protect himself? "Let's go inside and have a drink," he waved his hand encouragingly and James and I followed him without a word to the same kitchen and the same bench, which we had left only minutes previously.

Edward made himself a double espresso and pulled out one of the long larders, which were framing both sides of a silver American fridge. He stood there for a minute contemplating, before he finally took out a plastic box full of cakes.

"I love pastel de nata," I shouted almost too enthusiastically when he moved the contents of the box to a large plate and presented it to us.

"I'm slowly getting sick of them," Sophia murmured.

"She doesn't mean it," Edward smiled gently. "My mother just doesn't like the Portuguese woman I'm dating. She's such a great baker."

"Has she ever liked anybody you've been dating?" James asked with his mouth full of cake.

Sophia made a face, "No, I only think she's your rebound after Leona."

"Leona left a long time ago," he said nostalgically.

"But you saw her a couple of months ago," I said.

"I did, but now I wish I hadn't," he snapped. "Although, that's not true. We had a great time, and I was glad that I had a chance to see her again and explain what really happened in England all those years ago," he said and loudly licked his fingers after eating his second pastel de nata

– the gesture didn't match the picture of the perfectly groomed gentleman.

"How did she react?" James asked with curiosity.

Edward cleared his throat, "She slapped me on my face. Twice. Both cheeks equally hard," he said and then he turned back on his chair to glance at his mother, who for the whole time had been standing next to the coffee machine as if she was afraid to come closer to us, "mum don't listen... I put her head into my hands, kissed her and—"

"Whoa, whoa! We don't necessarily need to know more details," James interrupted him while stroking the wooden table.

"Are you trying to say she forgave you?" I asked. "She was too easy on you."

"That was exactly what she said to me after we had... I mean afterwards," he cleared his throat again, his cheeks blushing, "she said that it didn't mean she forgave me, but she had waited so long she couldn't wait a moment longer."

"But then she couldn't have been that pleased with the result of the..." I waved my hands above the table making everybody uncomfortable, "of the whole encounter."

"She was very pleased with the ENCOUNTER," Edward said offended. "She just didn't want to build her future with me anymore."

"But that's the thing. She shouldn't have come here if she didn't want to build a future with you," Sophia snorted, she couldn't help herself from blindly defending her son, but Edward ignored her.

"I never loved any other woman as much as Leona, and I'm so glad I had a chance to see her before she was gone forever from this world," he rolled his lips and covered his face with his hands. The way he said it felt staged to me, but I quickly chastised myself thinking that maybe he did really love her; that she was the love of his life.

None of us noticed Sophia walked over until she suddenly stood behind her son and slapped him gently on his back saying, "I told you, Brigida is just your rebound. I'm always right."

Edward raised his finger, "But you never know what the future might bring. She's smart, beautiful and has a good heart."

I wasn't interested in Brigida, she was most certainly an excuse not to talk about Leona, so I asked bluntly, "What do think about Leona's disappearance? You must have some theories on what happened. You saw her just a few weeks before she went missing."

"That's the thing," he started slowly, but his mother immediately interrupted him saying in Spanish that he might regret later what he tells us.

"You realise," James smiled, "how many people in the US speak Spanish?" and he turned to Edward, "You might regret not telling us the truth. Think about it, your mother didn't do anything good for your relationship with Leona. Telling us is the least you can do for the woman you truly loved."

Edward gasped, "His name is Octavio Buendia-Iglesias. His superyacht is currently moored in Puerto Banus," Edward rolled his eyes.

"And who is this guy?" I asked.

"The last time I saw Leona, she was having a romantic dinner with him on one of his smaller boats. She told me she was leaving and didn't let me drive her to the airport. Two days later, on a Saturday evening, I saw her with him. She either assumed I didn't ever leave the centre of Marbella or she just didn't care. I asked around, I've got a lot of friends in Marbella and in Puerto Banus," Edward was speaking slowly, I felt like every word was bringing him pain. "She stayed on his yacht for a week before she went back to America."

"That would be approximately three weeks before she disappeared," James said rubbing his chin.

"That's right," Edward nodded.

*Just before I met her in the Hamptons! She came back from the billionaire's yacht a few days before I switched lives with the real Selina. What happened on the yacht? What happened between Leona and her only daughter-in-law? Did the real Selina know where Leona was?*

"What are you trying to say?" James asked, his eyes narrowed, scrutinizing Edward's face.

"Even if he kidnapped and killed Leona..." Sophia exploded, her hands on her hips, her voice getting more high-pitched, "you don't want these kids to go there. They'll only expose themselves to more danger. Octavio is a powerful, sick, rich bastard. Nobody can tell *how* he made so much money. Apparently, he comes from a working-class family from a poor village in the north of Spain, but he also has some roots in Russia..."

"Mother," he said calmly with a patronizing tone, "I didn't say that he killed anybody. But he might've been the last person except for her family who spoke to her. They spent a week together and sometimes it's easier to talk to strangers."

Sophia was boiling with anger, "They weren't strangers. She lived a week on his yacht, and they shamelessly paraded around the whole town, despite the fact Octavio has a wife. Phi! They were both married."

"He's separated," Edward corrected her.

"Still married. People sometimes change their mind while separated!"

"Like you and dad? You were separated for six years before you finally let him go," Edward said clenching his fists.

"How dare you in front of these guests? We were talking about Octavio and Leona, and, in my opinion, there was really something wrong with her. She flew all the way from New York just to see you! Just to sleep with you on the very first day you saw each other in nearly forty years! And then... Then she left you for the first rich man who showed interest. The slut probably got herself into some sort of trouble and it has nothing to do with Octavio. She just seduced him when he was most vulnerable and going through a divorce."

"Just like you did, mother? Obviously, the man must have something else than money if two women in my life – neither obsessed with money – went to bed with him!" Edward punched the table and stood up. Sophia left crying. Her son was standing in the middle of the kitchen blowing on his fist, when suddenly the doorbell rang.

James looked like he wanted to run away, but I didn't move an inch from our bench – it was only getting more interesting.

"Excuse me, it might be a parcel I've been waiting for," Edward said and walked away, holding his bruised hand in the healthy one.

"I think we should go. I don't think Edward did anything to Leona. We can always call the police and tell them about Octavio..." James was whispering.

Edward shut the door and ran upstairs with empty hands. If he had received any parcel, he left it in the hallway. He returned to us pale and shaky. He was standing for a moment on the kitchen doorstep clearly wanting to say something, but not knowing how he should phrase it.

"Do you want us to go?" James tried to help. I suddenly felt like leaving too.

"No, you should stay," he said, and I noticed his right hand wandered slowly to the bottom of his back. I got nervous, anticipating something was wrong.

"Okay," I said slowly. "Do you want to tell us something?"

He cleared his throat, straightened his back and raised his chin up like Sophia had done a couple of times, "The police are on their way. If you try to escape, I might shoot you."

"What?" I screamed.

James glanced at me puzzled and then turned quickly to Edward, while talking clearly and slowly, "That's fine. Everything is going to be all right. Of course, we'll wait for the police and talk to them if that's what you want"

Edward's right hand moved up and then forward. Now he was pointing his gun at us. My throat and mouth were so dry I couldn't say anything. It felt like my tongue was stuck to my palate.

James was holding his hands up, speaking very calmly, "It's all right buddy. I told you, we're not going anywhere." Now I realised he thought Edward was crazy and maybe he had even made up the whole story about Octavio having something to do with Leona's death.

"You can go, but the girl needs to stay until the police arrives. You didn't tell him, did you? You – all women are the fucking same. You all play sweet, harmless and naïve, make yourself into victims, when the truth is you're the abductors. You trap us, you abduct our hearts, our souls and then you kill us for pleasure."

*It's official! He's crazy! I don't want to die! Not again!*

"Have you called the police?" James stayed unmoved ignoring what Edward was saying.

"Of course! I'm not a liar!"

"Cool," James replied cheerfully.

"Have you already slept with her? Do you think you're her Kevin Costner?"

"I don't understand... Ah, of course I'm Selina's bodyguard. Like in the movie. No, I don't think—"

"Yeah, that's exactly what you think!" Edward licked his top lip and wiped his forehead with his free hand. "The police have been looking for your girlfriend for the last twenty-four hours. Selina Woodhouse is wanted for killing her mother-in-law."

*I'd prefer to go to prison than be killed by this sixty-year-old Mommy's boy!*

"Trust me she wouldn't kill a fly. It's a massive misunderstanding. Could you please put the gun away? We're obviously not going anywhere and we're happy to wait for the police."

Edward stood silently for a couple of long minutes with his pistol aimed at us, before he finally decided to put it back in his trousers. When he did, I didn't feel any better – something was twisting my stomach and my throat, and I felt the only way to get some relief was to vomit. If not for the fact that I had a crazy man with a gun in front of me, I would have run to the toilet and puked.

"May I ask who knocked on your door earlier? I suppose it wasn't a courier? More like a carrier pigeon?" James asked.

"It was Jose, who's got a hat shop a couple of houses away from here. He said he recognised you, but initially didn't know from where, until he went back to his shop and looked at the news on his computer. Then he found you as a suspect in Leona's murder. God, you have to be sick – to kill somebody and write a whole book about it!"

I glanced nervously at James, who suddenly gave me a quick hand squeeze when Edward wasn't looking.

"Really Edward? You're almost sixty, haven't you learnt that the pseudo-journalists write anything to increase their clicks? Selina is the wife of the most famous senator in the US – every day her family have to deal with fake news. Leona read the book and she loved it. She was proud to be an inspiration for Selina. But if you want to believe a Jose from your local hat shop—"

"Jose was a chemical engineer before he retired and opened the shop, so don't be so disrespectful, young man. When he called the police they were very grateful, so I'm not so sure about fake news."

"Why aren't they here yet?" James glanced at his watch.

"They've found a mafia boss in Puerto Banus and they asked me to keep you here until they arrive."

"I doubt they asked you to threaten us with your pistol. Have you even got a licence for it? You don't want to shoot a suspect with an illegal gun. You let us into your house voluntarily."

"Edward let them go," we heard Sophia coming down the stairs. "It's not worth it. Even if she killed Leona, she probably had a good reason to do it, and it has nothing to do with us."

"Mum please go back upstairs, she might be a dangerous criminal," he said to Sophia who moved to stand in front of our table. "Mum, please don't come so close."

"If you're a bodyguard you should also have a gun," she said staring in anticipation at James.

"As you said, it's not worth it. Selina is innocent and we don't want any bloodshed here."

"Mum step back," Edward was getting nervous. He walked slowly towards the table with his right hand on his gun belt." I couldn't believe he had a gun belt and was actually wearing it! Was he enjoying this opportunity to play policeman?

"I'll make some tea," Sophia walked briskly to put a designer kettle on. It was made of blueish glass and matched the Swiss coffee machine. I thought about Nathan making a deal with the Swiss brand to advertise their products, when I heard a thud and saw Edward lying on the floor under the long wooden table.

"Run," James shouted. "Run for god's sake."

I felt like my legs couldn't move, it was like a bad dream, but James grabbed my hand, made me stand up and pushed me towards the hallway. Edward seemed to be harmless again, groaning from pain, a trickle of blood on his lips, and the heavy table lying on his waist, covering the pistol.

"Ouch," James swiftly bent forward to avoid one of the plates that Sophia was throwing at us.

"Edward, my child! Somebody help!" she was screaming out of her lungs while throwing crockery and glasses at us. I got hit with a piece of glass on the back of my neck. Warm blood flowed down my spine as I was going through the dark hallway and out onto the street running as fast as I could – I had no choice, otherwise James would probably have dislocated my arm or torn it out of my body and run away with it.

I was practically out of breath when we got to a square, where some high-school kids were throwing powder paint at themselves and dancing to some spiritual music. It looked like a mini Holi festival, except that none of these people were likely Indian and it wasn't the end of winter but the middle of summer.

"Here," James dragged me inside the circle where we stayed until our entire bodies were covered with paint. "Can I buy your baseball hat?" he asked one of the boys in Spanish.

"You can have it for free," the boy replied with a massive smile. "It's a present from me." James thanked him and we slowly walked away holding hands.

"We didn't attract any attention before, now everybody is going to look at us."

"It's only so we don't have to run for another mile. Now nobody is going to even be able to say what our hair colour is."

I wanted to ask him so many things, but I was so overwhelmed with the last hour that I couldn't pull my thoughts together and ask him a single coherent question. We strolled in silence until we crossed a busy road, climbed a few stairs and got to the most amazing little park that I had ever seen. We stood in the middle of a square with a fountain, surrounded by exotic palm trees and other high trees, which were dense enough to create a shelter from the scorching heat. Siesta was coming to an end, but the alleys in the park and benches tiled with traditional Spanish motives were practically empty. The only busy spot was a small carrousel full of smiley kids sitting on plastic zebras and horses. Before I managed to move any further James took my hand and dragged me on it. We both sat on a white horse, his hands touching my waist, his breath on my shoulder.

"Why did you do it?" I asked loud enough to speak through the music of the merry-go-round, but also trying not to be too loud – I was wanted for killing my mother-in-law!

"I'm going to call a friend of mine, who lives here. He'll find us a place to stay. We can't go back to our hotel," he was saying with his lips touching my right ear.

"No. I'm asking why you threw the table at Edward? Did you think he's crazy?"

"Might be, but he was telling the truth about the book, and you being wanted by the police." I held my breath for a moment, completely petrified. "That's why I wanted you to leave America."

"What?" I turned back to see his face, which turned out to be calmer than I had expected.

"Look straight and laugh occasionally when I talk to you and when I…" he planted a kiss on my cheek, "…do this. We need to act as normal as possible while I'm calling Antonio."

I reached into my bag to get my phone, but it wasn't there, "Shit, I lost my mobile."

"I took it out of your bag before I knocked down Edward and threw it into a fountain while we were running away. Now they can't track you."

"You really are my bodyguard. Why are you doing all of this?"

"Because I know you didn't kill anybody and somebody is trying to frame you, I'm just working on who it might be."

"Wait, did you know about the book before it went viral on the Internet?"

"I knew about Virginia Russel, but now if you'll excuse me, I need to make a phone call. Keep smiling and don't look around. You want to look like you're enjoying the ride, not like you're scared that somebody can identify you."

"Done," I said through a squeezed throat. *Who the hell are you, James?*

"Hi Antonio… yeah, we're already here… mhhh… In Almeda Park. Yes. We're all covered in some powder paint… Don't ask," he laughed. "Orange Lamborghini – is it the same one you showed me… oh right, fantastic! Thanks! See you in five minutes."

## CHAPTER 45
## New Lily

"The name and breed of your first dog," a male husky voice read out the question, and then I swear I could hear him on the phone chewing an apple. Fair enough, it had been a long conversation, and maybe in his time zone it was already lunch or dinner – but couldn't he have gone for a less noisy snack? A doughnut perhaps?

"A sausage dog called Hans Gruber."

"That's fifty percent correct," he said with a distinct dialect.

"What? It can't be," I looked again at my secret notebook that Gabriel made me take from Lily's flat. "Ok, let's try – a dachshund called Hans Gruber."

"That's correct," he said flatly. "Where was I... oh, question number twenty-five, the name of the girl who bullied you and other kids in your kindergarten by tickling and pinching."

"Violetta Green."

"That's correct," he said yawning, and then he started coughing violently as if he was choking on the apple that I was still imagining him eating.

"Are you okay? Do I need to call an ambulance?"

"I'm fine," he said, but continued coughing and puffing. "A piece of guava got stuck in my throat. I'm fine now."

"Good." Now I felt like yawning.

"Last question... Your favourite holiday with Nathaniel."

"A business trip to New York just before Christmas when we got stuck there for a long weekend because of a winter storm. The only Christmas and New Year's Eve I had with him," I read out loud from the notebook. I was thinking how sad the answer was, and almost forgot that it needed to be approved by the man called Rufi on the other side. "Is it correct?"

"Yes, yes... Sorry. I was just thinking about your answer. I've never spent Christmas with my partner and I've been with him nearly five years. He doesn't want to come out as gay to his family."

"Oh, my god. I'm so sorry."

"Thanks... I'll give him an ultimatum this year. I think I've had enough of hiding. Life is too short."

"I agree... Do you have any other questions?"

"No, that's all," he said with enthusiasm. "Now, you can ask me anything regarding your account."

"So... I logged into my account this morning and noticed a million pounds."

"Jeez, that's sounds like my ultimate dream, second only to spending Christmas with my boyfriend. No..." he laughed. "A million beats him."

"I wanted to clarify whether there has been a mistake."

"Nope. All looks good to me."

"Can you tell me who transferred the money?"

"No."

"Excuse me?"

"The only way for you to find out who sent the money is by personal appointment at a Bermuda Bank. Sorry."

"So why would you ask me all these questions and take an hour of my life?" I was hopping mad. "Why? If you can't answer this simple question. Why?" I shouted and punched the granite counter, bruising my knuckles, and went to sit on the floor with my back bent against a white wall, legs stretched in front of me and eyes set on the beautiful sea view, which I couldn't appreciate in that moment.

"I didn't know what the question would be," he said innocently.

"Because you didn't let me ask you anything without going through the security questions."

"I'm sorry, that's our protocol. I can't do anything about it. Would you like to speak to our branch manager?" he sounded as if he was pre-recorded.

"Can I at least know which country the money came from?"

"Only personally in our bank. The only thing I can confirm on the phone is that the million is definitely yours."

I gasped, said a quick goodbye and immediately disconnected to call Gabriel. He didn't feel like answering my questions either, at least not for the first half an hour of me pressing nervously on his number or calling his name with my hands raised to the ceiling of my villa. It wasn't until I angrily threw my *afterlife* phone at the wall that he finally appeared and caught the phone at the very last second before it hit the wall.

"This is the latest model, which is very time-consuming to produce."

"And completely useless if you don't answer my calls. You're my only number on that precious device."

"Sorry, but you aren't my only Soul to manage and it's hardly a crisis here."

"So, you don't think taking ransom money is a crisis?"

"What ransom?"

"Get up to speed! Morgan and Tusk paid a million pounds ransom for Molly to be released. Nobody knows where she is, but a million pounds magically appeared on my secret account in Bermuda... Why am I even telling you this?"

"No idea, I already know."

"This is not happening!" I grabbed my damp hair and screamed. I'd spent the last four days wearing a dressing gown, but I still showered every day. "Why would I even call the bank, if you could immediately confirm my biggest fear... well, at least after a half an hour waiting..."

"I didn't say you took any ransom. But, I know about the million."

"Where is the money from?"

"I can't tell you."

"So how am I supposed to manage Lily's life? Can I spend it to buy myself out from Morgan and Tusk?"

Gabriel took a seat on the sofa, "You could've easily done that if you didn't buy this house. It was too late for the Tuscany villa, but—"

"But then what? I don't have Lily's business and design skills. I can look into her portfolio, use Jane's help and my imagination to decorate the villas. Hopefully all that plus the Lily Rice brand can make me a profit on flipping houses... Besides, she had money and for some reason didn't buy herself out."

"She also didn't run away..."

"But I got pushed straight into her life, just after she threw the bloody chair at Molly, who then got kidnapped..."

"Yes," he stroked his chin. Today for the first time since I met him, he had stubble. It was more part of his new image than neglect, because he had a fresh haircut and a fitted sleek suit. "You're one of my most lost Souls."

"Is that supposed to be reassuring?"

"But we wouldn't put you in this role if we thought you couldn't cope with it."

"I feel like somebody who just inherited a billion-dollar company, but has never worked a day in their life."

"You're doing fine New Lily Rice. I believe in you."

*You could do better as my coach, guardian or whatever you are,* I thought, but quickly tried to redirect my thoughts somewhere else, just in case he could read my mind. I sighed, "Emma called today. She helped me finalize the sale of the Aston Martin and one of my paintings. I thought that I needed more disposable cash. I wish I'd known about the million earlier."

Gabriel bent back on the sofa and crossed his arms, looking outside my terrace window. Was he avoiding my eyes? "Well, in your situation the more disposable cash, the better."

"Should I know about something?"

"Check your emails from Ally more regularly. There are people out there who are trying to help you. Not everybody living in London is your enemy."

I scanned the mailbox with tired dry eyes – that was what I had been doing for the last four days – looking for some solutions online. There it was – unread and in bold, with three exclamation marks – sitting between angry messages from my mother asking why I kept ignoring her advice on Nate, and some random offers of cooperation from companies, which mostly I'd never heard about. There was one offer that could turn out to be very profitable, but knowing Susana and Nate – they would never agree to it. One of the most popular TV stations wanted to do a reality show with our office. The only condition was that we had to start immediately while Molly was still missing.

"So?" Gabriel was impatiently taping his fingers on the side of the sofa.

"Yeap." I clicked on the email from Ally and soon slowly raised myself to a standing position, "I need a glass of water."

Gabriel flicked his fingers and a glass of something yellowish appeared in his hand, "Here you are... My latest trick. I've been promoted."

"Should you really promote alcohol?"

"What? Oh, no... That's vitamin water."

I gulped the entire contents of the glass, which tasted like diluted orange juice. "Real Lily might be glad that they didn't let me do her show."

"Wow, it's really working." I gave him a questioning look. "The vitamin water made you more of an optimist."

"Considering how much she gets paid per episode, she might be fuming," I shrugged, feeling more tipsy than optimistic. "But who cares? I'm here now and I'm going to make the most out of my time in this body, and in this life with all its ups and downs... Ally says they don't have any strong evidence on me having anything to do with Molly's disappearance, but they're not going to risk their reputation in case I turned out to be guilty. Apparently, they can break the contract with me without any consequences... Goodbye another source of income. Have you got more of this vitamin water?"

## CHAPTER 46
## *New Selina*

"Are you the one who said we should keep a low profile?" I asked, sitting on an orange corner sofa of a Lamborghini limo.

"He said he didn't have any other cars available and it would be too risky to take a taxi. Besides, nobody would suspect that you're driving along the Costa del Sol in a limo. Nobody will link you to Antonio."

"You still haven't told me who Antonio is," I shouted excitedly, although I felt I should've been more scared than excited. James pressed his forefinger to his lips and glanced at our driver, who was wearing a black chauffeur hat and a dark leather jacket. I touched my nose – the paint was slowly melting. "I just worry he'll kill us for messing up his car."

"He said the leather seats are stain proof, and if the paint can be used for the body, it's going to be easy to wash off. He said that blood washes off no problem. Anyway..." he passed me a hot wet cloth from a box hidden inside a drawer on his side of the sofa. He also took one for himself and wiped his whole face. "With this traffic we've got at least forty minutes, so you can relax."

"Forty minutes..." I looked out of the window. "And we're going north so I suppose—"

"Torremolinos. It's all I can tell you right now," he said seriously. There was something in his voice that gave me shivers. *What if he's the one I should be afraid of the most? Claudia and Leo told me to keep my distance and I did the exact opposite.*

I had some freshly prepared fruit and canapés that James took out of the limo's fridge. He knew exactly where everything was. I drank some coffee, but refused wine and champagne. *Actually, I shouldn't be drinking anything at all,* I thought. *What if Antonio, assuming that's even his real name, put something in my coffee?* James only had some juice from a glass bottle he had opened himself. My coffee had been stored in a gold flask.

I must have fallen asleep because I opened my eyes when the car wasn't moving anymore. When I looked through the window, I saw a narrow-cobbled street with a line of white houses on both sides. The buildings were modest but very tidy, adorned with colourful flowers and dense hedges made of plants with thick juicy leaves.

"We've reached our destination," James said matter-of-factly. He appeared to be colder and more distant. *Did they add sleeping pills to my coffee?* I didn't have my phone, nobody but James knew where I was – including me! *Is it really Torremolinos?* I holidayed in the town once in my life as Lily. I stopped here with Nate on our way to Marbella, but I had never seen such a picturesque street before or such an empty street in the town!

I swallowed hard, my throat was dry. *Did the sleeping pills make it dry?* I was frantically thinking about how to escape but no reasonable or feasible solution was coming into my head. "Where are we?" I asked in a trembling voice.

"Get out of the car and I'll show you," he said now more softly.

I let him take my hand to get me out of the car. My legs were slightly shaking when we stood on the street. I took a deep breath, and while I was doing this, the limo drove off with a squeak of tires.

"I think you're dehydrated," James said concerned. "We've been running in the heat and you only had coffee in the car. "Let's go and get you some water."

"But where are we going?"

He released my hand and stood right in front of me, so I couldn't see what he was looking at on his phone. He took off his baseball hat and scratched his head, "Okay... so..." He turned to look down the street, which went all the way to the coast. The sea was beautifully shimmering in the late afternoon sun, but it seemed to be miles away from us. We were on top of a hill, and I guessed that Torremolinos was more in front of us. "We need to go all the way down and find a house with a green door and a picture of a bull across six wall tiles."

"Why didn't he drive us to the house?"

"This is the best place for the limo to stop and not get stuck in the narrow streets. I actually like the fact that even Antonio's driver doesn't know exactly where we're going. Antonio completely trusts him, but I get some comfort thinking that nobody knows exactly where we are."

"Except the people in the house?"

"We're supposed to find the key in a red plant pot on the windowsill," he said and grabbed my hand, but this time I pushed him away. "What's going on?"

"Yes! Exactly! What the hell is going on? I'm not going anywhere until you tell me what we're doing here!"

"We're hiding because..." he lowered his voice to a whisper, "the police are looking for you. Have you already forgotten?"

"How have you managed to organise all of this so quickly?"

"I knew that sooner or later we would need to hide. That's why I got us the flight to Paris instead of London. I know people who could help us in Paris, here and a couple of other cities in Europe, but I've got nobody in London," I gave him a questioning look. I wanted to ask so many things, but I didn't even know where to start. He gasped, "My ex-fiancée is Spanish. We studied together for a year in Madrid."

"Madrid is a long way from here, and why would she help you? Why would she help ME, your *neighbour*?"

"I didn't get in touch with her. Some of her friends have remained my friends. She wouldn't mind. I represented her mother when she divorced her second husband, and that was after we'd already broken up."

"Fine but why are you helping me?"

"Long story short, we might share an enemy or two. Emil is the reason I can't practice law, and I hired a PI to spy on him and his family. We can talk about it later when we get to the house."

"Is Emil my enemy?" I shouted, my voice turning into a weird high pitch squeak. "His family, you mean my family? And what's the guarantee that you're not going to kidnap me?"

"There's none. You either trust me or not."

*I don't want to die! Not again! Will I get another chance in heaven? Whose life am I going to get next?*

I didn't let him hold my hand, but I followed him, walking one step behind.

---

James turned the key as softly and quietly as a knife in butter. He pushed open the green door and we immediately found ourselves inside a living room with low wooden ceilings, a brown tiled floor, stairs going up and an arched doorway connecting the room to a small kitchen. There was not much light inside – metal bars and thick heavy embroidered net curtains created the atmosphere of a basement flat. The whole place smelt of a flowery air-freshener and it was pleasantly cool. The room was tidy and modestly furnished with two flowery double sofas, a chunky wooden chest functioning as a coffee table, and a chest of drawers with a TV on top so old that I imagined it would explode when switched on. The TV was covered with an embroidered tablecloth and had a collection of porcelain figures on top. I picked up one of them – it was a Spanish matador dressed in a light blue outfit and looking like he was dancing with his pink sheet. I counted twelve figures, they were all either matadors, bulls or women in traditional Spanish dresses.

"They're all perfectly dusted. Somebody must be living here," I said showing James the blue matador.

"The woman who owns the house is currently flying to a five-star spa hotel in Mexico. Antonio sent her on holiday in return for renting us the place. He told her he needed it for some photo shoots. He also works in media."

"Also?"

"He's invested in many businesses, and he's a good and generous man."

"Right," I nodded. "Tell me everything about Emil and—" I didn't finish because as soon as I said it, we heard a loud bang coming from upstairs. I dropped the matador on the tiles, it crashed into a few small pieces, leaving white powder on the floor. "I know what Antonio also might be involved with—" I shouted but stopped when I saw James standing on the first step of the stairs and holding a gun. He put his finger to his lips and started climbing up with the gun ready. The upstairs went suddenly silent, and all I heard was the cracking of the wooden steps under James's feet. For the second time that day, I felt like I could be sick. James reached the top of the stairs, his back pressed to the wall, both hands on the gun, moving from the left to the right, from the right to the left. I held my breath when I heard another loud bang, threw myself on the floor and hid behind the sofa that was closer to the front door. *Should I run from here or better crawl to the door*, I was thinking.

"It's a bloody cat!" James screamed from the top. "Fuck, he scared me."

I was still lying on the floor when a fluffy ginger cat strolled past me – I would swear he was smirking and looking down at me. The cat stretched his front paws, bent his back into an arch and jumped on the sofa behind which I was hiding. I stood up on shaky legs, the cat purred and looked up. The ceiling was making cracking noises under James' feet as he searched the first floor.

"It's all fine... bars in all windows, both bedrooms and the bathroom are empty. The entrance to an attic is locked with a padlock the size of the damn cat!" James was shouting, while walking down the stairs, his hands dangling loosely on both sides of his body with the right one still holding the gun at the height of his knees.

"When did you get it? Did you have it the whole time we were in Edward's house?"

"I got it in Paris after you asked me to go with you to Spain," he answered, wiping sweat from his forehead and taking a seat on the sofa that wasn't occupied by the cat."

I sat next to the cat, which scrutinised me as an unwelcome guest before he closed his eyes and started snoring. I had a feeling he had also switched lives with somebody, and I wouldn't be surprised if it was a human. I looked at James, who was texting with a smile on his face.

"Who are you texting? God, who ARE YOU James?"

He put the phone back in his pocket and glanced at the gun that was lying next to his right thigh. "The cat's name is Gengibre, which in Spanish means Ginger. He belongs to the lady who lives here, which Antonio had forgotten to tell us."

"Wonderful! I'm pleased Gengibre is not armed, his fur is real and he's a local fella. What about you? What haven't you told me?" I said with my arms crossed.

"Before I tell you anything else..." he said and suddenly stood up to open one of the drawers under the TV. "Here you are," he passed me a new looking smartphone, "I put in my number and your mother's. I'm down as your emergency. I'm sorry I haven't saved more contacts from your old phone, but we were in a rush."

"You're scaring me. You were planning all this time to get rid of my old phone."

"Of course, it's the first thing you should do if you know somebody is looking for you."

I nodded, feeling stupid that I hadn't even thought about it. "Were you going to shoot Edward if he became more difficult?"

"No," he laughed. "His gun and the whole stupid gun belt weren't real. They're actually a toy. I saw a similar one, if not the same, on a male stripper."

"Are you gay?" I asked shocked. *Leo's secret lover?*

"No. I was once in a gay strip club... If you really want to know, I can tell you about that experience later... I think at the moment you're more interested in..." he cleared his throat.

"In you and Antonio."

"Antonio is just a good friend of mine and—"

"And a drug dealer?"

"What are you talking about?" he asked, looking genuinely surprised. I pointed with my finger at the white powder on the floor. James reluctantly left the sofa, kneeled down next to the broken matador, licked his finger and touched the powder. He sniffed his finger at a distance so as not to inhale much. "I think it's cocaine… Don't look at me like that. I've never taken drugs, but I had some friends in college. I'll text Antonio…"

"No," I shouted with panic in my voice. He looked at me questioningly, his thumbs frozen above the screen of his phone. "He's helping us, we don't have to know his whole life history. We don't have to know everything about him."

He put the phone back in his pocket and returned to sit down on the sofa next to his gun. "Fine, I'll ask him about the cocaine after we don't need his help anymore, but he's a good guy and despite what some people are saying he made his money completely legally."

"Fine… I mean, nothing is fine. Is the gun legal? How did you know about my book? What have you done to Emil?"

"I can't handle more than one question at a time," he leant forward, his elbows resting on his knees, fingers laced together and pressing against his lips. "The most important thing is that I'm your friend and you're safe with me. You do get that, don't you?" I was sitting with my arms crossed, looking at him blankly and not knowing what to say. "To prove it to you, I've just given you a phone," I turned the mobile in my hands and checked whether it was working, it was. "You can also take the gun if you want. I know you're a very good shot."

"Am I?" *Selina can shoot?*

"I know that you spent a lot of time in the last few months at one of Long Island's shooting ranges, which unfortunately could be used in court as further evidence that you were prepping yourself to…" he paused as if he wanted me to finish.

"Oh, just say it! I was prepping to shoot my mother-in-law!"

"My theory is that you needed a hobby that could help release the anger that you accumulated spending so much time with your mother-in-law…" he paused for a moment like he needed time to consider whether what he was about to say was appropriate, "Let's face the truth, your husband is also far from perfect."

"Do I even need to say anything? You seem to know more about me and my family than me," I snapped.

"There's no point going into all the details, but you should know that Emil threatened and blackmailed me. I was the divorce lawyer for a woman, who happened to be the wife of one of his closest friends. Her husband is a politician and also a good friend of Richard."

"Richard? Claudia's husband?"

He nodded, "The man wanted a very discrete divorce and to keep his wife quiet he offered her a big share of their estate. She didn't accept. She was happy with half."

"I bet she had good reason not to take his offer," I said flippantly, while playing with my hair, which smelled weird from the spray paint.

"She did. The man was found guilty of beating up his wife, and currently is facing a further trial for molesting two of his assistants."

"Holly shit! Why would Emil try to protect such a son-of-a-bitch?"

"Well…" James made himself more comfortable by sitting sideways with one leg under his bum and his left hand embracing a flowery pillow, "he claimed that his friend pushed his wife at a wall only because she tried to attack him, so technically it was self-defence. Then he said that my client's husband didn't deliberately throw a plate at her, but he was angrily pointing at a wall behind her and threw the plate by accident. Neither of these claim are true, but obviously Emil couldn't tell me that he needed the friend of his to help him with Leo's campaign, both logistically and financially."

"Does Leo know about it?"

"I don't think so, he's not as fucked up as his father."

"You're talking about my husband, you know?" I said calmly.

"Who, as we both know, is cheating on you with Keanu." I opened my mouth but no words came out. "Keanu told my PI that you found out about their relationship, but instead of *leaving him*…" he said over-accentuating the last two words, I felt a slight disdain in his voice that made me irritated, *who are you to judge me?* "So you made some sort of a deal with your husband. I was going to use the information to blackmail Emil—"

"Hold on a minute, why do you have to blackmail anybody? What did he have on you? You wouldn't be afraid of him if you were all innocent." James squeezed the flowery cushion harder and blew his cheeks. "I need some more answers; otherwise how can I trust you?" I said staring at him with anticipation. "Maybe my best solution is to give myself up to the police."

"I forged some evidence for my client to win. Her husband was a serial cheater who sponsored several young students for sex. The problem was none of them agreed to testify, all but one was already married and had children, and the last one came from a very strict catholic family. We came up with the idea of hiring some escorts, who pretended to be students and attempted to seduce him. It didn't work because it was all done too late and he wasn't stupid enough to fall for it. In terms of his real *girlfriends* he always used cash to pay them, he was very careful. We couldn't prove he was the sponsor for over ten years, but we found a way to make him a gambler who loved sleeping with prostitutes on a regular basis. His wife was a doctor and she managed to forge some medical records saying he had several STDs that he passed onto her a couple of times... Don't look at me like that. None of this would be necessary if he didn't want full custody of his children and he didn't start investing in his parents' properties to hide as much money as possible from his wife."

"You seem to be quite emotionally involved in that case," I said scrutinizing his face. I couldn't work out whether he was regretting his decision, was embarrassed, or it meant more than it should for the average lawyer.

"I might have slept with the woman on a couple of occasions," he said meekly, trying not to show any face expression. "Fine, I was in a relationship with her for a year, but after the case was over."

"Why did you break up?"

"Why do you need to know?" he said it in a such a defensive manner that I suddenly really needed to know.

"She wasn't ready for a new relationship, she was too controlling and not able to trust."

"Did she have a reason not to trust you?"

"No, I've never cheated on anybody... Now, do you want to know something more about my ex-girlfriends or should we talk about Emil and Leona?"

I gasped, "I feel a bit lost. Emil blackmailed you with embarrassing details from your life that could have had a serious impact on your career, but you said you won the case, and he didn't act on his threats. Why would you need to blackmail Emil then?"

"He tried to destroy my career, but he and his friend didn't have any evidence that me and my client forged anything, so finally we threatened them with slander and he backed off. Then he was going to spread malicious gossip about my relationship with Sandra – but when he saw me with Leona and discovered she wanted me to be her divorce lawyer – he decided to use it to blackmail me instead. He suddenly stopped caring about his dear friend."

"God, people are really afraid of you," I laughed nervously. "And then you just stopped working, I don't understand."

"I decided to pause my career because if people found out about me going out with Sandra, it could damage my reputation as a serious divorce lawyer. And I just couldn't work with Emil constantly in the background, a shadow emerging each time he didn't like me taking on a case of one of his friends or family – and trust me he's got loads of mates whose wives are potential clients," he smirked. "I decided to give myself some time to find something on Emil, convinced that with a guy like him it wouldn't be too difficult."

"Have you got something more than his son being gay who uses his wife as a beard?"

"It was my best leverage against him."

"Why didn't you use it then?"

"Because Leona disappeared."

"She disappeared just after she tried to hire you? Did she find another lawyer?"

"She did and my PI discovered her new lawyer, Helena, had been corrupted by Emil. He was paying her at least double what Leona had agreed."

"You told Leona about it, she got furious with Emil and..." my heart started pounding. *Did I already meet Leona's killer? I had never met anybody's killer before,* I thought and swallowed hard. "Are you suggesting Emil got rid of Leona and now he's trying to frame me? I get the first part, he isn't a nice man – I mean not being nice doesn't make you a killer, on the contrary..." I was speaking faster and faster.

"Breathe Selina," he straightened on the sofa, with his feet on the floor and hands waving up and down like a maestro. "Take a deep breath in, and breath out. Take a deep breath in..."

"I'm fine, stop," I snapped, although taking a few deep breaths was making me feel better. "Why would Emil try to frame me? Am I just a scape goat? All in all, he didn't write the book or even read it, and so far, that's the only evidence against me... I'm not even sure how it can be treated as evidence, unless they think I'm crazy..."

"I hoped you would be able to tell me," James rubbed his chin, he looked good when he was deep in his thoughts. "You said once that he inspired you to write a book."

"Did I?"

"Apparently, he told you to put more energy into your writing – to write about something that makes you furious and scared. Something that wakes you up at four in the morning and doesn't let you sleep."

"Leona was annoying, but it wasn't entirely her fault that I was unhappy."

"But we like to find somebody we can blame, it's very human – you want to have a tangible enemy. You wrote in the book that you had nobody on your side, you felt alone with your problems and embattled by Leo's friends and family," he said, expecting me to at least agree with him by nodding, but I had no idea what to say.

"I..." I coughed to give myself some time to answer. *Basil should have briefed me on this! Have I ever shown James my book?*

"Sorry, I should've told you that my PI hacked your computer. I needed to know whether you could've done something like that."

"Something like that? You thought I killed Leona? And then what? You read my book in which I kill my mother-in-law. You saw my search history in which I looked for some info about serial killers and you still thought I definitely didn't do it? That makes a hell of a lot of sense!" I was shouting in fervour, not even noticing when exactly I stood up in front of James, throwing my hands in the air.

"No," he answered calmly, but now bent back on the sofa as if he was afraid of me. "I thought you did it until my further..." he cleared his throat, "my *research* indicated something else..."

I covered my open mouth with my hands, looking at James with eyes full of fear, but also hope that together we could find Leona's killer and put him or her behind bars. "Who is it?"

"Leona was afraid of Emil."

"Emil is the killer?"

"I think she ran away to hide from him."

## CHAPTER 47
## New Lily

Two hours – that was how long it took me to set up my YouTube channel and upload my first video with a short announcement about my upcoming vlog. According to Ally using any footage from my old TV show might cause trouble with the TV network, so I searched my laptop for some good content, and asked Jane whether there was any videos of my work that I could use. Bingo! That woman was amazing! She spoke to my most loyal clients, who apparently worshiped me, and they agreed I could use the images of their houses before and after my renovations. Not particularly computer savvy I hired a woman who edited the five minutes video and ta-da I was taking my destiny (and fame!) into my own hands.

My first new project was a wall mounted electric fireplace in the living room. Miguel recommended to me a local builder Jose, who would put a marble stacked ledger of stone tiles on the largest and most strikingly empty wall opposite the open-plan kitchen. I imagined sitting on the corner sofa, placed in the centre of the room, and depending on my mood, I could either admire the sea view or turn my eyes to logs crackling behind the safety of a thick glass screen. I intended to negotiate a discount if he installed a similar stone wall with a fireplace outside on the patio – that was my favourite part of Leona's house in the Hamptons and now I wanted to copy the same feature in my dream villa.

Jose agreed to meet me at half past five and reassured me numerous times he didn't mind answering questions about his job and life in Spain on my live stream. Miguel said Jose was not only an incredibly professional builder, but he was also a fantastic storyteller with a great sense of humour, who spilled out anecdotes like a jukebox. Exactly what I needed! I did my hair and make-up and spent a couple of hours revising the script, which I had been preparing till three in the morning. I was more excited than scared, which made me wonder whether Gabriel's drink of optimism had something to do with it.

By a quarter to five, nine hundred thousand people had already subscribed to my YouTube channel. Lily had created profiles on all major social media sites and before taking my body she had kept them very active. No wonder, she never stopped working. My posts announcing the YouTube channel were the first since we switched lives. I expected a good amount of traffic, but the numbers exceeded my expectations. At five, when over a million people were anticipating my appearance, I cleared my throat, smoothed my hair and started filming. I began by telling my viewers how much I needed a break from the hustle and bustle of city life, and that was how the idea for the new project popped in my head. I saved them the detail, I wanted to sound happy and casual. Then I took them around the house with my phone, showing them every corner of the villa, and while I was doing all that I felt like I was levitating a few feet above the ground. My light green dress made me imagine I was Tinker Bell, and my phone was a magic wand.

I was showing a million-euro house with a one-in-a-million view to my million viewers – adrenaline and excitement skyrocketing in my veins – until I glanced at my watch, and it suddenly hit me! It was five forty-five and no sign of Jose. *Has he rung and I didn't hear him? Has he forgotten? Has he mixed up the days? Is he still coming?* These and millions of other thoughts were avalanching through my head. I was standing on the terrace, legs shaking in uncomfortable beige stilettoes, arms stretched forward, too terrified to move, with the phone transmitting the Torremolinos sunset. The unsettled state of mind mixed with a mild anxiety had accompanied me since I jumped into Lily's body, but I managed to keep it in check. Each time I felt a surge of unexplained fear I focused my brain on a new task, and sooner or later it went away. Each time I felt the world was closing in on me and an invisible force was squeezing my throat, I closed my eyes, and started breathing steadily. It worked every time – until now!

My heart was going a hundred miles per hour, racing like a wild horse with no intention to stop, even if its rider was going to end up in a ditch. My mind went blank. I could feel my wet palms, a trickle of sweat going down my spine and my chest shrinking as if it was about to shut down and never again take a gasp of air. Every trace of reasonable thinking seemed *Gone with the Torremolinos wind*. I wasn't able to reason with myself and explain that the feeling would pass. *Oh, my god! What if I die on livestream? I don't want to die again! Please! Please somebody come and fix me. Fix me... Fix me. I can't breathe.*

"I froze your world for a few minutes. You've got time..." I heard Gabriel's smooth voice and saw on the horizon a flock of birds, their wings had stopped moving and they were suspended in the air like they were immortalized on a canvas. "I'll count to three and you're going to be fine. Do you understand me?" I nodded, taking fast short breaths. "One, two, three..." he clicked his fingers like he wanted me to get out of hypnosis, but it didn't work. "I'm not going to let anything bad happen to you. I promise. Take a slow breath in and out... Inhale and exhale... Put your phone on the floor... sit down, cross your legs, shut your eyes and keep taking deep breaths..." I felt dizzy and couldn't say a word. I was falling deep down into an empty space where Gabriel's words were reaching me only as an echo. "Open your eyes," I heard his voice in the distance like it had to go first through a heavy storm. "Take a deep breath... Look straight ahead of you. You can see from here a small white house with a red tiled roof and green shutters. It has a covered parking space with a cobbled driveway. A woman will drive in there in a few seconds on her red convertible chevrolet camaro..." I saw her. She had long dark shiny hair covering her back and bouncing all the way down the spine to her slim waist. She was wrapped in a beige bodycon dress, which at a distance made her look naked. "She's a very successful fitness coach from Berlin. Three children, two Yorkshire terriers. One husband dead, one divorced a few months ago. Last month she finally received the rest of her divorce money and a first fat cheque from selling her fitness and dieting book. She immediately bought the house, the car and enrolled her kids into a local school..." As Gabriel was talking, my breath was getting steadier, and I was hearing him more clearly. His calm face, his confidence and the story that captivated my attention were slowly dragging me up to the surface from whatever darkness I'd fallen into. I was regaining control over my body, and by the time he finished talking about Mia Muller I was back.

"Thank you, Gabriel."

"I'll count to three and your world will start moving again. Are you ready?"

"What about Jose?"

"With Jose or not, the world must go on, and you're more than capable of dealing with it."

Gabriel disappeared leaving a green fog. Once again, I was standing on my terrace, my arms stretched out with the phone streaming the glorious Torremolinos sunset. But, this time I had a plan. There was no time to think how brilliant or terrible the plan was. I had to go for it and later cut coupons from my success or count the losses.

"Thank you for giving me a minute so I can switch to my laptop. I need to use my phone to call Jose, who is late twenty minutes already..." I glanced at the screen. Many comments were appearing about unreliable builders who were always late or never pitch up. People were sharing their worst experiences and providing advice. "Jose is not answering. I haven't had any message from him, so I have to assume he's not coming, and unless he's got a good excuse I don't want him tomorrow, or the day after tomorrow." I bet the Real Lily had numerous stories about contractors that failed her and she could fill up hours with them. I had to go down a different route. "I was telling you how I took on the house project in Spain because I had enough of city living. I haven't been quite honest with you. I think I haven't even been honest with myself..."

## CHAPTER 48
# New Selina

"There are two common mistakes that humans make..." Basil was saying, "First is thinking that they can see right through other people. That their brilliant intellect is able to work out other people's motives and intentions. The exact reason why they are behaving in a particular manner. They know what mistakes they make and how to fix them."

"I'm the last person in the Woodhouse family to make assumptions."

"You asked me for some advice so I'm giving you it," Basil said with his mouth full of an energy bar. "Sorry, it's been so busy today I had no chance to have dinner, and to answer your next question – yes, I do have to eat. I wouldn't starve to death, but when I'm hungry I get grumpy, and my belly starts rumbling really loudly, which can be distracting." When he finished chewing the bar, he immediately reached for another that he kept in a large pocket of his green fisherman jacket. He looked rather comedic in his camouflage trousers, wellies and a bucket hat, while sitting on the roof terrace of the Torremolinos house. It was two in the morning, nobody was likely to walk down the street, but Basil gave me a cigarette so if somebody saw me, I had an excuse, as to why I was sitting alone on the top of my house in the middle of the night. "Take it," he insisted. "Otherwise, somebody might think you want to jump and the last thing you need right now is attention." I said it was only a two-storey house and I wasn't going to stand at the edge of the roof, but he didn't listen. I had to pretend to smoke.

"We're not looking for the Leona, who I met in the Hamptons. The woman who we want to find looks and acts differently. What I don't know is whether Leona changed because she needed to hide; or whether the escape gave her an opportunity to create a New Her – somebody she always wanted to be. Unless she naively hoped that Edward would help her and save her from Emil, she didn't have to get in touch with him. Then, what was she doing with Octavio? Why would she have an affair when her priority was to escape from Emil? Again, did she see her rescue in that man?"

"Don't dismiss anything that suddenly crosses your mind," he said and wiped his face with the sleeve of his jacket. We sat for a while in silence looking at the illuminated coast.

"What's the second mistake that humans make?"

"They assume that other people can view right through them; that they know what we can or cannot do. It's one of the biggest stoppers when people want to change anything in their life. You start dressing differently or you've got a brilliant idea about starting a course or even a degree at the age of forty, fifty or sixty; or you take on a new and unusual hobby... And then all the people, who until then had sat quietly never commenting on your life choices, suddenly start emerging, and what are they saying? That the new dress or the longer hair are *not really you*. Degree or art course, why now? Isn't it too late for a career change? Isn't it too early to fulfil your passions when you aren't retired? Have you got a midlife crisis? Are you doing this just to show you still can? They can understand you want to have a TV binge or go out for a drink every night to the same pub, but they can't understand that you would like to change your habits, lifestyle, or possibly even build a completely new you. People don't like being surprised – they've already classified their whole world – including you – and they don't need you to disturb the order. It would mean more thinking, analysing, reorganising... and they want to go forward, not to look back, not to think they might've been wrong about you..."

"Is this about Leona or me?"

"Both," he said without hesitation, and we went quiet after hearing a noise coming from the roof access.

The trapdoor flew open, and I saw James slowly materialise in front of me. "What are you doing here?" He was rubbing his eyes.

"Well, I could ask you exactly the same."

"I woke up, went to the toilet and I noticed that the door to your bedroom was ajar. I looked inside, you weren't there so I went looking for you. I found the ladder unfolded and here I am," he said cheerfully. Basil giggled and suddenly disappeared leaving a small cloud of dust that James noticed. "Where's the smoke coming from? Have you..." he stopped, his eyes fixed on the cigarette between my fingers.

"I haven't, but I've been thinking about it."

"I didn't know you smoke."

"You don't know a lot of things about me," I snapped, irritated that he interrupted my conversation with Basil. "Besides, I haven't smoked. I spent the whole time fighting the urge. The last time I smoked was at uni."

"Well done you," he said, took the cigarette out of my hand and threw it in the street.

"You threw my fingerprints and probably bits of DNA on the street," I said flippantly and saw worry painted all over his face.

"Nobody will... I'll go and clean it in a sec."

"Don't," I laughed.

"We need to be up in five hours."

"I still think you should tell me where we're going."

"You'll find out soon enough. Just remember to wear something comfy."

I examined my baggy pyjamas with tartan shorts and flowery top, "All the clothes that Antonio brought us are comfy."

"The good news is that he sent somebody to our hotel room and he's got all your clothes."

"Somebody broke into our room?"

"Technically nobody broke into anywhere but they did trick somebody to get the key."

"How many people are involved in hiding me?"

"We need to go to sleep. It's going to be a long day tomorrow."

---

I was sitting on a surfboard, my legs spread apart and moving lazily in the water either side of the board. A neoprene black hooded wetsuit that I was given half an hour earlier, was doing its job – despite the chilly wind and the cold water, which was only just starting to warm up with the first days of summer – I felt snug. There were three of us, sitting in the same position next to each other and facing the shore that was approximately a mile away. I had James on my left and Octavio on my right. Their faces were so stern and focused on looking into the distance that it crossed my mind they were about to drown me and say later it was a terrible accident.

It was just after eight o'clock in the morning on Thursday and the beach was still empty. The only noise we could hear were gentle waves and planes landing and taking off from Malaga airport. We were right at the north edge of Torremolinos, where the promenade ended.

"There aren't any sharks here, are there?" James asked with a slight nervousness in his voice.

"No," Octavio said. "Not unless they're injured or ill. We spotted one maybe a couple of years ago, but it's practically unheard of. Why?"

"I've cut my finger on the bloody zip." I saw a red spot on his wetsuit around the zip that was going across his chest. He put his right forefinger in his mouth and started sucking on it as if he wanted to suck every drop of blood out.

"You'll be fine," Octavio said dismissively.

James was initially very comfortable about meeting Octavio while floating on surfboards in the sea. He woke me up at seven in the morning with a cup of strong brewed coffee and said that Octavio agreed to see us in a safe place, where nobody would be able to eavesdrop. "Antonio knows Octavio. They did some business together and apparently Octavio owes him a favour." I felt a mixture of excitement and fear, which catapulted me from my warm bed, made me drink the disgusting brewed coffee and pushed me into an old colourful beach van with two surfboards tied to its roof. Now when I was watching James, who looked like he was about to be seasick, all the excitement was leaving me like the air from a pricked balloon.

"Thank you again that you agreed to meet with us," I said through a squeezed throat.

Octavio nodded. He was a handsome dark-haired man in his early sixties with the body of a twenty-year old. Apparently, he wasn't deliberately working on his muscles, but was passionate about windsurfing, kitesurfing and rollerblading – and for that reason he had a villa in Torremolinos. His yacht in Puerto Banus was less of a home and more of a place to socialise and entertain his potential business partners. He loved Torremolinos for being more laid back and less pretentious than Puerto Banus; and for the fact he was less likely to meet his uber-rich colleagues when he just wanted to relax. I found all this out from James, as we were driving to the beach – mostly they were irrelevant and random facts that didn't bring anything to Leona's case. "I don't want to rush you guys, but I've got a meeting at nine thirty so you might want to get down to business."

"Who was Leona for you? How did you meet?" I asked.

"A good friend of mine. I met her a year ago in a plastic surgery clinic in Marbella, where my wife had an operation. Please don't ask me what Leona had done there because I don't know. *En general*, each time I saw her she looked better. I don't think she had any major surgery; I doubt it – I would say she just started looking after herself and she was a naturally pretty woman." James and I glanced at each other. *Leona, naturally pretty? Were we talking about the same woman? A year ago?*

I took off a waterproof rucksack from my back and placed it on the surfboard between my thighs, I noticed my legs were slightly shaking. A small wave came suddenly, the board rocked sharply to the right, but I got my balance at the last minute and managed to save the rucksack and me from falling into the water. I took out my mobile and passed it to Octavio so he could see Leona's photos. I had done a few screenshots from Freya's Instagram, where she posted pictures from some family events in the Hamptons. I also had the photo that Sophia showed us.

"I never understood what she saw in Ed, but well... it was a while ago, they were kids," he said and strolled his finger on the phone to the left. Before he said anything, he made a face, chuckled and put his left hand to his open mouth.

"Have you ever seen the woman?" James asked. "I'm starting to think Leona has a twin sister. I wouldn't be surprised."

"At first glance, I would never say they're the same woman, but... She was fatter when I met her for the first time and her boobs were larger so if she had any boob-job it would be a reduction. She never had grey hair. Her nails were always done and she used to wear make-up, and by make-up I don't mean the excessively pink blush of a porcelain doll. Her clothes also changed with time. I think my wife influenced her in a good way, but I've never seen her in such a comical costume like this. She looks like a caricature of the Queen of England," he laughed.

"You're talking about her like she was a regular visitor here," I said.

"Because she was. She came here every month, normally for a few days, but sometimes for a week or two."

"So you've been lovers!" I exclaimed. "My condolences," I said with respect.

"What?" Octavio laughed. "She was originally my wife's friend. When I separated from my wife and Paloma moved back to Sevilla, I got closer with Leona but never in that way."

"You don't have to hide anything from us. We won't judge you. We're afraid that Emil might have done something to her when she tried to leave him for you," I said. I looked at James who squeaked like somebody had been cutting his throat, and straightened his back as if he had been wearing some sort of brace to improve his posture. He rolled his lips and was staring at me with his eyes round as golf balls. I thought that a little bit of provocation would be useful to make him talk, but obviously James thought differently.

"Emil? I've never had the impression she was afraid of him... Okay maybe once, but it was more my wife posing theories than Leona inferring anything about Emil being dangerous." Octavio was looking into the distance when suddenly he turned to me and asked, "Why was her hand in plaster last month?"

"Actually, I don't know."

"You didn't ask her? What sort of family are you people, if you never even asked her how she broke her arm?"

"She said that she tripped on a pavement and reacted nervously when we asked for more details." I couldn't tell whether James tried to rescue me, or it was the truth. Although, there weren't many pavements in residential areas of the Hamptons!

"Hmm... The same here. Paloma suggested Emil was a wife beater. Leona always depicted him as a power-greedy workaholic with an overgrown ego. Even recently Paloma said that maybe Leona was covering for him to protect her son from bad publicity. None of us thought though that he'd kill her, and Leona apparently had osteoporosis so it wouldn't be so hard to break an arm, but still..."

"Did you go back to your wife just after Leona was believed to have died?" I asked boldly. I didn't want to be so harsh, but it was Octavio telling us to get down to business. *Did they get back together not to instil any suspicions about Octavio being involved with Leona. Let's face the truth, if not the husband, it's normally the lover!*

"Stop making me into Leona's lover. I've never slept with her. She was the one who convinced me to go to therapy with my wife, and actually I could say that she saved our marriage."

"All right," James took a deep breath. "We're thinking that..." he took another deep breath, "I've learnt in my job not to exclude any possibilities, and it crossed both our minds that Leona might have faked her own death to get away from Emil. From what you're saying she never mentioned that to you, but her husband liked to threaten people if they did something against his will."

"She was nostalgic about her past and mulled over some life changes, but I can't believe she would abandon her children."

"They aren't children anymore," James said matter-of-factly. "Besides, maybe she didn't plan to fake her death from the beginning. Maybe she also wanted to teach her kids a lesson or two – from what I know they took her for granted. The problem was that it all went too far with the media attention, so the only way to put it to bed was to die."

"Yeah," Octavio murmured. He bit his lower lip and tangled his fingers while making circles with his thumbs – he froze like that for a long minute. "I've spent some time with her. When she decided that

Edward wasn't for her and I was still separated with Paloma, she came to live with me on my yacht and we got closer. Not in any romantic way," he added defensively. "If she wanted to run away, I don't believe she would blackmail her family for money, she would be too proud."

"Really? Too proud?" James scoffed. "I can't see Leona taking a job in a laundry or begging for money on the street. As a missing person, she couldn't use her account."

"She could have a secret account. I don't really know. I think the version with Emil hurting her is more probable," he said with a sad face. "He could kill two birds with one stone. Ransom money is tax-deductible."

"Seriously? How do you know that?" I asked.

"I was blackmailed once and my brilliant accountant told me... Look, if she is alive, and I would love that to be true, she doesn't want to be found. If she's dead, and Emil killed her, the police will sooner or later find out. Emil Woodhouse is a lot of things, but he doesn't strike me as a man who could commit a perfect crime. Nowadays it's very difficult anyway. The police are better and better at solving murders," Octavio said with his face deeply in thought. I felt shivers going down my spine, and when I looked at James he shuddered. We both felt it was time to go.

"Just one more question," I said.

"Please the last one because I need to start swimming back."

"Did Leona have any other friends here except you, Paloma and Edward?"

"Not really. But a couple of months ago Leona got friendly with a guy who owns a chain of fitness clubs all over Spain. He's got one in Marbella where she used to go for Zumba and belly dancing."

"Belly dancing? Okay, that's it. James must be right – Leona must have a twin sister."

"What's his name?"

"His name is Diego. You'll find his surname on the Internet or look for a fitness club with the name Diego. It might not be true, but some people speculated he would go into bankruptcy. I'm not aware of the whole story but he overinvested and had problems with paying off all his loans. Not many people knew Leona's real surname and when I think about it now, she made an effort not to reveal she was from the Woodhouse family. But that doesn't mean, he couldn't find out. He was friendly with her, and I didn't have enough courage to ask whether there was something between them."

"Because you fancied her," I said without much thought.

"I did actually."

## CHAPTER 49
## New Lily

"All that matters now is whether they can really sue me or not." Ally must have been more than just a lawyer to me, if she didn't mind giving me her legal advice on skype, while she was cycling on her stationary bike, her hair put up in a bun, red sweaty face and large boobs falling out of her tank top. "Of course they can. But, should they? Will they? I don't think so. Nate might be super pissed, but he's not stupid. Nothing that you said is factually incorrect. Nothing incriminates you or puts the company in a bad light, at least not directly. I watched it a few times, once with my boss. Many of your statements were vague and open to interpretation. Does it come across like she bullied you and the company tolerated it? Probably yes. Have you made it clear? No. You had a very turbulent and difficult relationship with her THAT..." she raised her forefinger, "on top of your other problems eventually caused you to have a nervous breakdown and THEN..." Ally slowed down her pedalling, as she was getting out of breath, "she disappeared into thin air... I read some comments and many people relate to you and are grateful you talked so openly. They're also grateful you shared with them that you've had panic attacks. Personally, I think it was honest and brilliant. We need successful people talking about their real life – real problems. Not about... oh, my god it's the end of the world, my stone-cutter hasn't pitched up today."

"It's just... maybe I went too far talking about my relationship with Nate." I took a sip of coffee, my third one that morning. I barely slept after my first YouTube performance. I should have switched off my phone for the night instead of reading Nate's angry messages and Liam begging me to speak to him.

"You've got over a hundred people in the firm. You could have had an affair with any of them. I'm glad you didn't say the man was married because it would narrow the search and... you don't want to destroy your reputation by coming out as a homewrecker. Just deny everything. There will be gossip, but nobody is guilty until proven. And even if they find out, we'll make something up. You didn't know he was still married. You said he'd never taken his wife to any company parties... We'll work it out. Before the law degree, I did a few years in PI," she said proudly with a beaming smile, and wiped her forehead with a towel.

I put my face into my hands and groaned, "I'm so mixed on what I've done. I feel relieved and happy with the positive responses... Well, mostly positive... Jane removes unconstructive negative comments and blocks all haters. I got carried away."

"Yeah," Ally laughed. "I've never seen you like that and we've known each other... hmm... something like twelve years? I think I like the new Lily."

"When I started the channel, it didn't even cross my mind I would use it to help look for a missing person."

"That might help YOU by making you more likable and showing that you care; and MOLLY because, who knows, there might be somebody out there who provides a valuable clue..." she paused to look at her phone. "I've got an important call coming. I'll be in touch."

That was my first chat with Ally that had left me feeling positive and relieved. The last thing I needed was a lawsuit with Morgan and Tusk, and from what she was saying even if it happened – there wasn't much to be afraid of, at least not yet. Besides, my inbox was expanding – soon to explode – from potential advertisers and sponsors. If Jose, the stone-cutter and social butterfly, had appeared at my door last night, none of these people offering me their fat cheques would have ever spoken to me.

---

"Thank you that you made me finally leave the house."

Liam stopped fiddling with the stem of his glass and raised his red wine above our round table laden with colourful tapas, "Cheers to you finally leaving the house."

"Cheers to my first time in Sevilla."

We clinked our glasses, holding each other's gaze – and the few seconds were enough to make my brain spin a hundred and eighty degrees before I even took my first sip of wine. Liam was the perfect mixture of a mysterious stranger, who I wanted to keep uncovering – layer by layer, and somebody so familiar and trustworthy that I wished I could tell him my whole life story, including switching lives with the real Lily. He reminded me of James, a neighbour from the Hamptons. I also didn't know him that well, but they were both easy to talk to, attentive listeners, and offered a persistent positive aura. Many people could stand ten feet away from me and yet I still felt like, somehow, they were violating my personal space. Liam was the total opposite. His close presence didn't disturb my space – he fitted in it like he was always meant to be there, bringing with him a sense of tranquillity and purpose. It was like he expanded my space – creating other rooms where I wanted to be.

Our table had a fairy-tale view of the Guadalquivir River with the Triana Bridge and the moon reflecting on its pitch-black water. We were surrounded by people having romantic dinners with candles. They were chatting in different languages and all kinds of laughter were melting into one pleasant sound carried along the riverbank. For a moment I had a chance to forget about my afterlife mission, Molly or the challenges that I had brought on myself by buying the villa and starting the YouTube channel. Liam told me about his Spanish course and kitesurfing lessons. It looked like he was really starting all over again and enjoying his freedom. He was a massive fan of Spanish architecture and his stories and photos inspired me to see more of the country. It was only the name *Miguel* that brought some friction to our evening.

"I can't blame Miguel for the fiasco with Jose. That wouldn't be fair... I barely know him, and he's already helped me so much... And it's not the first time a builder stood somebody up..."

"I'm sure he planned it all to the smallest detail," Liam laughed out loud. "I know the man. If he wanted Jose to be there, he would have personally driven him to your house."

"That's ridiculous. He's so busy with his job."

"Did he tell you that his grandfather was a stonecutter?"

"No, but why would that matter?"

"When Jose didn't show, Miguel was hoping that you would call him in desperation," Liam was so sure of his theory. "He was waiting all dressed up and ready to share with your viewers his grandfather's anecdotes."

"And how exactly do you know that? It never hit me you were such wonderful friends. On that boat..." I cleared my throat trying not to laugh, "I got this weird sensation you wanted to push each other overboard."

"He invited me in for a drink at his house in Malaga and said we could see your show together. I thought it was suspicious he didn't want me in his new villa in Marbella that he's bragged so much about. But now! It was just too far for his emergency rescue of Lily Rice. He only invited me in to see my face when I lost to him."

"Liam, that's just crazy."

"Nah, it's just Miguel being competitive. We used to like each other, but I think he's never forgiven me that I asked Naomi out when I already knew he was head over heels for her."

"Ouch!"

"To be fair, she asked me out and I just surrendered."

"Well, she's a beautiful woman."

"With a terrible temper," he said without hesitation and grimaced, "I'm sorry I shouldn't have said that about Miguel. I don't like you to think you're a..."

"A trophy in a competition between two alpha-males. Well, too late," I smiled.

Liam opened his mouth to defend himself, but a waiter came to his rescue by distracting us, "Everything okay with your meal?"

"Yes, thank you," I said quickly to brush him off, although the prawns were barely edible. One in eight tapas were terrible, not bad considering the other seven were delicious, and the view, wine and atmosphere excellent.

The waiter was about to leave us when Liam stopped him by gently raising his hand, "Actually, there's something wrong with the prawns. They're too chewy. We left them just in case they could make us ill."

"Oh..." the elderly waiter with a round baby face looked genuinely concerned. "I'll check with the chef. Of course, we're not going to bill you for it. Would you like something else instead?"

"Another portion of calamari?" Liam asked questioningly at me. I nodded.

"A portion of calamari on the house," the waiter gave us a smile and walked away, happy he resolved the problem.

"Oh, I should've asked for another wine. What would you like?"

"Actually..." I slowly stood up, my head spinning, body heavier than usual and legs softer, "could you ask for a glass of their fresh orange juice? And now if you'll excuse me..."

"Are you okay? Do you want me to help you?"

I smoothed creases on my tight black dress and noticed with surprise that after a big dinner my perfectly flat stomach was raised slightly like an underbaked muffin. Lily was a human after all. "No, thanks. I don't need you to assist me on my way to the bathroom yet."

As soon as I disappeared behind the restaurant's door, I took off my stiletto sandals. A vision of me falling on my face and knocking out my teeth was stronger than the prospect of dealing with unfavourable looks of smartly dressed customers in an upscale restaurant. Everybody was too absorbed with themselves to care about a woman passing their tables barefoot and on slightly wobbly legs. I stood in front of a bar. My eyes met a twenty-something barman, probably a local student, wiping glasses with a white cloth and giving me a smirky look a la, *you've probably had enough*. I had, so I asked him for a glass of water and espresso. It was either Lily having a light head or me starting on the wine before I had enough tapas to put a safe lining in my stomach. I took a sip of espresso and for the first time that evening I took the phone out of my rose gold clutch. Not wanting to destroy the evening by reading some disturbing texts, I clicked on a news app. I strolled through the first few political articles, thinking, *not now, nothing positive... no, no, no...* My eyes stopped on a photo of Nate and a large headline that put my stomach upside down like I was on a carousel. With my palm pressed tightly against my mouth, my legs carried me as fast as they could towards the nearest toilet.

## CHAPTER 50
# New Selina

Our hideaway Spanish house had two good size bedrooms but neither had an en-suite – we had one bathroom to share, and a tiny toilet downstairs. The house was far from luxurious, but it felt very cosy and lived in – its owner clearly loved thick fabrics, warm sidelamps and paintings in wooden frames. Unlike the traditional living room, both bedrooms were newly renovated – they were painted in subtle beiges and decorated with colourful cushions, bedspreads, fluffy rugs and heavy curtains. I took the bigger bedroom, which had a double bed, a chunky desk and a flat screen TV on the wall, while James slept on the bottom of the bunk bed in the other bedroom. I presumed his bedroom was normally used by the woman's grandchildren.

I sat with James on the edge of my bed, covered in a pastel pink bedspread and embroidered maroon cushions, watching an English news channel.

"Did Octavio say he was planning to go to a party tonight?" I asked. "I would prefer he didn't watch this."

"He goes to a party most nights."

"Ufff.... And the Spanish news channels don't seem to be that interested in the Woodhouses, at least not yet."

"Antonio told him you were a suspect," he said, and I held my breath for a moment looking at him as if he betrayed me. "Don't worry," he took my hand and squeezed it tightly, "I trust Antonio, and Octavio has no interest in giving you to the police. Besides, he doesn't know where we live and that we're going to stay here for a while."

"Are we?" I asked, but James wasn't listening to me anymore, his eyes narrowed and fixed on the TV. I heard a familiar voice and felt like somebody suddenly put my head under water – I could hear everything, but it was muted with words melting one into another.

"Pamela Goodrich!" I squeaked.

"When I think about Selina now, she's always been surrounded by a mysterious aura. She doesn't talk much and seems to be constantly thinking about something. I've always wondered what was on her mind. You know, I'm afraid of people who think so much and talk so little..."

"Not everybody feels an irresistible need to talk twenty-four seven, you bitch!" I shouted, but James hushed me, waving his hand in front of me and... purring? No, I realised – it was Gengibre sleeping at our feet, who was purring.

"She tried to make me believe that Leona killed herself..." Pamela suddenly started weeping, maybe I was being cruel, but I thought the tears were staged. She was wiping her nose with a blue cotton tissue that matched her pastel blue dress and nails. She had white pearls around her neck and a pearl bracelet on the hand that she was using to wipe her nose. She wasn't actually wiping, she was tapping so as not to ruin her professionally done make-up. "I knew Leona for so many years and I can tell you with certainty that she would have never killed herself. She didn't suffer from depression – I would have definitely noticed. We were very close," she raised a finger from the hand still holding the wet tissue..."

Pamela was still talking, but she was put on mute, as a journalist from a TV studio introduced another friend of Leona's. "Now, we're going to move from the sunny Hamptons to cloudy Toronto," a man in a blue suit with arms that were taking half of the screen said in a deep voice.

"Don't they have a weather forecast later?" I asked, and James put a finger to his lips.

"Michael Bloom is currently on the Toronto Islands talking to Patricia Lentil, who might have been the last person who saw Mrs Leona Woodhouse before she went missing. We wanted to talk to her because Mrs Lentil was asked by the prime suspect, Selina Woodhouse, to meet with her in private."

"I didn't want any secret meeting, nobody else from the family was interested!" I shouted to the TV as if Michael Bloom could have heard me.

"I had the impression that Selina was trying to understand how much I knew about Leona staying in my cabin. I had previously told the family I only saw Leona briefly to give her the key, so I was surprised when Leona's daughter-in-law asked me to see her in private..." Patricia was standing on a shore with yachts sailing in the background. She was dressed in a modest black dress and was holding tightly a grey Kelly bag – as tightly as if she was forced to cross a dodgy street in the middle of the night. With her large designer sunglasses used mainly to hold her hair, bulky Swiss watch and large diamond studs she was epitome of a businesswoman, but she sounded less confident than Pamela who had clearly enjoyed the attention and her TV murder-mystery debut. She was repeating the same story over and over again just using different words. "When we met, Selina suggested that Leona committed suicide. I obviously don't know but maybe she changed her tactics later because everybody was so sceptical about Leona killing herself. I've heard a lot of people saying that she asked for the ransom money just to buy herself some time to hide the body. I don't know, but it makes sense. I wouldn't think she threw the body into the lake as it would be too obvious and sooner or later the search team would find it and be able to tell that it wasn't suicide..."

"Were you surprised when you heard that Selina wrote a book in which she killed her mother-in-law by hiring a hitman?"

I took off one of my shoes and aimed it at the TV screen, "It's a book, pure fiction for god's sake! The fact I wrote it in the first person doesn't mean it's about me!"

"We don't have time to shop for a new TV," James said taking the shoe away from me and throwing it to the other end of the room. "People normally think authors mostly draw on their real-life experiences. I read somewhere that it's especially the case for younger female authors."

I grabbed my hair and groaned, feeling so powerless – it was like I was watching a skyscraper about to collapse on me and I had nowhere to go.

"From what I know, Selina had a very complicated relationship with her mother-in-law. There was a lot of tension between them. Once..." she hesitated. "Yes, there was a lot of tension between them."

"Mrs Lentil, the more information the police have, the more likely there will be justice for Leona."

Patricia took a deep breath and stood for a long moment thinking. The TV correspondent didn't look even a bit uncomfortable. He was patiently waiting. Just when I thought Patricia was about to faint, she said, "One night Leona called me crying, she had an argument with Selina. The very next day I suggested skype with a glass of wine. She reluctantly agreed. She tried to hide her hand that was in plaster, and when I asked what had happened, she said she tripped on the driveway the day before. I knew she was lying."

"Interesting," Bloom was nodding, encouraging her to talk more. Obviously, he didn't want to be the one who spread fake news about Selina Woodhouse, the wife of a US senator beating up her mother-in-law. *But would it be fake news?* I kept asking myself. I wouldn't be surprised to hear Selina lost her temper and pushed her mother-in-law without any intention of hurting her.

"I wouldn't like to misconstrue. Leona was lying but there might be many reasons why she decided not to tell me the truth. Do I think Selina could kill her? I don't know. Do I think the girl is troubled? Yes, I think so. She was brought up by a single mother, an egocentric artist. Apparently, when Selina was in primary school, she wrote a short story about her music teacher. It happened just after the teacher said in front of the whole classroom that Selina didn't have ears for music. In her story the teacher goes on a cruise, and the ship gets kidnapped by pirates. Actually, she's the only person who gets kidnapped. The pirates heard about her music talent, and they wanted her to teach their children to sing in tune. She spends the rest of her life trapped on the pirates' island teaching them singing, while they've got no music gift whatsoever and..."

"You seem to remember the story in such great detail," Bloom said smirking. "How did Mrs Leona Woodhouse find out about it?"

"Her son told her."

"Hmm... Don't you think it could cause some tension? A son telling his mother too much about his wife?" Bloom asked, the smirk wasn't going anywhere from his smug face. During the last few weeks I watched enough news to know this particular channel had become very anti-Leo-Woodhouse.

"At the time he probably found the story amusing," Patricia shrugged dismissively.

"You talked a lot with Mrs Woodhouse about her daughter-in-law?"

"Leona needed to talk to somebody," Patricia said proudly. "She didn't know how to handle Selina, she asked me for advice. As I said, the girl was troubled. If you want to know my opinion, Selina couldn't get pregnant. She couldn't get her chick-lits published and she took it all out on Leona, who happened to be the closest person around."

"I thought Mrs Selina Woodhouse wrote a crime novel," Bloom added, "and she hasn't sent this particular book to any agents yet."

"Oh yeah, a crime chick-lit," she said, and they put her on mute. Even the anti-Woodhouse channel thought it was enough.

"For those who joined us just now, Selina Woodhouse, the wife of senator Leo Woodhouse, is still missing and is now the prime suspect in the murder of her mother-in-law, Leona Woodhouse. Selina Woodhouse wrote a book about killing her mother-in-law, which she completed only a couple of weeks before her own mother-in-law went missing. Here's special live news... If you can provide us with any more information on this case, please call the number... or contact the police directly by dialling... We'll be back right after the commercials. Don't go anywhere."

The adverts lasted twenty-five minutes and I bet the channel was making a fortune on them. Selina's novel was making other people rich!

"This is crazy! Is this real?" I squeaked.

"They've got nothing, absolutely nothing. They found out about the book, and they latched onto it like a hungry baby to a big milky boob. Suddenly they've got something to exist for. The senator's wife killed her mother-in-law. It's brilliantly shocking, filmy and going to attract huge viewership. It has the potential to bring back newspapers on the edge of bankruptcy to life. People will click the shit out of this on the Internet."

"Thanks! That's exactly what I wanted to achieve with my book."

"No! All I'm trying to say is that we need to give them another story. They don't care what boob they're sucking on, as long as it gives them some milk!"

"What are you suggesting then?" I asked and let my body collapse on the bed with my hands resting above my head.

"Welcome back after the adverts. For those who are just joining us..."

"Oh, no..." I murmured, covering my face with my hands.

"No member of the Woodhouse family has agreed to speak to us yet. Senator Leo Woodhouse said that they are in mourning and too shocked to speak to the media just yet..."

"No fucking kidding! They don't speak to you, eh?" I raised myself again to the sitting position. Maybe because two members of the family are already on the run?" Wait, Leo has no way of speaking to me. I've totally forgotten that you threw my phone away!"

"We also haven't managed to contact Selina Woodhouse's mother. As one of her neighbours revealed to us – she went on a spiritual trip to Asia six weeks ago and there's no reception where she is."

"Good for her, but it only supports the point of the egocentric mother."

I threw myself back on the bed, my hands above my head, eyes closed and legs dangling above the floor. My heart was going at a hundred miles an hour and beating as loud as a drum kit. I suddenly imagined going back to Heaven, or rather the pre-Heaven place to hear that I had failed my mission, and the real Selina was going to take it from here. *But what's going to happen with me?* I was screaming terrified.

The whole bed started falling – it was going faster and faster, my body getting heavier, my belly pressed against my back and wind blowing my hair in all possible directions. The bed was a vehicle that took me back to Lily's body. I felt a warm breath on my face and Nathaniel's soft lips gently touching mine.

"You can't imagine how happy I am to be here, home..." I whispered and opened my eyes to see James' face. His eyes were closed, lips lightly open, both hands touching mine. I did nothing to stop him. It was like the walk of shame when you are making another trip to the fridge to pick up a piece of cheddar, but you're supposed to be on a diet. It was like binging with another episode of your favourite TV series late at night, knowing that you need to get up early in the morning. It was like jumping in a queue in front of a kid to buy the last piece of cake he also wanted. As we entered the second phase, which happened quicker than I would have intended, stripping our clothes and throwing them around the whole bedroom, less brain activity was involved, and the guilt surrendered. Stopping now would be like refusing oxygen twenty meters under water; like depriving yourself of sugar when you have hypoglycaemia; like not claiming a million-pound winning lottery ticket.

## CHAPTER 51
## *New Lily*

 **NATE TUSK IS BACK IN THE GAME**

**With the recent disappearance of Molly Sulivan, and Lily Rice on her spiritual journey to Spain, *Morgan and Tusk* might be going through a rough patch. But, for Nathaniel Tusk the moment has never been better.**

Nathaniel Tusk is a partner at *Morgan and Tusk*, the largest interior designer company in the UK and Europe, which has recently expanded its services globally. Its new branches in New York, Singapore and Dubai have already become one of the strongest players in their local markets.

Nathan holds an MBA from Harvard University and a BFA from the prestigious New York School of Interior Design. The highly educated, incredibly driven and successful businessman has also been known for years as a hot TV celebrity. His fans still remember him as one of the four judges on the *London Home Design* show, and as a venture capitalist on *Become the Next Big Fish*, an entrepreneurial reality show. However, four years ago while still at the peak of his career, he decided that spending quality time with his family was more important than fame and so he stepped back into the shadows. His co-worker Lily Rice took his place as a judge. The beautiful and talented interior designer was on the show for only one season before she was offered her own program, called *The Art of Design with Lily Rice*. Now, three years and five TV awards later, Lily herself needs some quiet time. While she's living her dream renovating properties on the Costa del Sol, Nate Tusk is stepping into her shoes to lead *The Art of Design with Nate Tusk*.

In his most recent interview for *A Man of Success* magazine he said that his early forties feel like the best time of his life. It's not only his career that's drastically accelerated. He's having a second honeymoon with his wife. They recently came back from a holiday in the Maldives and announced they're expecting their third child. To enable the family to stay close together, the couple has bought a six-bedroom riverside apartment in London, located just a few-minutes' walk from his TV studio and the office.

"Each time I read it – and I've done it like twenty times – it strikes me how the principal adjective used to describe me is *beautiful*. Am I not highly educated and successful? Am I not driven?" I asked, not expecting any answer and stuffed my face with a few green olives. Still munching them, but with a grimaced face, as they were filled with chili peppers, I grabbed a piece of bread and dipped it in olive oil. Normally a stressful situation would tighten my stomach to the point I wouldn't be able to digest anything other than water, but this time I needed to keep eating not to throw up.

Nate was giving me a merciful look from behind a table covered with a white cloth. A jar of Sangria placed in the middle was already nearly empty. When I accepted his invitation for lunch in Marbella, he sounded surprised. If he expected me to decline, at least I won by making him disappointed. Why would I save him an explanation? And what did I have to lose? The real Lily would probably forever shut the door to her heart for him, but I had the luxury of being emotionally detached and was able to listen to my head, at least most of the time. He was wearing a white linen shirt with long rolled sleeves, the first few buttons undone more for effect than because of negligence. His right hand combed his bushy hair – some would say he could use a haircut, I thought they were perfect in their messy imperfection. *Use your reason!* I chastised myself in my head as our vegetarian pizzas arrived. Nate grabbed a steak knife and a fork, but only to hold them vertically like he was waiting impatiently for food. "You can't blame me for it," he laughed, looking confident and empowered. There was no trace of the guilty puppy eyes he'd used to play me in my house. "And a woman wrote it... Lily?"

"Yes Nathan?" I said more sensually than I intended to.

"You still haven't asked me whether the holiday and buying the house with my wife are true."

"Correct," I gave him a fake smile. "I also haven't said the B word."

"You mean the..." he was looking at me in anticipation.

"Yes, the baby!" I shouted. "You're going to be a father again!"

Our waiter rushed to us with congratulations. Then he glanced at my half empty glass of Sangria and the smile left his face, "Do you know that Sangria is actually an alcoholic drink? It might taste like juice but it's wine."

"It's not me who's pregnant, it's his wife," I said with a forced grin. Nate looked tense, his confidence was evaporating with every sentence I uttered. That brought me some satisfaction. "I've been having an affair with him for a couple of years. Now he's had a vasectomy, so I can't even make him marry me by getting pregnant..."

"Lily, you've had enough Sangria. People are staring at us."

The waiter left with an apologetic smile.

"Wouldn't it be easier if we were just honest with ourselves and other people? We would save so much precious time... Why would I ask you about the house and the Maldives if I knew the answer?" I knew it was true, I saw him and his wife on her Instagram – but I wasn't going to tell him that – them sipping wine, having a romantic dinner and couple massages in an overwater bungalow, them getting the key to their London penthouse.

"So, you know it's not true? I thought you... never mind."

"Why would you lie to me?"

"I'm not... sorry I'm confused now. I assumed—"

"That I've seen the photos on her social media?" Now he looked genuinely confused and stunned. "Then you thought that maybe I didn't..."

"She faked them. It's just photoshop. The Maldives is all photoshop. I bought the apartment as an investment. You inspired me," he cleared his throat.

"And how *fake* is the baby?"

He took a deep breath and blew out his cheeks, "Look... That's what I've been trying to tell you this whole time, but you didn't want to listen to me... and then I just didn't have the courage. I'm a coward, Lily..." he said flatly without a trace of guilt. "I had the vasectomy because I didn't want her to try to keep me with baby number four."

"Didn't you say you hadn't slept together for months?"

"I did it to keep up appearances... not to instil suspicions in her... right? I thought she was on the pill for medical reasons."

"Well, at least now when our affair is over, we can keep working together. I clasped my hands, "After all we seem to make a great team and we can have a civilized relationship."

"What? No... I mean I don't want it to be over. I'm still separated with my wife. But... I also don't want to go to the media with it right now, it would totally affect my image... not when Molly is still missing... Oh, I heard that your lawyer, Alice..."

"Ally, her name is Ally."

"Ally successfully proved that the laptop you allegedly took from Susana is a standard company laptop and there's absolutely no evidence it was hers."

"I know, but thanks for sharing."

"But I still think it's a good idea that you stay here for a bit longer. The board agreed to extend your unpaid health leave for another two to three months."

"Oh, so now I'm on unpaid health leave," I laughed. "I thought the board froze my salary... And health leave is always paid!"

He gasped, "Technically they froze your salary until further notice, but I didn't want it to sound like that. Let's not focus on actual terms. They're just words. Treat it like a long-deserved health leave..." he said with such enthusiasm that I felt he expected me to thank him.

"I'll leave this to Ally. I'm not in a rush to go back, but I can't be suspended forever... I can't believe this is lawful. Molly was the one who bullied me, and you and Susana knew about it. And, quite frankly, I don't give a fuck what happened to her. Whatever has gone on, it has nothing to do with me. If anything, I'm a scapegoat here."

"I know, I know..." he was moving his arms up and down, before resting his elbows on the table. He didn't like what I said – more, it triggered in him worry that his face couldn't hide. "I promise you I'll work on the other members of the board. I know how to deal with them. Roger owes me a favour. But I need some proof you're trying to get better. Could you look for a therapist here? I've already checked, and they've got a few brilliant psychologists who speaks English. Actually some of them are English... You wouldn't believe how many English people live in Marbella... Why would you buy a house in Torremolinos, not here? There's such a lovely community here in Marbella... I know that your Spanish is good but..." the words were flowing out of him like a waterfall.

"Stop!"

"Lily, there's something you should also know. There's this rumour now circulating in the office, and soon it will spread to the city... hopefully not any further," he cleared his throat. "Some people think that Molly ran away because she found out about my wife being pregnant."

"Did you sleep with her too?"

*You son of a bitch!*

"Yes... I mean no... not now... you knew I dated her years ago. It lasted only a few months, but somebody in the office found out and now is spreading the stupid rumour. Pretty much everybody knew I had an affair, but not many know it was you. Actually… only Susana suspected you. It's better they talk about Molly than you but… well, it would be easier if she was here. Alive."

I nodded and started eating my pizza. *So now, you might become a suspect, I thought with satisfaction.* Karma? I didn't believe he would hurt Molly, but I was glad to know I was possibly no longer suspect number one with the most compelling motive.

"Well, I hope they don't suspend you on my show…Sorry, your show," I said, trying to suppress a giggle. "That would be a shame. The pay is unbelievable, and now more than ever you're going to need money. Baby number three. The penthouse."

Nate's face lost all colour, looking paler than ever. Or, maybe it was the sun shining higher? *So finally, you're not going to have the best time of your life, while ruining mine and stealing the show.*

"How's the pizza?" the same waiter approached our table. I bet he couldn't wait for us to leave. What if I wanted to share more revelations with him from my secret love life?

"Very good, thank you."

"Delicious. We'll definitely come back. Best pizza in Marbella," Nathaniel said with exaggerated enthusiasm. It was a good pizza, but nothing extraordinary.

When the waiter was gone, Nate grabbed his phone and started typing. Obviously, he wasn't in the mood to continue our discussion and he couldn't make it any clearer.

I realised in that moment he had nothing valuable to tell me and I had enough of this charade. "Do you need to be somewhere else soon? I don't want to keep you any longer if you're busy."

"No," he snapped. "The only reason I'm here is for YOU." He put the phone on the table. "I've been checking reviews of the restaurant. Four and a half stars. I'm thinking two stars. Some veg on my pizza are undercooked, and some overcooked. The base is also too thick for my taste."

"Oh, but you said… never mind."

## CHAPTER 52
## New Selina

I woke up to the ring of James' phone. I was lying with my eyes shut, eyelids glued to my eyeballs, and brain operating in the slowest possible mode. "Shouldn't it go to voicemail by now?" I moaned, while rolling from my right side onto my back, stretching my arm to the left and feeling only soft crisped sheet under my hand. Reluctantly I raised myself to a sitting position and reached for the phone that was getting apoplectic on a bedside table. "Who the hell is Lilliam?" I shouted. "Seven here..." I yawned. "In the Hamptons it's two in the morning!"

"She lives in LA," I heard a voice coming from behind the door just before it was flung wide open from James' kick. He was holding a silver tray with a mug releasing a gentle steam above two croissants and a jar of jam. "Were you shopping?" I asked, while pulling a duvet over my naked breasts. I was still uncomfortable with James seeing me naked. I had slept with a man, who was my family's enemy. The only person who my husband warned me not to sleep with. I was blowing the deal of my lifetime and putting my existence on an even more unknown track – and for what? As usual for a man! Although, he had some undeniably positive qualities, like helping me hide from the police after I was accused of killing my mother-in-law. Priceless. Not every man would do it for me.

"I found some frozen croissants in the fridge and a working toaster," he said.

"Nice," I mumbled with my mouth already full of croissant. Sex always made me hungry – so the more sex I had, the more I had to go to the gym to keep my weight off.

The phone rang again. James pressed decline, "Lilliam is my mother's younger sister, who lives in California."

"She's your aunt then," I said with doubt in my voice as I needed to double check that Lilliam wasn't his girlfriend or fiancée.

He nodded with a smile, probably reading my mind, "Anyway, where is the remote?" he looked around the room, suddenly leapt out of the bed and started picking up our clothes from the floor. "Ha!" he exclaimed finding the remote under his boxer shorts.

I was glad that I chomped my croissants before he switched on the TV – I knew the moment they start talking about Selina Woodhouse as a potential psycho killer, who broadly documented murdering her mother-in-law in her yet-unpublished-book, I wouldn't be able to digest anything.

"I've already forgotten it's the middle of the night in D.C." James said and switched off the news – they were repeating what we already knew about me.

"What are we going to do?"

"Well, you can call me your boyfriend now," he said, then sat on the bed and planted a kiss on my lips.

"I wasn't talking about that," I smiled, gently pushing him away to take a sip of coffee."

"I've checked for Diego gyms on the Costa del Sol, and I found out that the closest ones are in Marbella and Puerto Banus."

"Haven't we just run away from Marbella? I have absolutely no desire going back to Edward with his fake gun and very real crazy despotic mother."

"What about if we do a little make-over? Fancy dressing up?"

"Don't you think that the make-over makes us even more noticeable?" I said standing in front of a long mirror in the bedroom, examining my new look and fiddling with my freshly coloured red hair.

James was sitting on the bed, frowning his brows and scrutinizing a package of the hair dye that was supposed to make my hair chestnut brown – and it might well have done if we didn't leave it for ten minutes longer as we were going through possible scenarios to confront Diego. Would he also threaten us with the police? Would he try to stay away from the case and brush us off? Could he have any relevant information regarding Leona's disappearance?

"Hmm... I would say you look striking," he smiled flirtatiously.

"Oh, god. Is it about the boobs? It's all about the boobs, isn't it?" I looked down and realised I couldn't see my feet, James' grey T-shirt was significantly stretched forward and covering my toes. The push-up bra, which had some serious padding inside was part of a package that three hours earlier had been couriered from Antonio. The parcel, which was the size of a small washing machine, contained a portable spray tan applicator with two bottles of self-tan spray; ten tubes of hair dye so we could choose different shades of blonde, brown or ginger; several push-up bras and padding for a man's arms and thighs. I loved the branded make-up kit and multiple sets of sunglasses, but the clothes were ridiculous – we could dress up like a priest and a nun, a couple of hippies, silver street mimes (body paint was also provided), policeman and policewoman (another crime?) or some road workers wearing bright yellow vests.

"The boobs could look good in the nun outfit," he chortled, "or even better squeezed into the policewoman T-shirt."

"You're not considering wearing any of these clothes, are you?" I asked rhetorically, but when I looked at him, I realised immediately he did. "Really?" I asked high-pitched.

"You could wear the hippie dress," he suggested meekly. "I've already called the gym regarding a job and a very nice woman told me that they were just about to advertise for a yoga instructor. You look very spiritual in that dress, and I'm sure you know some yoga positions..."

"I'm sure Leona would love the floral dress. Well, certainly the

Leona I met. Not the one from the photo with Edward! I know so little about her..." I gasped, looked at James and burst into laughter. "I'm sorry but you look like a cheap version of Ken from Barbie,"

"Cheap? What do you mean?" he pouted, "Every Barbie would instantly fall in love with my biceps and curvy thighs!" He raised his right arm to me showing his silicon muscles. He made me laugh even more, now I was feeling my stomach muscles shaking. He looked hilarious. My tan was perfectly natural and streak free, which was just as advertised on its leaflet. I had light brown skin that worked very well with my red hair and deep green lenses in my eyes. James wasn't as lucky – his tan looked fake and yellowish, the brown hair didn't match his blonde eyebrows, and the biceps and enlarged thighs made him look like an off-duty superhero.

I wasn't going to mock him, all in all, he was doing it to help me. "What are you going to wear?"

"The tight silver pants and... I'm thinking that I'll keep my black top."

"The shiny silver trousers for street mime?"

"Have you seen any others?" he asked joyfully. "They'll complete my look of a man who tries hard to look good, but he somehow keeps making all the wrong choices."

"Fine, just don't say you're my partner of any kind."

"Don't make such a disgusted face," he said and showed me his tongue... tongue with a piercing!

"When? How?"

"I found it in the parcel. There are two magnets on both sides of my tongue."

"What if you accidently swallow it?"

"I'll poop it out the very same day, or max the day after. The leaflet says it's absolutely harmless."

"Okay, but please don't inform me about your pooping habits."

"I've read recently that there is one thing that good relationships have in common."

"Yeah?"

"People aren't afraid to talk about their bowel movements," he grinned.

"Delightful. I'm sure that rule only applies after you've gone through a certain number of relationship stages."

"Probably," he sighed and grabbed the TV remote.

"Oh no, please. The news is giving me IBS," I said without thinking.

"Aha! I told you! We're good!"

"No, I just feel like somebody is squeezing my intestines and making them into a plait."

"Senator Leo Woodhouse is here to talk to us about his withdrawal as a candidate for the presidency," I heard a woman's voice and my wide-open eyes wandered to the TV. I was standing with my back to the mirror, my hands along my body, fingers scratching my tights nervously, my skin was suddenly itchy everywhere.

"That can't be true!" I shouted reading again and again the breaking news from the red line at the bottom of the news channel.

"The whole country is asking today..." the woman paused for better effect, "...is it true that senator Leo Woodhouse is withdrawing?" She was wearing a white pencil skirt and a soft pink blouse which made her already pale skin look even lighter. Leo was staring at her blankly as if he hadn't heard the question. She crossed her legs, her right slim knee stretching the skirt to its limits. Then she slowly put one of her arms over the back of her blue armchair, while waiting for his answer with an inappropriately smug face. Leo was sitting calmly on a blue sofa in a morning show studio. He was looking sedated, or like somebody had pulled a plug out of his back and his battery was running on its last reserves.

"Senator Woodhouse—"

"Yes, yes, I'm sorry... To be honest I've been living in a phase of constant and utter shock since my mother went missing. I woke up today and couldn't believe she's been murdered," his voice started breaking on the last few words. "It felt like a bad nightmare – even more so now that my wife is also missing."

"Missing?" the woman's arm flew from the back of the sofa to her chest where she crossed both her arms, staring at Leo with disbelief. "I'm sorry, but don't you mean your wife is *wanted*? Not missing. I don't want our viewers to get the wrong impression."

"Last night me and my family received a phone call from the people who claimed to have kidnapped my mother. I can't say much, but we've been able to confirm that they weren't lying. And now they also have my wife hostage."

The woman opened her mouth not knowing what to say. Now she was the one in shock, completely unprepared for the bombshell he just dropped on her. For a minute the studio went so silent that we could hear the whispering voices of the TV crew.

"Emil doesn't fancy paying more tax?" James scoffed. "Is he going to launder more hostage money, this time in your name?"

"So now I'm not a killer, but a victim?" I sat down on the floor with my legs crossed. "What if I just go to the nearest police station and tell them I'm fine and have never been kidnapped?"

"Ha! That's exactly what they want you to do! It's a trap!"

"If they're the same kidnappers..." the woman was talking slowly like she was trying to gather all the information in her head to make something meaningful out of it, "you paid them a substantial amount of money and your mother was still killed."

"That's right. I wasn't ready to withdraw from the race, which was their key demand. And they had accepted significantly larger sums of money to allow my candidacy to continue. Ultimately, however, they asked me to resign, and I dragged my decision out for too long."

"Do you feel guilty?"

"Oh my god – what a bitch!" I screamed, feeling sorry for Leo, but reminding myself quickly that I wasn't kidnapped, somebody out there was lying and that somebody could be my husband.

"I think it's a trap," James said nervously. "Irrespective of what Leo does we need to follow our plan."

"Oh my god!"

"What?"

"Nothing," I said, "I just still can't believe..." I leant back against a wall and slid down to the floor. In the corner of my eye I spotted James' gun lying under the bed. I grabbed it rapidly, jumped up on my legs and aimed the pistol at James, who didn't even look particularly surprised. He silently put his hands up in an I-am-done-here and I-give-up gesture. "You're the kidnapper! Answer my question!"

"Sorry, I thought it was a statement, not a question," he put his hands up, while still sitting on the bed, but now with his back hunched and looking at me like a lost puppy.

"You tricked me, you used me to destroy the family! You kidnapped me! What else have you been planning to do to hurt the Woodhouses? I bet you know exactly where Leona is and that's why you're so sure that she's alive!"

He crossed his legs and grabbed his knees with both hands, moving back and forth on the edge of the bed, confident that I wouldn't shoot him, "Wasn't it you who dragged me all the way here to find Leona's high-school sweetheart?"

"I bet it was part of your plan – you somehow tricked me into thinking that it was my idea, while you were slowly guiding me to make certain decisions."

"Do you have any proof? Your theory wouldn't stand up in court," he said calmly.

"Apart from the fact that you've been spying on all of us?"

"Again, you've got no evidence."

"I don't need any!" I waved the gun and again he put his hands up, but this time he did it much slower and the hands stopped at the high of his shoulders.

"Fine, go to the police then. As soon as you get there, you'll find out it's a trap and they're going to arrest you."

"I won't let you mess with my head anymore. Even if it was a trap, I'm completely innocent. I know that!"

"YOU know that you're completely innocent," he laughed. "Well done that you didn't kill your mother-in-law while high on wine and cocaine." I must have looked like I was seriously considering the possibility – which I actually did – because after a long moment of silence he added, "God, if there is a chance you did it, then shoot me because when they find me, I'll spend the rest of my life in jail for collaboration!"

"Get dressed, we're going to the nearest police station." My voice wasn't as decisive as I thought because he didn't move an inch and you-are-not-serious was painted all over his face.

"Fine, but before we go anywhere, let me explain something."

## CHAPTER 53
## New Lily

"Why do you ask for my advice if you're not even going to consider it?" Gabriel asked amused. He was sitting with his legs crossed on a double sofa in my London office, sipping coffee that I'd made us in the company's kitchen a floor below – completely forgetting I had my own coffee machine next to my desk. I wondered whether the real Lily worked here at night. I would if I had an office like hers. I switched all lights off except a sidelight on a chest of drawers. I sat on a swivel chair, put my legs up and for a few minutes admired the night cityscape. St Paul's Cathedral and the Gherkin – I always loved a clash of historical and modern architecture – when well-thought out and carefully designed it could bring a dazzling effect.

Even if Lily didn't use the office late, other people in the building must have worked long hours. The security guard at the entrance wasn't even vaguely surprised when I slid my card at nine thirty in the evening. If not Morgan and Tusk, there were still three other fast-growing companies in the building. One of them was a promising start-up, which as Jane once mentioned, was employing hundreds of millennials working day and night. Apparently, the biggest traffic for them happened at five am when some were leaving – red-eyed and sleep deprived, and others were arriving – with huge aspirations and high caffeine doses flowing in their veins.

The office was wonderfully quiet and perfectly tidy, not a single dust particle on top of any mirror or painting. It smelled of pinecones and... there was a file with Steven's projects on my desk! At first, I didn't find it too weird. He might have left it here ages ago for me to have a look at and then forgot. It took me longer to realize that he had also left a couple of photos of his family. Initially, in the darkness I took them to be Emma's kids. I hadn't been in the office enough to know the contents of my drawers and shelves, but male lip balm, an electronic cigarette and a book on "Why crying is good for men", weren't likely to belong to Lily.

I suddenly reminded myself of Gabriel. He kept quiet the whole time I was lost in my thoughts. "I was just curious what you were thinking. I'm not going to do anything illegal, just look around while nobody's here. If my flight hadn't been delayed five hours, I would've looked for a hotel in the city. I was supposed to land in the early afternoon, but now it's so late. Besides, the couch you're sitting on is a sofa bed for a reason."

Gabriel smiled in disbelief, "One of your clients didn't like the sofa so you took it. Lily, you can be honest with me. You're not going to sleep here... And if you really want my advice, don't go into Susana's or Nate's office – they are the only two rooms on the floor with CCTV..."

"I guess I've been lying to myself. When I saw Nate, I felt like something was off and I needed to get here as soon as possible."

"Well, he shouldn't have shown his fake side to you by lying to the waiter about the food, and then posting that nasty review," he laughed.

"Yeah, it made me think... and it turns out I was right. First, he steals my show. Then Steven takes my office."

"Let's not draw conclusions too quickly," Gabriel raised his right hand and started vividly gesticulating, his elbow still resting on the sofa's armrest. "He might be using it now because his office has termites. You wouldn't believe how often something looks like one thing, and it's actually something completely different." Gabriel was dressed like he had copied my style. He wore a light blue tracksuit and white trainers, while I was wearing dusky pink joggers and a matching zipped hoodie. I bought the outfit at the airport, tired of wearing tight smart clothes and tired of waiting for my plane.

"Fine... I mean it's not fine, but I must choose my battles... Hold on. What's that sound?"

"Which sound?"

"Aren't you supposed to hear more than me?"

"I can't see through the walls and..."

"Shhh..." I pressed my finger to my lips, sliding quietly to the door in my new cashmere socks, a recent airport treasure.

Bizarrely the office door was made of solid wood that muted sounds from outside, but the walls were so thin I could hear Nate and Steven practically whispering. I pressed my left cheek to the wall, in the corner of my eye seeing Gabriel frowning his eyebrows and stretching his neck towards the door. Could he hear anything? Certainly, he was making the impression he could. I wondered what superpowers he had as he was always cagey about revealing them to me, as if I could use the information against him.

"Mate..." Steven was speaking loudly, his voice getting more high-pitched and irritated, "do you really think Susana had something to do with Molly's disappearance? That's just insane."

I didn't hear any answer, so I looked at Gabriel, but his face was telling me a big fat nothing. I desperately wanted to be invisible, open the door and see what was happening. It really wouldn't hurt them to give me one – just one – superpower of my choice! It would be nothing when compared to switching bodies! *Are they still here? Have they just arrived and they're now in Nate's office? Or were they heading to the lift, and walking past this office?*

"Steven..." Nate gasped, and my heartbeat accelerated. "My head is telling me that Susana *probably* wasn't involved. But my heart... I just feel it in my bones... and the feeling won't disappear, it's haunting me... Every time I look at her, I'm convinced she got rid of Molly, the woman never confronts problems. She prefers to get rid of people than deal with them when they get difficult to handle."

"That's great material for a leader," Steven laughed.

"Well, on the bright side we might get rid of her soon, and you would become my only partner," Nate said cheerfully. "Tusk and

Dunkin, or Dunkin and Tusk... Sounds a bit less posh than Morgan and Tusk. Have you thought about using your wife's surname? She comes from nobility, doesn't she?"

Laughter. Louder laughter. Blowing a nose. Laughter again. Clinking glasses. Loud slurp. Clearing a throat.

*The son of a bitch!*

*The sons of bitches.*

"The only person I feel sorry about is Lily," Steven broke the unbearable combo of sounds, produced by two tipsy men and their glasses full of whatever-they-were-consuming.

"I know, buddy. I know. But no matter how much I try to defend her, this one is on her. I begged her not to go to the meeting. She was unusually agitated the whole time, kept talking nervously about some pills she couldn't find. She told me she hadn't slept for a few nights. I tried to convince her to just leave. Go home. Go to bed. Lily please just take a break. Take some leave. I was begging her... but there was nothing I could do beyond physically stopping her from going through that door. Now, I think I should've done it. She ruined her chance to be partner in the foreseeable future, and I can't do anything about it."

"Hey, that's not your fault. You can't blame yourself. She's an exceptionally talented designer, but also a very moody one. If it's true what they say about artists being insane, she's always been on the edge... I mean, she's not completely crazy," he said defensively like he suddenly realized he was talking about Nate's lover – the Nate who was also offering him a partnership.

Something is pouring. Deep breaths. Tapping on a back? Shoulders?

"She's been on edge recently... but she's not always like that. Lily is a perfectionist. She's always got a very clear vision, hates compromises and once she makes up her mind, nobody is able to talk her out of it."

"You and her... Are you still..." Steven couldn't be such a buddy-buddy with Nate if he was chickening out about asking about me.

"I'm working on it," he sighed, "but so is my wife. So as you can expect it's not going well."

"Yeah, I've read the news... I can't believe she went to the press to save your marriage. Why does she even want to be with you?" Steven laughed, but Nate stayed quiet. *Whatever you're drinking Steve, you should stop before you talk Nate out of that partnership.* "But, what will we do with Susana? What if she's completely innocent when it comes to Molly? We need to find a way to get rid of that woman."

"Well, there will be two of us against her. Besides, she won't blackmail you anymore. Her only leverage against you was preventing you making partner."

"Are you serious? If she stays, I don't want to be a part of this. Look, what happened to Lily. She completely lost it. Everybody is saying she's having the time of her life, but I'm pretty convinced she's going through a nervous breakdown. And Molly? I bet she lost it too, ran away and she's the one demanding the ransom. Enough! Enough sweeping all the problems under the carpet. As soon as I become partner, we can build a lawsuit against her. She needs to pay for what she's done."

"Oh Steve, good but naive Steve... Susana's husband is a lawyer. Her brother is a lawyer. Her father is a judge. Not to mention how rich her whole family is and their considerable connections. I'm not going to ruin my life over one stupid bitch."

"So will we just let her sexually harass other men in the company?"

My heartbeat got louder, getting in the way of what I could hear. Luckily for me, Nate also got louder. Much louder.

"You and I managed to protect ourselves. Every strong man will, and if not... well, maybe they aren't destined for success. I'm not going to start another MeToo movement. I don't need that sort of fame..."

"Okay mate, chill. Do whatever you want. I won't ask you to testify against her, but when I'm a boss nobody is going to be harassed by Susana or anyone else."

## CHAPTER 54
## New Selina

"I don't mind that you're holding the gun, but could you please not point it right at my face?" James smiled forcefully. My hands didn't move an inch – as if my body was telling me he was dangerous, and I needed to stay focused. "No? I'm not going to convince you?" he said, the smile not leaving his face, but the voice stuck in his throat. I sat down on a chair, which was resting against one of the walls in the bedroom. Now I was aiming the gun at his knees. "Thank you. That feels much better... So where was I?"

"Are you taking the piss?" I asked annoyed and he shook his head with a serious face expression. "Because it very much looks like you're buying yourself some time and you don't really know what to say."

James fixed his eyes on the floor, his tongue making circles on the inside of his left cheek, his right knee moving up and down in a nervous tick. He took a couple of deep breaths and, looked at me like a wounded animal before saying something that I kept hearing constantly in my head for the next few days – the one short sentence became a dripping tap, drilling a hole in my brain, "Leona Woodhouse is my mother."

I dropped the gun and glanced terrified at him. It took me a few seconds to pull myself together. He had a chance to throw himself on the floor and get hold of the pistol, but – for one reason or another – he didn't. I picked up the gun, looked at him and got the overwhelming feeling he was telling me the truth.

I had hundreds of questions to ask him, but they were going through my head like tornados – before I managed to notice one, another was appearing and hitting me with even greater strength. "Keep talking," I whispered through my squeezed throat.

"Leona got pregnant the same month as Edward's secret girlfriend. I don't know whether the local shops ran out of condoms, or he ate something special. Or! He was just carefree and made two children with two different women at practically the same time."

"So, while the world was excited with fifty-year-old Hugh Grant impregnating his two girlfriends within three or four months, nobody knew that Edward Hasting had already done the Hugh Grant act in high-school," I said still feeling flabbergasted and overwhelmed with the news – each time I thought about Leona being James' mother I felt like I was getting electrocuted.

He smiled faintly, "Hugh Grant married one of his girlfriends, and bought them houses next to each other. Not that it would be sensible or even feasible for Edward to do the same at the time, no happy ending here, at least not for some. He's in touch with his daughter, but he still doesn't even know I exist."

"I sort of worked that out. Was the first time you saw him with me?" He nodded. "And during that time, he threatened you with a fake gun, and you threw the table at him."

"That's correct."

"Why didn't Leona tell him about you?"

"The pregnancy was the reason Leona's mother forced her to go back to the US. She hoped her daughter would have an abortion. Sophia knew Leona was pregnant, but she didn't tell Edward. It was enough one of his girlfriends was pregnant and wanted to keep her baby."

"Jesus! Leona and Edward were young, but they weren't children either."

"My mother..." he paused, "my biological mother was terrified and believed that she would never be good enough for the Hasting's family – while the truth was the Hastings weren't good enough for her."

"It sounds like you're defending her, but at the same time you're calling her your biological mother... so..."

"She gave me up for adoption."

"I'm sorry."

"Don't be. I got loving parents who gave me a great childhood and plenty of possibilities. I didn't need Leona."

"Then what brings you here James?" I asked and noticed his bottom lip was lightly trembling – he couldn't stop it, so he finally bit it and stayed like this for a while. I patiently waited because the last thing I wanted to give him were some guiding questions – there was still a chance he was lying.

"When a couple of years ago my mum died, I was devastated. Nothing was going to fill the gap after she was gone. That was when – for the first time – I thought about looking for my biological mother. Many people in my situation want to know earlier, but I was of an opinion that she didn't want me, gave up on me and there was no reason to upset my parents who gave me so much."

"I get it," I nodded. "How did you find her?"

"I knew the name of the adoption centre that my parents used. I didn't have much hope that my biological mother was even alive, let alone had any desire to meet me, but I decided to give it a go. It turned out that Leona left her details for me three years after she gave me up to my family in California. She updated the details every time she moved or changed phone number."

"Three years, isn't that when Leo was born?"

"Exactly."

"I could never give up... I'm sorry... I'm not here to judge anybody," I said, while judging Leona for being so judgy when she was the one who gave her son up for adoption!

"I couldn't give away my child either, but I forgave her. I only had one mother, but Leona gave birth to me and I owe her that."

*Well, it was the least she could have done*! I was still judging her, but well, I never liked the woman!

"Did you move to the Hamptons for her?"

"I always wanted to experience living in New York and had no problems transferring to my company's office in Manhattan. But I missed the coastal lifestyle, so I got the second house in the Hamptons. Those were the times when I could still easily afford it..." he sighed. "When I had to suspend my career and choose just one place, I rented out the New York apartment."

"And luck had it, Leo was your neighbour!" I clasped my hands.

"I tried to kill two birds with one stone. If not three. Leona, New York and... my previous..." he cleared his throat, "previous girlfriend lived in New York."

"What about Emil and the rest of the family? Do they know who you really are?"

He took a deep breath, and said reluctantly, "Emil knows."

"And still despite the fact—"

"He made Leona do DNA tests at four different clinics. Two is sensible, four is ridiculous. He claimed I was after their family's fortune, while he knew I was earning very good money, and my family run a successful software company in LA. He hated me from the very beginning. I ruined the idea of the Woodhouses as a flawless American family."

"Yeah, I bet the media and the political opposition would be thrilled knowing that Emil Woodhouse's wife gave her first child up for adoption. Then they would find out about Edward and his turbulent love life."

James nodded, "When we finally reconnected, Leona wanted to tell everybody I was her son, but I was less bothered. All I ever wanted was to get to know her."

"So, Emil going after you was a more personal vendetta than strictly professional."

"Both. I've been a massive inconvenience in his life – the biggest pain in his arse. But, I didn't want to be the reason her marriage collapsed..." he hunched his back, his legs moving, his heels hitting the bed and creating a dull noise. Suddenly he looked more relaxed, like he couldn't see the gun anymore that I was still pointing at his legs. "But she told me later that her marriage had been broken for years and they had many other disagreements."

"Like Leo..." I was thinking out loud. "Leo."

"What about Leo?"

"Seriously? You've said my marriage was a sham. How did you find out? You mentioned Claudia telling your mother Leo was gay... But obviously, you were lying..."

"Not exactly. We have the same mother and I hacked Leona's mobile."

"She knew?" James nodded. "She knew I was his cover-up. She knew it all along and just like that, let him get away with it? Oh dear god! Don't tell me she was the one who made him hide his sexuality. It actually sounds like Leona."

"I didn't have a chance to dig that deep. I got most of the info from my PI. Leona somehow discovered I was listening to her calls and then quickly changed her mobile and started using her landline. She might've found out after you were already married. Funny..." he giggled.

"What?"

"For the first time you don't mind her interfering in your life."

"I bet she knew, and I wouldn't be surprised if it was all her idea. She must have despised me for being so blind that I didn't notice anything," I said and raised my right hand up, before realising I was still holding the gun and now waving it in the air.

James straightened up, "Whoa, whoa."

I removed the magazine from the pistol. James watched me, his eyebrows slowly raising. I had learnt from watching YouTube videos after I was told by Basil that Selina was proficient with firearms.

"What? You told me your PI found out I was a great shot."

"Yeah, of course."

"We don't need a gun in this house. If you want to kill me, you'll have to do it with bare hands or stab me with a kitchen knife, which hopefully... you're going to find too much."

He burst out laughing.

"James?" I scrutinized him. "You said that Emil blackmailed you..." He nodded. "How is it even possible when it was *you* who had the trump card?"

"He knew it would hurt Leona the most if I said something. He knew it would affect my relationship with her if I deliberately hurt Leo.

And then he's my little brother who I actually feel sorry for..." he said with shiny eyes. "And then—"

"And then she was gone," I whispered.

"Also..." he hesitated, but I kept looking at him in anticipation until he started talking again. "I couldn't use the information because you would never forgive me."

## CHAPTER 55
## New Lily

"Nathaniel will never divorce me. I can fill you in on all *the case* details, just depends on how much time you've got. But I've heard so much about you, and if what they say is true – you're either at work or about to go to work," she giggled. "Always in a rush," she said with satisfaction. "Oh..." she sighed, "You could have more without killing yourself at work. You could spend your days playing tennis, doing yoga classes, reading, learning Italian... If you could only marry Nathan. Just screwing him doesn't bring even half the benefits."

"I love my job, I play tennis and go to yoga classes," I snapped. This woman was more irritating that I'd imagined. Lily, the Real or New, had nothing in common with Nate's wife. Nothing but the look. Melania was a tall slim blonde with big boobs. Her face, beautiful, symmetrical and unique, must have been the dream of every modelling agency. I'd found out from Jane – my assistant was priceless – that Melania pursued her modelling career in her teens and had a chance for a huge contract in Paris. The only obstacle were her parents – a very religious and conservative couple, who would never sign the modelling contract for their underage daughter. They considered it the devil's work and treated it on par with prostitution. So, she gained a PhD degree from an

Ivy League University and did what at the time must have felt perfectly natural... She talked herself out of any job prospects, and instead used all her knowledge to make the deal of a lifetime with – her future husband. Melania had none of the qualities that Nate attributed to her: lost, overly sensitive and vulnerable. She had never needed to fake her health problems only to keep a husband – she held all the cards.

"I'm thrilled I can share our story with you. Just please, don't judge Nathaniel for being stupid. We were both young and naïve. Well, I was the young one, in my early twenties, and he was the naïve one..." she laughed, weirdly friendly, like we were friends gossiping about other people's lives over a bottle of wine. "Once upon a time he was madly in love with me..." she smiled bitterly, revealing a glimmer of vulnerability. Maybe she wasn't a sociopath after all, "...and he was prepared to do anything to marry me..."

"Did he have to murder your previous husband so you could marry him, because your family would never accept your divorce? As crazy as it sounds, it would explain a lot."

"I see Nathaniel talked to you about my conservative family. Well, marriage is for life, women like you come and go... but where was I? Oh, I won't bore you with how much he would have to pay me for every year of our marriage, and each child if he wanted to file for a divorce. I can go straight into the detail of how much he's going to lose when it comes to an at-fault divorce. I've collected enough evidence to leave no doubt in any court..." Melania was in seventh heaven. When I asked her to meet me, I didn't realise I would make her dreams come true. It was like she lived for moments like this. *Did Molly leave Nate after meeting Melania?*

She wouldn't see me anywhere in public, didn't want to hear about going to my apartment – which, I briefly forgot was still rented. She suggested her house, which suited me the most. I was curious how Nate and she lived. All I knew was that the house was in Surrey, and they owned a large amount of land that Nathaniel inherited from his great-grandfather. When I got out of my Uber I wasn't sure whether they could still call it a house. It was more like a palace. Marble pillars and a fountain at the front. A tennis court and a pool at the back. Staff tiptoeing around the lady of the manor and bringing us drinks and canapés every ten minutes. Melania was sitting on a red and gold tufted chaise, her legs slightly bent at the knee and stretched along the length of the antique furniture. She was wearing a short black faux leather skirt with no tights, red heels, and a loose white woolly jumper with its sleeves rolled to her elbows. Her image was complemented with expensive gold jewellery that on her didn't look over the top. The whole time with her I felt completely underdressed. I had on light blue jeans with a silky blouse tucked in on one side, and no shoes. I left my heels in the hallway, despite Melania's maid assuring me that I didn't need to take them off. Easier said than done. Her shiny black stilettos with red soles were way smarter than my beigy heels, which I had already made dirty.

"I'm happy for you. I would expect nothing less from a woman like you. How long did it take for your PI to collect the evidence?"

Melania smiled mercifully, "I'm not going to reveal such details… It wouldn't be wise. So, where was I? Oh, except me taking the house, the villa in France and seventy percent of our combined wealth, I would get the majority of shares that Nathaniel has in Morgan and Tusk. And I would keep them. The company does and will provide me with a steady and substantial income without any need to work. I will also have a vote. Yes, I could have a lot more say in that firm than you. *Told Ya*, marriage is a much better deal. You just have to know how to play the game."

"Wow," I whistled. "With a deal like that, are you not afraid he kills you in your sleep? Or *accidently* drive over you?"

Melania sat up straight and I realized what I had just said.

"Did you come all the way here to threaten me?"

"I'm here to tell you that Nate is trying to rebuild my trust after what you sold to the press. He doesn't want to give up on me."

She laughed out loud like a witch would before turning me into a frog and throwing me into a boiling cauldron. "Enjoy. There are many ways to screw one man. I'm just telling you mine."

## CHAPTER 56
# New Selina

"If he doesn't leave in the next fifteen minutes, I'm out," said James, while fiddling with the broken air conditioning in a rented red mini cooper. He didn't have much hope it would suddenly start working, but he needed to do something with his hands to calm his nerves. "It's so damn hot, and everything is itching me under the bloody fake biceps and thighs. The stupidest idea ever."

"You chose the outfit and the tan all by yourself," I said without looking at him. Each time I saw a bit of his face in the left corner of my eye, I couldn't stop myself from giggling, and it wasn't just a nervous laugh in anticipation of Diego leaving one of his fitness clubs. "I can't believe I slept with that."

"Let's hope that the poopy hair will wash out after a week, and the tan…" he glanced at the insides of his palms, "it's already melting. Don't let me touch anything white."

"I'll try to remember." I gasped, "Fine, fifteen minutes and we're going. This silicone push up bra and polyester dress makes me feel like I'm wrapped in plastic foil."

"Your boobs don't need any silicon. They're perfect."

I was about to say *thank you*, but suddenly I felt a pinch of jealously. I only occupied the body on a temporal basis, and Lily had bigger breasts than me. *Would he like mine too? And why would I even care?* I took a sip of water and grabbed my new mobile. Nobody knew my number so for the first time since I remembered I had no messages to read. James kept his eyes on the entrance to the club, and I tried to distract myself by scrolling through Instagram. I typed the first name that crossed my mind: *Faith Woodhouse*.

On the most recent photo she was looking strikingly beautiful and... strikingly like the new version of Leona. Faith had loose wavy blond hair thrown over her sleek naked arms and small breasts entirely hidden under a fitted black dress. She was sitting with Jeremy in front of a large table bending from ornaments that were creating a romantic atmosphere: twinkling candles in silver holders, bunches of white flowers, tree branches sprayed with gold and wrapped with little lights. The food was beautifully presented but modest: cheese, olives, grapes and crackers, all accompanied by two bottles of wine. The photo reminded me of the one with Leona and Edward, Jeremy was even dressed in a similar style to Leona's lover – grey fitted jacket with white shirt and no tie. Was I only imagining it or was there something weird about that photo?

"Are you okay?" James suddenly interrupted my contemplations.

"Yeah, sure," I said not taking my eyes away from the screen. "I'm just looking at Faith... I mean your sister. Faith is your sister," I turned my face to James, who was giving me a faint smile. Somehow, I had no problem believing that I was in somebody else's body, but I couldn't make myself believe that James was Leona's first-born.

"Yeap," he smiled. "Half-sister. Although Leona says that a child is seventy percent mother and thirty percent father so—"

"That makes me doubt the value of her boarding school education."

James stretched his neck to glance at my phone that I was holding tight in both hands. "What's so intriguing about Faith's Instagram?" I showed him the photo. "Jeremy is a nice kid."

"Oh, she said it was just sex."

"She didn't," he said disgusted.

"Don't look at me like that. I'm only repeating what your seventy-percent sister said. And what's wrong with women wanting something with no strings attached?"

"Women can't do it. No free sailing, sooner or later they're going to try and moor their boat."

"Really? How many women did you include in your research?"

"I wouldn't dare conduct such despicable research," he said with furred eyebrows, but his lips were fighting a smile. "Just read it somewhere a long time ago."

"I'm afraid I can't trust you on that matter. Men are worse at retrieving information from their long-term memory, and that's a scientific fact."

"That's also a blessing. Otherwise, men would be as miserable as women... Ha!"

"Blah, blah, blah..."

"If you really have to impersonate a five-year-old, you should also cover your ears with your hands... Are you still looking at Faith? Anyway, I think it's time to go."

"No wait, I can't look at my phone when driving, it makes me sick."

"Then at least tell me what's so fascinating about Faith's social media profile?"

"I don't know. Just a feeling. Her mother went missing, then was pronounced dead, and... Faith is acting like nothing happened."

"Maybe it's just social media. Aren't they designed so people can legally fake their lives?"

"Maybe... but I've also watched her vlog. She sounds like a professional newsreader, not like she's talking about her own mother."

"Are you suggesting my half-sister is a sociopath? Everybody reacts differently to a tragedy."

Here we go. Already offended, #BloodIsThickerThanWater. "Of course," I said dismissively, at the last moment stopping myself from saying *whatever.*

"Can we go now?"

"Give me a minute. I mean, give Diego another ten minutes. We've made such an effort to get here... I've also looked at Jeremy's profile. He has more photos with Faith than with anybody else, some aren't even on her account. Another weird thing is that Faith isn't following Jeremy, although... she did say it was just sex... But then why would she put up a photo with him from a date?"

James rolled his eyes, "Shouldn't we focus on Diego?"

"Keep your eyes on the gym, and I'll keep mine on what your family is doing."

"It's mine no more than yours. At least they recognise you—"

"As a first-degree murderer," I snapped, and immersed myself further in my research.

Since Leona went missing, Faith had advertised products and services that were unusual for a young woman on Instagram: alarm systems, home cameras, getting your loved ones chipped with a tracking device, pepper sprays, self-defence classes, life insurance including for kidnaping and... reusable tissues guaranteed to prevent a red nose and gel for swollen eyes. I felt sick to my stomach. Sociopath was the only word in my head as I clicked on a photo of Faith wrapped in a large white fluffy towel saying in red letters: *Not going to give away my best years to college*. It wasn't even the photo that caught my attention, but the sheer amount of comments she received and how emotionally involved people were in the hashtag conversation.

> lady_in_pink_1980 If you can easily afford it, why not try? Maybe you'll like it! You don't seem to have any other ideas for your life at the moment.

> the_faith_woodhouse are you suggesting I should work my butt off because I have nothing better to do? Should I do it only because I can? Only because other people are doing it? #imnotafollower #iratherbefollowed

> lady_in_pink_1980 College is more than studying. Find something that you like and you won't have to work (hard).

> J_like_Jeremy And who are you @lady_in_pink_1980? A professor terrified that less people are keen to enter studenthood?

lady_in_pink_1980 I'm just a mature woman, who is concerned when celebrities denigrate higher education. Going to university is a privilege, not an obstacle. It can only bring good into your life.

Mona_Liza_1995 It brought me a massive bill and took away three precious years of my life that I could've used getting proper job experience or running my own start-up. Education is massively overrated, nothing that you can't find on the Internet. College is a waiting room that you have to pay for instead of living! #collegeisforlosers

the_faith_woodhouse @lady_in_pink_1980 I do appreciate your advice and concern, but please respect that not everybody has to have the same plan for life. It would be boring, wouldn't it? Also, I haven't said I wouldn't go to college at all, just not now. Maybe in ten or fifteen years, when I know what life is about, and what I really want to do. It's ridiculous that we're pressured to make life changing decisions in the middle of high school. How can you know what you want to do for the rest of your life when you haven't even started living, just spent your entire time at school?

lady_in_pink_1980 @the_faith_woodhouse Allow yourself to make mistakes. Anything that you learn can turn out to be useful when you least expect it. It can only add to your life. #Your body is what you eat, your brain is what you read. You're the sum of your experiences and the knowledge that you've got; the conversations you've had and books that you've read; you're what you believe in and what you pursue. Stay true to yourself and don't be afraid. You can always change your route later. Just keep moving forward.

"Ha! It's him!" James shouted making me jump.

"It's who?"

"Diego! Get out of the car before we miss him. He's walking to his Porsche."

"Actually," I took a deep breath, "I've changed my mind."

"You've got to be kidding me. You absolutely haven't! Not now after I spent nearly two hours in this outfit."

"Trust me. We've got more important fish to fry."

## CHAPTER 57
## New Lily

Gabriel decreased the speed on his running machine to a fast walk. He was still breathing heavily and steaming the glass in the room, while his face and neck placed in my mind the vision of a red lobster. I stretched out from my stationary bike to reach a towel from a pile lying on a chest of drawers on my right side. I bet Emma and Bob's housekeeper put them there. I didn't believe for a second that either of these busy doctors would care enough to put white and blue towels interchangeably, completing the marine atmosphere of their home gym. The whole room, in a basement of a traditional envy-worthy terraced home in Oxford, looked so perfectly designed that I wondered whether the real Lily had something to do with it. I particularly loved an exotic aquarium taking most of the front wall and some tropical plants in the corners.

"Here you are, yours is blue. Don't flood the floor."

Gabriel made a face, "I air dry very quickly. The towels smell intensely of some artificial sea breeze, and I've got delicate skin."

"Really?" I looked at him surprised, and my right foot fell out of the pedal.

He nodded. "Will you finally tell me why you went to Melania?

Instead of whining for an hour about how ungrateful she was?" he chuckled. "Just be honest with me. What did you expect to achieve?"

"I wanted her to know that I wasn't interested in Nate anymore and I was on her side. He's lying to us both. It's like he hates all women and I wonder whether it has something to do with Susana harassing him."

"Are you sure it's nothing to do with you wanting revenge? He took the show away from you and offered Steven the partnership. And if that's not enough, he betrayed you with his wife – ridiculous as it sounds, it's how you feel."

"He seems to get away with everything he's doing. Both Melania and I..." I said and it struck me how much I felt this life was already mine, "we finally need to set ourselves free from this manipulator and I don't know why it's so difficult. I thought that if we *worked* together, it would be easier."

Gabriel giggled, "Yeah, you could exchange dirt over a glass of wine. She could spill out some secrets that you could use against him to get your show or partnership offer back. Or you could get out of the job without paying a whooping million pounds. What's in it for her?"

"I could testify I had an affair with Nate so she could easily get the divorce money... She laughed when I said it, but I could see in her eyes that she was considering my offer. The problem is she didn't trust me, and I can't even blame her."

"You know you don't have to play dirty? The ends don't always justify the means."

"What's dirty in telling the truth?"

"Nothing yet. It's all about how you intend to use *the Other Truths* you get from people who are close to Nathaniel. Every stick has two ends, and you're angry now."

---

"Beautiful pad. Another investment?" Steven smirked.

"It's my sister's. I'm only staying here for a few days."

"Oh, great! Spain is a long-term project." There was relief painted all over his face. I bet he was thinking I was going to make problems about his partnership. Jane did all the numbers for me and over the last five years I brought the company six times as much revenue as Steven, but somehow he was the more suitable candidate for promotion. All he did was keep himself in check when Susana sexually harassed him and told no one, while Lily lost her temper with Molly. *Blessed* and *Promoted* will be those who can keep their mouths and eyes shut to the Evil of this World. Although, I admit that Lily could have expressed her anger in a more civilized way.

He sat down on a bar stool and rested his elbows on the granite island. The sun was coming through three Velux windows that took half of the kitchen roof. That part of the house looked like a brand-new extension. I couldn't help thinking about designs, part of the real Lily was rubbing off on my soul.

"That depends on many factors. Steven I'll be honest with you—"

"Lily..." he stopped me with an open palm, and his smiley face had this pregnant woman's glow or the sparkle that you can see on a man who has just met the woman of his life. A flow of fresh anger hit my body making me feel hot all over. He and Nate were taking what's mine and enjoying their undeserved success without even a pinch of guilt. "When we met last time. I know you were messing with me," he laughed.

"What?"

"You wouldn't tell my wife about our kiss."

At first I didn't realise what he was talking about, but then suddenly it hit me. When I saw him for the first time as the new Lily, I took him for Nate! I had that whole conversation with him about going public with our relationship. I recalled his face expression and it made me laugh. "No, not really."

"We made a mistake, and nobody has to know about it."

"Of course," I said softly.

Steven wasn't a partner yet, but something had already changed in him. He'd bought himself a new designer suit. I noticed he'd forgotten to cut a label from his trousers. He looked relaxed, confident and proud. The world was his oyster. *No, not quite yet.*

"Let's leave our personal lives alone, and talk business," his face was slowly losing the glow as I was speaking – calmly and confidently, "A couple of nights ago I slept in my office ... But is it really still my office?"

"Oh, oh... about that. You've seen my stuff. I'm sorry. There was a leak in my office and Susana moved me to your desk. I can assure you, that's a very temporary solution," he laughed nervously.

"Susana... hmmm... So, she doesn't know yet that it's her office you're after."

Steven looked at me terrified, "What?"

"The night I slept in the office, I had the pleasure of hearing you and Nathaniel. I recorded the whole conversation."

He swallowed hard. His confidence and pride disappeared like air from a deflating balloon. "That's fine because I have nothing to hide."

"That's wonderful and exactly what I hoped to hear when I asked you to see me. Why haven't you pressed charges against Susana? Is it because of Nate? Did he promise you the partnership if you stayed quiet?"

Steven gave me a long stare, put his palms like to prayer and pressed them against his mouth. As I was watching him, his eyes started wandering around the kitchen. He was looking for the best possible answer. He had something to hide, but I wasn't going to press and blackmail him just yet.

"You overthink stuff. I honestly don't know why I didn't do anything about Susana. I guess I was afraid of the reaction... and the fact it would be disproportionally large to any benefit I could gain. It would disturb so many people's lives and come with a certain cost."

"So, you were just afraid of her?"

He straightened on the stool and threw his hands up in the air, "What are you expecting me to say? Do I really have to defend myself? I was the victim," he shouted, flinching at the word *victim*. "I couldn't be bothered to face it. I was afraid of becoming the laughing stock. She's a beautiful woman. What was I supposed to say? I didn't want to get laid with our sexy boss to get promoted? I lost the opportunity of a lifetime because I wasn't prepared for a quickie with Sexy Susi? Every other bloke would have probably taken it."

"But not you. And not Nate..." I shouted with approval. Steven smirked. "He didn't, did he? Please tell me that he didn't."

"As far as I know he's always been faithful to you."

"Except that long-term affair with his wife," I laughed, but he wasn't amused. "There's something you're not telling me."

"Lily..." he stood up and glanced at his watch. "I've got a meeting soon. I'm sorry I can't be more help to you. I wish you all the best—"

"Sit down," I said decisively, but he didn't move. "You said you didn't want it to happen to anybody else in the company so stop pretending like it wasn't a big deal for you."

"What are you trying to achieve Lily? What does it have to do with you?"

"Everything. I was a victim too."

"We can't fix the whole world. Just focus on what's best for you and move on."

"At least we can try and fix our immediate environment," I snapped. "Just a quick reminder, I recorded your conversation with Nate. And I can still tell your wife about us, and by *us* I mean *having sex*. With my already shattered opinion, I don't have anything to lose, and who's she going to believe?"

"You are not..." he pointed his finger at me.

I jumped in front of him and pointed my finger, nearly touching his chest, "Try me." I was still wearing my gym outfit and trainers, and suddenly felt with my growing frustration and anger I could jump to the ceiling. I dreamed about a boxing ring where I could punch somebody on the face without consequences. Is this how the real Lily felt when she threw that chair at Molly? I took a few deep breaths. *I'll cycle again after he's gone.*

He put his head in his hands, his fingers making circles on his scalp like a hairdresser massaging a client during a hair wash. He walked twice around the kitchen until he bumped into the corner of a long wooden table, "Ouch! Fuck! You think you're different, while you're just like everybody else. You play the standard game – what's in it for me in somebody else's misery!"

"That's not fair."

"Okay. Fine. You want the truth. It's going to hurt! The man of your dreams, who you admire so much ..." Steven scoffed, "he slept his way to the top with Sexy Susi."

"But you said..."

"He was with Molly at the time, and she caught him red-handed walking out of Susana's room in the hotel, where we had a conference. He tried to make up some excuses, but Molly had already heard them having sex, she just didn't know it was her boss and her boyfriend."

"Oh my god!" I whispered and covered my open mouth.

"Molly was devastated. I met her at six that morning hectically packing bags into her car to drive away before facing another day of fun around people who'd betrayed her."

"I always thought Nate left her."

Steven shook his head, "She wouldn't listen to any of his lame excuses. It took her a year to realise what was really going on. She overheard Nate and Susana arguing in an underground car park. He was furious that she..." Steven cast his eyes down, "she tried to... she was also sexually harassing me..."

"Probably until then he pretended to himself that Susana really cared about him, and his promotion was inevitable."

"How is it that you've spent over two years with him and you don't really seem to know this man?" he gave me this look of disdain that was so hard to bear. I had to remind myself that at the end of the day I wasn't the same person he was talking about. I was brought to *this Life* later. "He was terrified anybody could find out how he got his partnership and a vote on the board. I knew he slept with Susana. She offered me..." he cleared his throat. "It wasn't a particularly hard puzzle to solve. At the time I wasn't close with Nate, I was more friends with Molly. If just one person spilt the beans, his reputation would suffer for eternity."

"Well, she didn't exactly force him to do anything. Was it harassment, or did they just have a deal?"

"It wasn't only about promotion. She would undermine him in front of other people and ensure he was the last person in the firm to get a new client. She did all this until he gave in."

"If you were so close with Molly—"

"I wasn't that close... it was more like we understood each other."

"Why would she hate my guts so much if she was the one who dumped Nate and wanted to have nothing to do with him?"

"She thought you were just using him to make partner."

"So, it was fine when she was dating him but—"

"Nate never told you?" I shook my head. Who knows whether he told me or not. He and the real Lily didn't seem to talk much. "Molly was with him when he separated from his wife and was renting a studio in London. When she left him, he went back to his wife. Molly could never understand why a woman like you would be with a married man who had no interest in leaving his wife. She found it suspicious."

"How about you?"

"What about me?"

"What do you think about me and Nate?"

"I don't know you that well, but I've got three sisters and plenty of girl-cousins. There are many women out there who appear strong and invincible... They get into any room and immediately make their presence felt as the Queen Bee, the Boss, the freaking God Mother – call it whatever you want. But, when they fall in love, they become vulnerable and.... Sometimes they make stupid decisions turning themselves overnight into small naive girls. They become the biggest enemies of themselves, making up excuses for all those men who don't deserve them. The men who feed their ego off a woman's strength and don't leave them until they've drained them of all their power, control and dignity."

"Wow..." I was standing agape with my hands hanging loosely either side of my body and staring at Steven. If somebody was watching us at that very moment, they would never have known that I had just blackmailed him into telling me company secrets. Suddenly, having got this burden off his chest, he became relaxed – like he had been waiting to say it for a long while and finally the moment came – he didn't have to pretend anymore. "Do you think he's already drained me of all my strength, and now it's time to get rid of me?" Steven didn't say a word. "When I threw the chair at Molly, I lost it. I let her win. Everybody saw my weakness... And it's like I deprived Nate of his power supply, so he needed to disconnect from me to survive. I'm not going to become his equal in this firm by becoming a partner. He's even taken my show. But the thing I don't understand is... why he doesn't let me go? Do I have to pay the million pounds to the company as his final victory?"

"It's not that simple. He's not all evil. The man is a narcissistic opportunist with sociopathic tendencies," Steven laughed.

"Are you sure you don't work for Morgan and Tusk as an undercover psychotherapist?"

"My parents are both psychologists, so some stuff just rubs off on you, whether you want it to or not... But about Nate..." Steven took a seat on a bar chair like he was preparing himself for a longer conversation. "When I said that you're like other people who try to take advantage of another's miseries, I also meant Molly..." he sighed. "Molly, Molly. It's always about Molly or Susana... Honestly, I hope they find her safe and sound, but since she's been gone and the police are keeping a close eye on Susana, I feel like I can breathe in the office without them scrutinizing me the whole time..."

"Okay. We were talking about Nate."

"I know, but all roads lead to Molly. If she didn't spread the rumour about you and Nathan... If she didn't tell his wife... a lot of things would be so much easier. Even if you didn't throw the damn chair at Molly, he couldn't actively participate in making you partner. People would dig into the decision and follow rumour to the truth. So, the current plan is that he and Susana will vote for me to become their partner. Then, when she goes, the board will be desperate to promote you. They want to have three partners and at least one needs to be a woman. With Molly gone, there is no one else except you."

"Hold on. Why will Susana go? Another kidnapping?" I giggled, but it was more a nervous laugh. How many dark secrets has the company been hiding?"

Steven raised his hands in a defensive gesture. "Even if she wasn't involved in Molly's disappearance, she'll have to take responsibility for her actions. Nathan said he would take care of that."

"And you trust him? He doesn't want the world to know the truth. He was loud and clear—"

"I'm slowly getting to the conclusion that the world doesn't always need to know the truth. It's more important that people get punished for what they've done, and *some Almighty Truth* doesn't need to be involved."

## CHAPTER 58
## New Selina

"Where is Leona?" I asked calmly and confidently, hiding the fact that my heart was racing like a rollercoaster. The fingers of my right hand were tightly entwined around James' gun, which I had put flatly on the wooden table. It was the very same table, on which Sophia once caught her son in a romantic embrace with his high-school sweetheart from nearly forty years ago. Sorry Sophia, but no matter how much you try, true love never dies.

Edward put his hands up in a defensive gesture, "I have no idea. You people are completely crazy. And what are you two wearing?"

"Ha! Rule number one when dealing with crazy and dangerous people is don't ever call them crazy Ed!" I shouted louder than I had intended, and James quickly shushed me. He was right. Although the walls in the house were concrete, it was a terraced house and people like the hat seller seemed to take great interest in their neighbours' lives. "Where is she?"

"I've already called the police. They know you're here," he said through a squeezed throat and swallowed loudly.

"No, you haven't," James said, and he wasn't bluffing. He would have never gone back with me if Antonio hadn't confirmed through a friend that Edward hadn't called the police last time. Antonio *happened to* know many useful people. Too many for a respectable citizen.

Edward glanced at his watch. "They've been following you since you landed in Paris. The only reason why you're not in prison yet is because they hope you'll lead them to the kidnappers you hired."

James gave me a fearful look.

"The only person you called after we left was Leona. You couldn't call the police. It wouldn't be wise considering you helped the mother of a public person illegally leave the country, faked her kidnapping and extorted serious amounts of money from a US presidential candidate. All to have your happy-ever-after with a woman you hadn't seen for forty years, and while her family is convinced that she's dead. To pull it all off you're clearly intelligent, so you wouldn't call the police."

"Well..." Edward smiled faintly. "They didn't want me in MI5, but I think I would have been pretty good at the job."

"So as soon as Leona arrived at her Canadian cottage by the lake, you put her on your floatplane and flew to the Military base at St. John's from where you transported her on a C-130 to Gibraltar."

"Wow, you're a good detective yourself," he said stunned.

"I do my homework, when the stakes are so high. I knew that till three years ago you served in the RAF, flying Hercules aircraft, and I dug further to finally discover you did an exchange tour with the Canadians. From there it wasn't that difficult... Once you add all the facts—"

"Are you both done with flattering yourselves with your grand ideas?" James interrupted me irritated. I could never understand men. I thought he would be glad to know I didn't drag him back to Edward in vain, and that my seemingly crazy idea turned out to be true. He reluctantly drove to Marbella, called Antonio on the way and refused to leave the car before confirming Edward hadn't called the police. He even more reluctantly handed me the gun and didn't let me break into the house before we saw Sophia leaving for an evening out. Apparently, Antonio happened to know that it was one of the days she was playing scrabble with her Spanish girlfriends. I had never seen anybody dressed in a mini silver sequin dress for a scrabble night out, but what did I know about the social life of eighty-year-old ladies, who looked like they were in their mid-sixties and acted like they were max thirty. Well done Sophia!

"Are you done with your grumpiness?" I sighed.

"Seriously? Am I grumpy? She abandoned her family! She let the people who love and care about her believe she was murdered. What sort of person are you to do something like that?"

"Technically only Leo doesn't know," Edward let his arms fall along his body and shrugged.

"So it's true?" James was looking at Edward. There was so much pain and anger in his eyes. He wasn't one of the children who Leona entrusted with her secret."

"What is true?" Edward's nervousness was back, he started slowly raising his hands up as if James' eyes could shoot bullets.

"Lady in pink is Leona," I gasped. She uses Instagram to communicate with her daughters."

Edward nodded, "I told her it was a bad idea."

"It was a great idea until she let Faith provoke her about not going to college. To be fair, I bet nobody but me has worked it out. Even James thought I was crazy. Lady in pink only opened her account two years ago and she's got over four million fans. There's no way of checking when Faith and Emily started following her. She never showed her face, but she still managed to become an inspiration for women of all ages. Leona as an influencer. Who would think, yeah?"

---

Lady in pink was posting at least one photo a day. She was always showing only her back or side, sometimes with a piece of her face deliberately blurred. Instagram is all about faces, but the nearly sixty-year-old woman somehow managed to attract millions of people who were motivated enough by what she was doing and writing. #No face attached – she posted under one of her first photos. She explained that although she did feel good in her body – especially after losing a few stone and looking after herself more than ever – she didn't want to be constantly judged by the way she looked. I took a screenshot of one particular photo where she was displaying her naked back, only her long blond

# A SWITCH MADE IN HEAVEN

hair covering the top of her lightly tanned spine and an undone pink bra thrown casually across her left arm. Her hands, with pink nail vanish and a small pink bracelet, were gathering her hair up into a loose ponytail.

 #IamMoreThanJustAFace #WomenAreMoreThanJustTheirFaces I don't want to waste anybody's time commenting on how my tits are changing by weight and years passed; or whether they're real or not. I don't need anybody to spot my new wrinkles and tell me about them. I don't want an ongoing debate about whether I age well or not; with or without dignity; with or without class; with or without a plastic surgeon. Who cares? What really matters is that #IamEnjoyingMyLife and you can too. #BetterLateThanNever.

If Leona didn't go missing and got involved in the so unnecessary – given the circumstances – conversation with Faith, I would never ever guess it was her. Lady in pink did kite surfing, water skiing and belly dancing in a hula skirt! She painted naked male models during art classes, tried dancing on a pole and sang karaoke in different languages. #LivingMyLife #WhileIstillCan she typed under photos that I suspected she took during holidays in Spain. #WaitNoMore she wrote under a picture with an equally mysterious date on a romantic dinner. With Edward?

---

"If nobody discovered for two years that Leona had been using all that padding to look fatter and wearing a grey wig, I guess Instagram is the last thing to worry about... except that you noticed," Edward said.

"The pregnancy belly!" I suddenly reminded myself. "It was hers and she told everybody I was faking MY pregnancy."

James was shaking his head in disbelief, "She had been planning it for years. The whole time I was thinking I was getting to know her, she was preparing to fake her own death."

Edward furrowed his brows and then he suddenly realised. He covered his mouth with his hands and took a long deep breath without exhaling. If not for the fact I was holding the gun, I would run to hit his back and make him breath again."

"Oh, come on," James shouted, and Edward started breathing. "Did you learn this from the boarding-school girls?" Edward was looking at us numbly, barely moving anything else than his eyes. "I mean fainting on demand, so you can avoid dealing with whatever you don't want to deal with?"

Edward cleared his throat and I practically demanded he go get himself a glass of water, which he drank in one gulp. "A few months ago, Leona finally revealed to me I had a son, but she never said who he was. She wanted to prepare both of us before we met each other."

James stood up and looking straight into his father's teary eyes said, "Well, she's done a terrific job, hasn't she?"

I tried, but I couldn't stop myself from nervously laughing. "This woman – she's been wasting herself as a housewife."

"I told her that and look what happened," Edward whispered with a squeezed throat.

"Edward," I sighed, "you have no idea how much you've messed up not only Leona's life, but also mine."

"I've made my mistakes, but I can't take responsibility for everything," He said loudly and confidently, his hands crossed on his chest, chin pointed up. "You've really scared me, you know?" he laughed full of relief. "But ufff... you're not going to shoot your boyfriend's father."

"How do you know he's—?"

"You're sleeping with each other, you have it painted all over your faces."

"Honestly, I don't know what Leona sees in you," I snapped. "What's between me and James is none of your business. I don't say I'm going to kill you, but I could shoot your foot or arm, which will hurt, and I'm not going to call an ambulance straight away. All I need you to do is to tell me where Leona is."

"Can you hear your girlfriend? She's threatening me."

James shrugged and I noticed that he did it in a very similar way to Edward.

"Just to feed your curiosity, there's no future for us..." before I managed to end my sentence both James and Edward looked at me stunned. These men never get used to being rejected. "What? Firstly, James is my mother-in-law's son... and yes, I know how it sounds! And if that wasn't enough, now you're telling me my mother-in-law is definitely alive. I'm not going to step in the same river twice."

"She's only my birth mother," James shouted outraged.

"Only? I beg your pardon son, Leona and I created you. Besides I've got genes reaching back to the Royal Family. That's something."

"It would at least explain your scandalous existence," I said.

"Selina, believe it or not, you and Leona have much in common. By the way, I thought you wanted her to be alive."

"I'm not so sure anymore. Maybe I just didn't want to be accused of murdering her."

"Well, tough luck. She's all safe and sound," he said with a smug face, and I was happy to get that confession recorded on my phone.

"So, where is she?" I was getting more and more impatient and for the first time I actually imagined – and wanted to keep it only in my imagination – firing the gun at Edward's foot.

"That's a secret I can't tell."

"Are you kidding me?" James shouted. "You're seeing your son for the first time in your life and you can't tell him where his mother is."

"Oh, when you put it that way..." Edward rubbed his chin and then his head. "The problem is I don't know exactly. I think she left me for Octavio."

"We've already spoken to him," I said with resignation. "He admitted he fancied her, but I don't think he's with Leona now. He's back to his wife."

"Which one?" Edward asked looking genuinely intrigued.

"Paloma," James and I answered simultaneously. "How many wives or ex-wives has he got?" I asked.

"Three. First one died during their journey to South America. The holiday was an attempt to save their marriage but unfortunately she tripped on her way to Machu Pichu and widowed him... Octavio did very well out of that *fall*..." Edward was talking, while James and I were staring at each other with disbelief.

No words were needed. We both were thinking the same. I just said it first, "Why the hell did you let Leona have anything to do with that guy?"

"He helped us smuggle Leona here from Gibraltar. How the hell did you think I could do that? I'm not an established drug dealer with a boat that no coast guard dares to get close to."

"I knew there was something unsettling about Octavio."

"But a drug dealer?" James squeaked.

## CHAPTER 59
## New Lily

"Beautiful house. Is it your—"

"It's not my newest investment," I said tetchily. "It's my sister's house, and we need to leave before the kids are back from school with their nanny."

"I was about to ask whether it's your design. The hallway it's spectacular."

Between seeing Steven and Liam I confirmed with Gabriel that, indeed, I did design the house, and was even involved in buying it based on its potential. "I did. Many said it was crazy, but I got rid of one of the sitting rooms to get the spacious hallway and a decent cloakroom. Instead, I put a two-storey extension at the back, so the new living room has a high ceiling and a mezzanine with a library," I was talking excitedly, reciting Gabriel's exact words. "The best part of the design are the glass and polished concrete spiral stairs with lit steps and..."

"Can I see it?" Liam's eyes shined. I glanced at a wall clock next to a double door to the cloakroom. It was modern and beautiful, but its design was so complicated that instead of showing me the time, it played with my eyes and prevented me from seeing the hands of the clock. Liam frowned his eyebrows, "Sometimes beauty comes before practicality," and before I managed to reply he glanced at his watch and announced that it was ten to one.

"I'll show you another time. We don't want to be late for our lunch."

"You don't want your family to see me."

"That's not true," I snapped. "Yes, fine. I don't want the kids to report to Emma that I'm seeing you. I think she's still on team Nathan.

"I can introduce myself as... let me think... I can fake a Spanish accent."

"You could, if you didn't just run away from the altar and leave a once famous model."

"Right... Naomi took care of my image. Have you seen her recent interview for a morning show?" I shook my head. I had stopped following the news and gossip columns. If something was important, Jane would text me anyway. The news was only distracting me from real life – it was noise preventing me from keeping my eyes on my goals. I couldn't control what people were saying, but I could control what I was doing. If nothing else, that was the lesson I got from Lily's life. "So..." Liam was saying as I was pushing him out of the door, "it was a discussion about men who are having trouble with commitment. She didn't use my name, but obviously she didn't have to. It annoyed the hell out of me. The psychologist who they invited to the studio... you could see she was totally on Naomi's side, and the woman never even met me!"

"You can always run a YouTube channel and tell your side of the story."

"About that..." he looked at me intensely, when we were already walking fast, pushing through crowds of people on a narrow pavement. That was the only downside of living in the center of Oxford – during the day it was never going to be quiet. "I thought you would stop the show when you're in England, but no! Instead, you smashed it at double strength. It was clever to do the tour around your office and talk about how somebody already took your desk in your absence. And then the live show in the kitchen with Emma. It was brilliant. So genuine and bold. It felt positively raw – like you weren't following any script, but somehow asked and said all the right things."

"Thank you. I've got many positive comments from the viewers, but you're the first person who knows me and expressed their support and enthusiasm," I laughed. "My parents hate it. They say I sold my soul online..." *Not quite, but I put it into a completely different body in order to save mine!* "Emma loved her five minutes of fame, but now she thinks we overdid it and I said too much."

"There was nothing controversial there. People loved seeing the real you, trying to manage the obstacles in your life, working out what's most important here and now... But also making long term plans..."

I was pretty sure the real Lily wouldn't approve of it. I told the whole world I needed to re-evaluate my personal life and career choices, which very much appeared to be one inseparable thing. No matter how much I loved my job it shouldn't interfere so much with my personal space. When Emma started questioning me on my love life, I admitted, I was involved with somebody from work and regretted the relationship. Although my sister didn't ask me anything from outside the script I'd given her, she looked sufficiently uncomfortable and curious for people to think it was all improvised. I was honest about taking the break from the office because of the mental distress that it had given me. "Years of not reacting to unhealthy interpersonal relationships in the company finally took its toll on me and other co-workers. When I lost my temper with somebody who bullied me for a long time and I tried to throw a chair at that person, I decided that it was the time to take a break." I had revised every sentence and consulted it with Ally.

Liam stopped just before the entrance to the restaurant I had booked for lunch, "Does it mean that you're done with Morgan and Tusk? Was it your attempt to get fired and avoid paying the million?"

"It's more complicated. If they fire me for misconduct or misbehaviour in the workplace or reputational damage to the company – they retain all my clients, who I then can't approach for five years. I've got some serious retail companies and very wealthy people on my account who keep coming back to me, so it would stall my career. I've been building the case against them with Ally for unlawfully freezing my salary and neglecting the fact I was bullied... And then... who knows... I've got a few ideas for my career that don't involve Morgan and Tusk, but if I leave, I want to do it on my terms."

The double doors to the restaurant swung open and let a group of Spanish tourists out, flooding the pavement. Liam glanced at the sign in the window, "You've been here only a week, and you're already missing the tapas. Something is telling me you want *to anchor* on the Costa del Sol for longer."

"I feel like it's the place where I could spread my wings for something more than here," I said mysteriously. I had a completely new plan for my career and had already investigated my options, but I didn't want to share it yet with anybody other than Gabriel. I did *it* successfully for a while as Selina and I was good at it. It had the potential of being a very profitable job that the real Lily could also enjoy and successfully link with interior design. My phone started buzzing in my handbag and I was glad for the distraction. I trusted Liam but wanted to talk about something else than our jobs. If it was going somewhere, we needed to know more about each other than just how we were going to make our money.

"Hi Jane, I'm about to have lunch with a friend, would you mind if I called you back later?" I was talking, while following Liam into the restaurant. "Oh my god! No! She can't be!" I shouted into the phone, drawing everybody's attention with my high-pitch tone, but also by nearly falling onto my face as one of my stilettoes got stuck between old wooden boards. *Bloody dressed to impress!* The whole loud and busy place went suddenly quiet. Forks and knives dropped on the tables with a clatter and all eyes were on me. Liam gave me a questioning look, and I saw no other option than just to get the hell out of there. I ran across the street to sit on a bus stop bench. My legs were shaking. Liam stormed out of the tapas bar and sat down next to me. "Was it something to do with Molly? Is she dead?" he whispered. He tried to hug me, but I pushed him away. I needed to gather my thoughts. "Lily, say something... Do you want to go back to your sister's place? Or go somewhere else to talk?"

I took a deep breath. "Susana has been arrested for arranging Molly's kidnapping... If Molly is dead," I swallowed hard, "then she will be charged with murder."

"Shit! Susana? Really? That's nuts! Why?"

"Molly blackmailed her for something," I said, still processing the information. It did make sense. At least to some degree. Molly had recorded a conversation that could be used as proof that Susana sexually harassed Steven. It would destroy her career and reputation. *But a kidnapping? Murder? Was she that desperate?*

"What about? What dirt did she have on Susana to get herself killed?"

"How can I possibly know that?" I snapped. "The police have a recording of Susana discussing some details of Molly's kidnapping."

"Bloody hell... I would never think that your workplace battles could end up at a cemetery and prison... So it's not you after all who's going to make national news."

"Nathan..." I whispered.

Liam jumped up from the bench, "Did he help Susana? Jesus, you really need to stay away from that guy!"

"No," I said calmly, looking into the distance. "I think he was right about her. She's pure evil. And she tried to frame me! And I helped her by attacking Molly!"

"The story of you taking her laptop was so weak..." Liam kept talking, but my thoughts got so loud that I couldn't understand much of what he was saying. *I need to check who transferred the million pounds to my account! Susana will do everything to defend herself. She tried to get rid of Molly, and she might try to get rid of me.*

## CHAPTER 60
## New Selina

I had to do it. I had no other choice. Time was running out, and we knew we couldn't wait until tomorrow. What if Octavio was gone by then and we missed him? What if Edward let him know we were coming? We couldn't entirely rule out the possibility that Octavio was still helping Edward and Leona. It would make perfect sense to ask him again for a little favour to provide Leona with some safe *lodging* – after their secret love nest was invaded by two unexpected intruders. What if Octavio was Edward's way to buy himself some time? We needed to know sooner than later.

If becoming a liar and imposter, who uses her connections from a previous life was going to push me out of heaven's door, well, at least I couldn't say I didn't try. What other options did I have? Knowing that Leona was somewhere out there, doing nothing was even more likely to become my *game over*.

Besides who were they to judge me? They put me into somebody else's body – for all I knew somebody who could have been a murderer – and they didn't give me a clue about how to deal with it. How ethical was it? And why do we always have to assume that *Up There* is good, fair and moral? What if they are throwing misfortune at us, while eating popcorn and placing bets – trying to guess which one of their puppets can endure the most pain...

"I feel so much better in my own clothes and without the extra body parts," James suddenly interrupted my life contemplations. He parked in an underground carpark in Puerto Banus and bent back on his seat like he wanted to have a nap. "What next?" he asked with resignation, which was unusual for the James I knew. "Are you sure you don't want to wait for my PI? He can be here tomorrow. He has a good network of people who can help him in Spain. He's experienced and unlikely to do something stupid."

"Why do you think I'm going to do anything stupid?"

He sighed, "You act in fervour. You're driven by emotions that you're not able to control when everything is still fresh – your pain, anger, the disappointment and disbelief. Honestly, I'm afraid that even if you find Leona, you're going to suffocate her with your bare hands."

"Well, I can't guarantee I won't but..." I paused and looked into his sad disappointed eyes.

"What?"

"I think you've been talking about yourself, not me. Anyway, move your butt. Somebody needs to finally tame this dare-devil woman, convinced she can pull all the strings in the world without any consequences... But first we need to find Alvaro."

"Who is Alvaro?"

"Who is Antonio, eh? Only you're allowed to have your little secrets?" James gave me a faint but honest smile, the first one since we left Edward's house.

---

I, the real Lily who was currently kept hostage in Selina's body, once designed an upscale restaurant in Puerto Banus, the luxurious marina to the southwest of Marbella. I still remembered the project as one of the biggest challenges in my career. The wealthy owners, a couple of just hitched chefs, desperately wanted their place to 'pop'. Easier said than done – how do you make a star shine more than the other stars surrounding it?

On the left side of the restaurant there was an opulent jeweller displaying in its windows million-dollar necklaces and diamond tiaras. Its entrance was adorned with two opulent-in-muscles bodyguards whose eyes shined like diamonds and set on every newcomer like they had robbery in mind. On the right side, there was a wine bar designed in a very minimalistic style: polished concrete floors, heavy wooden tables with Edison-style string lights hanging above them and expensive wine packed into wooden chests hanging on the brick walls. The bar could have been anywhere in the world when seen empty, but when it got crowded – it could have only been in Puerto Banus. The essence, the whole unique atmosphere of the place was created by the people who were spending thousands of Euros on fermented grape juice. They were chatting and laughing loudly, their fingers fiddling with their expensive haircuts and smoothing the creases on their silky jackets or gowns. It could be the middle of the day and people would be dressed like for a Christmas ball at Buckingham Palace or the Met Gala in New York. Besides, there was also the view to compete with – the most luxurious yachts shining in the bright sun, crystal clear water reflecting the high bare mountains and traditional white houses with terracotta tiles on their roofs. Swishing palm trees, sunbathed groomed bodies, the intensive smell of perfumes coming from every corner and…

"So many drunk tourists…" said James looking outraged at a smashed guy in his fifties leaning against a red jaguar, posing and pouting to photos taken by his girlfriend, probably thirty years his junior. "Oh, no. Can you believe it? He's going to put his sticky sweaty arse on the bonnet. Why would anybody park here?"

"Relax. The owner of this car probably has a few more toys like that."

"What are your chefs driving?"

"The last time I saw them they had one sports car to share and two SUVs for their twins."

"What are their names? Valentino and Ava?"

"Alvaro and Valentina Flores," I gasped. "What's going on with your memory today? You must have overheated your brain when you rinsed out the hair dye. You did it like fifty times too many."

"I've never been so glad to see my true hair colour. But what's going on with you, Little Miss Bully?"

"Why can't you just trust me?"

"Don't you think we've been acting a bit too hectically? Maybe we should slow down a bit."

"Getting cold feet?"

"Maybe... The thing is, I'm not sure whether it's a good idea to go around the marina and tell people we're looking for Octavio. Somebody is going to tell him, and we'll lose our chance..."

"Have you got a better idea to find his yacht?" He shook his head. We're only going to ask two people, who I trust." I wished I could tell James that since I re-designed the restaurant and gave it free advertising on my TV show, Alvaro and Valentina were able to entirely pay off their mortgage, both on their house and restaurant. They owed me.

For a few long minutes we walked in total silence. It was a warm pleasant evening with a gentle breeze that was somehow soothing my nerves – the wind felt like somebody was taking deep breaths and then releasing them slowly. The nightlights coming from surrounding businesses and yachts were twinkling on the dark water, which also reflected the full moon. Voices and laughter were melting into one another. I wanted to just be a tourist here. I missed my old life. I missed me.

"Emma Rice, we've got a reservation for nine," I said to a waiter at the door. He was tall, slim, had a dark goatee with a small moustache and was dressed in a sleek white suit. Before James managed to say anything, the waiter smiled, turned back to us and we followed him to our table next to a window with a mesmerizing view for the marina. I couldn't tell whether my date – who soon was going to improvise as my husband – was more surprised by the interiors of the restaurant or by me calling herself Emma Rice.

The entire floor was made of large panes of glass, underneath which we put thousands of real one-dollar and five-euro banknotes. To make the whole venture more affordable for the owners, there was a narrow hole in the floor, just next to the inevitable queue for the toilets, with a plaque encouraging people to throw in banknotes with their names written on. People helped their luck, and gradually improved my design. I couldn't see a single empty spot of bare concrete under the glass. All the walls were covered floor to ceiling with mirrors or gold bricks – one wall was actually gold-plated. The restaurant had three rooms separated with round, heavy metal doors – the Gold Vault wasn't just a name. I created something more than a design and completely re-branded the place. It was amazing to see it now filled to the brim with people laughing, chatting and enjoying their dinner in the surroundings I had created.

We sat at a glass box-table with fake, but very convincing, gold coins inside. James leaned back on his chair opposite me, crossed his legs and started tapping his fingers on the table with anticipation. "If you're Emma Rice, who am I? I thought you knew these people."

"You're my husband Bob, but we don't have the same surname. I kept my maiden name so as not to confuse my patients," I whispered. "I promise I'll explain everything later." He nodded obediently, but remained far from impressed.

I was incredibly grateful to see a waitress briskly walking in our direction, carrying a beaming smile and menus, covered with black velvet that I still remembered choosing.

James glanced inside the menu and shut it excessively loudly with a grimace on his face, "I don't speak Spanish." He spoke better Spanish than me but for some reason decided not to use it. He was just being difficult. Why? What was he trying to achieve?

"Of course, Sir," the waitress said with a shaky voice. She couldn't have been more than twenty-one. I noticed that her plump round cheeks reddened, and I felt embarrassed – this was the man who I was going to introduce as my husband! Or rather my sister's husband.

"I'm good with Spanish," I said, trying to rescue the situation. I put my hand on James' menu and, while taking pleasure from seeing his baffled face, I said to the girl, "I'll translate. It's good for James, he's taking Spanish classes and needs to build confidence."

"Our marriage counsellor said that I need to have more courage in saying *no* to my wife. I'll take the English menu, please," he said, while pulling the menu from under my hand, but I didn't let go. The waitress gave us a faint smile and slowly walked away rolling her eyes and exchanging looks with...

"Alvaro," I said high-pitched, immediately putting a smile on my face. Thanks god he hadn't changed much so I immediately recognized him. Still tall and well-built with strong cheekbones and a smile taking half of his face. The only difference was that he had started slightly receding on both sides of his high forehead, but his dense dark hair and a slightly different haircut was helping to mask it.

"Who?" James turned in his chair staring blankly at Alvaro, which made the whole situation even more awkward.

"Please act normal," I whispered through clenched teeth and raised myself from the chair. "Alvaro, it is so good to finally meet you in person," I said with a squeezed throat, feeling suddenly like I couldn't pull it off and was going to be exposed.

Fortunately, he quickly used all his charm to make me feel comfortable and familiar. "Emma Rice, I'm *muy feliz* to see you here... very happy, *muy feliz*..." He repeated, while squeezing both my arms and looking deeply into my eyes. Then he pulled me towards his toned chest and gave me a suffocating hug. All I could feel was his strong perfume mixed with a minty hair conditioner. *He's using the same stuff as two years ago,* I thought with nostalgia. I wished so much I could tell him who I was. During the three months I had been working on the restaurant and his house, we met up every single day and chatting till late at night. I got closer with him and his wife than I had ever done with any of my clients before or since.

"Hi, I'm Bob," James rescued me from the hug. He was now standing in front of Alvaro with his hand stretched out ready to be shaken. Alvaro grabbed James' hand and pulled him in for a hug and tapped him on his back.

After the warm welcome I was relieved to be back to my chair. I felt awful having to lie to him. *Although, is it really a lie?* I was thinking. *I'm Lily, just in a different body. My sister wouldn't mind in the slightest if she knew I was pretending to be her. And she'll never know. She's too busy with her work to ever take the invite and see the Flores family.*

Alvaro took a chair from a different table and sat between me and James. "What a wonderful surprise. I'm so glad you called. I just wish you told me earlier that you were coming. Valentina would love to see you, but she's now with her sister in Sevilla."

"Oh, such a shame," I drawled the last word, holding my right hand on my chest, and thinking – *What a relief, one person less to lie to.* "I'm here with work, a patient called me at the very last minute. I barely had any time to pack, but anyway... How is Valentina?"

Before he answered, Alvaro glanced at me with a mysterious smile, then at James and then at me again. "She's pregnant again."

I clasped my hands and jumped from my chair, "Congratulations. I'm so happy for you." I honestly was happy for them. Getting pregnant was the reason why I introduced them to my sister. They were frustrated with their local fertility clinic, and Emma was a brilliant, experienced doctor with a great deal of warmth and compassion. They never went as far as meeting in person, but apparently, they spent hours on the phone discussing their medical history and plan of action. Finally, she recommended a better clinic in Spain, but it turned out they didn't need it.

"Valentina is just over four months now and still not so happy," he laughed. "We didn't plan it and she's expecting two girls again."

"Wow. And your first doctor told you that you were never ever going to—"

"Get pregnant naturally! Yeah! Exactly. I'll never forget the moment she looked at my wife and asked her dismissively why she would even like to check her fallopian tubes. Everything was prepared for the test, laid out in front of her and she looked at Valentina like some sort of idiot and said, 'Whether your tubes are blocked or not, it's clearly not going to happen for you so what's the point?'"

"Well, so you don't ever wonder whether you need to use contraception," James suddenly chipped in.

"Are you a doctor too?" Alvaro asked with curiosity. I was sure I had told him Bob was also a doc. *Has he forgotten? Or does he know I'm an imposter?*

I heard a phone buzzing, and James immediately reached into his pocket. "I'm sorry but I need to take this," he said and left us without an explanation.

"Sorry, he's taken a last-minute holiday to fly here with me and—"

"That's all right, you don't have to explain anything," he put his hand on mine and looked deeply into my eyes. "At least, I've got an opportunity to ask now what your boyfriend's name is. I was so excited to see you that I didn't quite catch it."

*What the hell? I told him I had a husband.*

"Aaaa... I understand," he nodded.

I gave him a questioning look. I was so baffled that my mind went blank. *Help!*

"Ok, I know it's not your husband Bob. We only talked on the phone, so one day I wanted to see how you looked. I'm not a stalker, I was just curious. I googled you and found a couple of photos with you and your husband taken during a charity gala." He looked a bit guilty and embarrassed.

My whole plan was based on the idea that Emma wasn't on any kind of social media, and they only used phones to get in touch!

"That's fine," I forced myself to laugh. "I've also googled you." *I did. Last night. To check whether you were still running the restaurant.*

"To be honest, you definitely look familiar, but I wouldn't recognize you with that hair. My waitress, Antonia, pointed you out to me... But I love your red hair, and..." he lowered his voice to a whisper, "your new boyfriend is far more handsome than Bob," he smiled mischievously. "And hey, I love Valentina and my married life, but I would never judge anybody. I totally get it. You've got children with Bob and don't want to hurt anybody before you're absolutely sure..." I was listening to him flabbergasted. *Was he friends with my sister? How close did they get that she told him more than me?* "Besides, he made his choice when he slept with that nurse."

*Bob? The goody-goody Bob?* I felt sick. My head was spinning, but somehow I still managed to say, "His name is James... and the hair – I did dye them for a charity event and haven't had time to wash them off before coming here."

"Lily always used to say that she wasn't the really busy one, and that I had to meet her sister. I found it hard to believe how anybody could be busier than her... Anyway, what would you like to eat? You must be starving..."

I chose both for me and James a paella and a jar of sangria. He still wasn't back after I ordered, and I had a feeling he might have departed for good, disgusted with my lies. When Alvaro personally took our menus and went to make the order, I texted James that in case he did return, he had his old name back and wasn't my husband anymore. He was my lover. I had left my husband Bob at home. As soon as I sent it and read it again, I suddenly wished James just stayed out of it, wherever he was. He didn't, arriving exactly as Antonia was bringing our food.

"You're just in time," Alvaro said.

"I'm sorry. It was my wife. I had to take it. One of my children got into a fight at school," James said and smirked at me.

*Fuck you James.*

It wasn't what Alvaro was expecting to hear. He lost his voice for a long minute. He poured us all some sangria, while humming to the music. The food arrived just in time to fill the uncomfortable silence.

"How is Lily? Is she still with Nathaniel?"

"Yes. Her love life is more complicated than it needs to be. I have started believing that it might be hereditary."

Alvaro laughed out loud. "I was giving him max a couple of months, and it must now have been something like two years," he said and took a gulp of his sangria looking into the distance.

*Hilarious. Have you done a course for fortune tellers? What exactly was that prediction based on?* I wanted to ask, but I needed to butter him up.

"It's one of her longest relationships."

"Do you like him?" I could sense in his voice that he didn't.

"I don't know him well, but he's nice." Emma never properly met him. She saw him a few times and each time they only exchanged politeness. Neither of them was particularly fast to bond.

"Well, I hope he's not going to hurt her."

"I hope so too," I mumbled. "I don't know whether he'll ever leave his wife."

"Oh, no," Alvaro said, waving for the waitress to bring more sangria. "I'm more afraid he leaves the wife and gets hitched with your sister. He's so narcissistic."

"Sometimes... I mean, he might make such an impression, but when you get to know him, I don't think he is like that at all," I said, carefully choosing my words.

"You said, you didn't know him that well," James said, his elbows rested on the table, his left hand holding a fork with a large half-eaten prawn waving next to his curious face.

Alvaro was also looking at me with anticipation.

"Okay, you've got me. I don't like him at all," I said. "I just wanted to be loyal to my sister."

"You're with friends. You don't have to pretend anything," Alvaro gave me a genuine smile. I definitely had to pretend. Alvaro turned out to be more of a Gossip Boy than I had expected.

"You're right. I'm so glad that I called, and you were able to see me. It's just such a shame that I've got so little time and I'm here with work," I paused to instil his curiosity and took a few bites of my paella.

"Are you going to finally pursue your dream and try to move here? Our local fertility clinic would gain so much by having you," he sounded genuinely excited for me. *But, what? What have you just said? Is it my sister's dream to move to Spain?*

"So many things I still don't know about Emma, she constantly surprises me," James said with a hint of irony in his voice that even Alvaro noticed.

"Well, that's the beauty of starting a new relationship," my Spanish friend rescued me. "Tell me about the job."

"I'm starting a business as a concierge doctor, who can cover the whole of Europe. I haven't dropped my job in England yet, so I'm currently juggling both and trying to do them as best as I can."

"Oh, you mentioned that to me once."

*I thought Emma only shared the idea with me. Do I really know my sister?*

"I think I did," I said, glad that at least my imposter plan was working. "I'm looking for a man called Octavio Buendia-Iglesias. I'm supposed to see him tonight. The problem is I lost the details of his boat, he's still in a meeting and his secretary won't give me anything. I can't tell her who I am because he's a very private man and made it clear nobody should know about me. I'm worried to ask around in case he drops me as his doctor."

Alvaro was totally taken aback. He lowered his voice as if somebody was eavesdropping, "He's a very private man. No, I wouldn't tell anybody why you're here."

"I said exactly the same," James snapped, "but she told you."

Alvaro made a gesture of zipping his lips and throwing a key away. "Emma knows she can trust me."

"I do," I said as sweet as I could. "By any chance, are you aware, which yacht belongs to him?"

Alvaro bent back on his chair and rubbed his chin, "I think I might. When I see it, I'll be able to tell it's his. We could go for a stroll after dinner and try..."

"Perfect" I said. It wasn't perfect because I didn't want to parade with him and James for the entire evening around Puerto Banus looking for Octavio, but I didn't have a better option.

"I've heard some gossip about him and a Parisian blonde he was seeing when he was separated from his wife, but I didn't think it was true."

*Leona could speak French, but well enough to actually pretend she was from Paris?*

"I have no idea who I'm supposed to meet. Maybe it's him and his wife."

"Oh, I doubt it. His wife is in her early sixties."

"And the Parisian blonde? How old is she?"

"Early fifties. Octavio is not one of those old rich men looking for a much younger woman. I mean, he's dated some, but he never marries them. He is not stupid enough to think they would do it for love... How long has the freezing eggs thing been going on? Maybe she's done it."

"I bet if she is not through her menopause, she'll use somebody else's eggs," James said knowledgeably. "It's what I would do."

"At fifty I would use a surrogate, I think," Alvaro said, suddenly bonding over something with James. "Or maybe I would have a go with my own eggs first..."

"I can't make men pregnant. Not yet. Hopefully that's not what Octavio expects."

## CHAPTER 61
## New Lily

"Thank you for being here for me," I said.

Liam took his eyes away from the dessert menu and gave me a serious look, "I'm always ready to help. Although, I must admit, you've asked for a lot this time. It's a huge sacrifice to have dinner in a Michelin star restaurant. And a table with a view of Puerto Banus? It's killing me. And the fact that..." he leaned towards me and whispered, "we'll probably get the meal on the house because you know the owners? It's almost too much to take, but I can endure it all in the name of love."

*Love? Has he just said love? In which meaning of the word?*

"Is that like I-love-chocolate-cheesecake sort of way, or more like hey-I-think-I-am-going-to-marry-you?" I laughed, with a courage induced by Sangria.

"Hmmm... somewhere in between. More like... I definitely choose you over a piece of chocolate cheesecake." I must have looked disappointed because after a pause he added, "And I wouldn't bail on you at the altar."

"No?"

"I would just go with it, see what happens and divorce you if it didn't work," he said without hesitation.

"That's such a generous offer! Far more than I would ever expect from you. Let's make a toast to that!"

"What are we raising our glasses to?" Alvaro appeared out of nowhere, grinning and squeezing a third chair between us.

"Now I wish I'd designed bigger tables."

"They're perfect," Alvaro exclaimed! "They're only for couples requesting tables next to the window, and the more tables, the more *gold* for us," he smiled mischievously.

"Talking about gold..." I started, and Alvaro glanced at Liam and stiffened. I immediately thought it wasn't the right time to reveal the real reason why I was in the Gold Vault.

Liam stood up. "Would you mind if I had a cigarette? Or three?" he smiled, and looked at Alvaro, "I've been trying to be good for Lily, but I always feel like smoking after dinner."

That was the first time I heard it. I smiled to him gratefully, "Fine. Go."

"I promise I'm going to quit for you."

Liam knew exactly why we went to see Alvaro. I needed to confess it to someone except Gabriel and he was the only human being I trusted. He wasn't a member of my family or anybody working for Morgan and Tusk, which in itself was a lot. Also I was totally falling for him, but still didn't want to admit it even to myself. I didn't want to, but I wasn't going to beat myself up for it. If anything happened between us... Well, many people would manage to keep a happy romantic relationship going for a year. And then they would probably erase my memory anyway! So, nothing to worry about. Even from a rational point of view he didn't seem to be a worse choice than Nathan or Leo. *I'll sort out Lily's life and I'll deal with any aftermath of my infatuations later.*

"He doesn't smoke, does he?" Alvaro smiled. "I like him. He lets you have some space and is very tactful..." he was saying this, while scrutinizing my changing face expression. Was he trying to catch me lying? He certainly didn't look like he would trust me with his life – but I was still a good enough friend for him to give me a million pounds. I spent a couple of thousand quid for my last-minute round trip to Bermuda, but it was worth the investment. Two thousand to find out whether I could spend a million felt like a bargain. "You didn't tell him about the money, did you?"

"No! God! Of course not! Nobody knows!" I exclaimed with pretended exaggeration, but it was exactly the reaction he'd wanted to get as he grinned approvingly.

A waiter brought us three beautifully presented desserts that I didn't remember ordering. Alvaro followed him back with his eyes, and when he'd completely disappeared from our sight he moved closer to me with his chair – our elbows touching, his breath on my shoulder – and whispered, "Good. It needs to stay just between us. At least for now. It's all legit. But the way I manage my taxes is a bit complicated right now."

"Of course. I totally understand and I'm ever so grateful to you—"

He brushed me off with a wave of his hand like it was really nothing. Like he bought me three scoops of ice-cream instead of two, and I was making a big deal about it. "*De nada, cariño.* No problem…" He moved so close that his lips nearly touched my left ear and whispered, 'I'm not able *to process* that much money in such a short period of time, so treat it as a gift, not a loan. You helped us so much. Now it's my turn to give back a favour."

Was he still talking about me designing his restaurant? "I was just doing my job," I said, feeling like my oxygen levels were getting dangerously low. I was trying to take a deep breath but without much success. *What the hell am I involved in?*

"You did more than I could've ever asked for. You actually exceeded your clients' expectations and gave them exactly what they needed when they didn't even know what their needs were."

"I'm a bit lost right now," I murmured, wishing I asked Gabriel for more detail on Alvaro.

He nodded, pointing down to the floor with his nose. I frowned my eyebrows, and he gasped like he needed to explain the obvious to a child, "People often leave for luck twenty, fifty or a hundred euro. Those who come here, don't carry any low currency with them. On a few occasions I've found a couple of five-hundred-euro banknotes. I didn't know they existed. To my surprise, they weren't fake! Most owners would just keep the money and never declare them, but I'm an honest citizen and declare everything to the tax office. Everything and more," he said with a smug face.

"Well done you... What's the dessert?"

"Oh, I know you didn't order it, but I would really like you to try it and tell me what you think. This one is currently selling for a hundred euro ... For you obviously everything is on the house... It's a chocolate and caramel tart covered with edible gold."

I dipped my spoon into it and felt like a billionaire. I guessed that was the reason why people bought it as the edible gold had no taste. The cake, although delicious, wasn't worth more than ten euro. "Mmmm... I love it."

"Lily, listen to me..." Alvaro put his elbow on the table and rested his head on his hand. From a distance we must have looked like two people in love. "Buy yourself out from the company with the money from your main account, and..." he lowered his voice again, "use the Bermuda one for all the extra expenses to help you start your own business. We've already talked about it. I know getting a house in Tuscany sounds like a better idea for spending your hard-earned million than giving it away for nothing... but most of your clients are based in the UK or have some serious links to it. Italy seems to be close enough but holidaying and running a business are two different things. Brexit is also not going to help. Trust me. They'll get the money for nothing, but what I've given you is also easy-come-easy-go... Don't worry about it..." he was talking while I was staring at him with big eyes, afraid to say something that could expose my lack of knowledge on the real Lily and Alvaro relationship. "Seriously, don't worry. I run my business safely. I've got a family now that is about to expand so I can't risk anything. The guy who I'm helping is too powerful to get into any trouble, and I'm very precious to him. Both because of what I can do for him and because we've been friends since kindergarten."

"If you say so."

"I'll tell you what I tell my wife. You don't need to know anything else. It would only burden you with unnecessary thinking... Let's raise our glasses to new beginnings!"

I reluctantly raised my glass, "To new beginnings!"

"By the way, Valentina is expecting twins again!" Alvaro's face started beaming, and it gave me some new energy. This announcement made him look again like a normal dad and husband to me. We clinked our glasses.

"That's wonderful. Cheers to that!" I said and gulped the rest of my wine.

"How's your sister?"

"Emma?" He nodded. *Why would he...? Aaa... Gabriel said she helped them to find a fertility clinic.* "She went on a holiday with Bob. Luckily for me it was exactly when I needed her house," I laughed. "And even more luckily, she employed a full-time nanny a month ago, so I didn't have to pay her back with baby-sitting. Although, I don't know whether she would trust me..."

"With Bob, you're saying... hmmm..."

"Yes. Her husband." *Is it? Yes, obviously.*

"Well, she's a great girl. You're a great girl. Make sure you stay in each other's lives. Make sure you stay close." I was a bit taken aback by his preaching, but had no time to reflect on it as Liam returned from his smoking session. I wondered what he was really doing for the half an hour.

---

I sat with Liam in our car eating cheeseburgers with chips. We loved our free three course dinner in the Gold Vault, but it was a typical fine dining experience with tiny portions that only made us hungrier.

"I swear, I'm hungrier now than before dinner," Liam said and stuffed his face with salty chips dipped in ketchup from a plastic sachet. Speaking with a full mouth he asked me what I was going to do with the money.

I bent my head back on the headrest and gasped, "I feel stuck. I shouldn't really be using the money. God knows where it came from! But I can't give it back. He won't give me his bank details, and it looks like he almost wanted to get rid of the cash and I'd be causing him a massive inconvenience."

"Well, you've got the Bermuda account for a reason. Your secret is safe there..."

"What do you mean? I didn't open it to get a million quid of laundered money from Spain!" *Did I? Or maybe I did! Shouldn't I be allowed to have one phone call with the real Lily? Even prisoners get phone time!*

"I'd love to have a million for an emergency. For some unpredictable expenses. And probably for him, for *these* people, it's just pocket money."

"What if they come back asking for favours?"

"Like what? Designing them a new laundry?"

"I don't find it that funny."

"Speaking about funny. Nathaniel's wife kept calling you while I was outside of the Gold Vault."

"How do you know?"

"I felt under such pressure to leave you alone with Alvaro that I accidently grabbed your phone. You've got her signed as *Nate's bitchy wife* with three exclamation marks!"

"Have you answered?"

"Of course not," he said and stretched himself on the car seat to reach into the pocket of his jeans to find my mobile. "Here you are." I took it baffled, wondering how I could have mislaid it. I picked up my handbag from the floor, unzipped it, and to my surprise pulled out Liam's mobile. They were the same phones, but with different colour cases. Mine was blue, his green. I felt like I was tricked by a street magician.

I had twenty-nine missed calls from Melania and one voicemail. "What's so important?" I murmured and put the phone to my ear:

 Hi Lily... I really need to speak to you. You were right. It's important that we cooperate. I'm sorry I was a bit harsh to you the last time we spoke...

A heavy gasp and silence. She sounded beaten up and under confident. I could sense how hard she found it to ask me for help. And she wasn't the bad one here!

> I don't know what happened between you and my... (a pause) husband... God, you don't expect to deal with any of this crap when you accept a diamond ring, walk to the altar, give birth to his kids or... Anyway... He's got somebody following me or you, or most likely, both of us. He's got a video of you coming to our house and sitting in our lounge for a couple of hours. It doesn't help that we laughed. Damn my nervous laugh! It doesn't really look like we hate each other. Quite the opposite...

She was speaking quicker and quicker, breathing heavily like she was walking fast around a room:

> He's already been working with his lawyer on a claim that you and I made up his affair so I could get more divorce money in court. That I'm paying you to provide fake evidence and testify against him. He's a narcissistic sociopath and I can't believe I'm coming to this sad conclusion after such a long time. You might think that's actually a good result for you, and you get out of it with your reputation unscathed. But, he's still playing you and his every move has been carefully planned... God, he's spying on both of us!

Silence. A gasp. Blowing a nose.

I looked at Liam staring at me, impatient to find out what was going on. "I think Melania is going through a nervous breakdown and getting paranoid," I whispered, forgetting it was a voicemail and she couldn't hear me. "Maybe Nate wasn't lying about Susana and his wife. Melania sounds pretty unstable to me. She says Nate is following me and her."

> You're probably thinking I went crazy. That's what he wants you to think. Just think carefully about the day when you threw the chair at Molly. How did you feel that morning? Who did you speak to? Did you miss something? Yeah.... Right! He knows everything about you!

Melania wasn't beaten up anymore. She was preparing her guns to fire and feeling great about it.

> E-ve-ry-thing! When I found on his laptop a spreadsheet tracing your period I thought...

"What the fuck?" I shouted simultaneously with Melania.

> Could that really be your contraception method? It took me a while to work it out. But first, in case you don't trust me. You're on a twenty-nine day cycle with four days PMS and you normally don't sleep well the night or two before your period. The night before the memorable meeting with Molly, you couldn't find your sleeping pills. They should be in your bathroom cupboard but... Oh no! You'd forgotten to bin the empty package! Then you went to work and could barely function. You drank a couple of cups of coffee and reached out for your painkillers and some tranquilizers in a drawer at your desk, but again – there was nothing there! Could you have put them somewhere else and forgotten? When did you get so forgetful? You're completely out of control, and then Nate pitches up in your office begging you to move an important meeting. All because one of his kids has a doctor's appointment and he needs to be there. Reluctantly you agree, and he says 'great, see you in an hour'. You don't fret about it too much because you've got all your slides ready. Well, at least that's what you think. At the meeting you find out that you brought a previous version of your slides and the revised one on which you had worked for a week is gone! Molly starts picking on you, making some comments about you getting away with your incompetence because you sleep with the boss... She whispers it to a woman sitting just next to her, but at least half of the room can hear it.

Maybe you wouldn't lose it... But it's only been a

couple of days since somebody started spreading this terrible rumour about Nathan having an affair with somebody from the office... Actually, is it a rumour or the truth? Her words are like salt in your wound. And the terrible headache, you're all shaking and hate this stupid woman from the bottom of your heart... Can she just shut the fuck up? Can somebody stop her? But no. Everybody is staring at you, expecting to deliver as usual, and Molly and her friends – or allies – are giggling like malicious high-school girls.

Melania is getting louder and emotional. It feels like she's talking about herself.

> Maybe you would be fine if Nathan prepared you for the news... He eventually told Molly that he didn't give a damn about the whole world knowing about Lily and him. If he only told you what was coming... But not telling you was to his advantage.

The voicemail stopped, but I noticed there was another one.

> When was the last time you saw your therapist? She was good for you, helped you manage the stress of your job and relationships. The problem was that when you needed her the most, Nathan threw at you offers that you couldn't reject. A new huge client! A romantic dinner! A weekend away together! Why would speaking to a psychologist be better than an escape to a spa with the man you love? How do I know about that? He's got your therapist timetable on his laptop. No idea how he got it. Knowing him he had somebody hack into her computer or he bribed her secretary... He played similar tricks on me. Did he tell you he left the show for our family? Yeah, right! The success went to his head. He spent more time being photographed at TV parties than working. The

board asked him to leave the show and the company. They chose you Lily! He's been waiting for you to mess something up... Look what happened to Molly. Where is she? Where is Susana? Where are YOU going to end up? We need to act before it's too late.

## CHAPTER 62
## New Selina

"What's your plan now after you finally found Octavio's boat... or rather this floating five-star hotel?" James was staring at me impatiently, his arms crossed, feet spread apart. "At least Alvaro's nosy little arse is gone," he sighed relieved. "If his wife didn't call, we would never have got rid of the guy!" he said, looking agape at the four-storey superyacht. Its hull lights made the sea around it look vivid green, while the warm yellow glow from its many windows was illuminating the whole marina. I wouldn't be surprised if this *floating castle* was visible from space. It was moored between two other superyachts – naturally, birds of a feather flock together – but neither of them seemed to match its splendour. "And who is Emma?" James exploded, as if he was suddenly electrocuted by his thought. "You seem to know an awful lot about her private conversations, including these people's medical history!"

"My cousin." *What was one more lie of such low calibre?* "Look, we need to find Leona. She might be in danger. We've got so far. I'm not going back now."

"Why do you suddenly care so much? As far as I'm concerned, she's been having the fun of a second youth. In the meantime, her daughter-in-law's been accused of her murder, and her first-born son lost a lot of time and money to find her, not to mention all the stress and trauma..."

And then it suddenly hit me. Selina would do nothing. She would have obediently stayed at Leona's Hampton house, kept writing and waiting for somebody to save her and prove she was innocent. But the New Selina had a mission to accomplish! She was here to save Leona from the hands of a Spanish drug dealer! *Go girl!*

"Are you here?" James snapped his fingers in front of my nose.

"Hey, keep your fingers to yourself," I shouted. "James..." I gasped, "now is not the time to have your knickers in a twist. You've been so devoted to get to know your birth mother, then somebody tells you something about her you don't like, and what? You don't even give her a chance to explain herself?"

"I gave her a second chance and she has literally run away from me."

"Maybe she did, maybe she didn't. We've got so far and gone through so much that I'm not going to give up now. You're either with me or go home."

He bit his lower lip, ran his fingers through his hair and turned back to me, staring at the yacht. "There's a party on the top deck, but even if his bodyguards let us in, we can't just search the place..."

"We could tell Octavio that we know that Leona is alive, and he was the very last person who saw her. Then we need to politely inform him that everybody knows that we're on his yacht and—"

"Perfect plan," he burst out laughing.

"Have you got a better one?"

"We've passed a few boutiques on the way here. We need to get a suit for me, and a gown for you."

Half an hour later I was walking confidently towards Octavio's superyacht, my green silky dress sweeping the marina's concrete, loose red hair torn by the sea breeze, and a gold clutch squeezed under my arm. James was holding my hand and trying to make me walk faster, but in my six-inch nude stilettoes it was simply a mission impossible. I expected him to be in awe as I was putting my legs so elegantly in the shoes, which were clearly made by somebody who hated women, but he must have dated women before who were ready to die in the name of fashion. Unfortunately, they were the only shoes that we found in my size and matched the dress. *I bet real Selina would have face planted while trying to walk in them. She couldn't do it!*

James himself looked like a million dollars wearing his new black tuxedo that cost five thousand nine hundred and ninety-nine euros. When he was typing his pin number, the sale's woman kindly informed him that in order to give the tuxedo back, it needed to have all its ten tags. I saw him pausing on the last number and gasping heavily, but he did it. Suddenly, he was even more devoted to the plan than I!

"Edward Hastings and his plus one," James said to two bodyguards with arms so wide that together they masked our entire view of the yacht. He put on a posh accent, which I hadn't had a chance to hear before, and an arrogant face expression that somehow seemed to suit him. Like father like son?

The bodyguards looked practically identical in their sleek black suits, but the slightly shorter one eyed me up as if he was trying to see how I felt about being a nameless *Plus One*. Even with the red hair and Selina's body I was looking hot... *Oh, god... I feel like an escort now. But never mind...* I gave him a gentle smile, trying to keep my breath steady, but it was all in vain. He reached into his pocket and I gave a little squeak, thinking it would be a gun. He smirked and spoke to somebody on a walkie-talkie, "I've got Edward Hastings here with his..." he paused for a second, "his plus one. No, they don't have an invitation. Should we ask the boss or send them home? Mhhh... Yes... Right... Fine... I will wait then..." he was speaking in English with a Russian accent, "More people are coming, they're going to block the entrance... okay... fine..." The walkie talkie made a loud squeaky noise that felt like it was cutting through my brain, and we were again left alone with Octavio's bodyguards. I swallowed hard. The shorter one looked at James-Edward and said, "Walk straight to the lowest deck, go through security and leave your phones in one of the lockers."

---

A gold and glass elevator, which within seconds catapulted us to the top deck, made a ding and its door slid open. We walked outside into a living room with marble floors, a high ceiling with lit fresco-like paintings and crystal chandeliers. A half-asleep middle-aged man was playing smoothly on a shiny black piano in the middle of the room. He was accompanied by a beautiful young saxophonist with long straight ginger hair and dressed in an emerald-green gown similar to mine. If not for two jacuzzi baths filled with waxed torsos and big boobs squeezed in tiny bikinis, the place could be mistaken for a ballroom. There was also a massive TV with a football game on, surrounded by a group of men dressed in tuxedos and sipping champagne, which effectively stripped the place of its charm and added cheesiness. I stood for a moment with James, speechless, phoneless and shoeless. A security person said it was a shoe-free party – inspired by a few unfortunate events, when Octavio's guests had got drunk and fallen overboard. Apparently, it was mostly women wearing too high heels, but some men also like to add a few centimetres.

"Ladies and gentlemen, Olga is not only a talented saxophonist but also an incredible singer..." the pianist was saying, suddenly very awake and excited.

"I bet he sleeps with her," James whispered into my ear.

"He definitely wants to, but I doubt it."

The pianist wasn't lying, the woman's voice was incredible, but the choice of the song was awful. It was a teary musical hit that quickly introduced the atmosphere of a wake. Somebody was obviously thinking the same because I heard a man shouting, "stop her". There was unusual desperation in his voice, something unsettling that I felt, but couldn't quite describe. The woman kept singing even louder, like she was doing it purely for herself. She closed her eyes and put her right hand on the piano, her strong voice filling the room. I glanced at the crystal chandelier; it was as equally unmoved as the singing saxophonist. I turned my head back to see the bully, who was trying to shout through the song, "stop her, can somebody stop her?". I saw a distressed man in his forties moving slowly towards the piano, his left hand loosening his bowtie, legs doing zigzags and refusing to cooperate with his brain. I was about to point him out to James, when from the corner of my right eye I saw something flying above the people sitting in the jacuzzi and then a bullet went through the singer's chest. She fell into the arms of the pianist, never opening her eyes, mouth slightly open, and her emerald-green dress soaked in blood. Her microphone hit the floor with a bang, just as the pianist hit the keyboard with his left hand that was holding the woman. The place went deadly silent. I was the only person who couldn't suffocate her scream. My hand let go of the glass of champagne that I was holding, which I didn't remember picking up. *Was it before we got into the lift, or after?* James put his hand on my mouth.

"Ladies and gentlemen, welcome to our murder mystery evening," said Octavio, who suddenly appeared next to the jacuzzi. "For any sensitive souls, who have just joined us – Olga is doing well, just resting..." he said with a smug face and a wink, the audience started laughing.

James took his hand away from my mouth and looked at me with concern in his eyes, "Are you thinking what I'm thinking?"

"Did they just kill her in front of us pretending that it was a game?" I whispered terrified, and he nodded.

Octavio was explaining the rules of the game and giving some tips, "... there are eight double bedrooms on the second deck, the murderer is staying in one of them. No more than one couple at a time is allowed in a bedroom. Look for your clues in different places, check the whole yacht except the third deck, which is my personal space..."

"At least we know where we're going now," James smirked. Was he kidding? Somebody was just murdered in front of us. I wasn't going to be the next one in the line to knock on heaven's door, not yet. They weren't expecting me so soon.

"Olga, thank you my darling," Octavio said, and to my surprise the beautiful saxophonist came back from the dead. I squeaked but this time I covered my mouth myself.

"We better go now," James whispered, and we headed back to the elevator.

"No! Why would you press three?" I shouted at James, when we were alone in the lift. "We should wander around the second floor first; make the impression we're playing the game. People will become gradually more and more drunk and distracted and then we expand our search area."

"I'm pretty sure I pressed two. Well, my finger clearly disconnected with my brain. Let's search the place, while we still can. Before Octavio finds us and kicks us and our lame excuses out."

"I don't understand why you didn't just give him your name. He already agreed once to meet with us."

"On a surfboard in Torremolinos," he laughed. "There must be some kind of connection between Edward and Octavio. Otherwise, why would he be helping Leona? Even if Edward had any money, Octavio doesn't need it, and I don't believe in good intentions and free favours... not in this gilded world."

We entered the third floor. My bare feet immediately liked the feeling of the red deep pile carpet that was laid in the corridor, which was at least double the size of a standard hotel hallway. I couldn't resist touching the 3D white and gold wallpaper.

"You're leaving your fingerprints everywhere," James warned me.

"Why would anybody try to take them from this particular wall?"

"There might be cameras here."

"Fair enough," I said and abruptly took my hand away from the wall as if it was burning. "If they've got cameras, we better go."

"I hope Octavio doesn't have any in his private space."

There were only two pairs of doors on the floor, I pushed the one on my right. Somehow it didn't cross my mind I should've knocked first. Luckily, nobody was inside. The room wasn't as opulent as the rest of the yacht – plain beigy carpet, cream wallpaper with gold geometric shapes, a gold-framed bed with white silky sheets and a wooden bespoke wardrobe made of the same oak as the door to the en-suite bathroom.

The door shut loudly, and I jumped, "What the hell James? Why would you be so carelessly noisy?" He looked at me offended, or hurt or... "Is this how you look when you're scared?"

"Maybe. Probably..." he said high-pitched. "I didn't shut the door. Somebody pushed me in and slammed it."

## CHAPTER 63
## New Lily

I placed a magnetic card on the lock and opened the hotel door. I stepped forward but Liam stopped me by holding my arm, "What if Melania is lying?"

"Get inside before somebody sees us."

"So what? You're dressed like a cleaner and pushing a trolley."

"I think the green outfits are rather stylish. It makes us look like sexy surgeons."

"I'm glad you can still joke about all this. A sense of humour might be the only thing that will ensure you survive your time in prison."

"I'm going in," I said through clenched teeth. "And you do whatever you want." Liam swore under his breath, but followed me inside. I left the trolley with towels, toilet paper and cleaning agents outside of the door. People normally don't want to disturb cleaners.

Liam whistled, "Penthouse suite. He's doing well."

"I bet he found a way to take it off the company expenses."

"Not this time. I doubt there is anything that allows you to claim a luxurious hotel room as your home office after your wife kicked you out for being unfaithful."

"I bet there's something like that! The world is still predominantly ruled by men. But it's going to change…" I looked around, feeling an adrenaline surge and a flow of excitement. "I'll search the living room, and you do the bedroom."

"Do you even know what we're looking for?"

"Ideally he left his laptop or some other electronic device that could incriminate him."

"If Melania is being so helpful, why hasn't she copied any of these docs? Do you really trust her? She's got a vendetta against him and is trying to take him down at all costs."

"Everything that she's been saying make sense."

"I've read so many books and watched enough films to know that when everything makes perfect sense it's most likely to be the total opposite."

"Total opposite? Really Liam? So what? Melania is actually the bad one and she had it coming! She shouldn't have added so much salt to her home cooked meals! Or, she could do a better job at ironing creases in Nate's trousers! I paused feeling angry, "I still can't believe Nate paid Molly bonuses every year because she threatened to reveal he slept with Susana. That woman knew how to take advantage of every situation!"

Liam looked at me curiously, "I don't remember you mentioning that to me."

"We need to start searching."

"Lily..." he was staring at me with pity, "you spent a lot of time with him. Do you think he could hurt Molly? Like he might've tried to threaten her and then... you know... everything went wrong."

"I thought about that. Nate paid her from the company's money. Effectively he was paying himself... But..."

"But?"

"I think he would just kill her straight away to shut her up for eternity than try to threaten and kidnap her."

"Oh god..." Liam grabbed his head with both his hands. "What are we still doing here?"

"Okay, enough faffing," I clasped my hands ready to check every pocket of Nate's trousers, unroll every pair of socks and peer inside every pair of his shoes. The one thing that I hadn't predicted was him moving the entire contents of his closet to the hotel room. "We might need to move the trolley away from the door. In a few hours somebody might peer inside to check whether the cleaner didn't trip and hit her head."

"I'm leaving in no longer than an hour," Liam said categorically from the bedroom. "And I've already got something that might interest you."

"What?" I turned back from a closet. *Who needs a closet in a hotel anyway?* Liam passed me his mobile, "Unlock it, I can't see anything. Did Naomi text you again?"

"He left his phone, which does make me doubt Melania. He wouldn't leave it while he's on a business trip to Rome."

"Bingo!" I exclaimed enthused and took the mobile in my shaking hands. "It's his private phone that he never takes to work. He's got a holiday phone, and a work phone."

"By any chance, do you know his code?"

I shook my head, and then suddenly noticed on the screen a voicemail from... "Molly! Oh, my god! He's got—"

"Molly? I read *Melania*... Show it to me," Liam shouted and almost pulled the phone from my hand.

"That's the older version of my phone, has he got any speakers here? It looks like he's already made himself at home."

"What are you talking... Aaaa... I've seen one in the bedroom."

"Hey, Siergiej, listen to the voicemail," I said to a speaker plugged into a wall, just above the bedside cabinet. The speaker didn't even flash with a light. Liam pulled it out and put it in again. "Hej Siergiej, listen to my last voicemail," I said, overpronouncing every word.

Listening to your voicemail. You've got one new message, from Molly.

Hi Nathan. It's Molly. I'm sure I'm the last person you want to hear from and you're probably wishing me dead. But surprise. I'm alive. Still alive. Although not sure for how long. They took my phone, and yours is the only number I memorized in the last twenty years. You're my last hope. I promise I'll make it up to you. I'm being kept on a massive yacht somewhere in Spain, a few hours from Gibraltar. It belongs to a billionaire Octavio-Buendia-Something. I'm on one of the top floors. They say nobody has paid for me yet and they're running out of patience. They have a limited number of rooms for kidnapped people, and they will kill me to make space for somebody else more lucrative. I've got a million on my account, courtesy of your bonuses. *Nervous giggle*. My sister has all the details. Use this to pay them off. The police in Spain can't know anything. Some of them cooperate with my kidnappers. Please. Please. I beg you please. No police. Send them the money to this account...

## CHAPTER 64
# *New Selina*

"Oh, no, no, no... Why? Why would you be so stupid and get caught?" Leona was standing in the entrance to the ensuite, her left hand holding the doorframe, and the right pressed against her chest – a much smaller chest than I remembered. She was wearing a pair of blue jeggings and a loose ivory blouse, looking elegant and much younger than the Leona I remembered. "Who's going to save me now, when most people think I'm dead?"

"Well, I don't know mother. You managed to fake your own murder so damn well that maybe you've got another brilliant idea."

I sat on the silky white sheets, my hands rested on the bed, chin dropped on my chest. I closed my eyes and started taking deep breaths. The good thing about already dying once was that at least I knew where I was going to end up, most people didn't have the same luxury. That was good. I lay on the bed and kept taking deep breaths. The difference was that the last time it all happened so quickly I couldn't even remember any pain. That wasn't going to be the case if Octavio decided to get rid of us. My eyes opened. I sat straight up on the bed, "Has he given you a tour around the yacht before he trapped you in this room? Has he got a pool with sharks? A tiger locked in one of these large bedrooms?"

"Just three nosy Yorkshire Terriers," Leona started counting on her fingers, "Puddle, Strudel and Noodle. Lovely guys... I've seen most of the yacht, I think. Octavio and I..." she paused blushing. "I thought we were friends. I don't know whether he planned it from the very beginning, or he just took the opportunity. As he told me, he's a businessman and missing an opportunity to make money simply isn't in his character."

"You've always had fantastic taste when it comes to men."

"You're a fantastic outcome of one of my relationships, so it can't be that bad."

"Is this really the time and place to flatter each other? Get us out of here! It's all your fault Leona. I can't believe you tricked us."

She sat on an armchair opposite the bed, crossed her legs and put her elbows on the armrests so she could still vividly gesticulate with her hands. "Oh, please. Haven't you told him?"

"Told him what?" James looked at me anticipating betrayal.

Leona gasped, "Fine, I'll tell him if it's too difficult for you."

"I have no idea what you're talking about."

"You knew about my plan. You knew I was alive and that I ran away. The only thing I kept from you was how I was going to do it," she said proudly.

"That's not true," I said with hesitation, as it suddenly dawned on me – I wasn't the real Selina. No matter how much I felt Her at any particular moment, I wasn't Her. The truth was I didn't really know who Selina was, while the whole time I've been trying to blindly manoeuvre her life onto a better path. Why did nobody tell me? She stood with me *Up There* and all she said was "try not to kill my mother-in-law." Was it some sort of encrypted message? Stop my mother-in-law from faking her own murder and making you suspect number one? Why didn't she tell me? Was she afraid I would stop Leona?

"Selina," James was staring at me disappointed and flabbergasted.

"Oh, come on Mr Righteous. How much time did it take you to tell me she was your mother?" I snapped. *Isn't attack the best defence?*

"That's not the same," he yelled. "You knew. You knew this whole time and... That's it, I'm leaving," he turned the doorknob, but the door didn't move. He kicked it twice before he grabbed his hair and shouted into the ceiling, "Fuuuuuck!"

"The good news is," Leona started, totally unmoved by our distress, "that we have time to talk."

"What is he going to do with us? You don't seem to be particularly upset," I said.

"As soon as he's got the money, he's going to release us. The last thing that he needs is bad publicity in his circles."

"His circles?" James asked, walking back and forth across the room. "Don't they like chop people into pieces in his circles?"

"Oh, yes," Leona said, and then it hit me – she had some real mental issues. I felt sick to my stomach. This was really bad. Is it some kind of lesson? *Is this how I'm going to end up if I don't get help, keep working like a maniac, and not solving my problems with Molly?* "In the circles, where he makes most of his money, yes, but Octavio wants to start a political career. He's already got many friends in politics and killing us wouldn't do him any favours."

I giggled nervously. "That's a relief."

"I still can't believe you knew," James put his face into his hands and then started walking around the room holding the back of his head in his hands.

"I didn't know! But when she just mentioned it, I vaguely remember—"

"How incredibly convenient!"

"It's not like that at all. She said something on one occasion, when we were both drunk at one of those stupid Hampton's parties at her house," I was making it all up but actually it was also how I was processing what might have happened. It was the only logical explanation in my head. "She said she had enough and would love to be able to just run away and leave it all."

"Let's not trivialize my perfect conspiracy. I did exactly as I told you I would. I sent you money onto your Swiss account so you could immediately start your new life, even before you finalized your divorce. We both know Leo and Emil can afford the best lawyers and the whole divorce procedure would take ages. Your books are great, but they will go completely unnoticed without decent publicity, and here your genius mother-in-law comes to the rescue again with her perfect PR plan. You wrote about killing your mother-in-law and then ta-da! Puff!" she clasped her hands. "The mother of your famous hubby disappears. That's not all – I managed to make Leo resign from running for president. God, this little plan of mine, achieved more than I could have ever wished for."

"I thought that I would never be surprised again," I said astonished. *After I've been at heaven's door and switched bodies with a woman, who had driven into me at a crossing!*

"Did everybody know except me?" James was now more surprised than angry.

"I really didn't know," I said with despair in my voice, but James didn't believe me. "I worked it out when I realised you were communicating with Faith through Instagram."

"She should've been more careful. She hated the plan from the very beginning, and all the nonsense about not going to university was only to provoke me – now I can see that clearly. I shouldn't have responded... Emily also knows. But Leo and Emil have no idea."

"So, was it strictly a women's club and I was excluded because of my gender, or did you decide to keep me in the dark for some other reason?"

"I didn't know," I whispered.

"Fine," Leona said. "She might've been more drunk than I assumed, when I was laying out my entire plan."

James nodded, now looking more convinced. *Does he trust his mother more than me? Another reason not to get involved with him.*

I didn't believe her. For some reason she was protecting me. Bizarrely, the more she told me, the less I seemed to understand. "Why would you make Leo resign? Wasn't it like the Woodhouse family's ultimate dream? Were you afraid he would lose and couldn't take it?"

Leona rolled her eyes, "Please, it was Emil's dream. I'm not even sure whether Leo has ever really been interested in politics. I mean... he's got loads of money and the best possible connections – Emil laid out everything for him and Leo felt like he couldn't miss the opportunity and let his father down."

"I don't know, he looks pretty driven to me," James mumbled

through gritted teeth. "You two definitely know him better than I do, but Leo doesn't strike me as an oppressed little boy."

"No, but it could have been just a charade. Let's face the truth, we're hardly ever recognised for what we truly are. So often people rush to put others into little compartments to systemize and simplify the surrounding world for themselves. And so often they stick to their Great Order – no matter what – rather than disturb it and, god forbid, rethink their preconceptions. That would be just tiring," I sighed and made myself yawn, "and we don't want to waste any more time rethinking other people's roles in society. We need to focus on our own complex, unique and wonderful selves."

Leona gave me a genuine and friendly smile and nodded, "I couldn't agree more. Look at me. For all those years I couldn't get outside the frame of the old perfect mother and wifey, constantly running errands for the whole family and throwing networking parties for the men of her life." Suddenly her face flooded with sadness and disappointment, "Happy to live in everybody's shade, always eager to make other peoples' dreams her highest priority! Looking like her own caricature, never having enough time to look after herself, to get back at least a little piece of her younger self!" As she was talking tears started rolling down her cheeks. "I tried, I tried so many times to change, but at very attempt I was treated like a crazy old woman going through an age crisis or breakdown. Even Claudia thought that I was unwell when I suggested joining her at Zumba. My own kids hated my bright costumes, but they couldn't help staring at me askance when I reached for a pair of jeans or a red dress in a shop. 'It's not you,' they would say. As if they really knew who I was!" she scoffed. "When I refused to get involved in one Hampton gala, and instead decided to go away for a spa retreat, Emil immediately called Pam asking whether there was something wrong with me. The truth is – people don't like anybody to change and get outside of the lines that have been drawn, unless it really suits them – and me having a little bit of my own life didn't suit anybody. So yes Selina, I do agree with you."

"Wow," I didn't know what to say. Leona's outburst took me completely aback. "So you decided your only option to change and be your new true self was to run away from everybody..." I was thinking aloud, trying to collect my thoughts. "You set yourself free from the environment that was suffocating and suppressing you..." as I was saying it, I was thinking more and more about my life as Lily – no matter what I did, people always wanted me to remain the same. For my family I was always the childless old spinster, who starved herself to fit into designer dresses and sold herself to the devil to become rich. I was leading a meaningless life and their role was to remind me about that at every possible opportunity – all to prevent me from entering the gates of hell. For Nate I was this insanely driven interior designer who made her job into her religion. Also, I was so strong-minded and independent that I would never consider becoming restrained by an institution of marriage. At least that was what they wanted to believe. Otherwise, my family would have to face the brutal truth that they were bullying me only because I had different ideas on how I wanted to live my life; and Nate would have to admit he didn't really want to leave his wife for me.

"I'm glad you ladies are finally reconnecting. I'm really chuffed to bits," James said with a fake grin glued to his face. "But let's face *another* truth. Leona, you never made any impression as somebody living in her own shadow. As far as I remember, at least twice I had to comfort Selina after one of your outbursts of anger. Once, I heard you running out of the house and shouting pretty nasty stuff to your daughter-in-law. You seemed to be quite vocal about what you thought—"

"Stop," Leona stood up from her armchair and walked towards the bed on which I was sitting. My right hand was holding my rumbling stomach. I was taking deep breaths trying not to faint. What I really needed in this heaven game was an option to call a friend – *Basil, where the hell are you?* But it looked like I had already used that lifeline too many times. The only thing I had left was to turn to somebody from the audience, and I bet on Leona – she was telling me the truth. It was *her* story, but I bet there was something in there that could save us. I had to let her talk. She took my left hand and closed it between her palms – they were warm, soft and perfectly manicured. "Honey, do you really think I would be so cruel and bold with you if I wanted you to stay in the family, and if my son really loved you?"

I felt a heat wave going through my body. I stopped breathing for a moment which made me even more dizzy. James and I exchanged glances of disbelief before he rushed to the bed to hold my right hand. I sat like that for a moment staring at the locked door – the door behind which there was a drug dealer considering my to-be-or-not-to-be. I suddenly jumped to my feet boiling with anger. "When exactly did you find out Leo was gay? Why didn't you just tell me instead of putting on the truly unique shitshow that led us to this drug dealer's den? None of us would be here if you told me!"

Leona shrugged her arms, "Really my dear?"

"Of course," I snapped.

Leona raised herself slowly from the bed, pulled her fingers through her long dense hair and cleared her throat, "And when did YOU exactly find out Leo wasn't into women?"

"Oh, too late. Way too late. We were already married!"

"Too late for what?" she was speaking slowly, accentuating every world, "Are you trying to say that you didn't read the deal my son asked you to sign?"

James shot me an accusatory glance. He was staring at me with anticipation, but I was out of words.

I expected to see Leona's smug face, but she wasn't the same Leona I met in the Hamptons. With all certainty she wasn't going to leave the question unanswered, but she didn't seem to take any pleasure in torturing me.

"Have you actually signed anything legally binding? Why am I always the last one to find out about everything?"

"Are you going to tell him now or will you wait for a better moment?"

"What better moment? We don't even know how many moments we have left. What if Leo and Emil won't pay another ransom? They think you're dead!"

"Exactly. A better moment might not come, especially if you do nothing. What are you waiting for Selina?" she asked with mercy. "What have you been waiting for all those years? For Leo to change?" she scoffed. "When it comes to men, the only thing they let you change are their diapers, and the rest of the time you just have to deal with their shit."

"You weren't even there to change my diapers," James said through gritted teeth. I felt she deserved it but it even stung me.

"You're right James. I wasn't there and it's the biggest regret of my life, but maybe..." Leona started choking on her words, "maybe I gave you a better mother than me, better family, better opportunities. Look at us – look how damaged the family is. I did everything for Selina to finally find out Leo was gay. I sent her to D.C., I arranged for Keanu to come over and spend the night with my son so there was no way for her not to see it. And what did she do?"

"Fine! I sinned! But I'm not the only one in the family! He practically blackmailed me into doing it. He's got it on paper – signed, sealed, delivered! I agreed to be his cover-up."

"Seriously? So, what about us? Do you want me to be your Keanu, sneaking around—"

"Oh god, now's not the time or place to talk about what happened between us!"

Leona raised her eyebrows. "Of all the people in the world you decided to go for a son of mine. Again!" She started laughing hysterically. "Now, I'm convinced you're just doing it to be closer to me."

"I must have developed Stockholm syndrome. Not a common result of a relationship between mother and daughter-in-law, but the world is full of surprises."

"Tell me about it," James mumbled.

"Hold on a minute. Did Keanu also know about your plan?"

"He even helped me a little bit," she said with a guilty face. "Look, for one reason or another, Leo never trusted me enough to tell me the truth. But I've known since he was sixteen. I just wanted him so badly to trust me and tell me the truth, but the moment has never come," she said and rolled her lips, looking like she was pushing back tears."

"And it never crossed your mind it might have something to do with Emil being a homophobe?" I asked. Selina wasn't the only one in the family making an effort not to see the truth.

"I've tried to change Emil's mindset but what I really should have been doing was to talk more to my son. I just didn't know how. I didn't want to push. My plan originated out of sheer desperation. I had enough. I couldn't look at my child living a lie, and at another woman wasting her life with the wrong man. When I read your book about a woman who kills her mother-in-law and then runs away, I thought that maybe it was me who should run away. Nothing was working. I was a bitch to you, my son didn't react and you were still there. Like you tried to stay in the family, only to annoy me."

James burst out laughing, "That would be really funny."

"So you were such a bitch because you cared about me and—" I didn't manage to finish because we heard a terribly loud bang. James and Leona threw themselves on the floor that stayed completely still. That was a good sign as it indicated that the explosion probably didn't happen on the yacht. I squatted, looking around at James who was no longer amused, and Leona pressing her right hand against her chest and breathing hard. Then my eyes stopped at the round doorknob that started turning to the left and to the right and to the left again. I swallowed hard and glanced at Leona and James who raised themselves to their sitting positions, still blissfully unaware somebody was trying to get in.

"I think that somebody—" I was interrupted by a double knock on the door.

"Who's there?" asked a man with a happy singing voice. I thought he was drunk, which would make sense considering the party upstairs.

Leona was the first to get her senses back not to miss such an opportunity, "Can you open the door? I don't know how it happened but we locked ourselves in."

"But I don't have a key. I'll go and call somebody for help."

"No!" we all shouted simultaneously.

The man must have been surprised with our reaction because he went quiet.

"I cut myself on a glass and lost loads of blood," I shouted and moaned. "I might faint in a minute."

"Or even die!" Leona chipped in.

"Jesus, why didn't you shout earlier?"

"My wife fell on a glass after we heard the explosion! We've literally just noticed she's got a hole in her stomach!"

Leona rolled her eyes, "Your lying skills are like one out of ten," she hissed. "Let him go, if he can break the door, we can do it too."

"But if he leaves now, he'll go get some help," I whispered.

"Where exactly do you have the hole in your stomach? Are you sure it's not just your belly button?" the man asked seriously and then said something we couldn't hear.

"He must have smoked something," James murmured and went to the door to press his ear against it.

"What is he saying?" Leona was getting impatient.

"Nothing."

"Is he gone?" I asked.

James pressed his ear to the door even harder and stopped us from talking with his raised forefinger, and that was when we all heard a man with a posh British accent saying, "What are you doing here Dimitri?" James jumped away from the door, swearing silently through gritted teeth.

"Oh, I'm just messing with Octavio's hostages! They've been trying to convince me a woman inside is bleeding to death."

"Their family refuses to pay ransom so it might happen anytime," the Brit replied dead seriously, then said to us, "Hey you! I'll be back in an hour or so to make a video with you. You'll need to convince the Woodhouses that you're still alive. And if you don't cooperate with us or play tricks, look outside the window to see what has just happened with the detective that your son hired! Sorry guys! The engine was faulty!"

As soon as we heard the man's footsteps fading away, we rushed to one of three little round windows in the cabin. Leona gasped, covering her mouth with her right hand. I could nearly feel the heat from something that once was a motorboat but was now floating in flames on the black sea like a meteor in the night sky.

"It's Liam," James said through a squeezed throat. "It's all over now."

## CHAPTER 65
## New Lily

"That makes sense to me... Yes. Right. I'm with Lily, is it okay? Sure..." Liam was speaking into his phone, while I climbed on my toes and pressed my head to his chin (the highest I could go), desperately trying to hear what Miguel was saying. They both suddenly burst out laughing. I couldn't hear Miguel clearly, but on Liam's side it was definitely a nervous laugh. I gave up and put my feet flat on the hot tarmac of Puerto Banus. My feet, squeezed into stripy white leather sandals, were killing me. Every part of my body was killing me. Only a couple of hours before we had got off the plane from London. Then we drove straight from Malaga to Marbella – all just to see Octavio's superyacht sailing away from the marina. We jumped, waved and shouted but it was too late. The captain could never have seen us that far from the shore. Wearing shorts and creased T-shirts we looked like a couple of idiots, who drank too much and overheated their brains to the level that they thought they belonged on the superyacht of one of the richest people on the planet.

It was scorching hot. The sun was at its highest point of the day, and I was at my lowest. We had spent last night at a Heathrow hotel and neither of us slept more than a few hours. Liam kept making jokes and laughing that we should have called Nathan to find out at which point of our menstrual cycle we were, but in reality, he seemed to be even more concerned than me. Well, I'd already died once.

---

"There is a part of me telling me to do nothing – just wait. Susana has been caught, right? She hasn't paid the ransom..." I was thinking out loud, while lying on my back in the hotel bed and staring at the ceiling, "or maybe she paid it, but they demanded more. Or! She didn't pay it because the kidnappers were already paid by her and she kept the money. They must've taken some deposit, right? They wouldn't go and kidnap Molly just like that without the assurance that somebody pays them later..."

"Isn't it what they do for a living and risk is calculated into the job? If they don't get the money, they..."

"They will get rid of her," I finished with a squeezed throat. "But, there's no guarantee that she's on Octavio's yacht."

"You're already having trouble sleeping. Will you be able to sleep at all if they find her dead on this yacht? If we can get there before everybody else does, we should at least try."

---

"Well, at least we can't say that we didn't try," I tapped Liam on his arm.

He put the mobile into his pocket, stood in front of me and held both my arms, "You don't have to do this Lily and that's fine. I'll go. You can find a place in the marina and wait for me."

*Is he trying to prove he doesn't have problems with commitment? How is he even going to trick some gorilla-bodyguards to get to Molly?*

"Go where? They're gone."

"Miguel said we could hire a speedboat. The superyacht is moving slowly."

"Isn't it going to look suspicious?"

"There's a party tonight with a few big celebrities attending. I convinced Miguel that I need to do some networking to get back on my feet, and he'll be in touch with Octavio. They are businessmen, he'll understand."

---

Liam suddenly slowed the speedboat down, although we still weren't close enough to cruise into the garage of the superyacht. Apparently, our boat was about to enter the yacht without using a crane! The internal basin would flood, we'd park up and then eighteen-thousand litres of water would be expelled in just three minutes. *Some things are worth of dying for!* I thought, when Liam was explaining me the whole process. We had rented a motorboat for three thousand euros, I was grateful Alvaro put the money on my account. There's nothing like unexpected expenses to ruin the most careful plans. The owner of the boat rental claimed that nothing cheaper was available, but I knew he could sense our desperation and used the opportunity.

"We should jump into our party outfits," Liam announced and yawned.

I wasn't sure we were ready for a rescue-mission, but I counted the positives. It could buy me out of Lily's body. Maybe I could even score some extra points for the future with *Up There*. Lily rescuing Molly – it didn't get any better in terms of making up for the chair-situation. I would be the hero! I could talk about it in detail on my YouTube channel and boost my popularity.

"Would you like to go and change first?" Liam was staring at me with anticipation. Suddenly he looked like he couldn't be bothered anymore. He might have even changed his mind but didn't want to chicken out in front of me.

"Yeah, why not," I said reluctantly, and went down the stairs to the lower deck. It was better than any studio apartment I'd ever seen in London. Solid wooden cupboards in a kitchen with the newest appliances, a king-size bed with silky bedding and an en-suite bathroom with a hydromassage bath and a rain shower. I took the airport labels off and put my bag on the bed. I groaned – my back didn't like it. I unzipped the luggage, opened the case flat on the bed and... I had to press my hands to my mouth to stop myself from screaming. I was standing petrified, my legs trembling, throat squeezed and thoughts racing through my head at such a speed that I couldn't follow them. "Gabriel, are you here? Can you hear me?" I whispered. Nothing.

"Are you decent?" Liam screamed from the top deck, and I could hear he was starting to walk down the stairs.

I took a breath and managed to stop my voice trembling, "Not quite."

"Miguel called. Octavio's speedboat is still in the garage, so we need to wait a bit longer. His son is going out soon, so he'll make us some space. You can have a shower... After you paid three grand for the trip," he laughed.

"Okay."

"Let me know when you're in the bathroom and I'll pop downstairs. I want to take something from my luggage."

"Okay." *Please, just go. Leave me alone.*

I took the gun, which I'd found on a pile of pressed and perfectly folded shirts. I used to take shooting lessons in the Hamptons. It was the most effective way I knew to relieve my stress and anger after the time spent around Leona. Pointing a pistol at a target, pulling the trigger and watching a target fall was all part of my healing process – no matter how messed up it all sounded, it worked. I didn't want guns on the street, but I loved it in a controlled and safe environment. It was like dropping fuel from an aircraft so it could land safely or detonating explosives in a mountain to cause an avalanche so nobody would suffer later.

"Can I come downstairs?"

"Sure," I shouted, now with a clear head and ready to face him.

Liam ran downstairs whistling and stopped at the bottom of the stairs. He quickly raised his head, looked at me and his hands flew up involuntarily in a defensive gesture. "Where did you find it?"

"Our bags are very similar," I shrugged. "Do you want to tell me who you are and what you've been planning?"

"Could you put the gun down so we can talk?"

I shook my head, "As you probably know the gun is fully loaded. Do you know that I have been taking shooting lessons?" *Well, not in this life, but who cares!* "Sit down on the bed," I ordered and moved around the room so he could get to the bed and I could keep a distance. He could try to get hold of the gun, and I really hoped to do this without hurting each other.

Liam sat on the bed, his right hand stroking the silky bedding. He took a few long seconds to prepare himself for what he was going to say. "I told you that I've been working for my parents... They're researchers," he cleared his throat. "They have a private investigation company. Somebody hired me to find a missing person."

"Have you been using me to find Molly?" I screamed. Was I doomed to always pick the wrong men?

He put his hands up. "No, no...Jesus! At least let me explain before you shoot me... It's not Molly."

"So who is it?"

"Fine. Now when I know it's definitely not the job for me and I'm going back to sketching or... renting sunbeds in Marbella..." he sighed, "It's Leona Woodhouse..."

Saying that I was surprised would be a serious understatement. I felt like I was hit by a car again, but this time I didn't lose consciousness but experienced the full impact. "The Leona Woodhouse?" I squeaked.

"Don't you watch the news? She's the mother of the most likely candidate to become the next President of the United States."

*The bitch did it. She really did it!*

"Mhhh..."

Liam smirked, "I know. You would never tell that somebody like me could be hired to find a president's mother."

"He hasn't been elected yet."

"Apparently, the country hasn't had such an assured candidate for decades."

"Leo Woodhouse hired YOU?"

"Actually, it was her second son."

*Oh heaven! He's crazy! Thank god, I've got a gun. So handsome, but so crazy. Such a shame!*

"He's got two sisters," I said carefully, not wanting to hurt his feelings. I didn't want to use the gun. What if I accidently sank the boat?

"It's what everybody thinks, but Leona has a son from a high-school relationship. She gave him up for adoption. Long story short, he found her and soon after she went missing."

"Have you checked him out? What if he's lying and HE kidnapped her? Famous people and politicians attract all kinds of crazy."

"You're right. It was the first thing I did. I verified his story, and it seems to all be true. I even found his father, Edward Hastings."

"I heard about him!" I shouted, reminding myself too late that I couldn't have heard about him as Lily.

"Really?"

"They mentioned him somewhere on a gossip site."

"Oh, right..." Liam looked baffled and disappointed. "I haven't found anything about him in the press or online."

"I might have mixed up stories..." I said, and then it hit me, "Is it Octavio? The Big Fish you've been watching?"

"I knew you would make a perfect PI assistant."

"Assistant?" I scoffed. "The times when beautiful women..." *Have I just called myself beautiful? Oh, well...* "The times when beautiful women peak in their careers as assistants are hopefully over. I insisted on searching Nate's room and I found out about Molly... Molly, holy-moly! You think they've both been kidnapped by the same person?"

"I don't know it for sure yet. Octavio is not a typical kidnapper. He doesn't need the money. He's a drug dealer and this for him is just another source of revenue. He actually started this part of the business because people kept asking him to take somebody hostage for them; or keep them hostage – which Leona most probably did!"

"Pardon?" I shook my head in disbelief.

"He's got the perfect environment for it, with a team of armed bodyguards and a floating prison of soundproofed rooms."

"How do you know all this?"

*Leona paid him to keep her hostage? She can barely use the internet!*

"Miguel is a close friend of mine and a secret agent fighting drug smuggling. The Corte Ingles is his second job."

"Just another source of revenue, eh?"

"And a great cover. By the way... when we're being so honest with each other. Do you trust Alvaro?"

"He cares about me. He's a good guy."

"I don't doubt it for a second. But did you know that he launders money for Octavio?"

"Hold on a minute, I'm still processing the information..." I stopped him talking with my open left palm, my right hand was holding the gun even tighter. *So... I've got a million pounds from the same pot of money into which Leona put cash to get kidnapped. This is just hilarious!* I started laughing hysterically. *And the same pot to which Susana contributed to get rid of Molly!*

Liam looked at me concerned, "I know. It's a lot to take in."

*That's definitely my money. For all the pain these two women gave me, it's compensatory damage!* It took me a couple of minutes to calm down. Liam was watching me in silence. It was hard to blame him for being suddenly anxious about me. I've already had one nervous breakdown and threw a chair at a colleague. Now when emotions are running high, and I have a gun – the situation could easily get out of control. His phone beeped, but he didn't dare to make a move and reach into his pocket. "Read it. Might be something *muy importante*." I laughed again – involuntarily defueling my nerves and amused by Leona and Susana paying me all this money.

Liam did as I directed. The message made his body even tenser. He slowly raised his head up, without making any rapid movement, and said through a tight throat, "It's Miguel. Octavio knows what we're planning. We need to go back now before..."

"Before what?"

"Before they try to kill us," he squeaked.

"Show me your phone."

"I'm using an extremely private message app. All messages that I read are immediately erased."

"Bullshit."

"I swear. Look at the app, there isn't a single message," he put the phone on the floor and slid it across the room.

I picked it up carefully, not taking my eyes away from Liam, the gun still aimed at his chest. *If I accidentally shoot him, this is it! I'm going to hell!*

"What's your password?"

"It only works with my finger, and then face and voice recognition."

"Why would you have it so protected if you don't have any messages?"

"Lily, I beg you. Trust me. We need to keep moving. It's not worth dying for... I should stick to my old job. I was good at it... Lily please."

They say you can't *'trust no one'*. You can't survive in this world without a certain level of trust for other people. How, otherwise, would you get on a plane, walk over a bridge, put your kid in childcare or even eat something in a restaurant? Impossible. For my sanity and in order to survive I needed to trust somebody, just a little, but bad luck had it – nobody like that was on the horizon. Or, did I miss somebody? One thing was certain – if Liam had been honest with me earlier, I would have still trusted him.

## CHAPTER 66
# New Selina

"I can't believe you didn't tell me," I hissed to James. We were sitting on the edge of the double bed, arm to arm, leg to leg – not really wanting to touch each other, but feeling like being closer together was somehow building a stronger resistance against the enemy.

Leona was sitting with her legs crossed on the floor, her left hand in handcuffs and chained to a heavy wooden table. Alexei, who was responsible for filming us, thought it would add extra weight to the ransom message. That and Leona wearing a tracksuit dipped in fresh 'mud' – probably courtesy of Puddle, Strudel and Noodle. He also smeared her forehead with ketchup and made her say on camera she had been thrown at the wall. Three bodyguards accompanying Alexei, six-foot tall and three-foot wide in their shoulders, were smirking the whole time, and making even more ridiculous suggestions to create the most convincing hostage environment. The spectacle would be more comedic than scary – if not for the fact that half an hour ago their boss blew up James' PI and his, apparently, beautiful assistant.

"What would it change if I told you? Besides, you also haven't exactly been honest with me. Everybody seems to know way more than me. The worst is, Liam had something important to tell me and I asked him to wait because we were clothes shopping for this gala, where we're now hostage. I've been so stupid and reckless. It's not a movie, it's our life, but I realised it way too late," he put his head in his hands and rested his elbows on his knees.

"Do you think Liam wanted to warn you not to go on the yacht or was it something else? I don't even know if we can trust Leona. She sounds convincing, but—"

"It was Liam who helped us hide in Spain. He found Antonio... Now I think maybe Antonio tricked us all. He and Octavio are both drug dealers, they compete for business, but maybe sometimes it pays for them to cooperate."

"Selina, your turn now," Alexei demanded with a wave of his hand. "We're not going to do much with you. Clean off your make-up in the bathroom and we'll paint one of your eyes purple and give you some ketchup under your nose. It should be enough, you've spent only one day in captivity."

"I would stick some black tape on one of her front teeth, so it looks like we knocked it out," suggested one of the bodyguards.

"Great idea," Alexei nodded. "Let's do it," he clasped his hands.

I was moving slowly in the direction of the bathroom, when I was abruptly stopped by a loud bang and a gentle breeze on my back. *Another explosion?* Somebody broke down the cabin door, and it hit the floor. I held my breath, my muscles tensed – if it had happened a few seconds later, I would have been squashed under that door.

Alexei and his three bodyguards immediately pulled their guns out pointing them at the empty door frame, but there was nobody there. I moved slowly inside the bathroom. I didn't want to stand in the middle of a potential firefight.

"Edward?" Leona squeaked.

I peered out of the bathroom.

Edward pushed Octavio inside the cabin, made him stand on the mahogany door, while pressing a pistol to his head, "I've never liked making carpets dirty. My mother is very pedantic. It's rubbed off on me."

"Edward, I can still hear you," Sophia entered the room, looking nothing less than fabulous, hair put up into a high girly ponytail, tight jeans stressing her perfectly shaped legs, and a white V-neck top splashed at the front with – *blood?* It must have been, Alexei hadn't had a chance yet to spray her with his organic low sodium ketchup. I glanced at her hands – immaculate long red nails, and on the right hand a fresh trickle of blood going from her knuckles all the way to the wrist. Has she cut herself or has she just punched somebody in their face? "Put the guns down boys. If your boss gets killed, you might struggle to find employment," she said confidently with a smug face.

"Do what she asks you to do," Octavio said with a trembling voice. One would think he should have been comfortable in situations like this, but clearly, he had led a *sheltered* drug-boss life – hidden on his yachts, flying private jets between his mansions, always surrounded by armed bodyguards.

Alexei and two of the bodyguards immediately did what their boss demanded, but the third one with a bald head and a large scar across his forehead stood unmoved. He was in his early fifties and at least twenty years older than the other two muscleheads. It was hard to say how old Alexei was – his plump face, long blond hair in a bun and colourful string bracelets were giving him a boyish charm that could easily take even a decade off him.

*Unlike Octavio, this bodyguard has been here before. He knows exactly what he's doing. Will he shoot Edward before he manages to pull the trigger on Octavio? If he does, we're all dead.*

Sophia moved slowly behind Edward. Her grin faded away as she quickly realised their plan had flaws. *It's what happens Sophia, when you think you're an expert in every possible field. When you listen to nobody! Just like freaking Leona!*

Octavio must have doubted the shooting skills of his most experienced man because he asked in a begging voice, "Put the gun down, Siergiej. We'll let them go for now."

Was Siergiej a dare-devil, ready to risk the life of his boss – just so the enemy would definitely lose? He didn't say a word. His eyes were set on Edward, who was gradually losing his confidence – we could all sense it. The tension was practically suffocating, Siergiej was moving his gun in all directions but only in millimetres. I glanced around the bathroom. There was a window above the bath, but I couldn't smash it without making a noise. I couldn't spot anything I could use as a weapon. *A loo brush?* I could shove it into Siergiej throat but first I would have to disarm him.

"What's your plan old man?" Siergiej finally spoke up making everybody hold their breath. "If you pull the trigger on Octavio, you and all your mates here will die."

"If you let Octavio die, you're also dead Siergiej, so don't philosophize," Sophia was the only one who got her confidence back, or at least she was making that impression. "If logical thinking was one of your strongest attributes, you wouldn't spend your life protecting thugs and risking taking a bullet for them."

*Edward could shoot Siergiej and make Octavio into his shield*, I was coming up with a plan, but I wasn't the one who was holding the gun.

Siergiej narrowed his eyes, "Woman, you're giving me a great opportunity to get rid of Octavio and replace him. I've taken too many bullets for him," his left hand raised his T-shirt around his stomach to expose two thick scars. "I almost died for him once and never even got a pay rise."

"Because you're my best-paid man," Octavio was saying with a squeezed throat. "Are you going to kill us all now? Think about it, you're not going to be their new boss. They'll never trust you after pulling such a stunt."

Maybe they weren't going to trust him, but neither were they eager to kill Siergiej, an act which would most definitely be welcomed by both Octavio and Edward.

"I would never put us in a situation like this. We've got here because you're weak," Siergiej wasn't going to wait for a reply, he straightened his arms, widened his stance on the carpet and pulled the trigger twice. The first bullet went straight into Octavio's heart, Edward released him and let his body slide to the floor. Edward might have been too dumfounded to notice but his hip was bleeding. He managed to push Sophia out of the door – moments later Siergiej stood above Octavio and blew a hole in the middle of his forehead. When he turned round all three men, previously passive and petrified, now fired at him repeatedly not giving Siergiej a second to explain how he imagined their future cooperation. He wasn't going to become their boss after all.

Leona and James were both lying on the floor. She had her eyes closed and was crying silently. She must have finally come to the sad realisation that this little plan of hers wasn't a stroke of genius but an act of madness; and wouldn't make anybody free from their full-of-lies lives except by sending them to another world.

Alexei wiped sweat from his forehead and cleared his throat, "You can go guys. Playtime is over. You've had the adventure of your lifetime and let's leave it like that."

"Seriously? Are we going to let them go?" one of the bodyguards looked like he had already prepared himself to kill us.

"Seriously. Nobody needs ransom money from the Woodhouse family. The risk outweighs the benefits. Pass me your gun," he said to the muscleheads, and then turned to me, "Get out of the bathroom girl, you're going home. You were totally stupid coming here but it's your lucky day. I feel like I need to redeem for some of my sins and it's a perfect—" Alexei didn't finish, he fell to the ground from two bullets that went through his chest – unlike the bodyguards he wasn't wearing a bullet-proof vest. His pistol dropped just next to the bathroom door. I threw myself on the floor to get it. I got hold of the gun, and as I looked up, I saw Her.

"Oh my god! I cried, not even expecting I had so much strength in my lungs. My scream distracted her and made her move her pistol away from one of the bodyguards, who was trying to retrieve another gun from under Siergiej's body.

"Lily? I mean..." she squealed, jumped back and pressed her forefinger on the trigger.

## CHAPTER 67

## *Lily*

"What were you thinking? Oh, no! You weren't thinking at all! And again! You killed me! Again! How many freaking times can you get killed by one person?"

"Oh, don't be so overdramatic," *the real* Selina smirked. "You probably spent too much time in my body and the emotional and artistic part of me rubbed off on you."

"Ladies," Frederick gestured us to sit on two white chairs with their metal legs nearly fully immersed in a cloud. We were floating above Paris at night, and while passing the lit Eiffel Tower I felt a pang of sadness. *Is it really all over now? I didn't even have time to say goodbye to James. Will they erase our memories?* I bit my lower lip, trying not to sob like a baby. *It's not fair. The first man who saw the real ME - although, ironically, I was in a different body - and my memory of him was going to become a black hole. The first man in a while who made me feel the one and only, although... it would help if I didn't get involved with married men.*

Frederick sat at his glass desk on an invisible chair and put his hands together into a pyramid, "I was expecting to see you here a little later."

"I hardly invited myself," I snapped. "Why is she here? Did somebody also shoot her?"

Frederick smiled, "The current policy is that when one of you dies, you're both sent to us immediately. We tried other approaches but it always created a complete mess with the paperwork, our admin placed souls in wrong bodies or completely lost them and then it took ages to fix. That's how you get all the ghosts wandering Earth, freaking people out... but anyway down to business," he clasped his hands energetically, "Are you glad to be back in your own bodies?"

"It feels great, but I'm afraid to ask how long it's going to last," said Selina.

"Hold on a second. You said that we could only be back to our own lives when we both had completed our tasks correctly," I said.

"I did, but *Up Here* you're always in the bodies that you were given at birth. Again, it's way easier to keep order—"

"In your paperwork, I get it," I said irritated.

"Neither of you seems particularly thrilled at the prospect of getting your old lives back," he smiled. "You can always swap your lives forever, but it's permanent, there's no way back. Also, it would be so much paperwork," he gasped. "It would take eternity".

"No, no," Selina protested, fidgeting on her chair.

"Oh, come on! You must have enjoyed my luxurious apartment in London, the glamorous job, attractive boyfriend, your own TV show..." Oddly I didn't even mind her *enjoying* Nate that much. But I was happy to think that at least I had somebody out there to help me get over James – if I kept the memories after all. *Maybe I could find James... Maybe he would be able to SEE the real me again.*

"I didn't have much time to enjoy any of that."

I looked at her panicked, "What have you done to my life? I've been practically killing myself to get your life on the best possible track. Go to hell!"

"Lily, keep calm. Nobody is going to hell. Not yet," Frederick started raising his hands up and down and taking deep breaths. "We'll watch some video from both your times on Earth and soon you'll understand everything.

"What do you mean?" I screamed. "What have you done?"

"If you insist, I can give you a short trailer. I dumped your married twofaced boyfriend, rented out your excessively large apartment and left

England. You're welcome! I do hope you did the same for me because I had enough time to realise that I do have a choice and could just leave the Woodhouse family and start all over again!"

*The bitch just ruined my life!* I felt a flow of heat filling my whole body. I smirked, "Oh yes, you're going to love it. I signed a deal with your sweet gay husband that traps you in a marriage with him for years, and if you want to break it, there will be serious financial consequences. I made peace with your mother-in-law, and slept with your husband's brother! So even if you get yourself a new husband, the mother-in-law stays the same – alive and kicking."

"You wouldn't dare," Selina was looking at me like she was expecting me to suddenly start laughing and deny everything. "Gay?"

"Shall we see the films first," Frederick said nervously. Selina swallowed hard and rubbed her neck.

I was so close to resolving the Leona mystery and transforming Selina's life, and then she shot us! She shot me, while *wearing* my body! After Leo decided to step down as a presidential candidate, I was sure he would drop the deal – with or without Leona's blessing. James would be perfect for her. *He would be perfect for me.* He would make her happy. *He would make me happy.* He would support her in whatever she wanted to do. *He would support me in whatever I wanted to do.* He was her hope for a better future. *He was my hope...* But we were both dead, again! Dead and no less confused than when we arrived *Up Here* the first time.

## CHAPTER 68
## *Selina*

Frederick made us turn our chairs back to each other. We did what he said without asking anymore questions. He literally had our lives in his hands. There were no screens to watch the promised movies. I heard Frederick clicking on his glass tablet and a few seconds later I was surrounded by white fog that got denser and denser. Just as I started feeling claustrophobic and opened my mouth to scream, I saw Lily in my body landing on Leona's veranda in the Hamptons. I was sitting just next to her, still on the same white chair that Frederick gave me, my fingers squeezing its plastic frame, legs crossed underneath and eyes wandering around in disbelief. I glanced at my lap and saw a chunky remote control with large colourful buttons that allowed me to fast-forward, pause or go back to any selected moment. I could also use the remote to change my chair location. I pressed 'levitate' and the chair lifted a couple of meters above the veranda – thanks god for high ceilings as my head almost hit the spinning fan. *I presume I can't die as I'm already dead, but it could still be painful.*

It would be useful if everybody at least once could see their life from such a perspective – from this position everything looked so much clearer. Leo treated me like another task in his life, like another tool needed to fulfil his Grand Plan.

"I was such a fool!" I screamed and then immediately covered my face with both hands. "Ufff.... Nobody can hear me anyway. Of course! I'm a ghost. But how could I miss that my husband is gay? Really? Although, there's a certain relief and it puts a light on some—"

"Don't blame yourself. He was a master manipulator," I heard Frederick's voice shouting somewhere from above.

"Like mother, like son." I couldn't believe Leona pulled off her Runaway Mother-in-law Act, and nearly succeeded. She might have put some people into an early grave, but she ticked all the boxes she had intended to tick. I had never agreed to her plan, and quite frankly I thought she was bluffing.

"She's quite a thing, your mother-in-law. I've used her as a case study in my research on monsters-in-law. Women consistently blame them for ruining their lives and driving them on immoral paths," Frederick said, while I was still entranced watching Leona, James and myself kept hostage on the superyacht.

"Any interesting results? Which category of monsters-in-law does Leona fall into? She's pretty unique with her sheer rudeness."

"So far she's the only one in a category that I still haven't named. Mothers-in-law are normally less direct, because they typically don't want to actually get rid of their daughters-in-law. Firstly, better the devil you know, than an unknown angel. It's a lot of effort trying to work out the weak points of your son's wife. It takes time, energy and commitment. Hours of thinking how to stab the son-thief without anybody realising what you're doing. Have you seen Sophia in action on the phone?"

I nodded, "Yeah. I can't believe Edward's brother swallowed the bait and accepted that his wife exaggerated and totally misunderstood his mother. Sophia managed to make herself into a perfect victim!"

"Exactly!" Frederick said enthusiastically. "Secondly, no cat wants to eat their mouse as torturing it gives them far more pleasure. Finally, a daughter-in-law is a perfect institution to call on when things aren't going according to the script."

"I'm not sure if I understand that one."

"Your son said or did something, and you didn't like it – no problem! It was the cow who made him say it. It was the cow who made him do it! You've had a bad day – obviously you're not going to take it out on your own child. The daughter-in-law is always there ready to take another punch. She's accustomed to taking your hits so she can endure one more. The least she can do after she stole your son!"

"Frederick, where have you been all these years?"

"That's a secret I can't tell you. You're going back to Earth."

## CHAPTER 69
### *Lily*

"But what am I supposed to go back to?" I protested. "Shouldn't she first clean up the mess she made?"

"Seriously?" Selina scoffed. "If we're back to where we left off, I'm straight back into the middle of a gunfight, so don't tell me about messy situations."

"Well, I'll keep it simple. I promise I'm not going to shoot you!"

Frederick rounded his shoulders and stretched his arms in front of him. I was watching him with curiosity as he was lifting his arms up and slowly lowering them down, marking a semi-circle in the air. *Has he even realised we've both returned from our Life Immersions?* He stretched his legs under the glass desk, then bent them again at his knees, stretched them and...

"Frederick!" Selina lost her patience shouting angrily. *Has my no-nonsense approach to life rubbed off on her?*

"Oh, sorry. I've just been going through all the options we've got."

"I'm glad to hear we've got more than one option," I said cheerfully.

"Well, not exactly – there is one option that we can approach in many ways. I would suggest that the new Lily should wait outside the cabin and let the new Selina make a deal with Alexei."

"Alexei is dead," I snapped. *He feels so out of touch this time. Or is he just incompetent?*

"Only because the new Lily, so... Selina shot him."

"Oh, I thought he was going to shoot you," Selina said, and Frederick pursed his lips and shook his head.

Selina shrugged her shoulders, suddenly looking like she didn't have a care in the world. "I was convinced I was saving your life, so I hope Heaven appreciates good intentions."

"It doesn't really work like that," Frederick smiled. "Contrary to common belief nobody sits in your head twenty-four-seven to analyse every single intention."

"No? Does it mean that there are people out there who can get away with some nasty stuff, only because they're lucky not to be caught?" I asked flabbergasted.

"It's not that extreme. We search for specific keywords and images so you really can't get away with anything nasty."

"You need to erase my memories. I want to believe that the world is fair, at least *Up Here*," I said.

"It is," he said decisively, and after a short pause he added with a grin on his face "Most of the time."

"Can we just go back to the day when Selina drove into my car and killed me the first time? She could just wait a couple of seconds and let me go on my flashing green light."

Frederick shook his head.

"We could keep all the memories like bad dreams to remind us of what we need to do."

"And what do you think you need to do?"

"Get a better grip of my life, instead of just going with the flow," I said proudly, but Frederick kept staring at me, his hands shaped into a pyramid and pressed against his pursed lips.

"There is no such option," he said sternly. "There was a reason why you both got a second chance. There was a reason why you swapped your lives. Do you really want to go back to where you were?"

"No, not exactly. What Lily is trying to say, I guess is that we wouldn't mind doing it all by ourselves instead of handing away part of our lives to somebody else."

I nodded with approval. That was exactly what I meant, and I couldn't phrase it better.

"Your life is not a computer game. You can't press *delete* or *game over* and start from the level zero. The only way is to keep going, and you agreed to *keep going* in different bodies. You signed the deal."

"Well, we didn't have any other option," Selina said.

"Besides, even if it was somehow possible, there are too many people involved in your lives – we can't just make them all forget everything and change the course of their lives."

"I guess my life is no messier than before. I was just unaware of certain facts, or I just chose not to know them," Selina said nonchalantly. *Of course she's happy, she's getting a better deal than me. Molly still hasn't been found, my house projects are stuck in limbo because of the whole office-drama... In contrast to hers, my life has never been messier.*

"I got you an out-of-jail free card and gave you some real alternatives. You just threw my life completely upside-down," I gasped. "Fine, I'll deal with it. I can move to New York or San Francisco. It's not like anybody is waiting for me. Nate will find another girlfriend, and James..." my voice started breaking. I cleared my throat and started again, "James will probably like you, despite not being ME. Don't ruin it," I said with a bitter-sweet smile. "Shame that your Liam is gone, he was cute. Well, I hope he deserved Heaven."

Frederick didn't look particularly moved, but considering his job was dealing with dead people every single day I wasn't that surprised. Were they even *dead* for him, or rather just differently *packed*, and shaped into different *matter*?

"God!" Selina shouted, her head was turned to the right, eyes set on a Cloud overtaking us.

"God? No, no, no..." I screamed. "I'm not ready yet. I don't mind going back to the drug's dealer den. But I trust that you aren't sending us *down*, just so we get killed again and bounce back *Up here*."

"That's not God," Selina kept shouting, while Frederick calm and unmoved also watched the Cloud that now overtook us. Two men were sitting on white plastic chairs and talking to a woman behind a glass desk. "Can't you see them?"

"Oh my god! It's Octavio and Siergiej!" I stood up to see them better, but their Cloud suddenly sped up.

Frederick typed something quickly on his tablet and looked at us to say, "She's new to her job. She should've consulted her route with our Cloud traffic control. A situation like that should never happen."

"Siergiej and Octavio are getting a second chance?" I asked.

"Are they going to swap lives?" Selina laughed.

"I'm in no position to discuss that with you," Frederick said seriously, but I could see how the right corner of his mouth twitched. "I'm glad to see that somebody else will also have her hands full. I've been so busy with you two, we couldn't stop watching you for even a minute. You really threw your lives upside-down."

"And somehow we both succeeded?" I said still not fully understanding what we did to deserve another chance on Earth.

"Selina," Frederick called and paused for a moment. She gave him an inquisitive look. "Do you know why we think *Up Here* that you have both completed your tasks?"

She didn't rush with her answer, first taking a few deep breaths. "Quite frankly, the last few weeks have been so manic that I didn't have time to think about the task *per se*. All I was trying to do was to get Lily out of her toxic relationships. Nate, Molly, her family... I just couldn't believe that a young, beautiful, intelligent..." as she was saying this, I was slowly warming to her, "...educated, successful woman let all these people walk over her – over and over again. Why?" she asked still surprised and then turned to me, "Why would you let them treat you like that?"

"The truth is..." I bit my lower lip and swallowed hard trying not to burst into tears, "I don't know. I didn't feel that special when I was looking into their eyes. Quite the opposite, for Nate I was never good enough for him to fully commit to me. He kept saying he would eventually leave his wife, but I wasn't stupid, I knew the deal. Dah! For some reason I wasn't good enough to get that damn promotion, although I was already doing his and Susana's job. They had been promising me the partnership for over a year. Molly... hmmm... I think I just felt guilty she had been trying so hard and couldn't achieve as much as I did. If I only knew she was blackmailing everybody! I always felt she wasn't as lucky as me, I suppose…"

"Seriously?" Selina scoffed. "Do you really think you achieved so much because you were lucky? You never made that impression when you were talking to me. You come across so confident and—"

"I know," I cut in, "But sometimes I feel like an imposter. Not because I haven't done enough or worked hard enough, but because there are so many other people out there wanting to have my job and they're so good at what they do and…" I gasped heavily, suddenly thinking about all those nights when I woke up from the nightmares in which somebody younger, prettier and more famous took my TV show away from me, somebody with more experience suddenly became a partner in my firm or somebody who was just perceived to be cooler than me took my cushion collection claiming that I stole the idea from them. "I suppose, my worry has always been that the higher you climb, the harder you fall."

"I totally get it," Frederick unexpectedly chipped in, looking nostalgic. *I wish I could know more about his life before Up Here.*

"It's one thing not to push enough to become a partner because you were afraid, and another to let Molly bully you. And for all that to happen under Nathan and Susana's watch? It also took me a while to understand why Nathan wouldn't make you a partner. You would be equals at work. You could go with your relationship to HR, but—"

"But he wanted to have power over me," I smiled bitterly.

"That's what I guessed."

"I had to leave my body to see that," I sighed. "Nathan often introduced me as a *rising* star, and that is really the answer. Neither he nor Susana wanted me to become a star in their company. They felt threatened by me. I was ten years younger, a hundred percent committed and had already achieved more than them."

"The world is impossible. You want to have children, so they'll find a way to degrade you because you can't give work one hundred percent. You don't want kids and your work is the most important for you, so they won't let you progress because they're threatened."

"I've never really decided on having kids or not. I just wanted it to be my decision, not my parents, sister or a man. I wanted to be sure it was what I wanted."

"Of course," Selina said, and at that moment I realised she must have read my diary.

"Is that what you told Liam? Have you already talked about kids?" I laughed but quickly stopped giggling seeing pain in her eyes. She didn't have a better deal than me. She lost Liam. She didn't want to admit it, but I could see how they looked at each other. It was obvious! "I'm sorry."

"That's fine," she brushed me off, and quickly changed the topic. "It's odd," now she was laughing through tears, "I thought people were dismissive about me because they thought I wasn't good enough, but then I got your glamorous life with your splendid career and saw the same dismissive faces distorted by scowls attempting to belittle you, to make you feel bad about yourself, to wipe the smile from your face."

"And?" Frederick was staring impatiently at Selina.

"It's wonderful when people cheerlead you; when they support you in whatever you're doing, but so often they can't help but look at you through their own selves, if you know what I mean."

"Yeah, I think I finally get it," I said for the first time feeling an incredible connection with the woman with whom I literally had shared my life. "They look at you, but they see themselves. They envy you because you pursue your dreams, while they've already given up on theirs. They hate you because by what you're doing, you question their life choices. How could you not want kids when it's the only way to lead a full life, right? You could have one. Maybe. But then how could you do it to your child, how could you not give them a sibling? Isn't it selfish? How could you not want to have a regular job nine to five, or more likely nine to six, five days a week, when they've told themselves it is the only way to succeed? They hate you because you remind them that their way is NOT the only way."

"Ladies, to get to the point. I need to hear it from you before I send you back. You get your lives back, I get promoted. I really want to finalize this project like right now," he smiled.

"I'm enjoying the break," Selina gasped. "It's what I should ask for Christmas every year – to be able to put my life on hold."

"That's what meditation is for," I said.

Frederick kept looking at Selina and me with anticipation.

"Down to the point..." she suddenly broke the silence. "I'm just thinking loudly, hoping that one of my thoughts can turn out to be good enough so we can be released and back to our old lives. Our old-new lives... I wish I didn't let people hurt me. I should've been more empathetic to Myself. Trying to understand and forgive are wonderful qualities that I want to practice for the rest of my life. But, not at all cost."

"Not at the cost of my mental health," I added.

"Not at the cost of feeling bad about myself. Not feeling good enough for anybody... *Dismissing, demeaning* and *humiliating* are tools that weak people use, and I could so easily disarm them by disengaging, leaving or setting up clear boundaries," Selina was saying and smiling to herself.

Frederick hit a gong sitting on his desk. "*No one can make you inferior without your consent,* said Eleanor Roosevelt. Look after yourselves, ladies. You're ready now! Keep trying to be a better Self. I'm the best example that you can always change your life. I was working for *Down There* when one day a head-hunter from *Up Here* believed in me and—"

"You were a devil!" Selina and I screamed simultaneously.

He shrugged his shoulders and grinned, "We don't call anybody from *Down There* that anymore. It's not politically correct."

## CHAPTER 70

### *Lily*

"Really Frederick? I hoped that at this stage of our relationship you would have more mercy!" I scream, looking at the sky, my body trembling from the cold. I turn my back and quickly realise that it's not the time for complaining but rather to *Swim for your life!* The boat-explosion that I saw *Up There* suddenly seems to be a hundred times larger. I'm still so close to it that I feel I'm suffocating, hot air is filling my lungs. I look around, but there's no trace of Liam. Adrenaline kicks in and I start swimming using every muscle of my body. There is no way I could get to the shore. I swim towards the superyacht. *They're not going to kill me again!* That would just be wasting all the work they put into their project. I get close to the lowest deck with a pool and see a group of people sunbathing there.

"Hey, can anybody hear me?" Completely exhausted, I'm trying to keep myself on the surface.

A tall, slim woman with a long ginger ponytail is raising herself from a sunbed and walks to the edge of the deck. She's wearing a one-piece green swimming suit and is moving like a model on a catwalk. She's got sunglasses but still needs to put her hand up to her forehead to see me clearly. My eyes are dry and sore from the salt and the fire. *Didn't they notice anything?* I wave to her. *Is she seriously going to abandon me to a certain death?* She turns back, but seconds later a man is throwing me a life jacket and a rope. I can't reach the rope, but I put on the life jacket and for a sweet little moment lie on my back, letting the sea rock me. I start weeping, mostly from exhaustion. Suddenly an invisible force is pulling me back and moving me onto a surfboard. I slowly turn my neck, terrified of what I'm going to see, but it's just a muscly friendly looking man rescuing me. With his help I finally sit down next to the pool, and it feels like I've just switched my tickets from hell to heaven. Somebody is wrapping me in a soft warm towel and passing me a glass of Piña colada.

"Sorry, we've run out of soft drinks," says the supermodel in the green swimsuit. "I'm Olga..." she introduces herself, but it takes me a while to respond. My head is still spinning, now after taking a gulp of that drink, even more. I suddenly recognize her. She's the singer who got shot in the murder mystery.

"Selina," I say with a low fainty voice.

"Selina, right?" she asks me to confirm, and I nod. I realise that's not my name anymore but decide not to correct her. Her boss just tried to kill a woman called Lily.

"Poor you," she strokes my wet hair that smells of smoke. "Whoever threw you overboard... I hope one day he pays for it." I only nod. She's more helpful than she can realise – she has just given me an excuse for why I'm here. "Do you know what? Let's go to the party at the top. Some food and coffee will make you feel better. And then you'll show me the bastard who did it to you."

---

In a silky blue dress from Olga, with a stomach filled with coffee and grilled chicken – I finally feel like myself. Well, not exactly. It turns out I managed to get used to Selina's petite body. My boobs feel heavier. Each time I make a few steps with these long legs squeezed in a pair of high heels, the legs are tangling up. At least, I've got an excuse, or even two. I've been thrown overboard and drunk Piña colada!

"Everybody get down on the floor with your hands up!" A deep male voice materialises out of nowhere and starts giving orders. I look at the direction of the lift and see Miguel pointing his gun at me. Maybe not exactly at me, but somewhere in my direction. "Everybody! Now!" he screams, and I notice I'm the only person still sitting on a chair. The top deck is suddenly flooded with men in black military equipment, running around with massive guns and arresting people. Every few seconds I can hear, "You get up... handcuff him, get her out of here..." The music is still playing, currently, "Shut Up and Dance with Me." I imagine the whole place is a stage and soon everybody will stand up and dance in a video clip. Two-thirds of the guests get escorted out by the men with guns. It all happens so quickly I can still barely comprehend what's going on.

"Everybody..." Miguel says, standing next to the piano on the stage, "You're all safe here. None of you is under arrest, but we will need to interview each and every one of you. If you try to escape, you'll find yourself in serious trouble. Besides, you don't want to leave the room. It's still not safe. We're searching the yacht for dangerous criminals, and you better not move anywhere. Understood?"

Nobody says anything so I feel obliged to shout, "Understood!" Miguel gives me a warm smile, but it fades away quickly when we hear shots being fired. He asks us not to panic, but even I – who has died twice in the last few months – find it difficult to keep calm. *This is not how I imagined my big come back!* We are surrounded by an army of men with machine guns, but I suppose there are two ways of looking at it. One, that's bloody scary. Two, they're going to protect us. Miguel lets us stand up to have a drink. The staff recommence serving but only juice and water. Alcohol is not allowed. Obviously, they don't need any more drama. I look at the horizon. There are speedboats coming to us from all directions. It's like the beginning of a battle. The sky is red, orange and yellow. A plane is cutting the perfect sky, looking like it's about to fly into the sun and burn. It's how I feel. I should be glad I'm here, but I just want to disappear. I wish James was here. I already miss him so much. I close my eyes, take a deep breath and feel hot tears rolling down my cheeks.

Somebody puts a hand on my shoulder and says, "Hi, beautiful. You've done so well that you deserve to be promoted from assistant—"

"Liam?" I smile and throw my arms around him. We freeze like that for a moment before we hear more shooting and something that sounds like an explosion. People scream and once again Miguel asks everybody to stay calm. "I thought you were... I'm so happy you're fine," I sob into his arms, staining his silky black tuxedo. "How did you even—"

He pulls me gently away from his chest and says something through the dense noise of people crying, laughing nervously and raising questions in utter disbelief. We hear more shooting from the lower deck, but he looks calm. He looks straight into my eyes and then whispers into my ear the whole story about how he managed to swim to the yacht and a couple of people rescued him. They said he was the first man ever to have been thrown overboard so nobody is safe now, whatever the gender. I giggle nervously. Tears flooding down my cheeks. Liam is handsome, warm and charming but I miss James. *Oh, I can't wait for my memories to be wiped clean.*

We go sit at a table with a white cloth stained with something red. We agree it's Sangria, although neither of us really believes it. He takes my hand, squeezes it tight and starts talking with a shaky voice, "Lily..." he overpronounces my name. I flinch, it's like somebody pinched me. "Lily, I can't imagine my life without you. I don't know what I would do if I lost you..." *Oh, god! He's talking about Selina, and I can't tell him the truth.*

"I feel the same," I manage to say, thinking about James, seeing his face, hearing his laugh, feeling his body, smelling his aftershave. It's so painful. I've never felt like this about anybody else! That's the cruelest part of the experiment that *Up There* put us through. Hopefully they realise it before more people get hurt.

He gives me a faint smile that I seem to recognise. Maybe there is a chance for me and Liam. Time will show. First, they have to erase my memories so I can forget about James. He clears his throat, "I hoped you'd feel the same." At that particular moment I can't give him more. My mind is blank, and the heart is bleeding. It shows how much I changed. *One life earlier* I would think 'a bleeding heart' is just a silly, cheesy phrase. "I don't care how you look, I can see YOU."

"Great," I say disappointed. *You totally care how I look.*

"You don't know yet, do you?" he smiles. "James and I – we were also part of the Soul Management project. We're both home now."

## CHAPTER 71
## *Selina*

When our cabin is suddenly invaded by armed men wearing bulletproof vests and helmets, Alexei and two of the bodyguards are already gone. I quickly realise that them letting us live might have nothing to do with mercy and kindness. Somebody must have tipped off Alexei that the Civil Guard police was coming, so they needed their bullets for a bigger threat than us.

We put our hands up as the men demanded. Leona can't help herself and has to question their orders, "I'm a victim here. I'm Leona Woodhouse, the mother of..." she stops last minute and smiles to herself. I wonder if Leo will go back to running his campaign as soon as he knows his mother is safe and sound. But this time he'll probably lock her in a tower for the duration of the campaign and his presidency.

"Did you kill Octavio?" asks one of the policemen. He's got disappointment painted all over his face. Did he hope to kill him to get promoted? Oh, heaven!

Leona looks proud and I immediately sense she wants to take credit for it. It would make amazing headlines: Leona Woodhouse kills Spanish drug lord! But James stops her from talking by speaking louder, which is the only way to shut her up. "The bodyguard, the dead man next to her," he points with his chin as his hands are still up in a defensive gesture, "he killed Octavio. Then he was shot by another bodyguard, who escaped. Have you caught them?"

"I'm not in a position to tell you," says another policeman. "How did you manage to stay alive?"

"I'm not in a position to tell you," Leona snaps.

The man's curiosity wins over his professionalism, "We haven't yet. No. But, if you imagine that for every guest, hostage or criminal there are three armed policemen we've got a fair chance of getting them all. I've been waiting for this day all my life."

A head in a helmet and black balaclava appears in the place where once there was the door that nearly made me into a pancake. He turns to the policemen and says in a deep voice, "Only three of you need to stay here. The rest of you upstairs. We found another hostage. Another famous person. Molly something."

*Molly got famous? She eventually gets what she wants!* "How is she?"

"Shocked but fine. She keeps saying that she spoke to Nathaniel, and he saved her. I think she means an angel. You need to have faith, eh?"

I can't help but say, "Her surname is Guacamole. Molly Guacamole. You know just in case a reporter asks who you saved today.

"Thanks," he says seriously, and I feel a pinch of satisfaction. "Oh, there is also an Edward asking about Leona. I don't have another room, so I'll bring him here in a minute."

James and I sit on the bed with our legs stretched forward. He takes my hand and squeezes it. He's nice and good-looking, but I doubt that we've got a future together, which is probably best for all of us. Especially, when I'm going to completely cut myself off from Leona and her son. I miss Liam and I regret that we didn't have more time. Now when my emotions are fading, I can finally see how much he meant to me. I feel a pang of jealousy thinking that Lily might stay with him. Hopefully, one day I'll find *my Liam* too.

Edward runs into the cabin, straight to Leona, like there are no machine guns at the door, and James and I don't exist. "If anything happened to you… Leona, darling! I can't lose you again." She rolls her eyes looking bored, as if she hadn't contacted him to help her escape from her husband. Like they hadn't had sex on a table only a couple of weeks ago. Like they hadn't got a child together.

The policemen are just staring at them, it would be the perfect moment for the bad guy to kidnap us again.

"It's so weird to think that I'm locked here with my biological parents..." James says to me quietly, but all helmeted heads suddenly turn to us. I shush him. Their English is very good, and the world hasn't learnt about Leona's first-born yet.

Edward is holding Leona's arms and looking at her with so much affection that love fills the whole room, "Are you all right?" She opens her mouth to say something, but he interrupts her, "I knew from the beginning Octavio wasn't the man for you. I worried about you, but you needed to find it out for yourself. Such a shame it happened in this way."

Leona clears her voice and puts her hands on her hips. She starts loudly, not caring about the little audience listening to her, "I slept with Octavio's wife. Not him." I almost choke trying to swallow and can't stop myself from coughing. James burst into uncontrolled laugher, and the men guarding us, luckily, are holding their guns so they can't record it. First Edward looks like he's going to have a heart attack – if it's true, he's lost his chance at being with Leona forever! There are some things he just can't compete with. Then he starts laughing. "Edward, I'm not joking..." His smile fades away from his face. "But, I didn't like it enough to continue the relationship. I'm still not quite over you."

"I wonder why he would even bother to kidnap you. You're such a public person – if he thought logically, he would see right away that it was a terrible idea. But it was all personal. Love makes people mad."

"Actually, Edward... It was your mother who paid Octavio to kidnap me. She didn't even ask for a share of the ransom money... Alexei told me on his way out. I always liked him... Eh, the same old Sophia who would do absolutely everything to have her way!"

"I always knew you and my mother were similar in so many ways."

## CHAPTER 72
## *Selina*

When we finally moor at the Port of Malaga, the place is already rammed with reporters. Miguel tried to mislead them by asking Octavio's guests to post on social media that we were going back to Puerto Banus. #partyisover #goingbacktopuertobanus could do the job, but it's rather hard to hide a hundred-and-eighty-meter-long boat.

There are police vans ready to take handcuffed criminals, along with a variety of suspects. Other guests are being safely escorted to taxis and private cars. I'm grateful that they didn't just drop us into the paparazzi's morass. I haven't even had a chance to speak to Leo, and Leona is too busy talking to Edward, so I wouldn't know what to tell them. James keeps sending me merciful glances as if he could feel I miss my old life. He's in love, but I won't be able to help him. I'm not going twice over the same Leona-river. Maybe for Liam, but not for somebody I barely know and there is still time to avoid. I reach out to hold his hand because we're surrounded from every direction by reporters and police, I'm afraid that I could trip and faceplant on international news. I notice as we walk through the port, the crowds begin to thin until we're left practically alone. I can finally breathe but then I realise what's happening. We're in a cordoned area marked with red tape and guarded by an army of bodyguards. At a distance I spot five Land Rover Discoveries. James releases my hand and moves slightly away from me, that's when I notice that I'm walking straight into Hell – the entire Woodhouse family is gradually emerging from behind privacy windows.

"Liam must have tipped off the family that Leona was in Spain."

"Do you know where he is? I need to talk to him," I say to James, looking at Leo with a sinking heart. At least I know now that he's another victim of the Woodhouse clan.

James takes my hand, pulls me back and stops me from walking. We let Leona and Edward go in front of us, and they're happy to show their love to the whole world. James leans towards my right ear and whispers, "I'm here, New-Lily..." I feel shivers going down my spine. "I'm back with you. And I'll always, ALWAYS, have your back. No matter how you feel about me now. Whether you like my new look or not. I'm always here for you." I can't say a word. I'm staring at him looking for an answer. "The Soul Management," he whispers. They knew we would like each other..." he gives me a beaming smile. "And they don't like messing with love. It's too powerful. Look what happened to Leona..."

I glance at Leo welcoming his mother with open arms. Leona is weeping, he's weirdly calm. I look at James, take a deep breath and nod that we can start walking again. Towards a better future. One where I make my own conscious choices. Where I don't let people hurt me. We don't need to hold hands for me to feel safe. For the first time in a while, I know who I am, and I very much like the person. I will keep respecting and protecting *her*.

---

Leo and I are in a car alone. He sent his driver away and is driving us himself. The bodyguards weren't happy, but the Land Rover is bulletproof and we're moving in the middle of a president-like-escort. I'm glad I'm not going to be a part of it for too long. Today they will all fly on a private jet back to the US, but I'm going to *hide* somewhere in Spain for a bit longer. I need some space to think, and I would also like to speak to Lily, while we still have the memories of our previous lives.

Naturally Leona is disappointed she's not invited for this get together. The woman will never change. You could kidnap her, threaten her, put a gun to her head and her true manipulating-self will remain completely unaffected. She's so hard-wired to stay who she is that many would die trying to change her. My only solution is total separation. But, I've also learnt during the journey that my soon to be ex-mother-in-law is not actually the person who I thought she was, and that is the best part of it. I don't want to be near her, but I wish her all the best with Edward and her plans for the future.

"I don't think you've got time to run this year..."

"That's not important," Leo says calmly.

My head turns towards him in surprise. *He really isn't that bothered.* "You can always do it in four years."

"I'm not going to. It was my father's dream. Not mine."

"I'm sorry for what you've had to go through."

"It wasn't as bad as everybody thinks..." *He's still in shock. Or, is he just pissed off with Leona and going to play the phi-not-a-big-deal game"*

"Keanu collaborated with my mother. He couldn't keep his mouth shut for too long. He quickly reached the conclusion that this whole debacle would leave me traumatized and I'd require years of therapy. Not that I don't need it anyway, but maybe years can be compressed to months. Honestly, I don't know what she was thinking. Emily and Faith were aware of everything from the very beginning... Genuine conversation has never been a strong part of the Woodhouse family, but what the hell? To go to such length..." he looks at me in pain. I think he will suddenly burst into tears, but he just hits the wheel and swears loudly.

"Keep your eyes on the road!" I shout, thinking it wasn't a good idea to have this conversation while driving.

He takes a few deep breaths and reaches for a sip of water. "I resigned because I had an excuse. I thought that at least it would buy me some time to decide whether I really want it. And I don't. I really, really DON'T."

"Which is absolutely fine Leo. I'm completely on your side and obviously what she's done is terrible, but I also know that you would never let anybody talk you out of your plans. You almost managed to convince me that we were doing right..."

"I agree it went way too far. I don't know whether you will ever be able to forgive me or even understand, but now when I see so clearly I've been brought up in a toxic environment, at least I can comprehend myself, my own life... When I was fourteen and still working out who I was, I heard my father talking with one of his friends about a conversion therapy for his gay son. They both concluded that it was a wonderful idea for this boy!"

"Seriously?" I shout.

"All I wanted was to be Leo Woodhouse, not the gay-Woodhouse. I didn't want to be different," he starts sobbing.

"No, it's definitely better to be as miserable as most people who are just trying to fit in at all costs," I say, and we both start laughing.

"That's what Keanu says."

"I might like him."

Leo rolls his lips, "He's got enough of the drama. He wants a normal life and a family."

"Leo. Don't tell me you don't want the same! Your mother almost died so you could stop hiding. She was the one who sent me to D.C.!"

"Since when have you liked what my mother—"

"I don't but you're thirty-five! You are allowed to live a happy life on your terms."

"Don't worry, I've already destroyed our deal. We'll get the divorce and split everything fifty-fifty."

"I wouldn't expect anything less from the New You."

"I'm not going to announce to the whole world tomorrow I'm gay. It's not everybody's business. Nobody should give a damn who I love. But, I'm not going to hide it either. I'll go away for a few months, probably hike in South America and reflect on what I want to do in life. Being a politician is not for me. Hopefully Keanu will join me at some point..." he says with new energy and hope. "What about you?" I don't reply immediately, I haven't had enough space recently to think about it while switching lives. "I'm sure you'll find a publisher for your book now."

"I can't imagine better PR than Leona's little stunt," I laugh.

# CHAPTER 73
## *Lily*

 **SCANDAL AT MORGAN AND TUSK**

**How finding an abducted employee has opened a Pandora's box in the company.**

**As one mystery unravels, we find out more secrets that have shaken the Shark of Interior Design and left many speechless.**

Nathaniel Tusk has been charged with arranging the kidnapping of his employee Molly Sulivan. The woman was found a month ago on the Costa Del Sol, where she still remains under psychological care in a private hospital. She was trapped for weeks on a superyacht belonging to Octavio Buendia-Iglesias, a Russian-born billionaire drug smuggler. She was found during an operation to rescue Leona Woodhouse – the mother of senator Leo Woodhouse, who only recently stepped down as a candidate to be president of the United States.

Sulivan had been blackmailing Tusk and his colleagues for years for financial and professional gain. The specific nature of her blackmails is unknown to the public, but recent events and several accusations from co-workers indicate that she had plenty of options. Several senior members were involved in tax fraud, hiding their income in offshore accounts. Some were creating fake invoices for their clients who were using the practice to launder money, which is believed to be mostly from arms and drug trafficking. Through this enterprise Tusk met the billionaire Octavio Buendia-Iglesias and one day asked him for a favour. A proposal to scare one of his employees created a worldwide investigation and initiated the process of unravelling the company's darkest and ugliest secrets that many will wish were buried forever. Last week Susana Morgan was formally charged with multiple counts of sexual harassment in the workplace. The evidence provided by an anonymous source will likely keep her locked up for years. She has already received a wave of requests from prisoners around the country to support changes to prison cell designs. She is likely to have the time and motivation to take the project forward.

Over sixty percent of the employees of Morgan and Tusk have left during the last month, and many of them are going to submit claims for financial compensation for personal, psychological and discriminatory harassment. The kidnapped Molly Sulivan is one among many who will be facing multiple bullying allegations.

The most recent evidence suggests that Tusk will also be charged for trying to frame Susana Morgan with kidnapping an employee. He used a voice-changing app to alter his voice to Morgan in a conversation with Octavio I.B., during which they made arrangements to kidnap Sulivan. Subsequently, Tusk gave the falsified recording to the police as evidence against Morgan. However, Susana definitely wasn't helping her own case. When asked to pay the ransom, she transferred company money into her own private Bermuda account...

I take a sip of a hazelnut latte and press on my most recent call to speak to Selina. Since we left the superyacht, we called each other practically every day.

She answers yawning, and then I remember it's only seven in the morning on the East Coast. "I'm here and listening, but you need to give me a minute... or ten... or twenty minutes to fully wake up."

"I can call later," I say, not meaning it. It's been less than twenty-four hours since I found out about Nate, and I feel like I'm going to burst if I don't talk to her about it right now. Who could understand me better than a woman who was literally in my skin?

"No, no it's fine. It's about Nate, isn't it?"

"Thank you for dumping his arrogant-criminal arse! I spoke today to Steven..." I gasp, still finding it hard to believe, "and I found out that Nate also had recordings of my voice ready to send to the police. He was so pissed off I contacted his wife, he wanted revenge! But then he must have thought it through and went back to his original plan. Susana was the real problem that he needed to solve first.

"And very much in his own terrible way. How does Steven know that?"

"He and Melania joined forces and broke into his new apartment. After all, with her shares in the company and Steven becoming a partner, they're going to run the company now."

"Amazing!" she exclaims excited, and I know she really cares and means it. "It makes me wonder what team Nate and Leona could have made. Imagine them working together while hating each other's guts."

"Oh, how is she?" I ask too enthusiastically. I should strongly dislike the woman for making my time so difficult, but now when my emotions have calmed and I feel safe, I just find her amusing and peculiar. I'm honestly interested in how she's doing and have no other way of getting the information than through Selina. I'm not even supposed to know Leona! And there's literally nothing new about her on the internet.

Selina laughs, "I knew you'd be dying to know. She might soon become your neighbour."

"What? I'm curious about her, but it doesn't mean I want her anywhere near me!"

"Chill. No reason to panic," she's giggling, and I can hear a coffee machine in the background. "Actually, I saw her a couple of days ago when I was in the Hamptons to take the last of my stuff from the house... my half of the house."

"And?" I'm *boiling to* know. I need some distraction from thinking about Nate. I'm in love with Liam, I'm certain of that. I hope that when we finally lose our memories from living as Selina and James, we feel the same about each other. But, there is a part of me that still feels something for Nate and it needs time to heal. I flinch at the thought I could have ruined my life by staying with him.

"She's moving like wildfire. It's only been a month and she's already bought a house in Spain and set up her own dance school! I think she's had it in mind for a while."

"Spain? Like the south of Spain?" I squeak. "Soon I'm not going to remember her, not only her... Oh, Selina, I really want you and me to find a way to stay in touch. I think we have to come up with a plan about how we could meet each other! And I can't imagine you want to live close to Leona!"

"That's why she generously got her place on the Costa Brava and is setting up the school in Barcelona. Edward is helping her..."

"So you're still coming?"

"Of course," she sounds cheerful. I love hearing her voice and laugh. It's weird but it's like hearing myself! The better part of me. "James will close a few things in the US and as soon as I have signed the final contract for my book, we're in Torremolinos!"

"Brilliant! Just one more thing about Leona. What did you do to break her arm?"

"I didn't drop her shoes to a cobbler as she had asked me to, apparently that's why she slipped in her heels. It also doesn't help she's got osteoporosis."

"Should I even ask what stopped her from doing it herself?"

"She just wanted to annoy me," she sighs. "She told me last week she couldn't stand looking at me being so stuck in my unhappy life with Leo. I reminded her of her younger self... And then she called herself a family influencer!"

"That's why all people should be required to apply for a social media permit!"

*A year later*

## CHAPTER 74
## *Selina*

The villa that I rented for my book launch in Torremolinos looks even better than I imagined. My event organizer, Lily Rice, initially bought the house for herself to live in for a year, while redesigning the interior with a plan to sell. However, she quickly realised she could make more money by renting it out for events. One thing led to another, and now she successfully manages two careers as both an event organizer and an interior designer. She has two villas to rent and a YouTube channel that is ranked among the fifty most viewed in the world. We get on really well, she even offered me a job position on her events' team as her company is expanding. I'm going to think about it. Leo's guests used to be impressed with the parties I organised in the Hamptons. Needless to say, I gained no recognition or profit, my ex-husband and his mother took all the credit. But, that's the old story. So much has changed during the last twelve months that sometimes I barely remember my life in the Woodhouse family. The only thing I kept is the surname, as my agent accurately predicted it would help me sell over five million copies of my first book. That gives me the pleasant freedom to throw lavish book launch parties without going through the ordeal of trying to convince my publisher to spend a little extra for better food.

I glance at my watch. It's an hour till sunset, and the time when the guests should be arriving. Lily put soundproof walls on both sides of the garden and covered them with thick exotic plants, so apparently the neighbours never complain about any noise at night. I actually invited them all to the party, and everybody accepted. Lily says the place looks like it's prepared for a wedding, which wasn't intentional, but brings all the right connotations because my second book is predominantly a love story. There are lilies and candles floating in an infinity pool. Next to the pool is a long table covered with white cloth with more flowers and candles, and chairs set up only on one side to enable guests to admire the coastal view. Palm trees are decorated with gold twinkling lights, and the main feature in the garden is a gigantic bespoke bookshelf in the shape of a heart, completely filled with my signed hardback copies. It needed a team of muscly men to assembly and will need them again to get it out of the house.

The very first guest arrives, and my heart skips a beat. The woman is wearing a strapless long light blue dress, a diamond necklace and long diamond earrings. She can't be more than early twenties, but she's already got the chic elegance and walk of a successful woman, who is content with her life. I watch how the dress is sweeping the floor of the living room and then how its fabric moves with the evening Torremolinos wind.

"Faith," I throw my arms around her. She's the only person from the family I still keep in touch with. I would have never thought we could become such good friends, but life is full of surprises. "Thank you for trying not to steal my show," I laugh.

"Oh, please. You look fab!" she is eying me from my toes to the tip of my head. "I read last night that your dress was designed in Milan especially for you!"

I roll my eyes. Of course, some people will always care more about what I'm wearing than what I'm writing. I have on a long green dress that, on reflection, might be a bit too tight and overly accentuate my boobs, but who cares! It's my party and I'll wear what I want to. "I'm going to put it up for auction with a charity next week, so the more they write, the better..." A waiter brings us drinks. Faith takes a glass of champagne; I reach for orange juice. I can't be smashed while reading with Liam and Lily a scene from my novel. "So, how's everyone?" I ask for the first time in months. We've been in touch, texting each other every week and making occasional phone calls, but until now we've had this unwritten rule that our friendship is totally *separate* from the family that we once shared, and we don't mention any of its members unless we absolutely have to. I've just broken the rule and feel like I've touched an oil painting with greasy hands and got caught by a museum keeper.

Faith loses her effortless smile and grows tense, "I don't know where to start."

"Never mind," I say nonchalantly like I don't have a care in the world, which is partly true – I'm only curious.

"Emily ditched the whole idea of writing her blog. She screamed to mum on the phone that she absolutely hated every minute of it, and all she ever wanted was to enjoy her time with her kids while they're still so small. It turned out she did it only so people would stop asking her what she was doing while *sitting* at home with children." Faith suddenly starts laughing, "So she's the last member of the Woodhouse family to stop keeping up some stupid appearance that was making her utterly miserable... Mum's dance school is doing great. She's going to expand the business and rent a bigger place soon. Her courses sold out the very first day people could enrol online. She finally let Edward move in with her in Barcelona... Leo and Keanu have just closed a deal on a house in Boston and are looking to adopt. They are both done with politics. Keanu is going to lecture at Harvard, and Leo has started practicing law again. He's recently been doing mostly pro bono cases..."

"And Emil?" I ask meekly. He's the only person from the Woodhouse family who has been in the media spotlight for the past year. The whole of America is still quoting a chat that somebody overheard between him and his friend Richard Moon, the real estate tycoon.

**Richard**: 'Sorry to hear Leo had to resign... But, I like the woman your party appointed. Felicity has real potential to win.'

**Emil** (grunts): 'The world is changing so fast. I can't imagine a man being *a first lady*...

> **Richard** (scrutinizing Emil's face and frowning his bushy eyebrows): Felicity is married to a woman so if she wins, we're still going to have a first lady...
>
> **Emil** (looking like is about to faint): Well, it's high time. We should stop digging into people's personal lives and focus on who they are...

Faith looks into the distance and smiles, "Dad quit politics and has become happier than ever before." Other guests keep arriving but she's talking to me vividly and nobody dares to approach and interrupt us. "I mean, he would be truly happy if he didn't feel so guilty about Leo. He's trying to win his forgiveness. Currently he's making a tree house for their kids, who he hasn't even met yet, and is trying to work out the logistics of transporting it from the Hamptons to Boston."

"That's wonderful."

"Yeah, he's definitely growing into a man who I could introduce to my friends... and if you're asking about *me*," she says with a smug face, "I got into Brown."

I can't resist throwing my arms around her "Congrats!"

"If you don't strangle me first, I'm going into politics."

"What?"

"I'm going to make the bloody world a better place – for everyone. Before he quit, dad was supporting Felicity so maybe I could get an internship in the White House!"

"I couldn't stop you if I wanted," I laugh.

"Look who's talking. Your first book was so bold! Publishing a story on how your mother-in-law went missing in *these* circumstances... That was just wild." *Well, nothing was going to stop me. I've changed enough not to be threatened with a lawsuit and went all guns out there to take advantage of my five minutes.* "What's your new book about?"

"This time it's pure fiction. Two women get into a car crash, die and end up in a place called *Up There*. They don't deserve Heaven, and Hell is overcrowded. So, the management of *Up There* makes them participate in a new program called Soul Management, which offers them one more chance to go back to Earth. But, there is a catch. They need to switch lives for a year and rescue each other. One of them is a successful architect, and the other a struggling actress... One will land herself a position in a family from hell, and the other will find herself in the middle of a fierce office war..."

"Where do you take your ideas from?"

I smile and look into the distance, admiring the sunset. I bought this view. I don't own it anymore, but it doesn't feel any less mine. I negotiated with Frederick that I could keep my Up-there-memories for an extra year. They are still a big part of me, and I would be terrified to lose them too soon. But, I'm working hard on building plenty of new memories – stories that I can tell myself, that will make me proud, lift me up, give me a sense of purpose and make my life meaningful.

I hear a familiar voice and turn my eyes towards the kitchen. *Oh! James has made it.* He's looking exhausted after his flight from New York. He's vividly gesticulating and speaking to Liam, who's got his arm wrapped around Lily's waist. They're all laughing, their faces relaxed and beaming with happiness. Oh Lily, we made a hell of deal, and god only knows where we finally end *Up There,* but at least for now we've found our heaven on earth.

# Epilogue

Dear Molly,

Thank you ever so much for your letter. I just wish you wrote to me months, or even years earlier and tried to explain where your disturbing behaviour was coming from. Maybe together we would have managed to stop some of these terrible events that took place in the company. I understand your difficult situation, and I'm sorry you struggle with your bills, but I can't change our settlement. I'm afraid it's too late. I've already given the money to a charity that supports victims of workplace bullying. On the bright side, your half of a million pounds can at least partially redeem your sins — trust me, it's a good offer.

At the end of the day, I hope you still think that all you've done to Me, Nathaniel and every other person you hurt, bullied and blackmailed was worth it. Surely you can reflect on that — on how wonderful you felt each time you boosted your self-esteem by ruining ours. Contemplate on how you had your five minutes of glory, each time you made somebody else cry, suffer in quiet desperation and gave them sleepless nights. Hopefully it should give you a bit of consolation.

When you feel lonely or your money finally disappears, think about all those sweet little moments when you left somebody breathless. I know I wasn't the only one having panic attacks because of what you put me through. I hope all the memories will make up for all the inconvenience, burden and misery you have to deal with now.

You would never have got so far if you didn't fuel your tanks with so much envy and hatred. You think my life is better. But it's not better because I stole from you. There really is enough out there for everybody. But, you somehow decided it's better to invest your energy into putting everybody around you down; showing that they weren't as good as they thought. Wouldn't it be more efficient to just be a better person?

I really hope you still think that all you've done was worth it.

Because now that's all you've got.

Yours sincerely
Lily Rice-Malone

## THE END

# Dear Reader

Thank you so much for reading *A Switch Made in Heaven*! I really hope you enjoyed the story. If you did, I would be very grateful if you could post a rating or short review on Amazon.

If you would like to hear updates about my next book and any associated offers, please send an email to phillips.eva@hotmail.com and I'll add you to my mailing list:

Printed in Great Britain
by Amazon

63262417R00296